Just a Whistle Away

The Heirloom Farm Series, Volume 2

J. Kimalie

Published by J. Kimalie, 2024.

This is a work of fiction. Similarities to real people, places, or events are entirely coincidental.

JUST A WHISTLE AWAY

First edition. November 5, 2024.

Copyright © 2024 J. Kimalie.

ISBN: 979-8227780478

Written by J. Kimalie.

From the authors

We are very grateful to our friends who helped make the Heirloom Farm series better.

Thank you to Dini, Elizabeth, Karen T., Alyssa, Alicia, Judy, Karen C., & Pam. Your contributions to our project will always be appreciated.

Dear Veritas,

I have a friend with a toddler. He is completely in love with his child, as it should be. However, every time I call him to catch up with what is happening in his life, he thinks it is fun to put his toddler on the phone to speak with me. The child, at this point, can only babble nonsense. I've tried to tell my friend that I called to talk with him and not his kid, but apparently my hints are not getting through. Even though I think his child is adorable, it is irritating and frustrating to sit on the phone with someone who can't speak with you. Can you give me advice on how I gently tell my friend that I'd rather talk with him than his toddler when I call?

Signed: *Babbling Baby Blues*

Dear Babbling,

Hang up. The child is too young to know it is rude and your friend will eventually get the hint.

Chapter One

Ian grabbed his keys and wallet off the front table and hastily stuck them in his jeans pocket. He was late getting to Garrett's for the weekly Rook card game. He had spent the last few hours at the attorney's office going over a transfer of lease for the veterinarian clinic located below his apartment. Ian had many real estate interests, but the small building he was currently rushing out of was his favorite. It was a two-story building with a veterinarian clinic on one end and a bakery on the other. He had remodeled the upstairs to make one big apartment, where he currently lived.

He had used all his favorite materials in the remodel. The floors and molding were a warm oak, and the fireplace on one end was surrounded in stone with a built-in wall cabinet to hide the TV when not in use. The furnishings were big, leather, and masculine. The rooms contained many of the trappings of a bachelor pad, but it was tastefully done in a part lodge-like look and part gentlemen's smoking room with tones of emerald, maroon and brown throughout. The best thing about his home was the smell of cinnamon and sugar that wafted up the stairs every morning when the bakery lit up their ovens. One of the spare bedrooms had been converted to a workout room that Ian put to good use given he had a sweet-tooth, and the bakery downstairs was just too convenient not to pop in every day for a treat.

Taking the six-pack of Garrett's favorite IPA out of the refrigerator, Ian clomped down the back stairs to the door of the two-car garage he had built along with the remodel of his apartment. Entering the code into the keyless lock, he hit the garage door opener and jumped into his SUV. The weekly Rook games were sacrosanct among his friends and if you were late, you paid the penalty. The penalty being fixing the first round of drinks. So far, he had never been late.

Taking care not to get caught speeding, he made good time and pulled into Garrett's driveway just as Emmett was getting out of his truck. Emmett waved and waited for Ian to park. Grabbing the ale off the passenger seat, Ian swung his legs out of the vehicle, calling, "Hey Crank," as they shook hands. Emmett, who Ian had served with, had been a master mechanic in the Army and had earned the nickname Crank, as a result.

"All dressed up for the weekly Rook game, I see," Emmett said.

"I had business at the attorney's this afternoon and didn't make it home in time to change. I feel a bit constricted in these jeans, but that doesn't mean Donovan and I won't kick your ass in cards," Ian stated with a smile on his face.

"Dream on," Emmett chuckled.

"Gams is showing no gams tonight," Emmett shouted as they opened the door to Garrett's home. A chuckle sounded from inside the kitchen. Ian had earned the military nickname "Gams" due to his fondness for wearing kilts and showing off his muscular legs.

"Why all dressed up?" Garrett asked as Ian came around the corner of the kitchen.

"Can't a man wear something different once in a while? Surely, we men are above talking about our outfits?" Ian asked, raising one eyebrow. "I do have a story, however, but perhaps we can wait for Donovan, so I don't have to repeat myself."

"What story do you need to tell?" Donovan asked as he came up behind Ian. "And why are you wearing jeans?"

Garrett and Emmett laughed while Ian just rolled his eyes.

"I had business with my attorney, so I thought I would dress up a bit. You know Paolo, the veterinarian that rents a part of my building?" Ian paused, trying to move quickly on from the talk of his clothes. His friends all nodded. "He is close to retiring and turning his clinic over to his niece. He wanted to do the paperwork to transfer the lease into her name."

Garrett nodded his head and stated, "Paolo told me a couple of weeks ago that he is almost done working. I was sorry to hear it as he has taken care of my animals for a long time now. He assured me his niece was a better vet than he is. I'm not sure that's true, but I hope so. It is the only vet clinic close by and I've come to rely on their services. Have you heard anything about her?"

"All I know is her name is Olivia de Luca, she's a veterinarian and she'd like to rent a piece of my building," Ian said.

Ian moved into the kitchen, putting down the ale he brought. Turning to Donovan, he said, "Last one here has to make drinks and I think I would like a couple fingers of scotch, if you don't mind?"

"I'll help," Garrett said as he moved around the kitchen gathering glasses. "Emmett what will you have?"

"I'll take a beer, thanks," Emmett said.

The four men moved toward the card table with their drinks, continuing to tease Ian about wearing jeans instead of his usual kilt until the cards were dealt and the first hand was underway. As the men played, the conversation swirled around sports, animals, Garrett's latest search and rescue and another real estate investment Ian was thinking of making.

Dealing the cards for, what he hoped, was the last time, Garrett said, "Have you all seen the new column in the *Poulsbo Weekly Gazette*? It's like a Dear Abby column, but with a much less gracious tone."

"What do you mean?" asked Ian.

"Well, the answers to the readers are much more to the point and kind of hilarious. I don't remember Dear Abby being so humorous and incisive," explained Garrett.

"I've read it and it seems like a more sarcastic version of Dear Abby. I have to admit, I always wondered about the people who would call into a radio show or write to somebody for advice. Why would you want to put all your problems out there for millions of people to read or hear about? Maybe it's my age showing?" questioned Emmett with a shake of his head. "Whatever happened to personal business being personal?"

"Hah, old man, ever heard of Facebook, the internet or TikTok? People love putting their opinions, feelings, comments, just about anything out there for others to read," said Donovan.

"I kind of like advice columns," said Ian, "They can provide good advice to those who may not have somebody else to turn to."

"Don't tell me you would write to an anonymous journalist seeking advice on something?" questioned Donovan, "How do you know they're even qualified to give advice?"

"I probably would if I didn't have you knuckleheads all up in my business, giving me advice all the time," Ian snarked back.

"I find it funny," said Garrett, "but it's titled Dear Veritas. Seems a little pretentious." Garrett put his hands up, crooking his fingers in quotation marks, "Dear Truth. Obviously, the writer feels like they hold the market on truth."

"It's just an advice column not a scientific journal. I think it's helpful for people to have an outlet to ask their questions," Ian reiterated scooping in another hand.

"I'll have to read this new column. I must have passed over it when I read the paper this morning. I was more interested in the new advertisement spot for the Longhouse. Perhaps I can write in asking advice for a friend who has an atrocious wardrobe made up of kilts and statement tees," Donovan said, his lips turned up in a half grin.

"As I always say, you are all jealous of my mighty, masculine calves. If you had legs like these you would be showing them off every chance you got," and with that Ian threw down the rest of his hand full of trump cards, saying, "Read them and weep, my friends."

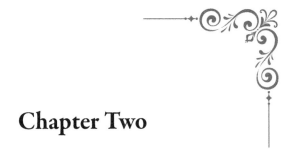

Chapter Two

When Olivia was a child, adults often asked her what she wanted to be when she grew up and she always knew the answer. At the age of 10, she was absolutely sure she wanted to train dolphins to perform and delight audiences at SeaWorld. She visited the attraction as often as she could convince someone to take her. At the age of 16, she was sure her purpose in life was to travel to Africa and be a wildlife photojournalist for National Geographic. A very bright and accomplished teenager, mastering the camera she got for Christmas came easily to her.

During her sophomore year in college at Fullerton, she discovered that activism was her true calling when she met Dillon, a charismatic senior who was an international affairs and philosophy double major. Her first love. He was the one who introduced her to the power of the people. She intended to support his fight to improve the lives of women in Micronesia through small business loans while he would help her fight to protect the planet's growing number of endangered species. A year later, Dillon graduated and moved away from both San Diego and their romance to live in a volunteer community in Bangladesh. Olivia was busy working hard on her biology degree and working part time at a local animal shelter, so her heart didn't suffer much at the loss. As she grew up, she changed career choices several times, but the draw to working with animals was a common thread. Nobody who knew her was surprised

J. KIMALIE

that her path, after graduating with honors, involved a dedication to animals. Thus, her entrance into vet school.

Fifteen years later, Olivia smiled to herself as she finally began decorating her new office with some of the mementos of her journey—photos from all the forays that had led her down the road to becoming what, in the end, was her dream career as a veterinarian.

"I always knew you'd make a great vet!" her Uncle Paolo told her at least once a week. He had always hoped his favorite niece would choose the same career he had and join him in business one day. In his opinion, the quiet, thoughtful young woman was the perfect combination of intuition, astute perception, and well-honed medical skills to be brilliant in the field. Although it took her a few years more than he'd hoped, she finally decided to move to the Pacific Northwest and join his practice just as he was beginning to wind down and focus on retirement.

"Dr. de Luca and Dr. de Luca—we are going to be an unbeatable team!" he pronounced when she finally committed to the plan. He was happy to know that he'd be turning his practice over to his very accomplished niece before long, and she was thrilled at the idea of owning her own clinic when the time came. Until it did, Uncle Paolo, or "Zio" as she often called him, would work a couple of days a week and also as a relief vet while she would attend to the majority of their clients.

Olivia had hit the ground running from the time she first arrived. Vet clinics everywhere were still feeling the impact from the pent-up demand and increase in pet ownership associated with the Covid pandemic. Since Olivia could attend to both small and large animals, she was often busy looking after the needs outside of the clinic. She was only now getting around to unpacking more of her office even though she had been here for almost six weeks. Thank goodness there had been no emergency calls for a change this Sunday when the office was typically closed. She had set aside the afternoon to work her way through more of the boxes in her office that had sat unopened since they had been delivered weeks ago. She enjoyed working in the quiet clinic today with only the sound of her beloved pup Dolce, a three-year old German shepherd mix, snoring softly from his bed near the window, shaking a leg and mumbling every now again as he dreamed his doggy dreams.

Her diploma from the U.C. Davis Veterinary College was already hung in the reception area, but her office was more of a personal space. She was enjoying thinking about the path she had followed that led her to this clinic as she displayed some of her favorite photos on the wall. The photos were from the non-profit shelter she interned at during vet school, the first clinic that hired her once she earned her degree, and the incredible year as Veterinarian in Residence at a retirement home for animal actors outside of Oakland.

On her desk was a framed photo of herself and Dolce at the end of a hike through the Hoh Rain Forest. They did the hike when she first scoped out the area and discussed the possibility of moving here to work with her uncle. The breathtaking beauty and magical allure of the rain forest ended up cementing the deal. Any place that offered something as special as that place just a short drive away was a location, she could be happy calling home.

As one of the few vets in town, Zio Paolo knew people from one end of the county to the other. All it took to find Olivia a home was asking a client or two if they knew of a place for his niece to rent when she came to join him at the clinic. Sure enough, Mrs. Duffy, who was a cat lover and one of his favorite clients, had a friend who had a cousin who had gone overseas on sabbatical to Florence for a year and decided to stay indefinitely. They were looking for someone to lease their charming little furnished cottage in Indianola and would be happy to have Olivia move in as soon as possible.

Olivia thought the cottage was perfect and she loved the shabby chic décor, the cheerful farm style kitchen, and the yard for Dolce to romp. As a bonus, the property had a medium sized, sturdy out building that would work when she felt the need to bring a farm animal home with her for observation outside of clinic hours.

At five foot four, many of her farm clients looked surprised when they met her for the first time as she didn't look big enough to handle a horse or a full-grown steer in distress. That impression was further fueled by her long brunette hair with natural gold highlights, deep brown eyes, and curvy stature typically attired in jeans, a long hoodie and a pair of bright color Wellies when she was on an assignment.

It became clear within minutes that the initial impression fell short as she confidently approached her new patients and introduced herself. In a soothing voice, she calmed them along with a steady hand, soaking in every detail while completing a visual assessment that was not only thorough, but reassuring. Olivia could perform a number of treatments in the field. The clinic van had a portable x-ray unit that could go wherever she went. The clinic was not outfitted for a large animal major surgery, so she diagnosed and referred any of her patients that required that level of treatment to an appropriate animal hospital. Those with more severe injuries or illnesses were often transported across the state to Pullman's Washington State University's College of Veterinary Medicine for assistance which was fortunately not a frequent event.

Olivia found a folded-up lab coat at the bottom of the last box she unpacked. It was clean and starched, so she hung it up in the small wardrobe in her office with her other lab coats. Also, where some spare "house call" clothes and her Wellies were stored. Just as she was smoothing out the wrinkles in the garment, she heard the bell on the front door jingle as someone entered. She was sure she had locked it behind her as the clinic was closed. Dolce lifted his head but didn't bark or get up so she deduced that it must be Zio.

"Hello?" she called out as she walked toward the reception area.

"Hello?" responded a low masculine voice who was most definitely not her Zio.

Olivia stopped short, surprised to see a medium height, stocky-built man with wavy red hair in his mid-thirties, wearing a khaki utility kilt, and a "Be Calm and Carry On" logoed sweatshirt.

"I'm sorry, but we're not open today," she said, "unless there is some sort of animal emergency I can help you with."

"No, nothing like that," the man replied. "I'm here to see Dr. de Luca."

"I am Dr. de Luca," Olivia responded. "Dr. Olivia de Luca."

The man smiled warmly and held out his hand. "Ian McKay, your landlord and neighbor. I'm supposed to meet the other Dr. de Luca here today. I'm sorry, I didn't see his car and he mentioned that if I got here first, I should let myself in out of the rain."

Olivia smiled back after shaking his hand and said, "Sorry, Zio Paolo didn't mention anything about your coming over today or meeting anyone. Why don't you have a seat and I'm sure he'll be along soon."

Instead of sitting on one of the waiting chairs, Ian walked behind the reception counter and sat down on one of the office chairs like he owned the place, which in fact, he did. It rankled her a little all the same as the clinic itself, was not his. Before she could formulate an appropriate reply, the door opened, and the bells jingled again as her zio came in.

"Ah Ian, I see you've met my niece. Sorry you beat me here."

"Hi Dr. P. We just met, although I don't think she was expecting me."

"No, she wouldn't. Olivia, I forgot to tell you that I asked Ian to meet me here this afternoon to update our lease agreement. I didn't realize you'd be working all afternoon, but it's good that we're all here. Ian, my niece is now a co-owner of the clinic and will be taking over the business sometime next year, so that's why I need to update our lease agreement before renewing."

Ian opened a satchel he had carried in with him and started digging through the papers. "That sounds fine. We've got another month before the existing lease expires so we can take care of the change and address any other issues we need to update."

He set a manila envelope on the counter and looked back at the lovely young woman who was studying him with an unreadable expression.

Olivia looked at her uncle then back to the stocky, confident man she'd just met and then back again. Clearly her uncle liked their landlord as was evidenced by his comfortable interaction and the thump on the back he gave him when he greeted him. Although she had never met the guy before today, he did look familiar. Poulsbo was a small town situated close to several other small towns, and a man running around in a kilt was not a common site. She vaguely recollected seeing him somewhere in the past and thinking him to be a little unusual, yet adventurous. The twinkle in his eye as he bantered with her uncle suggested he also had a good sense of humor.

"So Dr. Olivia, let me."

"I prefer Olivia or Dr. de Luca," she corrected but softened the interruption with a grin.

"Ok, Dr. de Luca then, welcome to Poulsbo. Are you from Washington?"

"No, actually, San Diego. I am really enjoying it here though and looking forward to getting to know the area better. I've been busy ever since I moved and haven't been able to get out much," she explained.

"I've kept my niece pretty busy trying to catch up with all our patients," added Uncle Paolo. "She's been a godsend."

"You mentioned we're neighbors?" inquired Olivia, "I don't understand. I thought I'd already met my only neighbor."

Ian hitched his head in an upward gesture, "I live in a unit above," he clarified, "but I'm in and out at all hours so I guess we just haven't bumped into each other yet."

A friendly bark sounded from the back of the clinic and Olivia turned toward it. It was strange that Dolce didn't bother to follow her out as he was normally quite protective, particularly around strangers. Perhaps he already knew that Ian was living just above them and had formed his own opinion.

"That's my call to get back to work," she said. "Nice meeting you Mr. McKay."

"Ian is fine," he replied, grinning at her. "I look forward to seeing you again."

Paolo waved a hand as Olivia retreated. He turned back to Ian and said, "so, let's go over the lease and maybe you've got time for a cup of coffee?"

"I'd love to but will have to make it another time," Ian said. "I've been running errands all afternoon and I've got a deadline today and need to get on it."

"Deadline?" inquired Paolo.

"Well, um, another few stops I need to make," Ian answered. "I'd love to have a coffee soon though. Why don't you look the paperwork over and we'll schedule some time to discuss it over coffee next week?"

"Okay, that sounds good," replied Paolo and walked Ian to the door.

That was strange, Paolo thought to himself. The use of the word "deadline" seemed a little odd when Ian had said it. Oh well, as much as he liked the friendly man, Ian was a little odd when he thought about it. Odd indeed, but in a good way.

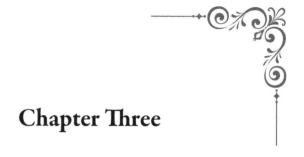

Chapter Three

Hot black liquid sloshed over the mug's rim as Ian set his steaming coffee down on the counter beside his, already booted up, laptop. The copy for his weekly advice column was due at noon and he had procrastinated long enough.

Ian's pithy replies to Dear Veritas had become an instant hit in the *Poulsbo Weekly Gazette* and now every local weekly in the county was running his column. At least the column was an instant hit with everyone it seemed except for his friends who were trashing the column the night before at their weekly card game. When Emmett compared Dear Veritas to a sarcastic version of Dear Abby, Ian barely had the control to bite back a scorching response. At this point, Ian was congratulating himself for not sharing with anyone that he was the wit behind the anonymous advice columnist as his friends would never let him live it down.

One night at the Longhouse, the neighborhood pub, when Ian was closing for his friend, the editor of the *Gazette* had overheard Ian dispense some sage advice to a talkative patron during last call. Then and there the editor pitched the idea for Ian to write an advice column from a bartender's point of view. Ian reminded the editor that he was not actually a bartender, he just poured drinks and closed when his friend, and owner of the pub, Donovan Hawk, needed an extra hand or Ian was bored. Ian was there frequently enough that many people mistakenly thought he actually worked there or even owned the place.

JUST A WHISTLE AWAY

It was shocking how many new and interesting people Ian met pouring drinks a few hours a week. Even more gratifying was catching up with the locals when he was in the mood to socialize.

The editor broke into Ian's introspection by saying, "You're missing the point, it's a male's nuance and perspective of their thinking that would be fresh and compelling to readers. You already dole out pearls of wisdom to troubled advice-seekers here at the Longhouse. You would be a natural."

After a couple of drinks and an hour of hashing around various ideas, the editor convinced Ian to try the column. Ian agreed with the following caveats: Ian would hide his true identity behind a pseudonym; the editor had to promise, in writing, that he would never, ever, divulge Ian's identity to anyone, and that Ian's responses would be his own – no editing allowed. With a clink of two glasses, the deal was struck. For a nominal fee, Ian would produce six columns. The fee would be renegotiated if the Gazette picked up the column after the six-week trial period.

Ian let out an exaggerated sigh as he ran his callused hands through his thick, wavy, mahogany red hair to get it away from his face. Before he finished off his mug of black coffee, he dispatched his weekly column – a smirk on his face as he thought about how his opinionated friends might react to Veritas' no-holds-barred advice. One task down, now it was time to get to his day job, the one that paid the bills.

Chapter Four

The sun was shining brightly and, but for the February nip in the air, one might think it was a beautiful late spring day. Olivia had to wear sunglasses as she drove the clinic van down the winding country road despite the shaded, tree-lined thoroughfare. She still marveled at her luck to be living in the Pacific Northwest with its readily available forestation and lushness without having to trek into the mountains. She always thought she couldn't live without big open skies, palm trees, and more than 300 days of warm, California sunshine. That was turning out to be anything but true.

"I could really get used to this," Uncle Paolo said, interrupting her musings.

"Living in the northwest? You've been here now for years," she replied.

"No, not that. I mean having a lovely lady chauffeur me around everywhere," he explained. Her uncle had suggested she do the driving when they went on house calls as he thought you learned your way around better if you were the one at the wheel. "It's going to be a real loss when I'm not on duty all the time and I have to drive myself everywhere."

"Oh Zio, you never have to do that if you don't want to," she teased. "I've seen the way all the single ladies look at you when they come into the clinic. In fact, I think some of their fur babies are not even sick and they just make something up so they can have some examination room time with you."

JUST A WHISTLE AWAY

"Oh, so you think that do you?" he retorted. "Well, you may be right. Who could resist my many charms? Take a right up here when you get to the T. Go all the way to the end and we'll be at Garrett's place."

Olivia laughed at him and continued down the road. "We've made pretty good time today and are a little ahead of schedule. Is it okay to show up this early?"

"Oh yeah, Garrett won't mind. He doesn't leave the place on Tuesdays as a general rule. He'll probably appreciate it actually and I wouldn't mind wrapping up early if possible."

"Hot date with one of your many admirers I suppose" she commented with a raised brow. "What's on the list to do for him today?"

"He has two rescue horses that he's been trying to put weight on and he wants us to check on their progress and do dental exams. While we're here, we might as well take a quick look at Sadie since she's been slowing down a bit, but on pace for her age."

"Sadie's the golden retriever he brought to the clinic a few weeks ago, right?" she asked.

"Yep. We always go the extra mile for her as she's saved more lives than I could count," Paolo explained. "Sadie's been one helluva rescue dog and has earned a premier retirement."

"I'm on board with that. I'm looking forward to seeing Garrett's operation. I think it's incredible how much good he does." Olivia stated.

Paolo had told Olivia all about Garrett's rescue operation. Garrett Olsen ran a small equine rehabilitation farm, and he also worked the past few years on mountain search and rescue teams with his well-trained dogs. He and his dogs had all served overseas in the military. They brought tremendous experience back with them, putting their skills to use in the community where the outdoors welcomed but sometimes caught even experienced hikers unprepared.

"That's his place right over there," her uncle said, pointing out a lodge-style house with big beams framing the entrance. Not far from the house was a decent sized barn surrounded by several small, separated paddocks and a fenced in field. A sheep paused from its lazy grazing to look up at them as they pulled closer to the barn.

"Does that sheep have a bandana on?" she asked surprised.

"Oh yeah, that's Pirate. She's sort of a fixture around here and is a calming influence on some of the rescues that come in. And before you ask, she's called Pirate 'cuz she only has one eye."

Olivia nodded and said, "Okay, why not?" She parked the van and they both got out to stretch their legs and let Garrett know they had arrived. Immediately, she saw movement and a black streak with a slash of white shot over their way and did a fast stop in front of them, hopping up in a barely restrained fashion to greet them.

"How you doin' Nitro boy," Paolo asked as he cuffed the lab's head teasingly and scratched around his neck and thick white collar, jangling the pup's I.D. tags in the process. "This is Nitro, Garrett's other partner who has mostly taken over for Sadie now. Speak of the devil..."

Garrett wasn't far behind Nitro and walked up to them smiling, hand reaching out for a friendly shake. "Glad to finally meet you Dr. de Luca. Your uncle has said only good things about you." His other dog Sadie wasn't too far behind him, tail wagging and eager to greet the visitors.

"Good to meet you Garrett, and I'm so glad I get to see your operation. We're a little ahead of schedule, but Zio Paolo thought you wouldn't mind," Olivia stated with a warm smile.

"Of course, he knows his way all around the place and you will too, soon. I wouldn't trust my animals with any other clinic and you're good to go with or without me," Garrett reassured her with a nod in Paolo's direction. "I think the new tenants are doing real pretty well, but you be the judge. The supplements you recommended seem to be working out. The filly is bouncing back fast. The twelve-year-old is improving, but just a little more slowly. Come see what you think."

Leaving the dogs behind, Garrett led them through the barn and out to one of the paddocks in the back where a small dun mare was nosing around the far end of the space and a red roan filly was laying down, soaking up the sun. The filly rolled over and got up when she heard their voices and nickered in response as she trotted toward them. The mare followed at a more discreet distance, sizing them up first.

"The little one's really socialized," noted Paolo. "She's beginning to fill out nicely."

"Yes, she's learned fast that people equal a good, square meal," chuckled Garrett.

Olivia opened the gate and put her hand on the filly's neck in a calming gesture. "Hey little girl, how are you doing?" She moved her hands over the animal, checking out her muscle tone and coat and letting them get to know each other. She pulled her stethoscope out of her vest pocket and listened to the horse's heart and lungs. "Everything is looking good," she said glancing at her uncle. "Let's see if she'll let me check her teeth." Olivia cupped her left hand under the young horse's chin and used her right to rub her nose, talking softly to her as she went. She eased the velvety upper lip back and the filly opened her mouth just a little but enough for her to get a quick peek.

"No need for an apparatus or to look deeper," Olivia announced. "All good."

The older vet slowly made his way over to the mare, hand extended with his fingers curled under to avoid getting nipped as she was unfamiliar to him. He approached her in an unthreatening fashion, slowly with his head turned to the side. The mare extended her neck and sniffed loudly but didn't back away. Before long, Paolo was giving her a good rub and quick check and came to a similar conclusion. "No broken teeth and while she could certainly put on some weight, she's not in any danger. I'm very pleased with their progress," he pronounced. "Keep doing what you're doing, and we'll look at them again in another month."

Garrett couldn't have been happier. He never would understand how anyone could neglect these incredible animals the way they sometimes did, but he welcomed each one he had room for with open arms and a determined commitment to see them through their troubles. The little filly hit him particularly hard. She had such a sweet nature, and it tore at his heart that she was so underweight when he took her in. The mare was not her dam, but she mothered her a bit as if she was. They each were helping the other adjust. Although they hadn't shown signs of physical abuse, they had clearly not been eating well and came from a farm where there were more animals than the pasture could support. They had not been getting the supplemental oats and vitamins they needed. He'd get them back in good health and then help find them a responsible home.

"Are you guys in a hurry or do you have time for a coffee or something?" Garrett asked once they were done in the paddock.

"I thought I'd do a quick follow up with Sadie while I'm here," said Paolo, "but yes, we can enjoy a little time after I'm finished since you're our last stop."

"That's great," said Garrett. "Let's go over to the house and find Sadie since she seems to have wandered off. Jacq is inside clipping things out of magazines, if I'm not mistaken." Garrett turned to Olivia and grinned as he added, "She's my fiancée and apparently there are a million wedding things that need to be planned."

"Congratulations! When's the big day?" she asked in return.

"We haven't quite set the date yet, but it will be sometime this summer. Jacq is an expert at planning events so all I have to do is answer a few questions along the way and she'll make sure it all happens on whatever timetable we decide. I'm glad you get to meet her today."

Paolo suggested that Garrett bring Sadie out to the van where he had a few things he needed. Garrett walked Olivia to the house to introduce her to Jacq and to find Sadie.

"Jacq are you still here?" he called out as he opened the door. "I want to introduce you to someone." He wiped his feet on the rustic mat but didn't step inside.

A beautiful, auburn-haired woman with the Golden Retriever at her side appeared at the door.

"We're right here," she answered and gave Garrett a quick kiss on the cheek. She reached out and took Olivia's hand in both of hers and said, "Hi, I'm Jacq. Come on in!"

"Hello, I'm the other Dr. de Luca. Please, call me Olivia," she responded feeling an instant connection to the woman who stood before her.

"It's so good to meet you! I've heard a bit about our new vet—all good things, small town, word gets around, you know..." She said with a sparkling laugh. "Come on in and let's get to know each other. Is Dr. Paolo here?"

"Yes, he's out at his van waiting for me to bring Sadie out for a follow up," explained Garrett. "Is there any coffee left?"

"I'll make some fresh," she responded. "Olivia, come in and tell me how you're settling in, and Garrett, no hurry so we girls can get acquainted, okay?"

Garrett nodded and headed back to the clinic van with Sadie matching his stride. Olivia took off her Wellies and stepped inside. "It's so nice of you to take time out of your day for us. I understand you're planning a wedding," she said. "I haven't really had many conversations with anyone outside of the clinic since I've arrived, and I appreciate this."

"Oh, it wasn't so long ago that I was the newcomer," Jacq noted. "I was going to stay just a few months while I settled my aunt's estate and look at me now! I ended up with a new town, a fiancé, started a business, and made a lot of new friends. All that in my first year."

"Impressive," noted Olivia. "I won't try to top that as I have my hands full with my uncle and taking over his business. Let's see if I'm as sane as you appear to be in a year's time."

Jacq laughed and invited Olivia to pull up a stool at the counter while she ground some fresh beans and made coffee.

"I don't think I'm ever going to regret coming here if for no other reason than the local commitment to making great coffee," Olivia joked. "It's almost ritualistic."

"We do like our coffee," Jacq agreed. "It did help coerce me into staying. Of course, meeting the man of my dreams sort of sealed the deal."

"Garrett seems just great, and he almost gushed when he invited me in to meet his fiancé. Where did you move from?"

"New York. It was quite a change of scene, but I found people here to be so welcoming and wonderful. I now own the farm next door and I met Garrett on my first day. Between him and my realtor, who was going to help me sell my aunt's house that I inherited, I quickly met a lot of their friends and now they are all like family. In fact, I was going to have some of the girls over later this week to catch up and spend a little quality time together. Do you want to join us? I know they'd love to meet you."

"I'd like that a lot," Olivia said, perking up at the prospect of meeting some women who weren't there to discuss only their pets. "We close the clinic at 6:00 so any time after 6:30 if it's a weekday works or anytime on the weekend. As long as I don't have an emergency to respond to, I'm totally available."

JUST A WHISTLE AWAY

"Wonderful," responded Jacq. "I'll see what works for the others and let you know." She grabbed her phone and said, "Let's trade contact info." That accomplished, she began pulling out mugs and setting up a little tray of treats that appeared to be home made.

"Do you bake?" inquired Olivia.

"I do, but mostly simple stuff. We have an amazing Scandinavian bakery in town that is a local institution, so I usually defer to them."

"You must be talking about Sluys," noted Olivia. "My nose led me straight to it my first day checking out the town."

Jacq chuckled and added, "The same thing happened to me! Now we've got another source of temptation—that new bakery by your clinic is good too and it's different enough from Sluys' that I'm sure they will also be a success."

"Oh, yes, I've tried it a couple of times and it is good. But there is something extra special about Sluys'."

Garrett and Paolo could be heard approaching and were soon opening the door and taking off their boots. Sadie, anxious to get in, squeezed past them and came over to rest her chin in Olivia's lap.

"Hello you soft girl." She stroked the silky fur on the dog's head and turned to Paolo. "Well, did she pass inspection?"

"Yes, that and then some," he said.

Garrett's eyes softened as he patted his thigh for Sadie to come over and sit by him. She nuzzled his hand and then lay down near his feet. "I know she's starting to get up there and has sure earned her retirement, but I can't imagine life without her. She's seen me through a lot and she's as much family to me as anyone born with two legs."

"I've been taking care of her since you came to town young man and she's got a special place in my heart too, even though we're told not to get too attached to our patients," Paolo added. "She'll always be one of my favorite patients and Livvie will take good care of her too."

Olivia nodded sincerely and said, "We always go the extra mile for a service animal."

Jacq filled all their mugs and they moved into the sitting room that was decorated with warm colors and lodge-like furnishings that just invited you to sink in and relax after a day of work. Olivia found herself enjoying the couple who made conversation easy and who were clearly so much in love that their warmth radiated out to embrace everyone in their orbit. It was nice to have an invitation to meet some other women and the prospect of making some new friends was as welcome as the smooth cup of coffee and the cozy room they were sitting in.

They wanted to know all about Olivia and, being animal lovers, couldn't get enough of her stories from her past jobs. Before long, a grandfather clock chimed the hour and Olivia realized they had stayed much longer than she was sure Paolo had intended. Her uncle got up and started gathering the mugs as he was planning an exit.

"Dr. Paolo thanks, but I've got that," Garrett said taking the mugs from him.

Olivia got up and walked with them to the door where their boots were next to each other, like soldiers lined up, standing at attention.

"Thanks for the refreshments," Paolo said, "and text me in a couple of weeks and let me know how all our patients are doing."

"Will do," Garrett nodded.

"Jacq, I can't tell you how nice it is to visit with you," exclaimed Olivia. "I'm really looking forward to meeting your friends, so thank you for the invitation."

"My pleasure and I'll get back to you tomorrow with the plan," she responded.

The two vets walked side by side back to the van and this time Paolo climbed into the driver's seat and backed up so he could turn around and drive straight out. It was nearing twilight, the sun had set and a few hints of stars were becoming visible in the fast, fading light.

"Really nice people," Olivia proclaimed. "If only all our clients had people like that looking out for them."

Paolo huffed and nodded in agreement. "Yup, that would be wonderful, but at least I can say that most of ours do." He pulled out of the long gravel driveway onto the main road and flicked the lights on as he headed home. "In fact, there's only one, now that I think about it that I have to prepare myself to see when they call to schedule."

"So, who do I need to brace myself for? A crazy cat mom?" she asked with a knowing look.

Paolo turned his face toward her with a gleam in his eye and began to answer when Olivia yelled, "Zio, look out!" All she saw out of the corner of her eye was a glimpse of movement— black with a white slash.

Paolo steered to the right and slammed on the brakes, bringing the van to an abrupt stop, but not before they heard a thud somewhere near the rear tires.

Dear Veritas,

I killed it. Or maybe it just died of old age but either way it's dead.

Against my better judgment, I let my neighbor talk me into watering his house plants and feeding his kid's goldfish while the family's away on vacation.

The fish lasted two days on my watch. What should I do? Flush it down the toilet; replace it with a look-a-like; bury it in the yard...? Currently, it's laid out in my freezer.

Signed: *No Good Deed Goes Unpunished*

Dear No Good Deeds,

Text your neighbor and ask him how he would like to manage the situation. He may know how his kid is likely to respond. The kid may want to bury it him or herself. Plus, his father can choose the best time to deliver the bad news.

If your neighbor wants you to dispose of it, put the fish in a paper bag and bury it in the yard. It might be a nice touch to mark the grave with a little cross made out of twigs or popsicle sticks so the kid can say goodbye. Do not flush it, we have enough unsanitary things in our plumbing systems.

JUST A WHISTLE AWAY

If there is a positive side to this unfortunate incident, you likely will not be asked again to watch your neighbor's place while they're away.

P.S. In the midst of your dilemma, don't forget to keep watering the plants.

Chapter Five

The next morning, Olivia gently picked up the sedated animal and slipped it onto a soft blanket inside a warm cage. The cat had broken its leg while trying to jump from a roof onto a tree branch and miscalculated the distance. The Tom had twisted mid-air to land on his feet but came down badly. The break was clean, but the leg needed to be pinned and stabilized. The cat wouldn't be happy when he woke up, so Olivia slipped a small treat into the cage's feeding bowl to make waking up a little less painful.

She looked at the clock by the door and swore. She was going to be late for her meeting with her landlord. Luckily, they were meeting for coffee at the bakery next door. She slipped out of her lab coat, put on a cream-colored cable knit sweater, and briskly walked out the door. Spying her zio Paolo washing down the medical van, she quickly made a detour to let him know she was leaving him with their patients for about an hour.

"I'm headed to meet Ian. Are you good to watch the clinic for a bit?" Olivia asked, making her voice heard over the hissing of the water hose.

Zio Paolo looked up, "Yep, the next appointment is a couple of hours from now, so I'm going to continue to try and get the smell off these back tires."

"It's a dirty job, but somebody has to do it," she said with a smile, "Not that I want harm to come to any animal, but I'm just glad what we hit was a skunk. For a minute there I thought we had hit Nitro."

JUST A WHISTLE AWAY

"It worried me there for a minute as well until I realized that Nitro is too well trained to run in front of a vehicle. I'll see you when you get back. Bring me a panne de chocolate on the way back, will you?"

"Of course, see you in about an hour," Olivia reiterated, heading next door to the bakery.

The smell of butter, cinnamon and sugar, overlayed with freshly brewed coffee assaulted her, in a good way, as she walked through the door. She was always impressed by the variety of Lily's offerings. Lily had trained as a pastry chef in France but had decided to return home and open her own shop after her parents had become older and needed care. Although trained in France, she had a variety of pastries that were her own special creations. Olivia loved her twice-baked croissants with dark chocolate, pecans and coconut. It was like a candy bar and croissant mashed together in one heavenly bite.

Lily smiled at Olivia when she walked in.

"The usual?" she asked.

"Please," Olivia responded as she looked at the other customers gathered around surprisingly comfortable, wrought iron café tables.

"Go ahead and sit down. I'll bring your coffee in a minute."

"Thanks," Olivia said.

She spotted her landlord in the back corner reading the newspaper with a steaming cup of coffee sitting by his hand. It looked like he had been there a while if the crumbs on the plate in front of him were any indication. He was leaning back in his chair with his legs stretched out, combat boots crossed at the ankles. He was wearing a plum-colored utility kilt, with a neon green t-shirt that proclaimed "*Once in a while someone amazing comes along...and here I am*" written across his chest in black, block letters. Olivia just shook her head. She had to admit he had great legs, but his wardrobe needed some renovation.

She put the folder she was holding down on the table. Ian looked up and jumped to his feet as Olivia pulled out her chair and sat down.

"Dr. de Luca, it's good to see you," Ian said, regaining his seat and sending her a smile.

"Olivia, please," she said as one of the cafe servers, with the name tag Heather, delivered her cappuccino and croissant to the table.

"Thanks," Olivia said as she smiled up at the woman. Heather smiled tightly back and gave a quick "You're welcome" before leaving the table. "I didn't realize how hard it would be working beside a bakery. It's everything I can do not to visit every time I smell butter and sugar through the vents in the clinic," Olivia said taking a much-needed sip of her cappuccino.

"Just imagine what it's like to live over the bakery. Impossible! Now, what can I do for you today?" Ian asked, thinking she was the prettiest veterinarian he had ever met. He hadn't met many since he didn't have animals, but he was sure she was extraordinary.

She opened the file folder she had put down on the table. He noticed it was adorned with flowers. It seemed regular manila folders didn't satisfy Dr. de Luca. He would have to remember that. Why it mattered to him, he didn't know, but it might come in handy in the future.

"I would like to make some improvements to the front of the clinic. I will pay for them, of course, but wanted to get your ok before I proceeded," she said as she turned some pictures to face him.

"I'd like to have some window planters built as well as bring in some large pots where I can plant small trees and edible flowers. I think it will add some cheeriness to the front of the building and I'll make sure it blends into the architecture." As she continued to lay out her plans for him, her face became more and more animated as she spoke about edible flowers, colors and textures. He was enjoying

JUST A WHISTLE AWAY   31

her enthusiasm, perhaps too much for somebody he had only met a few weeks ago.

"What do you think?" Olivia asked.

Ian had to mentally shake himself as he realized he had only been half listening to her. He was more concerned about the way her eyes sparkled, her hands emphasized everything that she said and, of course, her red, kissable lips that had him mesmerized.

"I think it sounds great. Are you up for some suggestions?" Ian grinned at her as she slowly blinked at him, not believing he had so quickly agreed to her ideas. She had thought she would need to do a little more convincing.

"Since I'm familiar with contractors and wood workers in the area, I can recommend a person who could probably make the window boxes. I'll pay for those. If we are going to enhance the windows on your clinic, then I think we should carry them through to Lily's space for continuity. They'll increase the value of the building, so that's on me," Ian responded. His grin had disappeared, and he was all business. "What do you think about wine barrels cut in half for the pots? I have a friend who owns a winery, so I can see if he has some available. They would probably be half the price of ceramic or concrete containers and might look better with the window boxes, especially if we go with distressed wood."

Olivia burst out laughing. She couldn't help it. It struck her as so funny, here was a guy who was wearing a stupid t-shirt in an eye-popping color but was intensely studying her ideas about some window boxes and flowerpots.

Ian frowned and looked up from where he had been writing ideas on her pictures. "What?" Ian asked in consternation.

"Sorry, I just didn't think you would be so quick to help," she said a little sheepishly.

He sat back and relaxed into his seat. Picking up his coffee cup, he looked at her through narrowed eyes. He raised his hand and circled his face with his index finger, "You were thinking this was just a pretty face," he remarked, nodding his head knowingly.

She raised her eyebrows and said, "Uh, I would say your legs are your best feature."

"I know, right, that's what I tell the guys all the time. If they had legs like mine, they would all wear kilts," he remarked with his trademark grin.

Olivia shook her head and stated, "I'm afraid you're a player, Mr. McKay."

Ian turned serious again and looked down at the pictures, "I'm really not. I just think life is too short to be so serious all the time."

She hoped she hadn't offended him, but decided to get the conversation back on track and asked, "Do you think the wine barrels will have too much residual acidity in them that will leach into the soil?"

Before Ian could answer, Heather came up to the table and asked Ian if he needed a refill on his coffee. Ian, thinking about barrels, soils, and flowers, looked up briefly and shook his head in the negative.

Heather stood by the table a little longer than necessary waiting for Ian to acknowledge her. When he continued to study the plans, she sighed and turned away, but not before Olivia saw the disappointment in her eyes. Olivia realized that Heather was attracted to the man and wanted Ian to notice her, but Olivia didn't think he was interested. She tuned back to Ian as he continued their conversation.

"That I don't know, but we could probably pressure wash the inside and possibly line them. I'm sure any nursery could give us some advice," Ian commented.

"Do you really want to help me out with this?" Olivia questioned. "I don't want to take you away from your work."

"I love a good project. But I'll back off if you would like to do it yourself. I just ask that you update me on your material selection," Ian stated looking at her warily like he assumed she would reject his generous offer.

"I'm all for partnering, as long as I get to choose the plants."

"Since I'm not a plant expert, I'll leave that to you," said Ian, "But I do have a question. Why edible flowers? That seems weirdly specific."

"I have a hobby where I use the flowers," she said.

Ian raised his eyebrows, silently asking her to elaborate.

"I make shortbread cookies decorated with edible flowers. I've been doing it for a while now and have built up quite an online following," Olivia explained.

"I love shortbread cookies. You do know that they are a creation from my home country? Pure Scots," Ian exclaimed.

"I'm not sure mine live up to the originals, but people seem to like them," Olivia said.

'Do you have pictures?" Ian asked, scooting his chair around the table to make it easier to see the images she was pulling up on her phone.

God, he smells good, Olivia thought to herself as he leaned closer. It was a clean earthy scent, reminding her of the smell of soft rain falling on moss and newly cut wood with a hint of leather. She found herself taking deep breaths, then stopped before he noticed, because how embarrassing would that be.

"Those are so unique!" Ian proclaimed, "I've never seen anything like them. Do you really eat them? Don't flowers taste like dirt?"

Olivia chuckled, "Of course they don't. Do you think people would eat them if they did?"

"I don't know, people eat a lot of crazy stuff. They drink expensive coffee from Indonesia pooped out of an animal's butt, so they may eat dirt," Ian remarked.

Olivia laughed at the dubious look on his face.

"They're delicious. I'll bring some to you so you can try them some time," Olivia offered.

'I'll take some in payment for my manual labor," Ian declared with a lopsided grin.

"Deal," Olivia said and held out her hand to shake.

Ian clasped her hand in his and gave it a gentle squeeze, feeling a bit of electricity race up his arm, making his heart beat a little faster. He liked that her hands were a little calloused, evidence of the work she did with animals. He was reluctant to let her go, but she pulled her hand back and stood up.

"When can we start?" she asked.

"If you trust me, I'll look into the materials and give you a call when I have something for you to look at."

"Sounds perfect. I look forward to hearing from you." Olivia gave a small wave as she turned to leave.

"Olivia," Ian called as she reached the door, paused, and turned. "Don't forget my cookies."

She gave him an enigmatic smile, turned, and walked out the door.

JUST A WHISTLE AWAY

Dear Veritas,

I want to be a good neighbor, but I've had it with the young couple who have moved in next door. They have been feeding crows for about six months now even though I have begged them to stop. Crows are loud, trashy, nasty birds that bully all the smaller songbirds and seasonal migratory species that used to delight us as they passed through. Their actions now result in about a hundred, yes, a hundred, crows coming each day! Naturally, they hang out in my yard too, dropping garbage and crow poop as they harass and caw at me when I try to work in my garden.

I've tried explaining this to my neighbors and have asked politely for them to stop feeding these pests, but they insist that their child adores the crows and claim a two-year old's needs must come first. I've suggested we work together and focus on less noisy and messy birds and offered to team up to create a welcoming environment for another choice. They are not willing to make any changes and just smile at me and tell me that I need to be more accepting of these amazing creatures and to appreciate the delight of a young child.

I've had it with these obnoxious, beady-eyed, winged monsters and I've had it with my irresponsible neighbors. I wouldn't harm the crows, although I often think they deserve it, but I'm ready to employ tactical methods to scare them away. Do you have any ideas? Ideally, something effective that won't hurt anyone or get me arrested.

Signed: *Too Young to Not Care, Too Old to Wait for Them to Move Away*

Dear Too Young,

Crows can be rather offensive, I agree, but not everyone sees it that way. Your neighbors aren't being very neighborly, but it is their property just as yours is yours.

As children, we were supposed to learn to play together. As a kid, my sisters and I really enjoyed playing with slingshots and super soakers—just saying. I have heard that a big, motion activated owl installation can be very entertaining to put in your yard. You can even put one right by your property line. Again, just saying.

Chapter Six

Olivia watched Ian's muscled back bunch and release as he picked up the bags of soil from inside the SUV and piled them next to the halved wine barrel pots in front of the clinic. It wasn't a particularly warm day, but it was one of those beautiful days that happened in the northwest where the temperature was in the high forties, while the sun shown gleefully down on the earth. Ian had been working hard to fit the window boxes underneath the sills as well as place the pots where she wanted them. As a result, he had removed his t-shirt. Something she was not unhappy about as she could watch the play of well-defined muscles in his arms, chest, and back. His skin was tanned with pronounced freckles looking like he was no stranger to working out of doors. Today he was in black cargo pants, but still wearing his signature combat boots, the leather showing nicks and scars from constant wear.

"I hope we purchased enough soil," Ian commented as he tossed another bag on the already substantial pile at his feet.

Ian had taken control of what Olivia thought was her project, but she was grateful. She had been busy at the clinic learning about clients, the finances, and working with her uncle to hire another veterinarian. She wanted to have another doctor in the office before Zio Paolo decided to hang up his stethoscope. Seeing that she was busy, Ian had sent her pictures of the window boxes and pots, asking her opinion along the way. She was steadily forming her opinion of Ian. He was solicitous of her feelings, was funny given the number and choice of emoji's he attached to his texts, he had a million different statement tees and was comfortable expressing his love and respect for his friends. It was also apparent he loved his motorcycle as Olivia couldn't mistake the sound of the engine as he roared out of the garage every morning it wasn't raining. And the muscles he sported spoke of a man who kept himself in top shape even though she saw him eating pastries as much as she saw him on his motorcycle.

"Earth to Olivia," Ian said, waving his hand in front of her face. "Whew, I thought I lost you," he said as she slowly turned toward him. "What were you daydreaming about?"

She shook her head, "I was thinking about the flowers and how great they are going to look," she said quickly, trying to make up for her lack of attention.

"Have you ordered the plants yet or do we need to run by the nursery?"

"I called the local nursery, and they have some of the starts I will need, but I may plant some from seeds. I'm thinking nasturtium, borage, definitely lavender and perhaps some blooming herbs like chive or dill. Of course, I'll need violas which will be at the nursery," rambled Olivia, "All of those should have a great flavor profile."

"What flavor profile is dirt?" questioned Ian with a smile.

"They don't taste like dirt," she scoffed, "Don't knock it till you taste it."

"No thank you. If it doesn't taste like chicken, I'm not eating it," stated Ian, going back to the truck for the last bag of soil.

"Well, no shortbread cookies for you then,"

"Now wait a minute. I think I'm due a reward for all the manual labor I'm putting in. Can't I have just one cookie for being so great at my job," Ian said, fluttering his eyelashes which, even though they were a strawberry blonde, were disgustingly thicker than hers, even with her Italian heritage.

JUST A WHISTLE AWAY

"That handsome face will not get you any cookies, but if you fill all the pots and window boxes half full with soil so they will be ready to pop in the flowers, I'll take you out for lunch," Olivia offered.

"Deal," Ian said as he grabbed a Swiss army knife out of his back pocket to slice open the first bag.

Olivia went back into the clinic to make sure everything was going as planned. Today had been fairly slow. Her uncle had said he would cover the office appointments so she could help Ian. They hadn't had any house calls come in, so her day had been largely free. She wandered in the back of the clinic to give some of the recovering animals a pat and a soft word of encouragement. Her uncle was just putting an orphaned kitten who had been bitten by a dog back in its cage.

"How's she doing?" asked Olivia.

"She'll be ok, but she may be afraid of dogs for the rest of her life. Time will tell how traumatized she is, but she'll make somebody a good house cat," Paolo stated.

"Ian and I were going to grab some lunch, if you think you can handle the lunch appointments?" questioned Olivia, "We'll bring you back something."

"Of course, it has been a light day. I'd like a sandwich and an iced tea when you return, if you don't mind," Paolo said.

"Thank you and I love you," Olivia stated as she leaned up to give her uncle a quick kiss on the cheek.

"Love you too, Livvie, now get out of here," Paolo said as he patted her on the shoulder.

Olivia stepped out of the clinic door, right into a hard masculine chest half covered in a neon orange t-shirt.

"Oomph," Olivia heard through the t-shirt that Ian hadn't quite gotten over his head.

"I'm hoping that's you Olivia or this could be really embarrassing," Ian was saying as his head emerged from the shirt and proceeded to pull the fabric over his torso that Olivia was currently eyeing.

"Are you ok?" he asked.

"Fine. Why do you have a poop emoji with a red cross through it on your shirt?" she asked quizzically.

"I'm a no bullshit kind of guy," he said smiling. "And I'm a little stinky from slinging dirt around. If you'll give me a minute, I'll go clean up."

"There's no need unless you feel like it. You are talking to a woman who deals in animal fluids and muck. I've smelled much worse things than you," she said without thinking.

"Um, I'm not sure how to take that comment, but I think you're saying I stink, but on the stink'o' meter it's not so bad," he commented and chuckled when he saw a pink stain start to bloom on her cheeks.

"Come upstairs with me for a second. I'll clean up really quick and grab the keys to my bike. We can take a ride into town for lunch. If that's ok with you?" questioned Ian.

"Sure," Olivia mumbled, still a little embarrassed she'd told him he smelled, but wanting to take him up on his offer. She had been dying to see his place upstairs and ride on the motorcycle he seemed to treasure.

She followed him up the back stairs and slipped through the door he held open for her. The first thing she noticed was the clean woodsy smell that permeated the space. Obviously from the cologne he used. Olivia hadn't known what to expect, but she was surprised at the designer quality furniture, warm woods, and masculine décor she observed.

"Make yourself at home. I'll just be a minute," Ian said as he made his way to the back of the building, presumably where his bedroom was located. "There is bottled water and maybe some soda in the fridge, if you are thirsty," he yelled just before a door snicked closed.

Olivia walked deeper into the apartment, running her hand along the back of the soft leather couch. There weren't many knick-knacks, but there were a series of black and white photos sitting on a table underneath the window. One of them was of his army brothers as she recognized a younger Garrett with his arm slung around Ian's neck. Another was of Ian and who she thought were his parents. The older gentleman had Ian's eyes and the woman was kissing a smiling Ian on the cheek. A smaller photo sat in between of Ian in full Scottish regalia, set against a forested back drop, playing the bag pipes. She lightly touched the top of the frame, thinking he looked rather lonely.

"Whatcha lookin at?" asked Ian as he sauntered back into the room.

Olivia jumped slightly, not having heard him. Turning around, she was about to comment on the pictures, but "Oh, hell no," popped out of her mouth.

Ian threw back his head and laughed. He was wearing a bright pink t-shirt with a rainbow unicorn encased in a sparkling cloud that read *I Suck At Fantasy Football*.

"Oh, come on, I'll wear my leather jacket. Nobody will notice!" he exclaimed as he donned said jacket.

Well at least he's wearing jeans, thought Olivia, as he escorted her out the door.

Ian backed the motorcycle out of the garage, stood it up next to Olivia, and ducked back into the building. He came out holding two black helmets and a smaller leather jacket.

"Here, put this on," he said handing her the jacket. "It's my sister's and she is about the same size." After the coat was in place, he dropped the helmet gently over her head and secured the strap.

"Does that feel ok? Not too tight or too loose?" he asked.

"No, feels fine," Olivia said.

"Have you ever been on a motorcycle before?" Ian inquired, securing his own helmet.

"Once I was on a dirt bike with my cousin, but that was a long time ago," Olivia stated, looking into his hazel eyes.

"Just hold on to me and move when I move, and we'll be ok. I'll take it slow since there's precious cargo on board," Ian said with a grin. She realized his voice was coming from inside the helmet. There must be some Bluetooth mechanism inside so they could hear each other on the road.

Ian slung his leg over the bike and started the motor. He held out his hand, pointed to the footrest, and helped Olivia get situated behind him. He drew her arms around him, enjoying the feel of her front mashed against his back.

"Ready?" he asked.

"Ready," she answered, tightening her grip.

Ian gently gave the machine some gas and eased out of the parking lot. Looking both ways, he headed toward town. He hadn't asked her where she wanted to eat but thought he would take her to the Longhouse to meet Donovan. After working all morning, he could use a meaty burger and a cold beer.

Riding the road on a powerful motorcycle with her arms wrapped around his solid core was a rush for Olivia. She had to admit, she was attracted to Ian and her libido perked up whenever he was near. But they were two very different people. She was the studious, geeky product of Italian immigrants who liked nothing better than to go home and curl up with a good book. He was the boisterous Scotsman who had his fingers in a plethora of pies and seemed to know everybody they encountered.

Before Olivia was quite ready to let go of Ian, they arrived at the Longhouse. Ian parked the bike then held out his arm to help her dismount. He followed, swinging his leg off the bike while at the same time removing his helmet and hanging it on the handlebars. He turned to Olivia, removed the strap from under her chin and raised the helmet off her head, putting it on the seat. She tried to smooth down her hair. Even though it was in a ponytail she was sure it was sticking up all over the place.

Ian grabbed her hand and led her through the front door. It was a little after the lunch crowd, so the atmosphere was more subdued than usual. Donovan was behind the bar with a newspaper unfolded in front of him.

"Ho, Hawk," Ian called as he walked up to the bar.

Donovan looked up and smiled at his friend. Then he looked at Olivia, then down at their clasped hands and raised his eyebrows. His scrutiny unnerved Olivia, so she pulled her hand from Ian's to smooth down her hair again.

"I'd like you to meet Dr. Olivia de Luca. This is Donovan Hawk. He's the owner of the Longhouse and one of my best mates," Ian said.

"Welcome, Dr. de Luca," Donovan stated in his quiet voice, clasping her hand between his hands.

"Just Olivia is fine," she said. The man was beautiful. Of American Indian descent, he had smooth brown skin, midnight black hair, with eyes so deeply brown they looked black. There was a calmness about him that made Olivia think he would be great with animals.

"What brings you two and your rainbow unicorn into my establishment this afternoon?" Donovan asked with a small smile that made his eyes crinkle at the corners.

"We were hoping to have some lunch and something cold to drink. We've been working on enhancing the front of the clinic with pots and flowers," Ian explained. "Any chance the kitchen is still open?"

"The kitchen is all yours. Take a seat and take this menu with you for the doctor. I assume you want your usual?"

"Yes, and Olivia, what would you like to drink?" Ian asked.

"Can I get an Arnold Palmer?" she asked.

"Coming right up," Donovan answered as he began to pour a dark beer from the tap. He handed the beer to Ian who grabbed the menu and led her to a table in the corner.

"How do you know Donovan?" Olivia asked, perusing the menu.

"I met Hawk when I moved to Poulsbo. Every once in a while he needs a stand-in bartender or someone to watch the place while he's away on business, so I help him out in exchange for free food and drink. We've been friends for a long time now."

Donovan approached the table with Olivia's drink and asked what she wanted from the menu. She ordered a BLT for her, and chicken club sandwich to-go for her uncle. Donovan disappeared into the kitchen and returned a little while later with Ian's bacon burger and Olivia's sandwich.

"Do you have time to sit with us?" Ian asked as he took a big bite out of his burger.

"Sure, just for a couple of minutes. I have a meeting in about a half hour that I need to jump on. Tell me Olivia, how are you liking Poulsbo?" Donovan asked.

"I'm actually surprised at how busy I am. When Zio Paolo asked me to join his practice, I thought it would be a fairly typical small-town clinic. I've discovered that there is quite the variety of animals around here that need a vet's care," she answered. "Of course, the area is beautiful and being with family so close by is a blessing."

Donovan nodded his head. "Garrett's animals alone could probably keep you busy for weeks."

"He definitely has some special cases," she remarked.

"What's new in Poulsbo? I saw you reading the newspaper when we came in," Ian asked, changing the subject.

Donovan chuckled. "I was just reading the latest Dear Veritas. Whoever writes it, definitely sees the funnier side of life."

"Isn't Dear Veritas the Dear Abby-like column?" Olivia asked.

"Yes, the other day somebody wrote about their neighbor feeding crows and the birds becoming a messy distraction. They asked Dear Veritas what to do about it," Donovan said. "The advice was sound. He advised them to get a big, motion activated owl and put it by the property line. I imagine before long, Dear Veritas is going to get another letter from the crow feeders asking what they do about the owl in their neighbor's yard."

"Seems like pretty sound advice to me," Ian stated emphatically.

Olivia looked at him and grinned. "What Veritas doesn't know is that as soon as the crows realize the owl isn't real, they'll ignore it. Crows are one of the smartest bird species out there. They'll either gang together and attack the owl so it no longer functions, or they'll ignore it, all the time thinking humans are dumb."

"No way crows can be that smart," Ian exclaimed.

"Oh, I assure you they are," Olivia said nodding her head knowingly. "They can even recognize and remember human faces."

"Well while you two debate the crow population, I have meetings to attend. It was nice to meet you, Olivia. I hope to see you again soon. And you, I could use your help at the bar tomorrow night, if you can lend a hand. It's live music night," Donovan stated looking at Ian.

"Yep, I'll be here," Ian said.

"Thanks," Donovan said giving Ian a slap on the shoulder as he walked away.

"You and Donovan seem close," Olivia remarked as she watched him walk down the hallway to what she presumed was his office.

"We are. He would be the perfect friend if he had a little more respect for rainbow unicorns," Ian stated with a dead-pan face.

"Yeah, I don't think rainbow unicorns are his jam," Olivia said with a sarcastic sigh.

Ian's eyes crinkled in laughter as he took another large bite of his burger.

Chapter Seven

Olivia had initially been delighted when Jacq invited her over to her house for coffee. The move to Poulsbo several weeks ago and the demands of the clinic hadn't left her much time to integrate into the community or make new friends. While she appreciated the opportunity to get to know Jacq better and get acquainted with her friends, the timing was less than ideal. She had been up half the night helping to deliver a bawling calf into the world who had stubbornly wanted to arrive tail first. The skittish cow and her willful offspring did not cooperate well with Olivia's efforts to reposition the calf to align with the birth canal. Olivia was a natural at intuitively knowing when to be aggressive and when to be gentle in order to reposition a breech calf. But last night's delivery, while successful, was challenging on several levels and the ordeal had left her exhausted.

Olivia was more of an introvert than most people realized as she was very much present and engaged in social settings. But meeting people for the first time was more draining for her than anyone might have guessed and today she was already lagging from lack of sleep. Olivia would have liked nothing more at that moment than to curl up with a good book next to a crackling fire. *Buck up*, she thought to herself, *you signed up for the job and lack of sleep is an occupational hazard*. With that thought, she stepped out of her red sedan and began walking up the steps to Jacq and Garrett's home.

Before she reached the front door a silver Subaru Crosstrek drove up and a smartly dressed woman radiating energy popped out of the vehicle and approached Olivia.

"You must be Olivia," the woman noted as she reached out her hand. "I'm Nicole. I've been excited to finally meet you and officially welcome you to Poulsbo."

"Thank you" Olivia responded as they shook hands.

Olivia took that moment to reflect on the woman standing before her. She was petite but exuded such confidence and vitality that she seemed much larger than her delicate frame. Her demeanor was warm and genuine, and Olivia realized, with some surprise, that she instantly felt comfortable around her. As Olivia met more people in the community, she would come to find out that Nicole had that effect on almost everyone.

Before the ladies reached the thick oversized door it swung open. An athletic woman with graceful movements swept Nicole up in an enthusiastic hug and then focused her attention on Olivia.

"Hi Olivia, I'm Lia. It looks like you've already met Nicole. Come on in, Jacq is the kitchen taking cookies out of the oven."

The smell of freshly brewing coffee greeted Olivia before the three women reached the kitchen. That glorious aroma was eclipsed by another one – Ginger Molasses Cookies. The smell instantly transported Olivia back to her grandmother's kitchen. When she was a young girl, it was her grandmother who taught her to make cookies. And it was cookies Olivia had always made when the academic rigor of her chosen degree stressed her out. Thankfully, it was stress baking versus stress eating that got her through becoming a veterinarian. If she was a stress eater, she was sure she would weigh 300 pounds. The cohorts in her program were huge fans of her baked goods, especially her signature cookie, Pistachio Shortbread, adorned with edible flowers and leaves.

Having removed her oven mitts, Jacq greeted Olivia with a tight embrace and then took coffee orders. When all were finally settled around the kitchen table with mugs of piping hot coffee and warm cookies on dessert plates, Jacq welcomed Olivia to the group and shared how she got to know both Nicole and Lia.

Olivia's fatigue melted away as she and her newfound friends chatted and laughed while getting to know each other. She found herself intrigued and entertained by their stories and gradually pulled into the group's supportive circle.

"You mean you each were married at Jacq's farm before she ever conceived the place as an event venue?" Olivia inquired.

"It's true. My husband, Brett, and I were married in her barn; it was magical! And Nicole and her husband, Matt, were married a few months later in her greenhouse," Lia gushed. "Jacq barely knew us when she generously offered her premises," she added.

"And now she is planning her own wedding to Garrett," Nicole interjected. Olivia looked over at Jacq, who was smiling and nodding her head in agreement.

"Jacq, you've got to tell her how he proposed," encouraged Lia.

Jacq chuckled at Lia's eager anticipation at hearing the story yet again.

"Lia is the hopeless romantic in our group," Jacq exclaimed before beginning her story.

"Unbeknownst to me, Garrett enlisted the help of my friend and business partner, Christopher, to come up with an 'unforgettable proposal' location. Christopher, knowing how sentimental I am, suggested my Aunt Rose's greenhouse. It was my Aunt Rose who left me the farm when

she passed away and that was her happy place. "

Jacq, Olivia realized, was fighting back tears and paused a moment to regain her composure. Her smile returned brighter than before as if a cloud passed out of the sun's rays, and she continued her story. "Garrett took me out for drinks," Jacq continued, "to give Christopher and his co-conspirators time to arrange things in the greenhouse. I could see the greenhouse aglow with flickering candlelight as we pulled up to the gleaming structure. Garrett took my hand and as we entered, I heard a violin arrangement of "To Make You Feel My Love." My senses were so overwhelmed by what I was experiencing that it took me a minute to realize the music was being played live by a willowy woman seated in the corner. The glimmer of hundreds of candles..."

"Three hundred and eight candles. I counted," added a contrite Lia feeling apologetic for interrupting Jacq.

Patiently Jacq resumed her story.

"The glimmer of 308 candles lit a rose-petal-strewn path to a small table set for two in the middle of the greenhouse. In addition to the enchanting candlelight, the potted plants had been rearranged to have Wedding Slipper orchids surround the table. I can't even begin to tell you how bewitching the setting was. When I looked up and into Garrett's eyes, he took both of my hands in his and got down on one knee and proposed. To tell you the truth, I'm not sure what he actually said, but I said yes! At hearing my affirmative answer, his face morphed into a relieved and then exuberant expression. And for some inane reason, we both started to laugh. I had never felt happier in my life."

Jacq sat there with a faraway look, obviously captured in her past. Lia jolted her back to the present when she stated, "Tell her about the chef that Garrett brought in from Seattle to cook a gourmet dinner and how you both talked for hours until the sun came up!"

"Well, I think you covered it yourself," Nicole intoned, giving Lia a reproachful glance.

"Wow, I don't think I have ever heard a more romantic proposal in my life," exclaimed Olivia. "I've met Garrett a couple of times and would never have guessed he was the overly romantic type. But good on him," she added.

Jacq affectionately grinned at her friends and replied, "I'm not sure he would have pulled that off without my 'fairy godbrother' and his merry band of helpers. You'll have to meet Christopher sometime; he's an old soul and also a hopeless romantic. He lives for pulling together unforgettable experiences. And the backdrop he created for the proposal was a wonderful gift to Garrett and me."

"I just had to hang around to hear the story one more time," Nicole announced. "But if I don't get going, I'm going to be late for a meeting with a client."

"I need to get going myself," Lia echoed.

Both women stood and Olivia and Jacq joined them. After hugs all the way around, Nicole thanked Jacq for hosting the gathering and said to Olivia, "I hope to see you again soon for coffee." Lia voiced similar sentiments.

Olivia responded, "I would love to get together again and next time, I'll bring the cookies."

Nicole and Lia were the first ones out the door, Olivia hung back to thank Jacq for including her in the get-together and for introducing her to Jacq's delightful friends.

"I hope you were serious about joining us again soon," Jacq stated.

"Name the date and time and I'll bring the cookies," Olivia promised. "And, Jacq, I would love to see your event site sometime."

"Well, if you have 15 more minutes, and would like to stretch your legs, I'll give you a quick tour of Heirloom Farm right now," Jacq offered. "Or maybe not," Jacq said, as she looked down at Olivia's midnight blue suede pumps. "I would hate for you to ruin your beautiful shoes."

"No worries," Olivia replied, "I always have a change of work clothes and a pair of Wellies in the trunk of my car. I never know when I may have to respond to an emergency that will land me in animal muck. Let me pop on my boots and I'll be good to go."

Chapter Eight

Olivia donned her favorite pair of Wellies decorated with vibrant Tuscan yellow sunflowers. Jacq put on her own pair of less colorful boots that were positioned near the front door. On the way across the damp pasture to the weather-worn, red-painted, barn, Olivia and Jacq chatted companionably. At Olivia's urging, Jacq elaborated on how she had inherited the farm from her Aunt Rose and had come out from New York to sell the place. Instead, she had fallen hopelessly in love with the helpful and handsome guy next door.

At Lia's wedding, Nicole had made a comment in jest about turning the barn into an events venue. The comment had planted a seed that eventually took root. It wasn't until the hotel Jacq worked for in New York was bought out and her career was about to take a new turn that her fellow employee and friend, Christopher, suggested that they go into business together and the idea bloomed into the fledgling enterprise of Heirloom Farm.

While pointing to the newest structure, Jacq explained that Phase I of the business had been to add guest restrooms and dressing rooms for wedding parties.

"Nice job at incorporating the new building with the existing ones," Olivia noted.

"Thanks," Jacq replied, "but Christopher came up with the design. He deserves the credit as I didn't make one change to the structural plans. We also modified the house. We greatly expanded the kitchen to make it conducive for catering large parties. The rest of the house we opened up to create a light, airy design studio for welcoming clients and planning events, as well as office space for Christopher and me. Already, the added conveniences are bringing in more clients and larger events. I am very glad our porta-potty days are over," Jacq grinned.

"You mentioned Phase I of the business, it sounds like you have additional plans," Olivia stated in a questioning tone.

"As soon as we have five consecutive months of running in the black, we have a landscaping master plan which will incorporate dedicated parking and paths linking all the structures. Phase III, at this point, is just a dream. But if all goes well, sometime down the road we would like to add bed and breakfast facilities.

As they neared the greenhouse, Olivia stopped dead in her tracks and let out an appreciative little whistle.

"I wasn't expecting that kind of greenhouse," Olivia admiringly breathed.

The English antique greenhouse was reflecting the sunlight, and the beveled panes of glass acted as prisms reflecting various colors of the rainbow.

"It was my Aunt Rose's pride and joy," Jacq stated, a tinge of reverence in her voice.

"Now it's yours and more importantly, part of your story," Olivia declared. "I can just picture it at night lit by candlelight," she added. "Now I have a visual to go along with your romantic engagement story. It must have been breathtaking!"

"The setting was a fantasy come to life but the man I will spend my life with is a dream come true," Jacq added as her throat and cheeks began to color at just the thought of Garrett. "What about you?" Jacq asked, determined to change the subject, "How are things going at your clinic?"

JUST A WHISTLE AWAY

Olivia smiled and replied, "It has been a very busy few weeks. My zio is getting more and more anxious to turn the reins over to me. He will stay involved as needed but is ready to slide into semi-retirement. He thought it was going to be harder to relinquish control of the business he built, but as I assume more and more responsibility for the veterinary clinic, he is happily letting go. I think having a family member to continue his legacy has allowed him to relax knowing the practice is in good hands."

"Are you making changes to the practice?" Jacq further inquired.

Olivia nodded her head as she stated, "Not so much to the operations, but I've been working with the landlord to spruce up the frontage of the clinic to make it more welcoming."

"Well, Ian is a reasonable guy. I'm sure he was fine with whatever changes you wanted to make," Jacq said encouragingly.

"I saw a picture of Ian and Garrett in his apartment. They were in military fatigues," Olivia stated.

"They served in the army together and have been best friends ever since," Jacq offered.

An unbidden visual image of her kilt-wearing landlord came to mind. The first time Olivia had met him, she was surprised by the utility kilt he was wearing but she had to admire his well-toned calf muscles on full display under his highland attire. At the time she had wondered if his quad muscles were equally well-defined.

"Almost every time I've seen him, he is wearing a kilt," Olivia voiced in a dubious tone. "Is that his normal attire?" Olivia surprised herself that she had asked that question aloud but too late to take it back.

Jacq chuckled knowingly, "Yes, it is. I must admit, it took me a while to get used to his eccentricities, but now, on rare occasions when I see him in trousers it just seems off. You'll get used to him; Ian is a bit of an acquired taste. But I have come to think of him as my crazy and extremely loyal brother. He's a good guy to have in your corner."

Olivia had experienced that first-hand with all the upgrades he had done to the front of the clinic without much persuasion. However, in her mind, jury was still out regarding her unconventional landlord.

Olivia was delighted by the tour and pleased that Jacq kept it to 15 minutes as she needed to head over to the clinic before going home. Her zio had asked her to stop by at the end of the day as he had a surprise for her.

As the evening's brilliant-colored twilight was being cloaked by dusk, Olivia thanked Jacq for the lovely afternoon and hopped into her car. She was becoming more curious by the moment about the surprise waiting for her.

Chapter Nine

What the heck, Olivia thought as she steered her red sedan to a parking spot directly in front of the clinic. Before sliding out of the front seat, she could see her headlights were illuminating yuck all over the front door. The top part of the door was glass, and the bottom half was metal. Her initial thought was that most of the door looked like it had been splattered with vomit. Perhaps a pet had been sick in its owner's arms and had...no, as she cautiously stepped forward, she realized it was something else. It looked like someone had hurled a giant coffee with cream at the door and it had splashed the glass and dripped down puddling on the cement. Her nose confirmed what she was seeing. She smelled sour milk that overshadowed the fainter aroma of roasted coffee.

Surely someone wouldn't have done that on purpose, would they? Well, either way, she needed to get the mess cleaned up. And then, she wanted to get home to Dolce and curl up by the fire with a good book.

Olivia let herself into the clinic, exaggerating her steps as she entered to avoid the puddle and grabbed the hose. She was grateful she hadn't changed out of her Wellies. The clinic was the last business on the south end of a strip mall. Just around the corner of the building was a water spigot. She connected the hose to the spigot and adjusted the nozzle to high pressure.

As she set to work, starting at the top of the door, she spotted it – her zio's surprise. She had been so focused on the gunk on the door that she hadn't actually focused on the door itself. In crisp new lettering, painted above her Zio Paolo's name, in slightly larger lettering, was her name and credentials: Olivia de Luca, DVM.

She stood there for a moment overwhelmed by her zio's generosity in placing her name above his on the door and in larger lettering. He was the one who had established and grown the business into the respected clinic it had become. Seeing her name in the prominent position made it all seem real. Until this moment she had thought of the clinic as his, even after they had signed the papers officially making her the majority owner a couple of months ago.

Now the responsibility of the clinic did feel like hers, and the feeling was a bit daunting. Olivia wondered why the clinic hadn't felt like hers when she had turned over her life's savings and signed the papers making her the majority owner, but for some reason, it hadn't. Seeing her name on the door brought reality into sharp focus. Zio Paolo was doing all he could to set her up for success, but the future success of the clinic was up to her. The major steps that brought her to this moment flashed through her thoughts: her family's immigration from Argentina when she was a young girl; years of study at UC Davis to earn her doctorate; long, long hours of residency at the clinic where she worked in San Diego; and the move to Poulsbo to launch her own practice. She was determined to throw herself at her work serving this community and she was confident she would make herself and Zio Paolo proud.

Olivia adjusted the nozzle of the hose to reduce the water pressure to avoid ruining the freshly painted glass. After removing the gunk from the door, she adjusted the nozzle once again and blasted the cement clean. If there was one thing a veterinarian knew how to do it was deal with gunk, not the most glamorous part of her job but a bigger part of the job than most people realized.

Task completed, she locked up the clinic and began her commute home. She would call her uncle on the way and thank him for the thoughtful surprise and all that he had done for her.

Dear Veritas,

I'm reaching out because I don't know where else to turn. My brother is ex-military. He was medically discharged from the Air Force about six months ago. He was a helicopter pilot and was hurt during a training mission. His chopper had mechanical issues and he went down in the desert. He was able to land, but his foot was crushed in the crash landing. He was fitted with a prosthetic, went through all of the rehab, but now he's struggling with what to do next. He was trained to be a soldier and doesn't know how to make the transition into civilian life. I've watched him become more and more depressed. I've encouraged him to get help, but I'm his younger sister and he brushes off my concerns. Knowing the high suicide rate for veterans, I don't want anything to happen to my big brother. Can you help?

Signed: *Out of Answers*

Dear Answers,

You are right. The transition from military to civilian life can be almost impossible for soldiers and soldiers with life-changing injuries have that much more to deal with. There are people who can help and relate to your brother's struggles. The Honor Organization and The Best Defense Foundation are just two. Please call the managing editor of this paper and give him your contact information if you want me to provide you with additional resources. Your brother still has so much to offer this world. Don't lose hope.

Chapter Ten

Ian sat in the Adirondack chair with one foot propped up on the footrest watching Garrett grill burgers. It had been a long day and he was happy to sit and play armchair chef while sipping on his Guinness. Sadie and Nitro lay around his chair looking as worn out as he felt.

"Where's Jacq tonight?" Ian asked, taking another pull of his ale.

"She and Christopher are over at Heirloom Farm putting the finishing touches to the barn. They are hosting a 50th wedding anniversary party tomorrow night for a couple who met when they both joined a square-dancing class. Apparently, they still dance, so their kids are throwing a square-dancing shindig for their parents," Garrett explained, gesturing with the long spatula he had used to turn the burgers.

"Well, then the barn seems fitting," Ian said. He sighed as he looked toward the farm even though he couldn't clearly see the buildings through the trees.

"What's up man?" Garrett asked, looking at his friend with concern.

"Just tired, I guess. I didn't sleep well, too many dreams."

"Deployment dreams?" Garrett asked, leaning against the deck railing with his arms and ankles crossed.

"Deployment dreams that morphed into apocalyptic nightmares. Not sure why they decided all of a sudden to come back, but they did with a vengeance last night," Ian sighed again, putting a hand to his forehead as if trying to rub the memories away.

"Yeah, well we both know they come and go with stress," Garrett said. "What do you have going that's got you twisted up?"

"Nothing more than the usual. I did decide to put an offer down on the Williams Building downtown. It's a fairly hefty investment, but the space is all rented and the businesses all seem stable."

"What does your sister say?" asked Garrett knowing Ian always asked the advice of his investment banker sister before he pulled the trigger on any real estate purchase.

"You know her. She's all for brick-and-mortar investments as long as they are in a place that is vibrant and growing and the businesses all have a sophisticated online presence," Ian explained. "She checked it out and gave me a thumbs up."

"So, it doesn't sound like the purchase is a big enough deal to throw you off. What about Olivia?" asked Garrett.

"What about her?" Ian asked, looking back over toward Heirloom Farm.

"Donovan said the two of you were pretty cozy at the Longhouse."

"Donovan is seeing romance where there is none. We just went for a friendly lunch," Ian explained.

"Why would you not consider romance with a beautiful woman who loves animals?"

"Come on Garrett. I don't even know how to do relationships. It's been too long. I'm more like a couple of dates, couple of drinks kind of guy," Ian said.

Garrett looked seriously at his friend. "You would make a great husband and father, but if I can't convince you, then at least give the pretty veterinarian a chance."

"Maybe," Ian said as he heaved himself out of his chair. "Can I get you anything to drink?" he asked as he walked toward the French doors leading into the house.

"No, I'm good. The guys should be here in a minute," Garrett stated as he watched his kilt-clad friend enter the house. Garrett turned back to the barbeque with a worried frown marring his face. It wasn't like Ian to be so taciturn. He wondered if something else was going on.

A few minutes later, the back door opened, Ian stuck his head out and pronounced, "We've got company."

Garrett opened the barbeque, determined the burgers were done and flipped them onto a tray. Where his kitchen had been empty a few minutes before, now it was full of his friends. "Hey, make way for the meat," Garrett said in an unnaturally low voice, putting the tray down next to the buns and condiments. All conversation stopped as plates were filled with burgers, broccoli salad and potato chips.

"What's for dessert?" Emmett asked, stuffing a potato chip in his mouth.

Garrett raised his eyebrows. "You haven't even eaten dinner yet."

"I was hoping Jacq made cookies," Emmett said with a hopeful look on his face.

"Molasses chews," Garrett stated. Emmett smiled and gave a thumbs up as he made his way to the dining room table.

Emmett sat his plate down, began to sit and immediately stood back up. "I forgot. I picked up the latest paper. I wanted to read it to you. I'll be right back."

Three heads turned to watch him walk out the door, then they resumed eating and drinking. Soon Emmett walked back in with the *Poulsbo Weekly Gazette* folded in his hand. "I suspected the writer of Dear Veritas was a dude and now I'm convinced," he said, "Have you all read the latest?"

All but Ian nodded their heads. "It must be hot off the press," Ian stated, washing down the bite of burger he had just taken with a long drink of ale. "I haven't received my paper yet."

Emmett nodded and handed him the paper. "It's from a gal who's worried about her brother who got hurt pretty bad in training. It sounds like he's really struggling."

The four friends were silent for a moment, each lost in their own thoughts.

"I've never served in the military," Donovan said, breaking the silence,. How did you three manage to make the switch?"

"I relied on a good therapist and my family," answered Emmett. "Going to therapy was looked down upon when I made the break, but luckily, a family friend convinced me that talking to somebody was the way to go. It doesn't seem like a profound solution, but I'm happy to say it worked."

"Ian and I had each other," Garrett explained looking at Ian who nodded. "We got each other through and, of course, I had the animals." Garrett looked down, with a soft smile on his face, at his dogs laying at his feet.

"Do you think we do enough?" asked Ian looking down at his empty plate.

"What do you mean?" Garrett questioned.

"I don't know," Ian answered, getting up from the table to put his dishes in the kitchen. "It just seems like something more can be done to help."

"The best thing, I think, is to hook people up with professionals who can help individuals work through their struggles. I think Dear Veritas has the right idea. Seeking help is the first step. I hope the sister reaches out," said Donovan.

"I do too," Ian said sitting back down with a prominent frown line between his brows.

"Do you guys feel like playing cards tonight?" Ian asked.

JUST A WHISTLE AWAY

"Not really," Donovan said with a sigh.

"How about we head to the deck," Garrett suggested. "And speak of happier things."

"Here, here," Emmett agreed softly.

Chapter Eleven

"Oh no, noooo," Olivia loudly lamented catching Ian's attention as he was walking down the steps from his apartment. From the tone of her voice, whatever it was, it wasn't good. Ian could see Olivia was looking down but couldn't see what she was looking at on the ground. Picking up his pace, it wasn't until he passed the front door of Lily's bakery that he saw the focus of Olivia's exasperation.

A colorful array of blooms was scattered on the ground near the planter boxes. It looked as though someone had haphazardly hacked off every bloom and bud of every plant. Ian turned his head looking back at the planters in front of the bakery. None of those plants had been molested. *What on earth*, Ian thought to himself.

As Ian neared the clinic's front door, Olivia was on her knees carefully collecting beheaded and abandoned blossoms. Ian could tell that some blossoms were flattened as if they had been stomped on and others were so badly damaged that it appeared that someone had deliberately ground them into the concrete with the toe of a boot leaving only a smear of color behind.

Olivia started and quickly leaned back on her pastel-colored polka dot Wellies as she sensed someone approaching from her side. She readied herself to stand up and then relaxed when she saw it was Ian. Relief flooded through her at the sight of him.

"Who would do this?" she contemplated aloud.

JUST A WHISTLE AWAY

Ian looked down at her hands cradling the blooms she was able to salvage and then back up to her solemn face. Ian's heart contracted as he looked at Olivia's pained expression. At that moment Olivia looked as delicate and vulnerable as the petals she was safeguarding. But in the short time Ian had known Olivia, he knew that characterizing her as vulnerable was a fallacy or at least a grossly incomplete picture of the woman before him. She was first and foremost resilient, intelligent, and strong, which Ian found incredibly appealing on a visceral level. *Dang*, he thought, *her looks also appeal to me on a physical level.* As she was leaning back on her heels, her jeans were pulled tight against her curves and because she was looking up at him her breasts jutted out in a pose that made her look like a 1940's pin-up model. A knotted fabric headband holding back her glossy dark brunette hair completed the look. He never thought a woman had appeared more captivating. She even rocked her Wellies in a way that was sexy. The whole package that was Olivia, Ian found desirable on several levels.

"First the coffee gunk hurled at the door and now this!" Olivia continued. "I wonder if someone is trying to send me a message?"

"What! What do you mean first the coffee gunk?" Ian questioned; his full attention refocused on her words.

"Oh, last week someone hurled what looked like a latte at the door of the clinic on the very day my name was painted on it," Olivia clarified. "I don't know if that was a coincidence or not, but now this..." She let the unfinished phrase die on her lips, her forehead scrunching in irritation.

Ian glanced at the door, not seeing any lingering residue of the previous incident. "If it wasn't a coincidence, who do you suspect would have done this?" he asked.

"I haven't a clue," Olivia insisted. "I haven't been in town long enough to make any enemies," she added.

Something about her phrasing and delivery of the last statement made Ian grin. "How long do you need to be in town before you'll have a list of enemies that I can start checking out?" Ian joked. His attempt to bring a little levity to the situation fell flat. Ian hurriedly went on trying to make amends for his regrettable quip. "Sorry, that wasn't funny, nor is this whole situation. You should probably be hyper-aware of anyone following you or taking more interest in you than normal."

Ian watched Olivia's features change from irritation to concern at his words. He clumsily went on, "It's just that growing up, I watched my two sisters dodge unwanted attention from a variety of Neanderthals. So, I tend to be overly protective. Not that you need protection," Ian hastily added. "Of course, I would protect you if it came to that," he stammered.

Olivia found herself looking deeply into Ian's hazel eyes. She could see genuine concern in them and the tint of embarrassment spreading on the rest of his face as he clumsily rambled on. She was touched by his sincerity.

"Oh heck, let me help you clean up," Ian said clamping his big mouth firmly shut and extending a hand to help Olivia stand.

After cleaning up the mess, Olivia and Ian headed into the bakery for croissants and coffee. Situated at a bistro table, Ian asked, "Do we need to replace all the plants?"

"No, I can trim up what's left. Nothing was pulled out by the roots. It will just take a while for the plants to bloom again."

Ian was dubious as the plants looked ruined to him, but *what did Ian know about green growing things*, he thought to himself.

"I'm sorry your morning got off on such a dreary note," Ian stated. "But I was serious about you keeping a lookout for anyone taking undue interest in you or the clinic. It's probably nothing, but better safe than sorry."

Chapter Twelve

Olivia entered the building and a smile bloomed all across her face. The Longhouse was clearly a cheerful gathering place for the entire community, with no specific age range, and people from all walks of life interacting, joking, and even dancing together in an atmosphere that defied a label. She'd been there once before when she came for lunch with Ian, but she'd been so focused on him that she hadn't paid much attention to the venue. It also seemed to take on a different look and feel at night. She looked around and took in the blend of northwest Indian art, European antiques, country kitchen and even a little industrial that somehow formed an environment that was uniquely welcoming and perfect. Clearly, the patrons were all relaxed and in fine spirits and there was an overwhelming sense of belonging.

"Olivia, we're over here!"

Olivia looked to her right and saw Jacq waving her over. She was sitting at a tall, round table with the two other women she had met at coffee the week before. Lia hopped down off her bar chair and pulled out another one, patted it, inviting Olivia to sit next to her. "I'm the weakest of the lot and can use all the reinforcement I can get," she quipped, "So please bring those brilliant doctor brains over near me and maybe I will absorb some extra knowledge," she joked.

Olivia smiled and sat down and said, "I have a feeling you can hold your own just fine. In fact, I'm counting on it as I've been so busy getting caught up at the clinic that I'm a little out of touch with all the latest scoops and that might be a problem tonight if they have current pop culture questions. I just hope I can contribute something helpful tonight."

Jacq piped up and said, "Who knows what to expect since it's the first trivia night they've had here. When you mentioned the other day that you enjoy these things, I knew we had to snag you for our team before anyone else did!"

"Well, since nobody else really knows me around here, you didn't have to worry," Olivia responded, "but I'm so glad you invited me to join you. And what a great place, I can tell this is going to be fun."

"I've got the entry form," said Nicole waving a paper around. She had taken on the job of getting them organized and registered, a natural role for her. "We need a team name. Anyone have an idea?" Everyone turned and looked at Olivia.

"Me? Well, I used to go after work with some of my girlfriends in California and we had pretty good luck together. We called ourselves 'Let's get Quizzical.' We could always recycle that one."

Nicole put her thumb up and nodded enthusiastically and the others followed suit. "Done," their organizer proclaimed. "I better get the sheet in as I think they are about to start. We ordered a bottle of prosecco to share but can I get you something else while I'm up?" she asked Olivia.

"Prosecco sounds great," Olivia said as Jacq started filling everyone's glasses.

Nicole was back in a flash with another piece of paper. "Looks like we have 12 questions, and we answer them all and turn in the form in 20 minutes. The honor system is in play and winners get gift certificates for food and beverages. Okay ladies, let's do this!"

Everyone raised their glasses and cheered "Let's get quizzical" together and laughed.

There appeared to be a number of other teams preparing to compete as well seated at tables discreetly spaced apart.

JUST A WHISTLE AWAY 71

"Okay, first question," said Nicole in a very serious voice. "Which one of the following is NOT one of the seven wonders of the ancient world: The Hanging Gardens of Babylon, the Great Pyramid of Giza, the Temple of Artemis, or the Taj Mahal?"

The women looked at each other and shrugged.

"I haven't traveled all that much so I'm not sure on this one," pronounced Lia. "I just hope the Taj Mahal is not the right answer. It deserves to be one of the wonders since it's such a romantic story."

"I'm not sure either," added Jacq. "I think the Temple of Artemis seems the most unfamiliar to me for some reason so if I had to guess, I might choose that one."

None of the others were very sure so they decided to go with the Temple as their answer and move on.

"Question two and this might be in Olivia's wheelhouse—how many bones do sharks have?"

Olivia laughed and said, "I've never worked on sharks and don't ever intend to. Not something we general service vets typically train for, but I do know the answer from my previous trivia tourneys. They don't have any."

"Well done, I knew you'd be a great asset," Jacq pronounced., making Olivia feel good.

"Okay, one maybe and one for sure that's right, so let's move to the next one." Nicole continued, being the good organizer she was, and kept them moving along. "In *Romeo and Juliet* which family is Juliet from? Malvolio, Capulet, or Montague? I know it's not 'Malvolio, but I don't know if it's Capulet or Montague," she added.

"Lucky for all of you I wanted to be an actress when I was young," Lia chirped. "And yes, I got the part of Juliet Capulet, thank you very much."

"How old were you?" Jacq asked.

"Thirteen. I thought I was destined to be a star, but I dreaded having to kiss Peter Musser who played Romeo and was a year older than me."

They all laughed and commented that they were glad she did and chalked up another correct answer. They had just worked their way through seven more questions with a fairly high degree of confidence when a bell rang and none other than Ian announced a five-minute warning 'til the sheets had to be turned in. Olivia hadn't noticed him up until now and was surprised that he seemed to be the trivia master. "Ian's in charge? She asked, puzzled. "He told me that Donovan owns the bar, but does he own this building too?"

"He thinks he does," Lia answered with a smirk. "No, this is sort of his second home and he helps us out a lot. It was Ian's idea to try trivia night, so I'm not surprised he's running the show. If there's fun to be had, most likely you'll find Ian in the center of things."

Olivia noticed that Lia had said Ian helps "us" out a lot. She must work here in some capacity as well, but before she could ask, Nicole moved them along.

"Talk later, work now," Nicole reminded them. "Two more questions and then we gotta get this in on time. Which of the following is not a U.S. president on printed currency: Andrew Jackson, Ulysses S. Grant, Benjamin Franklin, or Thomas Jefferson?"

"Wait, I thought they were all on bills," Olivia pondered. Which one is Grant on?

"He's on the fifty," answered Nicole.

"They are all on bills," Jacq added, "But were they all presidents?" she asked with a sly smile. "Benjamin Franklin was not."

Nicole whooped with joy and marked the form. "One last one, and thank heavens, it's an animal question." She paused to read it first and frowned. "I don't know if even you will know this one Olivia. Which mammal has no vocal cords?"

Olivia raised both her thumbs in the air. "Guess working in a zoo was meant to be. Giraffes, final answer."

Nicole whooped again and completed the form. "Okay ladies, here goes nothing!" She hurried over to find Ian and turn in their answers and then returned with another bottle of prosecco. She expertly popped the top, trapping the spent cork in her napkin with everyone applauding the satisfying sound, and held the bottle high in the air. "Here's to our team's first tournament, win or lose, best team ever!"

The competing team sitting closest to them looked over and raised their glasses good naturedly. The ladies cheered back at them, settled in to enjoy their drinks, and chatted while they awaited the results.

"So," Olivia began, "Tell me again what Ian does here?"

"You explain it Lia, you're the one who spends the most time here," nudged Nicole.

Lia turned to Olivia and explained that she worked at the bar full time before she was married and now helped out part time as needed while she was taking some classes at the community college. She wanted to learn more about the catering business and thought it was a logical progression after working at the Longhouse for several years.

"As I said, Donovan owns the place and Ian is one of his close friends along with Ian's old army buddies, Garrett and Emmett. You've already met them I believe. I'm sure you'll meet Donovan tonight once he gets a chance to wander around and say hi. He's a great guy, very smart, very good looking, a little quiet and mysterious actually, and very single." She waggled her eyebrows as she described him.

"I actually have already met him," informed Olivia, "But we only spoke briefly."

"Oh, that's wonderful!" continued Lia. "As for Ian, well, he is so outgoing, friendly and he always pitches in. I think most of the people who come here think he's the owner rather than Donovan. By the way, Ian is single, too."

Jacq laughed and clarified, "Now that Lia is happily married, she wants everyone she cares about to be in paired up and in love too."

"I do not!" exclaimed Lia.

"Yes, you do!" chimed Nicole and Jacq simultaneously.

Lia laughed along with them and admitted, "Well yes, maybe I do. So Olivia, do you have anyone special in your life? Maybe I should have asked that before suggesting anything with some of the guys I care about."

"No, no guys in my life at this time outside of the handsome lad I live with. And he's got four legs."

"Okay then, you've got to get to know Donovan better," Lia noted. "You're already getting to know Ian since he's your landlord. Any chance there's a spark there?"

"He does seem like a great guy, but not really the kind of guy I typically go for."

"Is it the skirts?" asked Jacq with an exaggerated grimace. "At least you know he has strong, muscular legs."

"Okay they are a bit unusual, but they somehow do seem to suit him once you get to know him," Olivia commented. "No, I just don't get the impression we fit together. But in all honesty, I'm not really out there looking."

Nicole's attention seemed to be somewhere else and Lia nudged her and asked, "What do you think Nick? Know anyone who might be looking for a girl like Olivia?"

Nicole looked directly at Olivia and said, "I'm not sure who that guy in the blue sweater by the window is but he certainly seems to be looking at you."

JUST A WHISTLE AWAY 75

Olivia glanced nonchalantly toward the window to see who Nicole was referring to and then turned back to the women, frowning in recognition. "I know who that guy is and he sort of gives me the heebee jeebies."

"Who is he?" asked Nicole. "I thought I knew almost everyone around here."

"His name is Wayne Hoffman. He's the accountant that my uncle Paolo used until I fired him. Let's just say the numbers didn't add up," Olivia said, keeping her focus on her friends, and ignoring the man staring at her.

"Well, I don't recall ever seeing him in here," added Lia. "He does look like a bit of a dweeb."

"I'm sure he's harmless," added Olivia. "We reported him but didn't make a big deal of it, just ended our business relationship, and went our way. I'm sure he was curious about Trivia Night and seeing him here is a coincidence.

"Coincidence or not, he appears to be leaving," noted Nicole. "We are going to stay a team if they keep up the fun and games, right?"

"You bet we are," said Jacq. "We're just getting started!"

"Count me in," Olivia added. "I love this place and I think we're a great team."

"I love this place too," said a deep, rich, masculine voice from behind her.

"Donovan!" Lia jumped off her bar chair and motioned for him to come over by Olivia. "I heard you already met Olivia, but I bet you didn't know we recruited her for our team."

Donovan offered a strong, warm hand in welcome and it enveloped Olivia's in a perfect clasp—not too firm, not too limp. His dark, knowing eyes crinkled slightly as he smiled at her.

"Welcome back Olivia, I'm so glad to see you again. It makes me happy to hear you like my place." He said it in such a simple and honest way that it felt incredibly sincere.

"I'm really happy to be here and I'm thoroughly enjoying tonight—you've got a wonderful pub."

"It's the people that make it wonderful," he responded. "I'm glad you like it. It looked like you ladies are having a fun time tonight. Good luck to you although I'm sure you don't need much of it. There's a lot of knowledge at this table," he said as if he knew the depth of their wisdom. "I'm going to go help Ian finish up with the results."

Olivia turned back to the ladies as he walked away. "Boy, did you describe him to a T. What an interesting guy."

"He is," Jacq said thoughtfully. "He has depths beyond most people I've ever encountered, and he is just as thoughtful as he is deep. He and his buddies are quite the brotherhood. They are also about the most caring and responsible men I've ever met."

"And that's why you're marrying one of them," added Nicole.

"Got that right!" nodded Jacq.

"Speaking of what we got right, look girls, Ian is getting ready to announce the winners." Nicole pointed to Ian waiting for everyone's attention over by the Jukebox that had been temporarily silenced.

"Ladies and Gentlemen, may I have your attention," said Ian in a loud and theatrical voice. "To begin with, I'd like to thank you all for joining us tonight at our first ever Longhouse Trivia Night." He waited for the applause to die down. "Now, some of you were here to observe, and some of you came to play!" He was dressed all in black tonight with a gold lightning bolt emblazoned over the front of his t-shirt which was stretched just enough to show off his toned abs and muscular arms. He wore a black utility kilt and the usual black combat boots with black wool socks peeking out of the tops.

JUST A WHISTLE AWAY

"We had 10 teams competing tonight and prizes will go to both the winners and the runners up. So, without further ado...let's announce the results. Second place and a prize of $50 worth of food and beverages at our fine establishment go to the team who got 9 out of 12 answers right, the Poulsbo Legends!"

The crowd cheered and chanted, "Legends, Legends" as three men and two women stepped up to take a bow and claim their prize.

"Do you think we missed more than three?" asked Lia with a concerned note in her voice.

"Shhh," said Nicole, "don't jinx us. We're about to find out."

Ian motioned for the house to quiet down and then continued. "And now, without further ado, the winners of our first Trivia Night with 11 out of 12 answers right, the winners of a prize of $100 worth of food and beverages, the team to beat the next time we try this, the team who has..."

Donovan stepped up and put a hand on Ian's shoulder. "Can you please just announce the winners now?"

The crowd laughed and stomped on the floor chanting "Winners, Winners."

Ian looked at everyone in mock disgust, "I was just getting there. Okay, the winners with 11 out of 12 questions right is (pausing briefly) Let's get Quizzical!"

Once again Lia leaped off her chair and began jumping up and down. "We did it!" she proclaimed. The four ladies made their way to the front to claim their prize and retrieve their form so they could see which question they missed. Ian offered a group bear hug to all the ladies, and waved and said, "That's all folks," to the cheering crowd.

It took a while for the winners to navigate their way back to the table as so many of the patrons wanted to congratulate them. By the time they returned, Ian had pulled up an extra chair and presented them with another bottle of prosecco.

"Good job ladies!" he said. "You really know your trivia."

"So which one did we get wrong?" asked Lia.

"The first one," Nicole said after reviewing their submittal. "It wasn't the Temple of Artemis, but The Taj Mahal."

Jacq wrinkled her nose up, patted Lia on the back, and commented that she would have guessed that one last.

Ian complimented them one last time and said they were a hard team to beat. "Even me and the guys would have had trouble beating you had we been allowed to play," he said gallantly.

"Oh really!" exclaimed Nicole. "We could always go to trivia night somewhere else and put that theory to the test."

"That sounds like a plan," Ian countered, "and I won't even complain if you bring your ringer."

"Our ringer?" asked Nicole.

Ian gave a knowing look at Olivia and then turned back to Nicole. "Yup, your ringer. Dr. Paolo told me his niece was a fierce trivia player. Didn't you know?"

"We do now," laughed Nicole.

Olivia blushed slightly and said, "I think my uncle exaggerated a bit. I played a little with friends in the past and he thinks everything I do is wonderful. I'm family after all, and we are Italian," she joked.

Ian looked at her thoughtfully and softly commented, "Oh, I don't know about that. You seem to know what you're about."

Jacq turned slightly and gave Nicole a pondering look.

"Well, we're just glad we got her first." Lia threw an arm around Olivia's shoulders and gave her a squeeze. "And we're gonna crush you guys when we get a chance, just wait and see."

Ian laughed and said, "You're on! Okay, I gotta go back and help at the bar. Good job again tonight ladies. I'm glad you won!" He smiled at Olivia and nodded to them all and went off to whatever duties he intended to fulfill.

"We will beat them, won't we?" asked Lia.

"We might or we might not." Nicole answered. "Either way, we'll have a great time trying."

The winners continued to enjoy talking about their victory while they finished the prosecco, sharing it with the runners up who had stopped by to meet them and smack talk in jest. Finally, they called it a night and walked out together, pleased with their performance and making a commitment to defend their title at the next trivia event.

Jacq walked with Olivia to her car and suggested that they meet for coffee sometime soon. Olivia said she'd reach out once she had a handle on her schedule and waved goodbye. It had been such a lovely evening, and it felt good to make friends so soon after moving. As she pulled out of the parking lot and headed home, she thought about the easy camaraderie of the night. She smiled as she recalled Ian's handling of the awards and thought about how he had looked at her when he commented on her trivia experience. She was so lost in thought that she didn't notice a car had pulled out right behind her and was following at a discreet distance, even though she had long since turned off the main drag.

Dear Veritas,

Writing to you is a bit of a last resort. I'm hoping you can help me with an embarrassing problem as I really don't have anyone else I can ask to advise me. I'm 32 years old and I work at the shipyard. I'm an electrical engineer and I make a good living. I'm a responsible, nice guy and I'm caring and decent. I'm just a regular guy. I know I'm not particularly exciting or attractive, but I'm not horrible looking and I don't have weird hobbies or anything like that. I'm painfully shy and always have been. I've never dated, but I've always wanted to. I did invite a girl to a high school dance once and got publicly shot down. I tried again a couple of times in college, but I only got sympathetic looks and awkward excuses.

I'm a grown man now and it's time. I really like a server at a coffee shop I go to and I'd like to ask her out. She seems very friendly to me and she always draws a heart on the foam of my drink. I know it's probably because that's her job but how can I tell if she can actually see past my protective barrier? I don't have any sisters or friends who are women to advise me and I'm hoping you can help. How can I ask her out in a way that won't ruin my ability to stop at my favorite coffee shop if she says "no" or better yet, get her to say "yes?"

Signed: *Latte Love to Give*

Dear Latte Love,

JUST A WHISTLE AWAY

First, don't think for a minute that you're the first guy (or lady) who has yet to find someone they click with. It can be a long and frustrating journey and there is, unfortunately, no magic phrase that I am aware of that will guarantee you success. You've made a successful career from a very challenging subject. Clearly, you've got brains! It's time to try to let go of the unhappy memories from your youth and focus on the fact that you're an educated, successful man.

Maybe the lady you'd like to go out with will be interested and maybe not, but you will never know until you try. Have you had any conversation beyond your coffee order? If not, start there. See if you have anything in common. Then, when you have an opportunity to ask her privately, just be friendly and ask her if she would like to have someone, somewhere else make her a coffee for a change and offer to treat. If you don't make a big deal out of it, you won't risk too much, and she won't feel pressured. If she isn't available, she isn't available. You at least got some practice and are better prepared for the next time you meet someone. If she says yes, well, there you go!

Latte luck to you!

Chapter Thirteen

Ian sat in front of the computer going over his books. Bookkeeping wasn't his favorite occupation, but with the help of his sister he had found a system to keep track of his buildings and the leases attached to each. When he had retired from the military, he had invested in his first rental building. It was a small house that somewhere in its long life had been converted into office space. The building had been well used and needed rehabilitation. Luckily, Ian was handy with a power tool, so was able to do much of the renovation himself. When he was finished, he leased it to a small legal firm specializing in estate management. They had been his tenants ever since. His holdings grew from there to a total of seven buildings, including the one Ian used as his home base.

His older sister had been a huge help. She was an investment banker and had helped him with all the paperwork associated with buying a building. She had also negotiated with the bank for attractive loan terms. Ian had paid her back by providing her with her favorite single malt Aberlour 16 which she shared with him when he visited. Ian's younger sister was a chemical engineer, working for a start-up space exploration company. She had always had her head in the clouds, so it seemed fitting she was reaching for the stars.

Ian's parents were a combination of conservative Brit on his mom's side and kilt wearing Scots on his dad's. Although his sisters took after his mom, Ian embodied his pure Scottish dad. With his red hair, and his barrel-like build there was no mistaking his Celtic

JUST A WHISTLE AWAY

heritage. He was happy that he had gained a little more height than his Scottish ancestors. Although he didn't tower over people, he usually wasn't the shortest one in the crowd either.

In his teens, Ian had decided to wholeheartedly embrace his Scottish heritage by learning to play the bagpipes. His family had toured Edinburgh Castle while visiting his father's family and he became fascinated by the piper bands and their history. He was determined to learn the pipes and his parents indulged his wish, buying him his first instrument when he turned fourteen. Ian started on the Border Pipes and, after three years of complete dedication to his art, graduated to the Great Highland Bagpipes. Playing the pipes was his way to relax and let his mind concentrate on nothing else but the music. His parents had also purchased for him the McKay tartan kit complete with a *sgian dubh* with his family crest etched in the handle. He looked up from the computer and spied the dagger in its ceremonial case sitting on the bookshelf.

Ian had gone to college, but after a couple of years had joined the military. He had finished his degree in international studies while serving his country. Ian had never been a great student, but he was able to graduate with decent grades. What surprised him the most was how much he relied on his financial studies and on his sister while managing his investments. Ian wouldn't say he was terribly wealthy, but he was more than comfortable for the lifestyle that he led.

Ian's phone rang, pulling him out of his reverie. "Well, hello," Ian answered with a smile in his voice. "What's up, oh sister of mine?"

"Do I have to have a reason to call my favorite brother?" his sister answered.

"I'm your only brother, but it's nice to know you love me," Ian said, chuckling.

"I wanted to let you know, I'm sending over the estate documents for your new building. I need you to look them over and, if everything looks good, sign and send them back."

"Ok," Ian said. "Thank you once again for your help. This probably means I need to send another bottle of scotch over?"

"That would be lovely. I'm almost out of the last one," she acknowledged. "I also called to discuss Mom's birthday. What do you think about sending Mom and Dad on a cruise?"

"They've been on cruises before."

"Yes, but I was thinking we could send them down the Mississippi on the big paddle boat."

Ian laughed. "It sounds like you're sending them down the river, never to return."

"I'm not sending them down the river Styx, just to New Orleans. Dad loves to sing the blues, and the cruise starts in Memphis. They can listen to music, eat great food, and perhaps see a ghost or two."

"I'm in," Ian said. "Let me know what you need me to do."

After making a few more plans, they rang off promising to speak later.

Ian saved his spreadsheet, closed his computer, and went in search of a snack. Stacked by the door were boxes filled with cameras and surveillance equipment. He may have gone overboard, but Olivia's safety had become his top priority of late. The fact that only the flowers in front of Olivia's clinic were decapitated seemed rather suspicious. His goal now was to catch the person who was vandalizing her clinic, and by association his building, especially if the perpetrator decided to try something else.

As always when his thoughts turned to Olivia, he conjured up the image of their motorcycle ride together and the feel of her plastered to his back. Many a night he lay in his bed trying to calm down his body and trying, but failing, to think of anything else but the curves of her body, the whiffs of lavender and vanilla he'd catch when he leaned close, and the softness of her skin when he would brush up against her. He found his dreams filled with Olivia and his mornings looking forward to when he would see her again. It had been a while since he had been so intrigued by a woman.

It's about time I manned up and asked her out, Ian thought to himself as he began unpacking the boxes. But first he needed to concentrate on keeping her safe. His spidey sense was telling him that something was wrong, and he never ignored his gut instincts. He had learned that lesson well during his tour of duty in the Middle East.

Packing the equipment in a satchel and grabbing his toolbox, Ian trotted down the stairs to get started on Operation Keep Olivia Safe. Putting down his equipment, he retrieved a ladder from the garage. He already had a few cameras up in the back that pointed toward the green belt at the rear of the property and still others that pointed toward the parking lot, but his new equipment would give him an almost 360-degree view of all the building entrances and exits. It wasn't as if Poulsbo and the surrounding areas were hotbeds of crime, but under the circumstances, Ian thought going a little overboard was warranted. He hadn't told Olivia that he was beefing up security, but he didn't think she would put up too much of a fuss. However, he was going to broach the subject of placing cameras at her home as well. If these pranks were directed at her and not the building, he wanted to make sure she had some security to fall back on.

Ian was just placing the last camera near the veterinarian clinic back door when the door opened and knocked into his ladder.

"Hey, whoa there," Ian exclaimed as his ladder rocked to one side.

"What are you doing?" questioned Olivia, peeking out of the crack in the door.

"I'm setting up additional security around the doors," Ian said, jumping off the ladder and moving to the side out of the way.

"Why?" asked Olivia.

"If you hadn't noticed, somebody is playing some pranks on your clinic. I want to make sure if it happens again, that we catch them."

"Don't you think that is a little overkill? It was just a splashed latte' and some clipped blooms. It doesn't seem to warrant additional security," said Olivia.

"I know it is a cliché, but better safe than sorry," Ian stated.

"You think it is more than just a few pranks, don't you," Olivia enquired, looking at him with a frown.

"I don't know what it is, but my gut tells me there may be something more to it," said Ian, "so I'm not going to take any chances."

"You're giving me the creeps," Olivia looked at him then back to the almost invisible camera on the door.

"I don't want to scare you, but I want you to stay on the lookout for anything that seems suspicious or somebody hanging around that shouldn't be. Just promise me you'll stay vigilant," Ian said gently squeezing her arm in comfort

"I will," said Olivia just as a loud grunt sounded behind her and she pitched forward into Ian's chest. Ian caught her before she could face plant onto the concrete walkway. There was snuffling sound behind her. Ian looked over her shoulder and spotted a black and white pot belly pig rooting around Olivia's feet.

"Who do we have here?" asked Ian, making sure Olivia was steady before he crouched down and held his hand out to the animal.

"Darn it Pork Chop, how did you get out of your cage?" Olivia asked in exasperation as she scooped up the little pig.

"Pork Chop?" Ian questioned incredulously and then outright laughed as the little pig squirmed in Olivia's arms.

"I have to go, I'll see you later," Olivia said as she gave one last concerned look up at the camera and went back inside. The last thing Ian saw as she slipped through the door was a wagging, black curly tail.

Grinning, Ian took a couple of more minutes to calibrate the new cameras with his phone making sure the video worked. He looked around the back of the clinic thinking that anybody could approach the building through the trees. The foliage was dense and a great place to hide. Shaking his head, thinking he was seeing ghosts where there were none, he turned his back on the forest to break down the ladder and put it away just as a shadow moved through the trees.

Dear Veritas,

I find myself attracted to a guy who is definitely not my type. Should I pursue a relationship or keep my distance?

Signed: *Wanting a Ring Someday not Simply a Fling*

Dear Wanting,

You left me wanting a lot more information about why the guy is not your type. Lacking specificity, my response is going to be more general than normal and probably less satisfying than usual.

Perhaps the reason you're still single is that you've pigeonholed yourself into a "type of guy" that has needlessly limited your dating pool, missing out on Mr. Right.

If his looks are not your type don't be so superficial. If he's a bad boy, with a prison record, your mom would probably say he's not your type and you may want to listen to her.

Expand your perspective and don't prejudge a type. Tamp down your preconceived notions and pay attention to compatibility, personality, chemistry, and common goals. You might find you need to redefine "your type."

Chapter Fourteen

Dolce was curled up in his dog bed watching every move Olivia was making in the kitchen. One never knew when a tasty morsel might accidentally fall to the floor. Besides, it was nice to be close to the action and the delicious aroma that wafted through the room as his favorite person on earth did her baking.

Olivia hummed along with the music streaming softly through the house—a nice mix of soft rock from the 80's and 90's that always reminded her of being around her parents. She had just pulled a tray of shortbread out of the oven and was getting ready to decorate the final batch. She had salvaged as many delicate blossoms as she could from the planters that had been vandalized outside of the clinic. Slim pickin's, as it was still early in the year, but she had salvaged some violets and pansies. She'd also found some clover at home that would do. Before long there would be some lavender and nasturtiums, two of her favorites, but what she had, would have to do for now. She still couldn't believe someone would be so mean as to destroy all the beautiful flowers in the planters the way they did. Ian surmised it was kids up to no good, but he obviously was concerned enough to already install some security cameras. Oh well, things happen, and plants grow back.

One of Olivia's favorite ways to unwind was to bake shortbread cookies and decorate the top with tiny, edible flowers or portions of them. She enjoyed the act of selecting a delicate blossom and gently pressing it into the light egg wash she'd brushed over each individual cookie. Once they were affixed, she lightly sprinkled some sugar on top and then baked them into beautiful, tasty, little works of art. Later in the afternoon, she'd be taking them over to Jacq's for coffee with the girls and she was looking forward to sharing them with her new friends she knew would appreciate the effort.

"Just a few more minutes Dolce and we'll go out for a romp," she said to her faithful companion. He really was a sweet-tempered dog, but he made her feel safe all the same, living out away from town as she did. She dug into the lower cupboards where she remembered putting a little vintage tray away when she unpacked that would be perfect for loading up with the cookies. She'd made enough to take to her coffee date as well as fill a small box to take to Ian tomorrow as a thank you for being there after the planter episode. *Nothing more than a simple thank you*, she clarified for herself. After all, he'd seemed like a bit of a renaissance man who would appreciate the design of the cookies as well as the taste which he would learn was nothing remotely like dirt.

After finishing up in the kitchen, she went outside with a tennis ball and an enthusiastic dog for a good 30 minutes of play. She loved watching her pup show such delight in something as simple as fetching a ball and chasing her around the garden playing a version of tag they'd come up with together. She'd always felt drawn to animals of just about every kind, but when she met Dolce at the shelter, it was absolutely love at first sight. Once the dog was thoroughly exercised, she put him back inside where he bee-lined over to his comfy bed. Olivia freshened up and put on a clean, long-sleeved T and pulled her hair back into a tortoise shell colored clip. She locked up and secured the tray of cookies in the backseat of the car and headed over to Heirloom Farm where she was looking forward to meeting up with the gang. They'd had such a great time at the trivia night event, and she was anxious to get to know them better.

JUST A WHISTLE AWAY

Her mobile phone rang over her hands free and she answered, "Dr. De Luca, may I help you?"

"Olivia, it's Jacq."

"Oh, hi Jacq, I'm glad it's you and not an animal emergency. I'd hate to miss our coffee date. I'm on my way now, is everything okay?"

"Yes, everything's fine. I just forgot to tell you that you're welcome to bring your dog along if you want to. I'd love to meet him, and we're used to animals around here. As long as they are good around others, they're welcome."

"That's so thoughtful," Olivia answered. "But since I'm already on my way, how about next time? I'd love to bring him then."

"That sounds great. I think Nitro, in particular, would enjoy a play date."

"Perfect. That would be good for Dolce too. He's always got some extra wiggles to get out. Ok, I will see you soon. Probably in about 15 minutes."

"Looking forward to it."

Olivia smiled to herself thinking about how well work was going and how nice it was to begin settling in and meeting people. Her uncle Paolo was already cutting back his hours to just a couple of days a week and all their clients seemed comfortable with her taking over. She wanted a few more months to really get established and then she planned to invite her parents up for a visit. They were a close family and her parents had always been so proud of her. They would be thrilled to see how well she was doing, and it had been a while since they had seen Zio.

The move to the northwest did put more distance between her and her parents than they'd ever had before, but she felt it was a good thing and the timing was right. Although she'd always had an independent nature, striking out on her own in business and starting a new life a little further away suited her at this stage. Besides, they were only a few hours' flight apart and had plans in place to spend the holidays together. Her parents had hoped she would have met someone special by now, but they didn't harp on the idea of getting married and starting a family the way some parents do. She wasn't opposed to the notion, but it wasn't her raison d'être either. If she met the right guy, then she was open to the idea. If she didn't, well, her career was very satisfying to her and that would be enough. It couldn't be much better than being a vet and spending time around so many beautiful and interesting creatures.

She wondered if there was any chance the right guy was waiting for her somewhere around here. She thought about Lia encouraging her to take a look at Donovan and she had to agree, he wasn't hard at all to look at. His dark hair, chocolate brown eyes, and his mysterious ways did sort of make a girl pause and catch her breath. But if she was honest with herself, she had to admit that he wasn't the one she found her thoughts frequently turning to. Strangely enough, it was the crazy guy in the kilt who seemed to have many facets to his personality that were starting to capture her attention. And while he wasn't handsome in the head turning way that Donovan was, he was still a striking looking, fit and interesting man who did, as Jacq had pointed out, have nice legs.

Olivia chuckled to herself at the prospect of introducing her parents to a guy who wore kilts. She imagined her mother would be a bit taken aback but would try to act as if she didn't notice, while her dad would probably ask him to explain the choice of attire as if there was some particular, defensible need to dress that way. Just the thought of it made her feel mischievous enough to consider going down that path should the opportunity present itself. Strangely, she had a hunch that it might. While a date or two with Ian might not go anywhere, it sure could be fun.

Heirloom Farm came into view and Olivia drove around to the back of the farmhouse where she noticed the others had parked. Jacq was waving to her from the door of the beautiful, restored

JUST A WHISTLE AWAY

greenhouse. She hoped this meant that's where they would be having coffee.

"Olivia, we're in here," Jacq called, beckoning her over to the greenhouse once Olivia stepped out of the car. She removed her denim jacket and left it in the car since the day was unseasonably warm, and reached for the wrapped tray of shortbread she had prepared. As she approached the greenhouse, she could see Lia and Nicole sitting at a table in the center of the structure along with a handsome man who looked like he stepped out of a fashion magazine. He wore skinny jeans and what looked like a custom-made button-down shirt.

"Come in. We're just about to pour coffee. I want you to meet one of my closest friends and business partner, Christopher Parks.

The man, who was somewhat slightly built, stood up and touched her shoulder and then gave her a casual brush of a kiss on each cheek, Italian style. "Ciao Olivia, I'm so glad to meet you," he said with a smile, "I hope you don't mind my crashing your coffee date."

"I'm happy to meet you as well, and not at all," she responded. "What a lovely setting for coffee and such a beautiful table." A white, medium sized iron bistro table was draped with a vintage French provincial cloth. There was an old stoneware pitcher filled with pussy willows and ivy in the center Five Italian ceramic mugs, small plates and spoons, and a matching creamer and sugar bowl were on a tray as well as a plate of several types of biscotti and a stack of chocolate truffles. Olivia set her tray on the table and sat down to join the others.

"Christopher came by to go over a few things and I invited him to stay so he could get a chance to meet you," Jacq explained, "Plus, he always adds a little somethin' somethin' to any party," she added fondly, nudging him with her shoulder.

Turning toward Olivia, Jacq asked, "What did you bring us?"

Olivia removed the wrapping on the tray to the delight of all and said, "I finally got a chance to whip up some of my shortbreads."

"Those are exquisite!" exclaimed Christopher extending an elegant hand to select one. "If they taste as good as they look, we're going to have to talk." Taking a bite he gushed, "Delicious. Not just beautiful, but buttery and light. Best shortbread ever. Olivia, what is your secret?"

Olivia laughed and said, "I'm glad you like them. No secret really. I use rice flour which makes them a bit lighter. If there is any secret at all, I guess it must be that I have so much fun making them."

"Would you ever consider making them to fill orders? These would be perfect to serve at some of our events," Christopher added.

"Well, I'm not sure how much time I'll have for a while, but I could produce some now and then. I used to sell some on Etsy when I was looking to make a little extra money in college," she responded.

"Pass those cookies this way," said Nicole.

"Absolutely," piped up Lia. "So, Olivia, I hope you've been well. I'm still lording our trivia win over the gang who came in second whenever I see them at the Longhouse."

Jacq filled their mugs with coffee from a large carafe and began passing around the cream and sugar while Nicole set a small plate and spoon in front of each of them. She also passed around a stack of beautiful napkins decorated with cheerful lemons and vines.

Lia made sure that Olivia's tray of cookies went around as well and soon everyone had a few delicious morsels piled onto their plates to go with the aromatic cups of hot coffee. The sun filtered in through the glass of the greenhouse. White chairs were stacked off in the corners and large, potted ferns were lined up near the door. The remaining space was filled with shelves full of orchids, a number of which sported beautiful, colorful blooms. The overall scene was artfully unintentional and totally delightful. A speaker somewhere behind the chairs provided happy, light classical music and Olivia felt that she had landed somewhere in a movie set of a European get away.

"So, Olivia, I won't ask you to tell us everything about yourself, but do catch me up on all the particulars," Christopher asked in a "just us girls" sort of way.

"Well, where do I start?" Olivia responded with a theatrical raised brow.

"You could always start with the juicy stuff," he encouraged.

"Oh, stop Christopher," chastised Lia. "We don't want you to scare her off after we've just met her!"

Olivia laughed again, enjoying the teasing banter and said, "No chance of that. If he wants me to talk about sticking my arm inside of a pregnant cow and..."

"NOOOO!" exclaimed Christopher. "I'll behave."

"Serves you right," added Jacq. "Seriously Olivia, you're really among friends here and Christopher usually has perfect manners when he meets someone new. For some reason he feels comfortable getting personal with you."

"I'll take it as a compliment," Olivia said grinning at Christopher. "And the basics are this—I'm happy I've moved here from California, I'm swamped most of the time with my work as a vet, I've got a beautiful dog named Dolce, I'm contentedly single, and so far I've met the nicest people. Anything else?"

"Hmmm, contentedly single," Christopher echoed.

"That's right, but we're going to work on that one," Lia added.

Olivia coughed as her coffee went down a little wrong when she heard that. "But we're not going to work too hard on that too soon," she added. "I'm a firm believer that when it's meant to happen, it happens."

"What Delilah says," Jacq noted.

"Excuse me?" asked Olivia.

"What Delilah says," added Christopher. "She's Jacq's favorite therapist."

"She's not a therapist," Jacq explained. "She's a radio host and she's really very smart about these things."

"Jacq really connects with her," Christopher explained. "She's listened to her for years and she takes most of what she says to heart."

"Me and a bazillion others. She hasn't steered me wrong yet, and between the two of us I'm the one who found true love, so there's that," Jacq said pointing to him teasingly.

"I'm familiar with her," Olivia told them. "In fact, I was at her farm yesterday on a consult to her vet who needed my assistance with her zebra. She really seems like a lovely person and she clearly has a giant heart with a soft spot for kids and animals. I enjoyed meeting her."

Everyone else at the table except for Nicole froze with their mugs in various elevations looking gob smacked.

"Zebra? You met Delilah? And she has a zebra?" asked Christopher. "Oh, this just went from good to great."

"Yes, to both questions and didn't you know she lives around here?" Olivia asked.

"Oh, we knew, but not exactly where and we haven't ever seen her around," Jacq replied. Nicole was suspiciously silent. "Nicole, you know everyone. Have you met her?"

Nicole took a sip of her coffee and lifted a biscotti in the air. "Well, yes, as a matter of fact I have. But as you all know, I don't talk about my clients."

"She's your client?" exclaimed Jacq. "What? Have you just met me? Did you not know what a huge fan I am?"

"Settle down darling. Aren't you glad to have reassurance that your friend and favorite realtor is so trustworthy?" Christopher offered. "I'm sure she would have said something if she felt that she could have."

"Correct," said Nicole. "And where she lives remains private at her request."

"Same here," added Olivia. "I won't say anything more than what I already have other than meeting her was a really enjoyable experience."

"And if you ever need an untrained but caring assistant with your vet duties in her vicinity..."

"You will be the first person I think to ask," Olivia reassured her. "How about passing those truffles over here? Now Christopher, your turn to tell me a bit about yourself."

"Oh, there's not much to tell but if you insist...Let's see, I grew up in New York but I'm loving being here in the northwest, I have a great business partner and the work is fun, I'm still waiting to meet my Mr. Right, and I have a feeling that we're going to get along famously."

"Christopher couldn't make it to Trivia Night, but we'll get him on the schedule for next time. He's good with all the F's—food, fashion, fine art, and finance," added Nicole with a wink.

"That's wonderful," Olivia said with thumbs up. "We'll be invincible!"

Jacq disappeared and returned with a fresh carafe of coffee and the group enjoyed another hour of sharing stories about when they first moved to the Poulsbo area, work, and the weddings that both Lia and Nicole had in the past year. It was such an easy group to talk to and they all agreed that this should be a regular thing.

"How about we get together at my place next time?" invited Nicole.

"Yes, let's do that. She's got a very nice house with a view of the water," Jacq said. "It's always fun to watch the boats go by."

Christopher offered to clear the table for Jacq as her guests got up to leave, so she could walk the other women out to their cars. "I'm so glad you all came today," she said warmly.

"Thank you for having me over again," Olivia replied as she picked up her now empty tray. "I thought we were going to go out, but when you suggested we meet here I had no idea that I'd get to see the others and get to spend the afternoon in such a delightful setting. No coffee shop could compete with this."

Jacq smiled and gave each of her friends a hug and replied, "Anytime."

As the women drove off, Christopher came outside and offered Jacq a kiss on the forehead. "I like our new friend."

"I could tell," she responded. "She's a good one; I think we'll keep her."

"And she knows Delilah," he quipped.

Jacq socked him lightly in the arm. "We're not going to harass our new friend to make introductions that she's not at liberty to make, no matter how much of a fan girl I am."

"I wouldn't mind spending some time with a zebra though," he added.

"I'm not sure that zebras and unicorns actually get along," she said thoughtfully.

"Good point. Maybe I should hold off on that," he noted as he climbed into his white Tesla and pulled the gull wing down. He waved goodbye, backed out, and headed home while Jacq went over to close the gazebo and go find Garrett. It had been a most spectacular day.

Chapter Fifteen

The day had been long, exhausting, and emotional. Olivia's morning was booked with routine care for domestic pets. Before lunch, not one but two emergency walk-ins imploded her schedule. One of the emergencies resulted in a young woman making the agonizing decision to put down her beloved lop-eared rabbit rather than prolong its suffering. Olivia felt the owner's painful and heartbreaking decision was the right one for the pet, but the compassionate decision did not ease the trauma of the loss.

Olivia always scheduled lunch on her calendar knowing she would not always get one. Emergency drop-ins didn't happen every day, but often enough that Olivia kept a box of protein bars in her office. Olive grabbed two bars and filled up her stainless-steel water bottle with cold tap water and headed out the door. She was determined to get back on schedule with her afternoon field visits.

Olivia had to stop by three farms, and all were geographically spread out, which would take her a while to make the rounds. While all the farmers were long-term clients of her zio, she was meeting each one for only the second time. The first time was when her Zio Paolo took her on a tour introducing her to his regular clients, but this was her first time flying solo. She knew she would need to win over the clients herself if she wanted the practice to continue to thrive.

At the end of a long tiring day, Olivia pulled her car up to the backdoor of the clinic. Darkness had fallen quickly as clouds obscured the moon and any twilight that normally lit the horizon. She could see no bright lights on in the clinic, only the dim glow of overnight lights. Her zio had arrived at noon to cover the afternoon shift, so he must have made it out of the clinic at a reasonable time. She had not been as fortunate.

Olivia leaned her head back on the headrest, closed her eyes, and exhaled a protracted breath. *Onward* she thought as she mustered the energy to exit her car, feeling emotionally spent and weary. She wasn't feeling hungry until she got a whiff of something garlicky her landlord was making in his apartment; the heavenly aroma made her realize she was famished. Her stomach rumbled, punctuating the fact it was empty.

First things first, Olivia thought as she moved to the neatly coiled hose next to the back door of the clinic. She efficiently sprayed off the muck from her bright yellow and aqua-checked Wellies. As she leaned over to recoil the hose, a rock ricocheted off the wall not too far from where she was standing. She froze, straining to hear any other sounds. The rock had ricocheted almost straight back from the wall which meant the rock came from somewhere behind her. She quickly whirled around and saw no one in the wide ally behind the building but the hairs on her arm and neck were standing on end as she felt eyes upon her. *Was it her imagination*, she wondered as she scanned the stand of trees and bushes just beyond the pavement. *Well, the rock didn't throw itself*, she reasoned. *Someone must be out there.*

Peering toward the trees, looking for movement, another rock came hurling in her direction. Olivia went from tired to hyper-alert as adrenaline flooded her system. She could feel her heart pounding and willed it slow so she could better hear the noises around her. Frozen in her tracks she felt like a sitting duck. She fumbled in her pants pocket for her keys as she moved to the front of her car and crouched down using the car as a shield. She pressed the alarm button on her key fob and a loud, sharp, repeating tone pierced the evening's quiet. Two things happened at once. A large Great Horned Owl took flight screeching as it swooped down from a tall cedar into the open, likely startled by the unnatural racket of the car alarm, and someone, perhaps startled by the alarm or the owl, began running through the trees in the opposite direction from Olivia. She strained her eyes trying to make out who the assailant might be, but the shadowy figure was obscured by the vegetation and wore something that provided good camouflage.

The threat removed, Olivia slid to the ground and took deep breaths attempting to slow her pounding heartbeat. Even though the night was cool, sweat broke out on her forehead. Before she had time to process what had just happened, above her and to the left, Ian's back door swung open so violently that the door bounced off the building's exterior siding. Ian was already through the door and running down the stairs before the door could rebound into him.

Ian caught sight of Olivia sitting on the ground leaning against the grill of her car and vaulted over the railing skipping three steps to reach her more quickly. Squatting next to her he took her hand and asked with urgency: "Are you all right, what happened?"

As Olivia recounted the events, she saw Ian's muscle tense and his free hand contract into a fist. His features contorted into an angry but controlled mask. He was torn between pursuing whoever was out there and keeping Olivia safe.

Ian stood, not releasing Olivia's hand, and said, "Come on, let's get you inside" as he pulled her to her feet and quickly led her inside. With the crisis over she began to tremble.

"You're shaking," Ian noted, "no doubt coming down from an adrenaline rush" he added. "Come here," he said, opening his arms wide and she automatically fell into them. "I just opened a bottle of Merlot, and you look like you could use a glass."

Ian was warm and he held her tightly yet tenderly. She leaned her head on his solid chest and the two stood there for several minutes, neither moving nor feeling the need to speak. Olivia was taking strength from his calm and reassuring presence. It wasn't long before her elevated heartbeat slowed and matched the steady rhythm of his.

When Olivia felt more in control of both her emotions and physical self, she reluctantly leaned back from Ian's comforting embrace and said, "I'm ready for that glass of wine now."

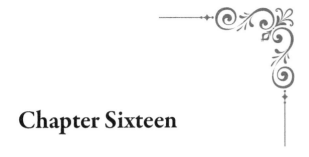

Chapter Sixteen

Ian was able to offer Olivia more than a glass of wine. He had a whole chicken in the oven on a bed of garlic cloves, lemons, and thyme surrounded by carrots and red potatoes. Ian donned a set of hot pads and pulled dinner out of the oven, setting it on the counter. He loosely covered the roasted chicken with foil as it needed time to rest allowing the juices to redistribute into the fibers of the meat.

"Dinner in fifteen," Ian announced, grabbing his laptop to check the footage from the security cameras. With Olivia looking over his shoulder, they reviewed the footage. Disappointingly, the cameras captured a very clear shot of the owl, but nothing of the assailant who must have approached from the backside of the greenbelt and never left the cover of the trees.

Over dinner and a bottle of wine, Olivia and Ian discussed the disturbing events of the past few weeks. Both were now convinced the escalating events were not a coincidence. Olivia was definitely being targeted. Ian encouraged Olivia to park her car in front of the clinic where there were more motion detector lights and fewer places for someone to hide. Additionally, traffic on the street in front of the clinic might deter someone from loitering in the shadows.

Ian was furious that some coward was harassing Olivia. He was so frustrated by the gutless creep that it was all he could do not to punch something. What concerned him most is that the events were intensifying and next time the attacker might find his mark. He was frustrated that these events were happening on his property –

practically under his nose. He would not be able to forgive himself if something happened to her, especially if it was just yards from his apartment.

Abruptly, Ian stood up and said, "I'll be right back," and rapidly disappeared down the hallway. Olivia took the opportunity to stand up and stretch her legs. She wandered over to the fireplace and was warming her hands near the crackling logs when Ian returned.

"I have something for you," Ian said as he reached for Olivia's hand and reverently lowered his gift into her palm, curling her fingers around the present. While Ian was looking down at Olivia's hand, she had been looking at Ian's earnest face trying to decipher the meaning of his intense expression. When Ian looked up and met her eyes, he could see an unasked question in them.

As Olivia unfurled her fingers, Ian said, "it's a whistle and a damn loud one. My grandfather gave it to my grandmother on their first wedding anniversary. They had recently seen the movie "To Have and Have Not," Bogart and Bacall. There's a famous line in that movie where Bacall's character says: 'If you want me, just whistle. You know how to whistle, don't you...?' Olivia joined in on the last line and recited along with Ian, "You just put your lips together and blow." For a long moment, that felt much longer, neither one spoke. The current between them was electric. To break the unintended and quickly growing sexual tension, Olivia slowly brought her hand up to examine the whistle dangling from a silver rope chain. While she inspected the beautiful sterling whistle, embossed with a thistle on its cylinder, Ian continued his story.

"My granny couldn't whistle, so my granddad gave her his father's Scottish officer's whistle on the chain so she could blow it if she wanted him," Ian paused, hitched a shoulder, cocked his head, and continued, "from that day forward she always wore it. It's old, but I guarantee you it works well. So, if you need help, and you're not near your car to hit the panic button, just blow and I'll come running."

Olivia's heart swelled until she thought it would burst. She had never been given such a solicitous and generous gift. She was so touched by Ian's sweet spontaneous gesture and his sincerity the bottom of her eyelids barely held the pooling tears.

"I can't accept this gift. It was your great-grandfather's whistle. Clearly, your grandmother treasured it. I can't accept a family heirloom no matter how generous the offer."

Olivia handed the whistle back to Ian. Ian took the chain and spread it wide and gently put it over Olivia's head and around her neck while saying, "Then consider it a loan."

Olivia stepped toward Ian and gave him a long kiss on the cheek. When the kiss was complete, she didn't step back. She leaned her cheek into the spot she had just caressed with her lips. She could feel his "five o'clock shadow" prickling her skin. The sensation sent a chill up and down her body. Her arms lifted around his neck as if controlled by a force other than her own. At the same time, she felt his muscled arms encircle her waist and their bodies merged. Olivia firmly kissed him again on the cheek in the same spot. She continued to plant kisses on his face, moving maddingly slowly toward his lips. Finally, their faces turned as if caught in a strong magnetic pull, answering an urgent attraction until their lips locked. She was completely lost in the moment. The force of their attraction surprised her and was so powerful she was defenseless to resist and found herself wanting to surrender.

Later when her libido was back in control and her mind could focus on something other than the feel of Ian's lips and the sensations he created with his tongue, she characterized their attraction to herself as an invisible natural force. *My gosh*, she realized, *that's literally the textbook definition of animal magnetism. Well, animal magnetism isn't just for animals of the four-legged variety.*

Ian thought no kiss would ever match the one, well, ones he had just experienced. The first kisses started out sweet and wholesome and they ended feverish and fiery. They were the type of kisses that normally would have resulted in clothing being ripped off, leading to ardent lovemaking. Instead, they held one another, neither one wanting to break the spell, each panting and trying to catch their breath.

Ian wondered if Olivia had just as much trouble keeping her clothes on as he did during their "mighty nice getting to know you better" session. Ian hadn't wanted to take advantage of a woman who had been seriously rattled just an hour ago; so, he had let Olivia set the pace and tone of their encounter. He never wanted her to look back and think, 'what did I do when I was emotionally compromised?' It took every bit of control he had not to do what he wanted to do to, and for, Olivia.

Ian was the first one to speak. Squeezing Olivia a little tighter he playfully warned, "I'm not letting you out of my hold until you promise to go out with me next week," his eyes twinkling with mischief. An instant later his features softened, and the tone of his voice sobered.

"Will you do me the honor of going to dinner with me Olivia?" Ian entreated, while a very small part of his brain debated if the tactic he was using to secure a date was taking advantage of the situation.

"Oh yeah," Olivia gasped between her still labored breathing. "Consider it a date."

Ian's internal debate evaporated. He had a date with the most intelligent, desirable woman he had ever met, and it hadn't even taken any coaxing.

Chapter Seventeen

A mournful meow interrupted her thoughts as Olivia updated the last patient chart of the day. That would be Ren, Mrs. Duffy's white and black spotted cat, who was waking up from his dental cleaning and letting it be known that he did not appreciate being locked inside a kennel. He was one of those cats with "attitude" that always looked around as if he owned the place and all creatures were there to serve his needs. He was a good boy though, so Olivia went along with it and treated him like the prince he thought himself to be. Even royalty had to submit to dental work however, and in another hour his observation time would be over and his favorite person would be there to chauffeur him home.

Olivia had planned to close the clinic a little early today because she was meeting her zio at four o'clock next door at Lily's Bakery to have tea and go over a few things. She needed to tell him about the rock throwing incident, that in light of the other rude pranks, was beginning to seem not so random. She didn't recall ever hearing about the clinic having issues in the past, but then again perhaps they just never seemed big enough or frequent enough for Zio to mention them. She didn't want to worry her uncle just as he was winding down and entering retirement, but she needed to know if there had been any other nefarious activities that she should be aware of.

Olivia finished up the chart she was working on and went over to check on Ren. He got through his dental cleaning like a champ and managed to down all of the softened kibble they'd left in the dish in his kennel. She opened the door and he got up and gave her a nice head butt and then rubbed his face across the back of her hand to let her know that he appreciated the attention. She scratched him behind the ears, told him what a good boy he was, and then shut the door to let him relax the remainder of the hour. He was the last patient left in the clinic today with no over-nighters to attend to.

After emptying and wiping down the remaining kennels, Olivia thought again about the idea of hiring a part time clinic tech that could do this work for her. She'd been considering it might be a good idea to start an intern program to give young people who were thinking about a career in veterinary medicine a chance to get some hands-on experience. Most of the vets she had trained with were just like her—they had a powerful love for animals and once exposed to the career, they became hooked.

As she finished picking up around the clinic, she found herself fingering the little antique whistle that hung around her neck. It fell just past the neckline of her shirt and nestled right at the top between the swell of her breasts. It was warm from lying against her skin and although she had only been wearing it for a few days, she felt as if it was already a natural part of her. It was such a thoughtful and endearing gesture for Ian to give it to her, particularly because of the sentimental value it held. He seemed so sincere and sure of the gift, but she barely knew him. She would never want him to later regret giving her something that was so special. Her thoughts turned once again toward the way it felt when their lips had met. It wasn't a sweet kiss by anyone's definition. It had been full-on, magnetic attraction like she had never before experienced. She was surmising now what would happen when they had their date. Would she feel just as drawn to him the next time or had it been his rescue and the magic of the moment, so to speak, after she was so shaken from having the rocks hurled at her? *Just roll with it*, she told herself. It wasn't the first time she'd kissed a man for heaven's sake. It was, however, the first time a kiss had jolted her the way that one did. That was one update she did not intend to share with her zio today.

The little bell on the door jingled merrily letting her know someone had come in. Sure enough, Mrs. Duffy had arrived right on time to collect her cat. Never had she seen a bond stronger than the one between this cat and his owner. Once she'd settled the bill and reminded Mrs. Duffy when and how to administer the medication, she saw them to the door and locked up the clinic for the day.

She glimpsed from the window Zio's dark gray Tahoe driving by just as she was getting ready to walk over to Lily's, so she picked up her pace, not wanting him to have to wait for her. Lily's closed at five o'clock so they only had an hour to enjoy their tea and go over the things she wanted to discuss.

When Olivia entered the bakery, she was surprised to see most of the little bistro tables occupied. She didn't expect it to be this busy late in the day. Fortunately, there was a table for two at the back of the room where it was a little more private and where her uncle was headed. While she loved running into clients, she wanted some uninterrupted time to talk things over. She knew if either of them got stopped by a client, it would be hard to get away as everyone loved to talk about their beloved pets. She focused on her destination and moved quickly toward it, arriving in unison with her zio.

"Ah Livvie, I'm so glad we could meet today," Zio Paolo said, wrapping her up in a big bear hug and kissing both of her cheeks.

"Me too Zio," she said hugging him right back. "I've looked forward to this all day."

"So, tell me Dr. de Luca, how are things going at the clinic?"

"Well Dr. Deluca, you were just there a week ago. Things were running smoothly then, and they still are," she responded. "Let's sit down and figure out what we want and I'll tell you all about it."

110 J. KIMALIE

A young woman that Olivia vaguely remembered seeing one of the few times she'd been in before came over to take their order. She was rather slim, narrow faced and wore her hair pulled back into a slick ponytail that made her face look even thinner. She had a big bright pink lipstick smile that appeared suddenly on her face as she approached, locking eyes with Olivia's uncle. She was dressed in soft pink jeans and a white top with a ruffled neckline that had a nametag pinned to it that said "Heather."

"What can I bring you?" she asked, still looking directly at Paolo.

"Why don't I let my niece order first?" he responded with a smile, always the gentleman.

Heather turned to Olivia and offered a brief smile. "Miss, what would you like?" she asked in a more serious tone.

Olivia scanned the little table tent menu and requested a cup of jasmine tea and a lemon scone if they had any left.

"I think we do," Heather responded succinctly and turned back to Paolo. "And what would you like? We have several pies that were baked today and I can tell you from personal experience that they are amazing!"

"Well, who can say no to amazing?" Paolo answered with a grin. "Bring me whatever you have that sounds good as well as a cup of Earl Gray please."

Heather gave him another big smile and left to go fill their order.

"Oh my," noted Olivia. "I think she has the hots for you Zio."

"Why do you say that?" he asked.

"Didn't you notice that she barely had the time of day for me but was completely focused on you?"

"Oh, I don't think a cute young gal like that would be interested in an old man like me," he chuckled. "She's just being nice to her customers. She must be new as I've never seen her working here before."

JUST A WHISTLE AWAY   111

"Hmmm, first off you're not an old man and second I don't think that's what is going on. Besides, you've got plenty of charm, and women of all ages are going to notice a hunky gray fox like you. Now that you're not so busy with work, why don't you get back out there and have some fun. You have lots to offer any lady, plus you love to dance. You can't do that so easily all on your own."

"Who knows what I'm going to do with my retirement. I'm just getting used to sleeping in on the days I'm not in the clinic, but if I do start dating it won't be with somebody my niece's age. I have thought about taking some ballroom dance lessons though. What do you think? Do I look like I could be the next Fred Astaire?"

Olivia laughed and assured him she thought he could do anything. Regarding Heather, she admitted she was mostly teasing him, but added, "Let's just agree that the new waitress was flirting with you."

"If you say so," he said. "Now, tell me what's going on in the clinic."

Olivia went over all the relevant activities of the week including the schedule for the rest of the month, so he'd know when she needed him. Heather swung by and delivered their order without interrupting them, but she did squeeze in another smile for Paolo. After all the current clinic business had been covered, Olivia told him about her ideas for expanding staffing.

"I did have an assistant a couple of years ago," Paolo told her, a really smart young woman who was a student at the University of Washington. She worked for me part-time a couple of days a week around her class schedule and then all day on Saturdays. It worked out quite well until she went off to attend vet school herself at Washington State. I never did find anyone who seemed right as a replacement, but I didn't really search very hard. I think if you looked you could find someone who would be a good fit."

Paolo thought the idea of some student interns was an interesting notion but recommended she find an assistant first and then see what she thought she could manage beyond that. Olivia agreed his recommendation made sense because he was still willing to work as a relief vet whenever she wanted. He always accomplished a lot whenever he was in the clinic, so there was no hurry to organize an intern program. Plus, it made sense to hold off on an intern program until there was someone who would be around long term to help supervise.

As they talked, Olivia noticed that their waitress was investing quite an effort to clean the table that had emptied that was closest to them. While there wasn't really anything they needed, she did seem to be spending a lot of time there as if she thought she should stay close. She reminded Olivia a little bit of a girl she knew in college, and she couldn't help glancing over at her again. Their eyes caught briefly, and the waitress quickly turned and left. Who knows, maybe she really did have a little crush on her zio.

"Zio, there's something else I need to discuss with you."

"What's that Livvie?"

"Have you ever had any problems around the clinic, you know, like vandalism?"

"Vandalism, why no, nothing I can think of. Why? Did someone do something else to your flowers?" he asked.

"The flowers are fine and growing back. It's just that they weren't the only incident."

"What else has happened?"

"A couple of weeks ago someone threw a coffee drink or something against the window where our names are engraved. It left quite a mess for me to clean up. I didn't think much of it at the time other than what a nuisance it was. But then the flowers got hacked up and then there was another incident."

"What kind of incident?"

JUST A WHISTLE AWAY 113

"Well, a couple of days ago I was in the back parking area and someone threw rocks at me."

"What? Are you sure they were meant to be thrown at you?"

"I can't be certain, but it felt like I was the target. I couldn't see anyone, and it rattled me. I triggered my car alarm and fortunately Ian was home and came out. I think that scared whoever it was away."

"Livvie, this is disturbing. I just can't see anyone around here trying to hurt you like that."

"I know weird, right? This was worse than the window or the flowers. I don't know if all of these incidents are related or not, but it does start to seem like someone has it out for me. I can't imagine why as I don't even know many people around here. All our clients seem wonderful and the few people I've gotten to know are terrific."

"Can I get you anything else?" asked Heather, popping up unexpectedly.

"No, just our bill," answered Paolo. She went to get it for him, and he noticed it was approaching closing time. "Maybe we should call the police. I know a couple of the officers—they're long-time clients. I'm sure it wouldn't hurt to mention it to them. They would have some advice."

"Not quite yet, Zio. I don't want them to think I'm going to be one of those people who call every time the wind blows and nothing really bad has occurred. Ian put up security cameras just in case. They didn't catch anything this time, but if something else happens, then yes we should talk to them." She mindlessly touched the little whistle that was under the soft fabric of her top. "I think then it would make sense."

"Okay then, we'll wait. But I want to know if anything, and I mean anything else, happens," he said firmly as their waitress returned and placed their check on the table in front of him. The waitress hesitated as if she was going to say something, but changed her mind and left.

"I promise," Olivia assured him. "I just can't think of who would want to hurt me or the clinic. After all, we help people's pets."

"You know, Wayne was not very happy when we parted ways," Zio Paolo said thoughtfully. "But if anything, he should be grateful he didn't end up in jail and just got off with probation since the amount he embezzled technically could have included serving some time. Lucky for him we caught him early before a lot more money was stolen. I'd think he'd want to avoid us at all costs."

"Hmmm, I hadn't thought of that," Olivia mused. "I was the one who reviewed the books and raised the issue. Maybe, but you're right, it doesn't make a lot of sense. Let's just see if this is the end of it. I'm on alert now for flying rocks and beverages. And the flowers are growing back."

"Don't make light of this Livvie, I meant what I said. Anything else, no matter how small..."

"Yes, I promise Zio. Okay, let's pay and call it a day. Your new admirer keeps looking over here and I think she's the last one here and is trying to close up. If you don't escape before she locks the door, she may try to keep you."

Uncle Paolo laughed and claimed "My treat" leaving a twenty and a five on the table and walked his niece out to her car. Her news troubled him, but he understood why she didn't want to make a bigger deal out of it than it was. The rock thing was the most concerning, but perhaps it was an isolated incident with a logical explanation. If nothing else, it had been a wakeup call for her that, even in a small town like Poulsbo, you have to be careful. He decided it might be a good idea to swing by Lily's in a day or two and ask her if she'd had any problems. Besides, if memory served him (and it usually did) Lily, an attractive 50's something widow, enjoyed ballroom dancing and oh mama could that woman bake!

When Olivia got home, Dolce was at the door ready to greet her as if she'd returned from the war. On days when she didn't take him with her to work, he stayed home and her neighbor, who was retired, came over to let him out and check on him. This arrangement suited the neighbor just as much as Dolce as he loved dogs but was at an age where he didn't want either the expense or responsibility of a full time dependent. For that reason, Olivia left Dolce home more often than she actually needed to.

Telling Zio about the rock throwing incident needed to happen, but Olivia didn't want him to be overly concerned. She considered what he had said about Wayne possibly having a beef with her. Their former accountant was sort of a creepy guy, no doubt about it, but would he be so juvenile as to play malicious pranks on her? And throwing a rock like that was dangerous. If he'd actually hit her there could be serious ramifications. Would he want to draw attention to himself after what had transpired when he was working for her uncle? It didn't seem likely, but then again, who understood the mind of a crazy person? She remembered how he'd been staring at her at trivia night but then jetted out of the Longhouse.

Perhaps for a while, she should bring Dolce with her to the office whenever possible. He was fiercely loyal and, although sweet, big enough and the right breed to be intimidating and responsive should anyone approach her in a threatening manner. As if he were reading her thoughts, Dolce froze and focused on the front door, emitting a low growl.

"What do you hear boy?" she asked looking over and trying to discern if she could hear something herself.

He continued to just stare at the door for another ten seconds or so and then emitted a soft "woof" and went back to nuzzling her hand for more affection.

"I must be jumpy," she chuckled, "You had me worried there for a moment."

Dolce put one of his paws up on her thigh and made it clear that dinner time was on his mind. Olivia agreed and went to the kitchen to rinse and fill his dish. She wasn't sure what to make for her own dinner tonight but was thinking comfort food might just fill the bill. She decided to throw together a simple mac and cheese casserole and a green salad and call it a day. A glass of rose' might be in order as well. It was early, but she double checked that her doors were locked and then closed her front blinds. As she turned toward the kitchen to start dinner she decided that closing the blinds while it was still daylight was overkill, and opened them again. Glancing out, she thought she saw movement behind the foliage that obscured her house from the road but chalked it up to her imagination and her state of mind lately.

Deciding that she'd feel much safer and more relaxed if she had more security cameras at the cottage as well as the clinic, she proceeded with getting dinner together. She'd ask Ian if he'd be willing to help her out. Olivia realized she was touching the little whistle once again, and she was confident that he'd be there for her. It was time to relax and put this out of her mind for the day. A glass of chilled wine was definitely in order.

Dear Veritas,

My neighbor planted lilacs next to our shared fence. The roots from her plant have spread to my side of the fence and are sending up shoots. I love the fragrant flowers but I'm allergic to them. What is the best way to prevent the bush from spreading?

Signed: *Sneezy, Wheezy, and in Needy of a Solution*

Dear Sneezy,

I hope you're downwind from the breezy 'cause I've got nothing for you that ain't cheesy.

What comment have I ever made that would lead you to believe that I have a green thumb or know anything about the plant world? Heck, I just recently learned that some flowers are edible. If you need a gardening solution check with an expert at your local nursery. If you've got a question regarding animals or minerals, I might be able to help. But the vegetable kingdom? You're barkin' up the wrong bush.

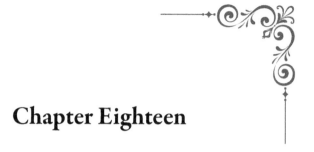

Chapter Eighteen

The spring morning was cool and rainy befitting the quintessential stereotype that most people had of the Pacific Northwest. Jacq wasn't sure how she would acclimate to the weather when she decided to move to Poulsbo from New York. She found herself not missing the punishing winds and snow of the "nor'easter" storms the East Coast experienced in the winter and the humidity and heat of the summers. In general, she preferred the milder weather in the Pacific Northwest, although she was ready for more sunshine. Spring seemed reluctant to shed winter's grasp and embrace the fabulous summers that were worth waiting for and were the envy of the rest of the nation.

"Today's weather punctuates your astute decision of a July wedding since you want it outdoors," Christopher commented, as he watched raindrops run down the office windows.

Jacq and Christopher had just finished their second appointment of the day when Chistopher revealed he had formally scheduled Jacq as their 11:00 AM client. Refilling their coffee cups, they settled down to business.

"July is going to be here before we know it and we have some details to nail down and a couple things I want to run by you," Christopher declared.

"Alright," Jacq said, "fire away."

"Did you get the invitations in the mail?" Christopher inquired.

JUST A WHISTLE AWAY

119

"Yep, I found some cute floral stamps at the post office and got them all in the mail the day before yesterday, so we can check that off the list," Jacq acknowledged.

Christopher had opened Jacq and Garrett's wedding file and was perusing the to-do list. "Have you decided if you are going to have someone walk you down the aisle or have Garrett meet you halfway down the aisle?" he questioned.

"I vacillated back and forth on that detail, but finally asked Emmett if he would walk me down the aisle," she stated. "I'm glad I asked him, he was so touched, he could hardly speak," she added. "And I'm sure I will need the extra support he will provide on my wedding day."

Christopher leaned over and covered her hand with his in a gesture of comfort. No words were necessary, he knew that his friend's wedding day would be bittersweet.

A little more than three years ago, Jacq lost her beloved family in a tragic car accident. The sudden and unexpected loss of Jacq's father, mother, and her Aunt Rose had almost irretrievably shattered her. About a year ago, Jacq had discovered that her Aunt Rose and Emmett had fallen in love before her death. Her devastating loss touched both her and Emmett in different ways, but shared grief had also united them in a special bond.

While the love of Garrett, her friends, and her new community had restored joy in her life, nothing could ever fill the hole in her heart left by the loss of her family. Not having her father walk her down the aisle was yet another reminder of that loss. Christopher gave her hand a squeeze, sharing a knowing melancholy look, and then got back to the tasks at hand.

"Let's talk about the aisle. I have an idea I want to run by you," Christopher said with a good dose of enthusiasm. "Your entrance has to be dramatic – that's a given," he grinned, cocking his left eyebrow. "What if we created an aisle out of potted white blooming French lilac bushes? I consulted an extremely helpful gentleman at the local nursery, and he recommended using a varietal called 'Madame Lemoine.' Their bloom time is Spring to Summer. If our order is large enough, he will guarantee he can deliver them a few days before the wedding covered with blossoms. En mass, they would be gorgeous and add such a lovely fragrance."

Jacq found herself caught up in Christopher's energy and his proposed concept. "How can he guarantee they will be blooming?" Jacq asked.

"The timing of the blooms can be controlled somewhat by judging when to take them out of the greenhouse and by placing them in the sun or shade. He said it wouldn't be a problem," Christopher assured her.

"What's the minimum order?" Jacq inquired.

"Three dozen," Christopher replied.

Now it was Jacq who raised an eyebrow.

"I know, I know," he quickly continued. "But hear me out. After the wedding we could plant them on the property. We already have a master landscape plan for the business, and we can just accelerate a portion of the plan – we don't have to execute the entire landscape plan all at once. Plus, we get some plants going and established where we want screening from the road sooner rather than later. And since it is a business expense, I'm in for covering half the cost. Just so you know, I'll be decorating the bride's side of the aisle. Come on, can't you just picture it?!" he concluded with a self-satisfied smile.

Jacq could see the lovely scene in her mind. She could almost smell the strong, sweet, heady scent that would be too cloying indoors, but the flowers would perfume the breeze of an outdoor wedding in spectacular fashion.

Jacq stood up and went to Christopher. Ignoring the risk of wrinkling his impeccably ironed robin's egg blue cotton jacket she gave him a big hug, "I think it sounds perfect!"

JUST A WHISTLE AWAY

"Okay, since I have you in a good mood," Christopher said, "I want to make sure you won't reconsider your gown. Are you absolutely positive you want to wear your mother's gown? I know it's sentimental, but is it you?" Christopher ended his question with an almost comical expression on his face, his features scrunched up as if there was a foul smell assaulting his senses.

"No, it's not me, not in its present form. But I found a local woman, on Etsy of all places, who can transform it into a more modern look that will be me. I sent her pictures of mom's wedding dress with a photo of a gown I saw in a Paris issue of Vogue. She sent me a sketch of how she can alter it to resemble the Vogue couture gown. You've got to trust me on this one, Christopher. I know I am cheating you out of a 'say yes to the dress' shopping trip, but how about we shop for shoes once the dress has been altered?"

Doubtful that Jacq's mother's 1980's era gown could ever be altered enough to suit Jacq's sophisticated tastes, Christopher knew his friend well enough to know that he would not win this battle. So, he reluctantly relented and said, "Well, I suppose that is a decent consolation prize. Consider it a date."

"Beth and I have a couple of things we would like to contribute to the wedding, but we want them to be a surprise," Christopher noted. "Do you trust us?" Christopher grinned in a playful and challenging way.

"Completely," Jacq replied without hesitation.

Beth and Christopher were Jacq's two closest friends. Back in New York, the three had been practically inseparable.

"You two know me better than anyone, probably even better than Garrett. A couple of surprises will add to the fun of the day," Jacq reflected.

Christopher was so sure that Jacq wouldn't mind a surprise or two at her wedding, that he had already called Olivia and asked if she would be willing to bake six dozen of her exquisite shortbread cookies decorated with a riot of colorful edible flowers and petals for the wedding. Olivia had enthusiastically agreed and flatly refused any compensation, explaining that both Jacq and Garrett had been so welcoming and kind to her as a newcomer to the community that she was thrilled to contribute a surprise to their special day.

Jacq and Garrett had chosen an elegant garden party theme for the wedding, but Jacq was uncharacteristically leaving Christopher and Beth to take the lead on many of the details. Jacq claimed that she was more focused on being Garrett's wife than on the wedding and she would be just as happy eloping. Christopher and Beth stepped up and planned to create a magical atmosphere for the wedding where everyone's senses would be engaged in subtle ways.

"Have you and Beth coordinated your outfits for the wedding?" Jacq inquired, breaking into Christopher's thoughts as he was making a mental note to have floral ice cubes for the pre-wedding drinks to compliment the cookies. She had asked them if they would stand up with her on her wedding day. They each had expected she would ask them at some point, so it did not come as much of a surprise when on a group video call Jacq entreated them to do her the honor of attending her at her wedding. "You both have become the only family I have left in this world. Not only do I want you both at my side on my wedding day, but I'll also need you by my side," Jacq had tearfully declared. Her softly spoken words had started the waterworks. All three cried together for what Jacq had lost when her parents and aunt had died the horrific accident and the wonderful life she had found with Garrett. After shedding many belated cathartic tears together, they made a pact of no sobbing, weeping, blubbering, or ugly tears on the wedding day.

"We have indeed," Christopher declared, responding to Jacq's question about the outfits. "Since you only dictated the colors (navy blue for the groom and groomsmen and pink for the maid of honor), and left the style choices to us, after a round of strategizing, Beth and I have it all sorted."

"Well do tell," Jacq said.

"We are going to do one better than that," Christopher declared. "On our next group video call, we are going to model our looks for you. Beth's dress should be delivered this week and we thought it would be fun for you to see what we came up with. Then you can finalize the flowers."

"Well, now I can't wait," Jacq mused. "Anything else to go over right now or can we grab some lunch before our two-clock appointment?"

"Lunch sounds perfect," Christopher declared. "I'll drive."

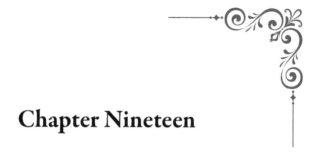

Chapter Nineteen

Olivia ran her fingertip along the raised thistle that was designed into the whistle hanging on a fine chain around her neck. Looking in the mirror, her head tilted to the side, she remembered the serious look in Ian's eyes as he explained the gift and why he thought she needed to keep it close. He had sidled up next to her to place the chain over her head. She relived the shiver that ran down her spine as his chest had brushed hers, how the air had thickened between them with anticipation and the heated look in his eyes as she leaned in close capturing his lips in a soul-searing kiss.

This evening they would go on their first date, the one she had promised him while her mind had spun with the effects of sharing that moment of amazing intimacy. Ian had told her to dress casually, so she wore her favorite jeans and a fuchsia silk blouse unbuttoned just enough to frame the beautiful whistle hanging from her neck. She finished off her ensemble with brown leather wedge sandals. It was a simple outfit, but one that made her feel pretty and feminine. She pulled her curls back in a pink headband the same shade as her blouse and finished her outfit with large silver hoop earrings that swayed as she walked. Even though it had been unseasonably hot, Olivia grabbed her jean jacket, not quite sure what Ian had in store for their evening.

Olivia heard Dolce give a quick, high-pitched bark of greeting just before the doorbell rang. She placed her hand on her stomach trying to quiet the butterflies fluttering there as she walked toward the front door. Swinging open the door, she was startled and then laughed as she came face to face with a flat of blue and purple johnny jump-ups. Ian's smiling face slowly came into view as he lowered the box to his waist.

"These are for you," he said. She put out her hands to take the box and Ian used that opportunity to lean forward and plant a soft kiss on her cheek. Before she could say anything, he let go of the box and bent down to give Dolce's head a rub.

"How ya doin' pup?" Ian asked Dolce, scratching the dog behind the ears.

"Thank you for these," Olivia said softly, looking down into the happy faces of the flowers.

Ian straightened up and looked down at her bent head. "I didn't know if you had replaced all the flowers that had been destroyed. I thought these were better than cut flowers that would just die. Plus, I didn't have to ask the lady behind the counter what color they were."

"You're color blind?" Olivia asked.

"Yep, I can see blue, though," Ian smiled, "and pink. You look beautiful, Olivia."

She thanked him and smiled back."Come in for a second while I grab my coat and put these in the back yard where they will get the morning sun."

Ian looked around as Olivia made her way through the French doors to the back. He had been stunned by the abundance of beautiful flowers and foliage in her yard and the quaint little cottage nestled among them. It was small, but comfortable. Her décor definitely had French influences, from the linen covered chairs to the muted color palette set off by black accents here and there. He was charmed by her house, much like he was by the woman who lived in it.

"Where are we going?" Olivia asked, walking up to him with her coat and purse in hand.

"That's for me to know and you to find out," Ian said mysteriously as he ushered her toward the front door with a hand on the small of her back.

"Really," Olivia said drawing out the word with one eyebrow raised. "We aren't going somewhere strange like alien hunting or spelunking, are we?"

"My, my Miss Olivia you do have an imagination," Ian said in a bad imitation of a southern drawl. "I was saving spelunking for our second date."

Olivia laughed as she turned around to give Dolce a farewell pat and closed and locked the front door.

Ian opened the passenger door of his SUV for her to climb in. When he was sure she was settled, he shut the door, rounded the front of the vehicle, and hopped in the driver's side.

As he pulled out of her driveway, Olivia glanced in the back seat and spied a woven picnic basket and a small cooler. It was one of those old-time baskets, hinged in the middle, so you could open it from either end. On the other side of the cooler was a rolled-up blanket secured by leather straps.

Olivia turned back around to face front as Ian asked, "How are things going at the clinic?"

"I think I'm finally getting used to the routine. I was a little overwhelmed with all the different kinds of animals that come into the clinic. Everything from reptiles to bulls. I really hadn't expected for Zio Paolo's practice to be so diverse."

"It must keep things interesting," Ian commented. "I've heard you are not only a great veterinarian, but that you've also volunteered to help with Jacq's wedding."

"Yes, I spoke with Christopher about providing some of my signature cookies. He thought they would be a perfect complement to some of the other things he has planned."

"Can I have the rejects?" Ian asked.

JUST A WHISTLE AWAY

"What? What makes you think I'll have any rejects?" Olivia asked.

"When my mom makes cookies, there are always one or two that aren't perfect. She makes me get rid of the rejects," Ian stated.

"She makes you get rid of them?" questioned Olivia. "Probably more like you steal them fresh from the oven."

"A guy has to eat," Ian stated emphatically.

"I bet you were a handful when you were little," Olivia said with a smile in her voice.

"I was perfect. It was my older sister that was the handful." Ian looked over at her and grinned.

"Uh huh," Olivia commented giving him a sidelong look. "I don't believe that for a minute."

After they had been on the road for about fifteen minutes Olivia asked where they were going, again.

"Be patient, my little animal lover, we're almost there."

Olivia realized that she had totally relaxed on the drive to wherever they were going. She had been so keyed up before the date, but Ian's teasing and easy manner had allowed her to unwind and enjoy the scenery passing by outside.

Before long they entered a narrow road forested on each side. As they drove through the trees and back into the sun, she could see a lighthouse at the end of the spit. Further out she spied the beach and tidelands with seagulls swooping among the air currents.

"Look," Olivia pointed out the windshield, "there's a lighthouse."

"That's Point No Point Lighthouse," Ian stated, "and our destination."

The scenery was beautiful with the blue of the water contrasting with the green of the grasslands surrounding the building. There were a few people beachcombing, but the park was fairly deserted for a beautiful spring evening.

Ian parked and walked around to open her door. She was glad she had worn a headband as the wind whipped her hair around and plastered her clothes to her body. Ian reached in the back, snatched her jacket off the seat and held it out for her to put on.

"You're going to need this until we get out of the wind," he said as he settled the garment on her shoulders. He reached back into car and pulled out the blanket, handing it to her. "Do you mind carrying this?"

"Anything else I can do?" Olivia asked.

"No, I can get everything else," Ian stated as he donned his own jacket and grabbed the picnic basket and cooler. Locking the vehicle, he led her to the door of the lighthouse. He fit a key into the lock and pushed open the door.

"I'm afraid to ask where you got the keys to a historic lighthouse," commented Olivia.

Ian looked back at her and said, "It's one of the perks of volunteering in the park and at the historical society every once in a while, and it just so happens the park ranger is a friend of mine."

Olivia looked around curiously. The building was mostly deserted with a few artifacts on shelves bolted to the concrete walls.

Ian took the blanket from her, unfurled it, and laid it out on the floor. She watched him open the cooler and take out a bottle of prosecco and retrieve two champagne glasses from the basket. He also pulled out a small candle, lighting a match to the wick and placing it on top of the cooler.

Holding out his hand to her, he asked, "Will you come sit with me?"

Olivia smiled, put her hand in his and kneeled on the blanket beside him.

"Nobody has ever taken me on a picnic before," she said.

"This is the Point No Point five-star restaurant," Ian remarked, "would you like some prosecco to start?"

"Please," Olivia said.

Ian handed her a glass filled with prosecco into which he had dropped a blackberry.

" Salude," Ian stated, clinking the rim of his glass against hers. She took a sip and let the bubbles rest on her tongue before she swallowed.

"What else do you have in that basket?" asked Olivia, making herself comfortable on the blanket.

"I think we will start with burrata and crackers, then move onto the main course of gourmet sandwiches and fruit salad," Ian listed as he began pulling containers out of the basket.

He handed her a bottle of wine and opener and asked, "Could you open this so it has time to breathe?"

Olivia looked at the label and giggled. "Did you think it was a good idea to bring a bottle of Dead Horse wine on a date with a veterinarian?"

"Hey, don't knock it. It's a great wine despite the name," Ian said grinning at her as he opened the cheese and crackers. He handed her a china plate and a bright orange napkin with poppies on it. Putting a cheese spreader in the container he set it between them along with a plate of crackers.

Ian was sitting with his back against the wall with his long legs stretched out and crossed at the ankles. Olivia liked this relaxed look on him. He wasn't wearing a kilt today, but rather sand colored cargo shorts with a rather subdued blue and white Hawaiian shirt. His ever-present combat boots encased his feet.

Ian continued to pull food out of the basket.

"That basket is like Mary Poppins' magic carpet bag," remarked Olivia.

Ian looked up and smiled as he pulled two wine glasses out of the hamper. "I have some magical stuff in here. I'm trying to impress a certain woman."

"Oh really," Olivia said, "what's she like?"

"She's beautiful, full of life, sometimes a little too serious, but she loves my clothes, especially my t-shirts although she would never admit it," Ian said.

Olivia gave an unladylike snort.

Ian continued, "She loves animals, has a soft touch with hurt creatures, is strong and brave and has a green thumb. All in all, I think she's pretty amazing."

Olivia could feel the heat rise in her cheeks as he smiled at her.

"...and she likes my cooking," Ian ended his monologue.

Olivia laughed as he handed her a cracker piled with cheese and popped one in his own mouth.

"Can I ask you a question?" Olivia inquired. Ian nodded. "What exactly is it that you do for a living?"

Ian swallowed and said, "Lots of things, but mostly I'm a landlord. I have several real estate holdings. As you know, I'm also the trivia king and help Donovan when he needs me. I volunteer, do odd jobs, and play the bagpipes. When I got out of the service, I didn't really know what I would do, so I started investing my money and the rest is history."

Ian handed her a plate with a sandwich and fruit salad and proceeded to pour the wine. They ate in companionable silence for a while, listening to the wind race around the lighthouse.

"Do you regret moving here?" Ian asked out of the blue.

Olivia thought carefully about her answer. "No, I miss the friends and family that I moved away from, but I've made more friends and am so glad to be with my zio.

Ian took her now clean plate and stacked it back in the basket. "I have some dessert, but you have to be sitting beside me in order for this to work," he said as he patted the blanket beside him.

She changed places, miscalculating how close she was to him when she ended up with her thigh plastered up against his. She went

JUST A WHISTLE AWAY

to move away but he put his hand on her leg keeping her in place. He took a thermos and two demitasse cups out of the basket and poured rich, thick chocolate out of the thermos. Handing her one, he said, "This is my favorite dessert or at least one of them. I hope you like it."

Olivia watched as steam curled up and over her cup. She smelled the richness of the sipping chocolate, taking a small drink and moaning as the chocolate coated her tongue. It was like drinking a candy bar.

Ian didn't think he had ever seen such an erotic site as Olivia sipping her chocolate. He shifted positions so as not to make it obvious what her actions were doing to his body. He picked up the thermos to distract himself.

"Would you like some more?" he asked.

Olivia opened her eyes and smiled as she held out her cup. "This is the most delicious thing I've ever tasted," she exclaimed.

Ian couldn't help it as he leaned over and kissed her smiling mouth, tasting her grin and the rich chocolate she had just drank. He deepened the kiss when he felt Olivia lean into him. He went to cup the back of her head so he could sink deeper into the kiss when he realized he was holding the thermos of chocolate. He slowly pulled back, looking into her dazed eyes. "It does taste delicious," Ian whispered, his eyes crinkling as he smiled.

She grinned back and held up her cup for a refill.

Packing up the dishes and folding the blanket, Ian hooked the cooler over his shoulder, picked up the basket and took Olivia's hand as they made their way out of the lighthouse. They both blinked in the waning sunlight, stopping to let their eyes adjust from the gloom of indoors.

They began to walk toward the car when Olivia stopped abruptly. Ian looked at her in concern and then looked where her eyes were staring. Standing by the car was a slim non-descript man dressed in khakis and a t-shirt hurling rocks at nearby driftwood.

"What's wrong," Ian asked, all his protective instincts coming to life when he picked up on Olivia's concern.

"That's Wayne," stated Olivia as if Ian should know who that was.

"Tell me about Wayne," Ian said quietly positioning himself between her and the car.

Olivia looked at him. "He was Zio Paolo's accountant. When I took over the books, I found that Wayne had been skimming some of the profits from the clinic. It looked like he started out stealing just a few dollars, but the amount kept getting bigger and bigger. We reported him to the police. That was months ago, but when I was at the Longhouse for trivia night, I saw him in the crowd and now to see him again..." Olivia's voice trailed off.

"You're thinking he's behind your trouble at the clinic," stated Ian.

"I don't know, I hadn't thought seriously about it until I just saw him, but it would be a way to get a little revenge on Zio and me. He didn't seem the type to resort to physical violence," Olivia said quietly, not wanting to alert the man they were discussing.

Ian looked at the man, who was now sauntering away from the car, committing his face to memory.

When they reached his vehicle, Ian quickly helped Olivia into the passenger seat, stowed the picnic gear and prepared to go. Olivia was staring out of the windshield with her hands clasped in her lap.

Ian put his arm around her shoulders and pulled her as close as he could without dragging her over the console and into his lap.

"Don't you think it's weird he was here at the same time? A man that clearly could hold a grudge against me?" questioned Olivia.

"It seems too much of a coincidence. But I'm not sure how he would know we were here unless he's been following us. I don't know him, but I'll ask around about him. I won't let him hurt you or your zio, I promise," Ian said.

Olivia put her head on his shoulder and sighed, glad that, even though she could take care of herself, it was nice to have another strong man in her life to lean on. As they sat in his SUV watching the sun go down over the water, Ian silently vowed that nothing would happen to Olivia now that he was here to watch over her.

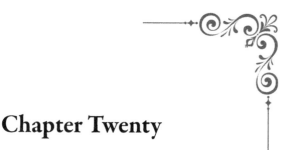

Chapter Twenty

Wednesday had been a long one for Olivia who worked in the clinic all day and then did house calls the remainder of the afternoon. She stopped for takeout from a Teriyaki place on the way home and sat back in her favorite chair to enjoy it while watching "Jeopardy" on TV to tune up her trivia skills. As usual, Dolce was lying on the carpet by her side resting comfortably after spending the afternoon with their neighbor.

Dolce raised his head slightly at the sound of a text coming in and then put it back down between his paws. Olivia had left her phone in her purse and decided to finish her dinner before she checked it. Hopefully, it wasn't a client call that couldn't wait until tomorrow. She was bone tired from her busy day and just wanted to disconnect from all things work related. After polishing off the last delectable bite of chicken and applauding herself for correctly answering the final question, she took her plate to the kitchen to rinse and deposit it into the dishwasher. She decided to raid the snack drawer for a chocolate bar as today certainly warranted one, plus she deserved a reward for her final Jeopardy answer. She grabbed her phone and went back to her chair, pulling over a big ottoman to rest her feet and checked her messages. She had a couple of ads, a reminder to order some office supplies for the clinic, and a text from Ian. She opened it excitedly.

"Hello lovely, how's my favorite tenant? I was just looking at the weather forecast and Saturday looks to be a good one—not too warm, not too cool, and hardly any chance of rain. I would love to have someone join me on a little adventure. They need to be highly observant, appreciate the outdoors, not afraid to get their feet dirty, and have a healthy sense of honor. A friendly disposition is also one of the requirements."

Olivia smiled and responded with a smiley emoji writing, "I think I can satisfy those requirements. What time do you want to leave?"

She watched while the dots indicated Ian was there now and responding to her answer.

"Oh dear, this is a little awkward," he wrote and included an emoji that looked embarrassed. "I was actually extending an invitation to Dolce. I guess we could accommodate a third if you'd like to tag along."

Olivia laughed out loud and wrote back, "I don't want to be a third wheel, but it does sound like fun. Dolce says it's okay with him if it's okay with you."

"Consider it a date then," Ian shot back. "I'll pick you both up at 9 a.m. and make sure you have room for breakfast. Dolce can have his ahead of time."

"We're on!" she replied and reached down to scratch Dolce's head. "Looks like we are going on an adventure my friend."

The rest of the week flew by without running into Ian, which oddly enough, hardly ever happened since he lived above the clinic in the same building. Saturday morning arrived before she knew it and she got up early, enjoyed her coffee and ate a granola bar to take the edge off while Dolce downed a bowl of premium kibble. She thought about what to wear on the adventure that Ian hadn't really defined. That man certainly liked to surprise her on their dates, but so far, the outcome had been good. Given the little he had told her, she decided to wear jeans, a white t-shirt with a soft, lightweight baby blue pullover that had cute pocket details on it. She wore leather sneakers but put a pair of ankle high Wellies in a tote bag along with a rain jacket just in case she needed them. The bag had straps that could transform it into a backpack if desired, so she'd be ready for whatever awaited. It had a zipped compartment for other things like her wallet and phone, and there was the perfect space to stash a couple of chocolate bars and dog biscuits in case they all needed a treat along the way.

At 9:00 AM sharp she heard the sound of a car pulling up. She liked the fact that Ian was always on time. It told her that he valued her time as well and that was always important to her. She waited for the cheerful rap at the door and then opened it to find him standing there in a dark grey utility kilt, plain black tee, and a black and tan plaid Pendleton shirt unbuttoned over it along with his usual choice of combat boots. His hair looked to be recently trimmed, disguising the fact that it was actually rather wavy, and he looked oddly enough a little debonair.

"Is everyone ready?" he asked, leaning in and greeting her with a quick kiss to her cheek.

"Yes, we are," she answered. "I just need to grab Dolce's leash and water bowl."

"Leash yes, water bowl no," Ian replied. "I've got all that covered. As I said, I was looking forward to spending the day with Mr. Dolce. But for the record, I'm very much looking forward to spending the day with you too."

Olivia tilted her head, grinning, and asked him, "Are you sure, or just being nice? I am sort of crashing the party."

"Our lucky day," Ian proclaimed and led them to his SUV. He had the seats folded down in the back so that Dolce had lots of room and a cozy rug for him to curl up on. "I'm used to chauffeuring dogs around since I sometimes need to do that for Garrett. "

JUST A WHISTLE AWAY   137

"Dolce will be perfectly comfortable here," she said as Ian opened the passenger side door for her and assisted her into the car. He secured Dolce in the back and got in himself.

"I hope you brought your appetite," he said as he started the car and headed down the road. "We're headed to Bremerton to one of my favorite little diners for breakfast first, so we're well fueled for our adventure. They make a coconut almond waffle that is to die for. That is, if you like waffles, toasted coconut and almonds, coconut syrup, and whipped cream and that sort of thing. They've got all the boring stuff too though, just in case that's what you want."

"You had me at coconut," she answered.

Ian smiled at her appreciatively. He loved being around women who didn't pretend they only ate like birds and rabbits.

"So, tell me more about this adventure you're taking us on," she probed.

"Okay, we're going hunting."

"Hunting? That's why you wanted to take my dog?" she asked incredulously. "We don't hunt animals; we try to keep them healthy."

"I agree. We're not hunting animals," he told her, briefly glancing her way and then focusing back on the road. "We are going to be hunting for orbs."

"For orbs. What exactly are you talking about?" she asked looking confused.

"We are going hunting for beautiful glass orbs," Ian announced. "The Bainbridge Island Museum of Art has this program where they hide hand blown glass orbs, like floats, in a bunch of different parks and we get to hunt for one. If you find it, you can keep it, but only one at a time is allowed. The orbs are made by young artists from Tacoma and this helps their development. If we find one, we take our picture with it and send it in. "

Olivia squealed like a child with delight, "Ooh, I love this idea, it sounds perfect!"

Ian smiled at her and said, "I thought you might. We're going to a park in Chico where Dolce is welcome as long as he's on his leash and not around the playground equipment. It's a beautiful park with a river where you can view salmon spawning in the fall. There are lots of other places to hunt if you like doing this. We can go again to one of the other parks."

"I absolutely love this and it's so nice that Dolce can come along too. What a thoughtful idea Ian. You made my day, no, our day!"

Ian's smile grew bigger, pleased that he had come up with the perfect second date. They talked about their week all the way to the café. He told her about how busy he'd been between taking care of his own business as well as filling in for Donovan who had left town for a few days. She told him about the spike in house calls she'd wrangled as well as going a full week without Zio Paolo's help for the first time as he had other things going on. It had been a hectic week for both of them and the prospect of being out in the woods on an adventure was just the antidote.

Soon she found that they were driving into a small commercial area where Ian pulled up in front of a fifties-themed place called the Big Apple Diner in an area called Kitsap Lake. It looked kitschy and fun. Her stomach was already starting to growl at the thought of food.

"Dolce is fine staying in the car, right?" Ian asked as he rolled all the windows down just a smidge.

"Yes, he'll be fine. Your car too, because nobody thinks twice about messing with a car with a German Shepherd in it," Olivia quipped.

Ian jumped out and came around to open the door for Olivia. "I'm really getting hungry," he said patting his belly and taking her hand in his. "I need these waffles at least every other month or two to maintain my mojo."

"Your mojo for what?" Olivia asked in a teasing tone.

"You know, my mojo for all things manly. Chopping wood into even pieces, wrestling bears and rescuing damsels in distress. All of those kinds of things."

"I see," Olivia nodded, "We better get in there and get you those waffles. I'd hate to go out into the woods with you without your mojo working at optimum levels."

"No, you would not," Ian assured her. They went in to find the place busy, but not too crowded. It had checkered floors, neon lights, painted wood ceiling, quilted and stainless steel walls, and vinyl booths—everything you'd expect the place to be right down to the music and red and white waitress outfits.

One of the waitresses was walking by with a plate in each hand and a few more balanced on both arms. She smiled and nodded to Ian, recognizing a regular when she spotted him. "Take any open booth you want guys," she called and continued on her way. Ian pointed to a big comfy booth by the windows where they could keep an eye on Dolce and took a seat across from Olivia. There were menus already on the table, but Ian set his to the side since he already knew what he wanted.

"I think I'm going with the waffle too," Olivia said, opening her menu, "but I just want to see what else they have for future reference."

"Of course," Ian said, "and please get whatever you want. Don't feel pressured to get what I'm having just because I love it."

"Oh no pressure here," Olivia replied assuredly, "I am totally in on the waffle. In fact, if somehow you get the last one they have, I'm stealing a bite."

Ian took her hand across the table and said, "If they are ever for some reason down to one last waffle, I'll split it with you and give you the bigger half. As long as I can get a little for my mojo, I'm happy to share."

Olivia loved his silly sense of humor and didn't pull away when he held her hand a little longer than normal. Her other hand went to touch the little silver whistle that was tucked under her t-shirt without even being aware she was doing it. Ian noticed though, smiled, and said, "I see you're wearing your whistle."

She pulled her hand back to join the other and rested her chin on them looking at him earnestly, "Yes, I wear it every day. It was such a thoughtful gift. I do feel better having it always close. It's so beautiful that I'd love it even if it didn't make me feel more secure."

Ian was about to say something more when the waitress came by to take their order. "The usual?" she asked Ian.

"Yes, two waffles for me and another for my beautiful date," he announced. "Or perhaps you want two as well?" he asked respectfully of Olivia.

"Oh no, one should be fine," she assured him.

"Also, a couple of mugs of your coffee. And don't feel like you have to ration the whipped cream," Ian teased the waitress.

"No, I remember," she said. "I'll bring extra whip and extra coconut syrup over. I don't know of anyone who appreciates our waffles the way you do hon' so don't worry about getting enough topping." She gathered up the menus and headed back toward the kitchen calling out to the cook, "Three alohas, a two on one, and a one, extra whip, extra syrup."

"I don't come here THAT often," noted Ian. "And there are a number of servers here so I'm surprised she remembers me or my order."

Olivia looked right at him and realized he was serious. "Noooo, it's such an amazing feat," she teased him. "After all, just about every other guy in here wears a kilt, has a devastating smile, and orders two fancy waffles every time they come in."

"You think I have a devastating smile?" Ian asked surprised.

"As a matter of fact, I do," she answered without hesitation.

Ian sat up straighter in his seat and grinned broadly. "You just made my day," he said happily.

Olivia laughed and leaned back, taking a sip from the sturdy mug of coffee that had appeared before her. She really liked Ian's personality. He could be so serious and protective when there was reason to be, tender and caring when he wanted to be, and just plain silly and fun much of the rest of the time. He was a wonderful combination of capabilities, heartfelt caring, and absolute playfulness. She loved how much he just seemed to enjoy life and all that it put in front of him.

"I'm glad I could make your day," Olivia told him. "You are certainly making mine."

They got to know each other a little better by talking about some of the best days from their past. Before they knew it, their waffles were delivered, and the conversation abruptly stopped as they inhaled the glorious scent of the plates before them. Well, a plate full of deliciousness for her and a platter with twice the deliciousness for him.

"Dig in and enjoy," Ian encouraged as he raised his fork. "Hey, you're not one of those women who needs to photograph her food first are you?"

Olivia rolled her eyes as she went in with her fork and knife, loading up the perfect bite. She cut off a big bite of the crispy edge of the waffle, drug it through the oozing syrup that had run onto the plate and dipped it into the whipped cream. She then looked Ian directly in the eye as she lifted the laden fork to her face, paused just ever so briefly, and then delivered the divine forkful into her mouth, closing her eyes, slowly chewing to savor the first bite and then swallowed before opening them again.

Ian just watched the entire performance, transfixed by how sensual it appeared.

"First you introduce me to the most decadent chocolate on earth and now this! Are you trying to ruin me?" she asked coquettishly, going in for another bite.

Ian just shook his head and started in on his own waffles. "Oh lady, I think I know who is being ruined here, and it certainly isn't you. How can I ever imagine coming back here and eating alone after that act?"

Olivia just smiled and took another sip of the bold coffee that helped to balance the sweetness of the breakfast. "You don't have to. I think it's safe to say I'm always willing to ride along and join you for this breakfast."

They continued to tease and talk their way through the sweet repast and then decided it was time to work some of it off on their hike and hunt. Ian paid while Olivia excused herself to freshen up and then they were back on the road, heading the short distance to Chico's Salmon Viewing Park where one of the orb hunting trails was located.

They got to the park and let an excited Dolce out to stretch his legs and look around. Olivia snapped the leash on her dog, adjusted her backpack and put it on, while Ian also put on his pack and secured the car. Ian pointed in the direction they'd be going and off they went. It was nice out, but still a relatively cool day, and there weren't many people in the park. There were a few parents with kids in the playground and they smiled at the excited shrieks and laughter from the children as they climbed and interacted with each other. The kids were no different than the dogs at the dog park she sometimes took Dolce to. They all had fun and played together as if they knew each other well even if they'd just met.

Before long, they were well down the trail that was wide enough for them to walk alongside in most places. She allowed Dolce to strike out a little in front of them or trail a couple of steps behind depending on where his nose led him.

JUST A WHISTLE AWAY
143

"So, as I was saying," Ian continued, "We're looking for glass orbs of various sizes, but most are about like a softball. They are in all different colors and designs. They are very well hidden so don't expect one to scream out to you, but you also don't need to go off the path or disrupt the plants to actually find one. They sort of hide in plain sight, but in a way that most people wouldn't notice if they weren't actively searching. Hence, the keen sense of observation needed. Even with that, don't expect to find one this first time out. Many people hunt every week and never find one."

The woods smelled wonderful with the mossy, earthy scent of having just recently rained. Big tall ferns and wild rhododendrons were plentiful along with a hundred other species of plants that she couldn't name. There were little drops of moisture that glistened in the sun every time they walked through an area that wasn't densely canopied by fir, hemlock and cedar trees. She told herself for the thousandth time how special the northwest was and how happy she was to be living here.

Dolce barked at a chipmunk sitting on a log just out of reach before it scampered up a tree. Ian gave the dog an affectionate pat on the head and told him that chipmunks were off limits and probably too fast to catch anyway. As they continued along the trail, Olivia found she could look closely all around her and still enjoy conversation with Ian without having to make frequent eye contact to connect. She told him more about her time in vet school and some of the interesting stories from being a zoo vet. Ian told her about starting to figure out life after leaving the army and how good it was to be able to live close to a buddy like Garrett since they had both experienced the challenge of coming back after overseas service. The conversation flowed so effortlessly between them and included both the serious and the comical. After about an hour and a half of walking along the winding trail, they arrived at a very small clearing where the sun could penetrate. There was a large, moss-covered boulder just wide enough for two people to sit on if they didn't mind being cozy.

Ian took off his pack and pulled out a collapsible dog bowl and a container of water. He poured a bowl full for Dolce and set it on the ground much to the pup's content. "I've got one for you too," he said to Olivia, "a water that is, but not the bowl." At her nod, he took a couple of La Croix's out of his pack, popped them open, and offered her one which she gratefully accepted. He put his hands around her waist and effortlessly lifted her onto the large rock.

"This is just what I needed today," she said inhaling deeply. "It feels wonderful to be out here in the park and to stretch my legs. I couldn't have asked for a better day. I'm so glad you let me join you, and Dolce, of course," she said teasingly.

"We're actually quite glad you invited yourself along too," Ian told her. "It's nice sometimes to just be guys out and about, but you do have your certain charms," he added.

They were sitting side by side right up against each other as the boulder allotted just that amount of space. When she nudged him, she pushed just hard enough that he would feel it without being knocked off. He nudged her equally hard back only it caught her a little off guard, causing her to lose her balance. While she was leaning perilously off the rock at a crazy angle, Ian's arm shot out, quick as a flash, and stabilized her. He started to pull her up when she said, "Wait, don't move, I think I see something! Okay, pull me up now please."

Ian's strong arm pulled her upright again and she handed him her can of water, hopped down and hurried over to the side of the trail where she stepped a few feet into the foliage. She bent over and straightened back up, lifting a beautiful glass orb into the air. It was about the size of a grapefruit, and it was a pale, peach colored orb with shots of purple, lavender, and mauve swirling through it like a magnificent sunset. Her eyes sparkled and her face was a portrait of

JUST A WHISTLE AWAY   145

delight as she did a little happy dance back to the rock where Ian was cheering. Dolce's tail was wagging furiously, caught up in infectious happiness of the moment as well.

Ian had hopped down and parked their beverages so he was free to wrap his arms around her and lift her in the air in celebration.

"This never happens! I've never heard of anyone finding an orb on their first try." He put her down and hugged her again. "Well done. You have crazy good observation skills."

"I do, don't I!" she exclaimed, still grinning from ear to ear. "Course, it took almost falling off a boulder and you catching me at just the right angle to see it."

"Happy to be of assistance, my dear," he said enjoying her absolute delight at the discovery. "I've got a cloth in my bag that we can polish it up with and then we have to take care of the business side of things."

"What business?" she asked as he retrieved the cloth and made sure the orb looked its best.

"Well, first, we need to take a photo of you holding the orb to send in to the officials. They document all the finds and celebrate the discovery by sharing it with all other hunters and everyone who follows the hunt."

Ian took out his phone for the shot and asked her if she wanted to stand on top of the boulder for her photo. She agreed it was the perfect location, so he helped her back up and photographed her in several different poses, all of which looked beautiful to him.

"Okay, what else?" she asked.

"Well, we finish our drinks, wrap up your treasure for its journey home and then we need to do a release." He clarified.

"What do you mean by do a release?" she asked with concern in her eyes. "I thought I got to take it home for keeps."

"Oh, you do," he assured her. He reached for his pack again and pulled out a box and opened it to reveal another orb that was nestled in a foam bed. This one was a deep purple with swirls of green shot through it.

"That is gorgeous," she exclaimed, "So what is the story?"

"I found this one when I went hunting in Manzanita Park on Bainbridge Island. The rules are that you can only keep one at a time. I've enjoyed this one for almost a year, so it's time to hide it again and let the next adventurer discover it."

"That is so cool, but why are you letting go of yours when I'm the one that found something today?" she asked.

"Because we're a team and I'm hoping we can keep doing this," he answered. "Do you agree?"

"Yes, absolutely yes!"

"Okay then, we need to find the perfect hiding place for the next person."

"Sounds good," she said. "I think finding them is the most fun but hiding them seems really fun too."

"It is," Ian agreed.

"What, you've hidden them before?" she inquired.

"Yep. I've been doing this for a couple of years now and have found three before yours today. So this will be my third time hiding one. If you find one you don't like as well as the one you have, you can just photograph it and log it rather than exchange it, but they are all so beautiful that I don't think I would ever have an actual favorite. And for the record, all my previous hunts have been solitary ones. I've never invited anyone else to go with me," he said softly.

Olivia felt oddly relieved at this piece of information. It felt good to have this be a shared, special experience just between her and him. She reached for him to assist her off the rock and it felt natural to do a small leap into his arms. From there, it was also natural for her to lift her face for a kiss, which he willingly obliged her. He began by placing a kiss on each corner of her mouth. Then he pressed his lips softly against hers and smiled. When he felt her smiling back, he gently ventured inside her mouth with-his tongue. He kissed her slowly and deeply and she returned the gesture. When he pulled away, she was smiling and her eyes were still closed.

"Dr. de Luca, I think kissing you is even sweeter than those coconut almond waffles," he whispered.

She opened her eyes and saw that he wasn't teasing; his look was filled with warmth and sincerity. Before she could respond, Dolce pushed his way in between them and looked up as if smiling, tail wagging and looking for affection. Olivia reached down and ruffled his fur, retrieved her pack, and pulled out a dog biscuit.

"Yummy," said Ian, "too bad you don't have one of those that would work for me."

"After all that sweetness you were talking about?" she quipped. Then she reached in and pulled out a chocolate bar and handed it to him. "I wouldn't shortchange either of my dates today."

Ian whooped and peeled open the chocolate bar and offered her a bite first. She declined, so he bit into it, clearly enjoying the offering. They finished their la Croix's, packed up the cans and turned back toward the trail head, bantering and looking for the perfect hiding place along the way. About halfway back, Dolce stopped and sniffed a wild huckleberry bush that had small berries starting to form.

Olivia suggested that Dolce may have found the perfect hiding place since the orb Ian had found sort of resembled a giant huckleberry. Ian agreed it was entirely apropos and so they found a wonderful soft spot to nestle the orb, leaving it both protected and just a wee bit exposed.

When they finally made it back to the car, Olivia leaned into a good stretch and yawned deeply, not because she was tired so much as relaxed. Ian helped Dolce get settled into the back again and stowed their backpacks behind the seat. As they left the park and headed back north toward home, Ian asked her if she needed anything. She suggested a Starbucks stop for a coffee and bio break which was an easy enough request to fulfill.

By the time they pulled up to Olivia's cottage, it was nearly five o'clock. The day had whipped by. Not only did they have a lot of fun and found the beautiful orb, they had begun to know each other much better. Ian got out, freed Dolce and carried Olivia's things to the house. Olivia unlocked the door and gestured him in. Ian stepped inside, put down her pack, and opened his arms inviting her into another hug.

"I need to go home and shower and change and get over to the Longhouse," he announced. "Donovan is back but I told him I'd handle things tonight, so he had a short day after being gone most of the week." He held her tenderly and swayed side to side for a minute. "It was a perfect day."

"It was a perfect day," she emphasized. "And I know Dolce loved getting out into the forest. You made both of us very happy."

Ian gave her a quick kiss and said he'd better get going or he might not be able to make himself leave. Olivia smiled and accompanied him out but remained on the porch. He walked toward the car, looked back over his shoulder and blew her a kiss. He turned away and did a little jig, his kilt swaying side to side as he moved, got in his car, waved and drove away. Olivia laughed, and then sighed as she wondered what would have happened if he didn't have to go. Well, it was clear that there would be more times together, so she'd just have to wait and see. She went back inside, retrieved the beautiful orb from her backpack, and set it safely in a shallow bowl on her coffee table. It was a stunning reminder of her unexpectedly wonderful day and the unusual, compelling man who had shared it with her.

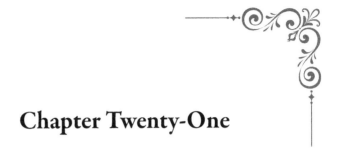

Chapter Twenty-One

Olivia added a log to the fire and returned to her plush chair-and-a-half. Her favorite chair had a wider and deeper than usual seat. The dimensions were perfect for her to snuggle into the corner and pull her legs up in the opposite corner or share the chair with Dulce when both were in the mood. Tonight, Dulce was content to stretch out on the area rug in front of the fire while Olivia looked forward to finishing a novel that had captured her attention.

The log popped, crackled, and sent up sparks like miniature fireworks. Olivia set the book in her lap to watch the show while she sipped on a red zinfandel she had poured herself after dinner. The wine was fruit forward with notes of cherry and currant with a hint of cardamom at the finish. She decided it would pair well with dark chocolate. She almost got up to fetch a Theo's dark chocolate and cherry candy bar she had left in her backpack from the weekend's orb hunt, but the comfort of the chair and fire had her rooted in place.

Watching the dancing flames of the fire and the curling smoke disappearing up the chimney combined with the relaxing effect of the wine made her sleepy. She squirmed further into the corner of the chair, pulled a soft, well-worn quilt over herself, and began to doze off, the book abandoned in her lap.

Before her mind could connect the scattered thoughts that were forming into a dream, Dolce let out a low, menacing growl that yanked her back into full wakefulness.

Dolce leaped up and his growl turned into a quick succession of low barks. The pitch of his insistent barking was usually reserved for intruders into his space or a pesky squirrel tormenting him from tree limbs just out of his reach.

"What is it boy?" Olivia asked as she followed Dolce toward the front door. *At this time of night, it could be a host of things,* Olivia thought as she pulled back the curtain on the front window and peered out into the front yard. No deer, bear, or squirrels in sight and nothing seemed out of place.

As Dolce's barking subsided with one final warning woof, Olivia dropped down onto a knee and began gently rubbing Dolce's ears and then vigorously scratching behind them. "Good job," Olivia praised. "That's the way to defend the home front. You're not a bad security alarm are ya boy?!"

Dolce's tail wagged at the praise and then he turned and trotted back to the living room. Instead of returning to his spot in front of the fire, he settled down next to Olivia's chair, taking up a protective position.

Olivia couldn't help but smile, thinking about her two male protectors just a whistle away. The promise of Ian's words warmed Olivia's heart as she felt the familiar weight of the whistle hanging around her neck while at the same time having her faithful companion on guard at her feet.

On impulse, Olivia leaned over the arm of the chair and grabbed her cellphone. She started to phone Ian and then hesitated. While she had a sudden urge to hear his voice, she really didn't have a good reason to call him. She sighed and put down her phone. She didn't want to appear needy or clingy after their date—every guy she knew fled from needy. Little did she know that Ian was at home trying to come up with a reason to give Olivia a call without sounding lame. At almost the exact same moment, both Olivia and Ian audibly sighed and put down their phones – an opportunity lost.

Early morning appointments on tomorrow's schedule would have Olivia up and moving. *It wouldn't hurt to get to bed at a decent hour*, she thought. Her first stop was the back door to let Dolce out to do his business. When she opened the door Dolce raced out of the house and dashed around the corner of the structure instead of heading to his normal spot at the corner of the lawn.

Olivia slid her feet into the broken-in slippers she used for such occasions and walked in the direction Dolce was headed. Not hearing any barking, she ambled around the corner of the house toward the front yard. As she suspected, Dolce was sniffing the ground, no doubt trying to discern the nature of the earlier intruder into his domain.

Picking up a scent next to her car, Dolce started heading for the woods next to the cottage's small front yard. "Come," Olivia commanded. She didn't need Dolce hunting the evening's earlier interloper at this hour. "Good boy," Olivia praised when Dolce obediently returned to her. She once again knelt, to reinforce his good behavior with an ear scratch and that's when she saw it! Her breath caught in her chest. Protruding from the now flat tire, on the back passenger side of her car, was a knife.

Her hand spontaneously rose to finger the whistle around her neck. Now she had a reason to call Ian. She sincerely hoped he would answer.

Ian was sorting through a pile of Dear Veritas letters identifying the ones he would respond to when his cell phone rang. He was pleasantly surprised when he looked down and saw the call was from Olivia's number. "I was just thinking about you," Ian said by way of greeting. "How are you?"

"Shaken," Olivia responded.

Ian could tell from the tone of her voice that she was serious. He bolted forward in his seat and said, "Tell me."

As Olivia recounted the events leading up to the discovery of the knife, Ian deliberately slowed his breathing when he felt his blood pressure precipitously rise. He didn't interrupt Olivia's succinct yet detailed account of the events. He listened to her voice with his whole being. When she described the knife protruding from the tire he leapt from his chair and had his car keys in his hand before his brain consciously registered his movements. "I'm on my way over," Ian said, the hardness in his voice stunning Olivia for a moment.

"Dolce and I are both fine," Olivia responded. "Dolce scared off whoever it was, and he will know if anyone comes back."

"I need to come over," Ian stated, steel still in his voice but with a softer edge than before. "I won't be able to sleep until I see for myself that you are safe."

"And I won't be able to sleep if you do come over," Olivia responded in a tone that Ian took a beat to absorb.

My gosh, how could she be flirting at a time like this, Ian thought. *Or am I misreading what sounded like seductive banter?* The sudden changes in tone from shaken to all business to flirting had his thoughts muddled.

After a bit of an awkward pause, Olivia said in a more neutral voice, "Ian, I really do need to get some sleep and Dolce will give me early warning if anyone comes near the place. I was shaken, but hearing your voice has calmed me down. And hearing the concern in it," ...she paused thinking, *has spun me up to the point neither one of us would get any sleep tonight if you came over,* but instead she said, "...is so appreciated. Would you be willing to come over soon and install security cameras outside around the house? I am taking this seriously enough that I want to catch whoever is doing this."

"Of course, I will," Ian responded, "I'll get right on it. But are you sure you don't want me to come over. I could sleep on the couch or just outside your room. I need to know you're safe, Olivia."

JUST A WHISTLE AWAY

"I'm sure I am safe with Dolce here," Olivia replied. "Whoever this coward is has not come out of the shadows. They are getting bolder with their spineless aggressions, but I don't get the impression they will crawl out into the light of day."

"Okay," Ian relented. "But will you call me after you get into bed before you fall asleep? By then, if no one comes back, they probably won't tonight." Ian wasn't sure that he believed his own words, but he delivered them with conviction in his voice.

"Then we will talk soon, Mr. McKay," Olivia said in an unmistakably come-hither tone. Then the call ended, with Ian staring at the phone screen—seeing nothing.

After twenty minutes of pacing in his living room, trying to work off the tension produced by his wandering thoughts about Olivia's faceless tormentor, his phone rang. Ian pressed the button to accept the call.

"I'm in bed and almost wishing I would have taken you up on your offer to come over, but I really do need to get some sleep," she purred in an indisputable alluring voice. Her voice changed and with complete sincerity, that seared his heart, she ended the call with, "Ian, thank you for being here for me. Goodnight."

"I can also be there for you tonight," Ian retorted, a new edge in his voice.

He heard the soft tinkle of her laughter before she said, "Goodnight."

For the second time in a half-hour, he was left staring at his phone screen. Now he had an entirely new tension to walk off before he could get any sleep.

Dear Veritas,

My buddy and I decided to leave it to you as to which of us should replace my tent.

Here's what happened. After a challenging and exhausting six-hour hike to a pristine lake we pitched my brand-new tent, made dinner, put out the campfire, got into our sleeping bags, and crashed. The night was young, but we were bone-tired, and it was pitch-black outside with not a lot to do. When we turned in there was not a soul in sight, even though the campground was a large one. We just figured that the strenuous hike took most campers out of the equation. Unbeknownst to us, there was a roadway that led all the way up to a parking lot just out of sight of the campground.

While we were sleeping, four busloads of girl scouts arrived and pitched their own city of tents and lit multiple campfires. My buddy, let's call him "Sam," woke around 9:30 pm and thought we were in the middle of a forest fire. He saw the impressions of dancing flames on the tent walls and started screaming "Fire! Fire!" as he wrestled himself out of his sleeping bag. Then he claimed to have seen a huge shadow projected onto our tent (of an alarmed girl scout as it turned out) and yelled "BEAR" as he ran out of the tent without his pants or bothering to unzip the tent flap. Of course, I purchased a waterproof polyester premium constructed tent that would not stretch or sag, but it did rip. He literally ripped out of the tent and scared the heck out of dozens of now screaming and hysterical girl scouts and startled the now pissed-off chaperones. The place was absolute mayhem.

Long story short, after threats of the police being called for Sam's indecent exposure (but to be fair he was wearing briefs and a tee-shirt) and talk of instigating a riot (which seemed to be overstating a bunch of screaming and crying girls), we cleared out of there mighty quickly. Since my tent was already ruined, I said, "leave it" as we just wanted to get away from the angry chaperones and out-of-control females.

Now Sam is saying that the tent was salvageable and I'm the one who said to abandon it. I contend that he ripped it and leaving the tent and replacing it was a whole lot cheaper and less hassle than getting arrested for God knows what. So, do you agree with me? Does Sam owe me a new tent?

Signed: *Tentless in Seattle*

Dear Tentless in Seattle (which I have concluded is not a bad thing),

Given the inexhaustible number of ridiculous camping fails and mishaps (a seemingly limitless number chronicled on YouTube alone), do yourself and the camping world a favor, and stay in the city. If you must get out into the great outdoors, make a reservation at a lodge or cabin and write the tent off as a lesson learned. Mankind (especially women of all ages), you, and Sam will be safer for the upgrade.

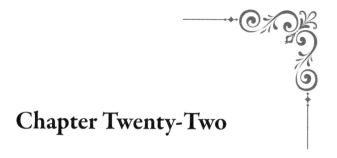

Chapter Twenty-Two

Ian was greeted by Dolce as he stepped out of his SUV in front of Olivia's cottage. The dog had a tennis ball in his mouth, and it was apparent by the slime on the ball he'd been playing with it for quite a while. But dutifully, Ian picked it up off the ground where Dolce had dropped it at his feet and threw it as far as he could into the side yard. With an excited yip, Dolce bounded after it. Ian wiped his hand on his kilt and reached into the back seat for his duffle bag of security cameras and installation tools. By the time he turned back around, the slimy tennis ball was back in front of him with a panting Dolce begging him to throw it again.

"Ok. One more time, then I must get to work," Ian said, picking up the ball and chucking it toward the back yard.

"He'll have you throwing it all day, if you don't cut him off," Olivia said leaning against the porch rail and chuckling as Ian, once again, wiped his dripping fingers off on his thigh.

She painted a beautiful picture standing there in the mottled sunlight of the porch. Olivia was wearing a summer yellow silk tunic over black capri leggings. The yellow made her olive skin glow and, even from this distance, Ian could see her brown eyes sparkling with humor as once again the dirty tennis ball rolled against his boot. Ian couldn't take his eyes off her as he bent down and rooted around for the ball for, what he hoped really was, the last toss for Dolce.

As he walked toward her, he felt his body tighten in arousal. He didn't know how long he could keep his hands off her. The few kisses that they shared had just whetted his appetite to run his hands and lips over her body to see what made her moan in pleasure.

Olivia didn't know what had put the intense look in Ian's eyes, but she loved his expression. He was dressed all in black. Black t-shirt that couldn't hide his muscular biceps and a black utility kilt that didn't hide his powerful calves. Any woman would appreciate the pure masculinity of the man and Olivia was no exception.

"I come bearing gifts of video cameras and all the trimmings," Ian said as he stood at the bottom of the porch steps trying to get his thoughts back to the business at hand. "I want to make sure if anything else happens, that we catch the guy. I don't feel good about you living out here on your own."

"I have Dolce who is a built-in alarm, a whistle to cry for help, and Zio also taught me how to defend myself along with what is probably a year's supply of pepper spray," Olivia stated.

Ian walked up the steps and couldn't resist giving her a quick peck on the lips. "It shouldn't take me more than an hour to install and test the system. You'll want to make sure your phone is charged as we'll need to set up your device so you can pick up the video feed when you need to."

Olivia was trying to pay attention to what Ian was saying, but his smell of woodsmoke and amber was like catnip to her senses. Since their dates, she had been trying to keep the erotic daydreams at bay, but they stole into her brain any time she let her mind wander.

"Olivia, do you have a ladder I can borrow?" Ian asked. After a pause, "Olivia," Ian said a little louder turning around to look at her.

"Hmm," Olivia slowly looked up at him, blinking to bring his face into focus. "I'm sorry, what?"

"Do you have a ladder?" Ian asked again looking at her quizzically.

"Um, yes, in the shed, in the back," Olivia said snapping out of her daydream. "I'll get it."

"No need," Ian said, squeezing her shoulder as he jogged back down the steps. "I'll find it."

As Ian made his way to the back with Dolce at his heels, Olivia shook her head trying to get her thoughts back on track. She ducked into the house to get her phone and try to shake off some of the tension in her body. The urge to wrap her body around Ian's when he got out of the truck was almost too strong to resist. The sexual tension between the two of them had been ratcheting up every day they spent in each other's company. She had to remind herself that he was here to do a job, not play a starring role in her fantasies.

By the time she got back to the porch, Ian had the ladder set up in the corner of the deck, marking the place where a camera would face out to the side yard. She watched him competently move around the cottage placing cameras in strategic locations, making sure they captured the places in the yard where somebody could sneak up on the house.

"If you'll get your phone, I'll set up your device to record the feed and we can make sure the cameras are placed correctly. You'll have access to the videos anytime you want, and can turn them on and off at will, but I hope you will leave them on," Ian said as he stretched to adjust the camera lens above the front door.

"I have my phone right here," Olivia said handing it up to Ian.

Standing on the ladder, Ian fiddled with her phone, adjusted the camera looking up and down between the phone and the camera a couple of times. Seemingly satisfied, Ian moved to step down off the ladder, while at the same time reaching up to make one last adjustment. Distracted, he missed the bottom step and came off the ladder quicker than he had anticipated. Grabbing for something to regain his balance, he clutched Olivia's shoulder for support and almost came crashing down on top of her. They both staggered for a few steps and came to a halt when they hit the waist-high railing of the porch.

JUST A WHISTLE AWAY

159

"I'm sorry, are you all, right?" Ian asked as he ran his hands up and down her arms.

Olivia was a little stunned to find herself pressed up against two-hundred pounds of hard male body. She looked up into Ian's concerned eyes, took advantage of their circumstance, curled her hands around his neck, and pulled him close. For a frozen minute, he just looked at her and then took her up on her unspoken invitation and melded his lips to hers. Olivia melted into his embrace and lost herself in the kiss.

Ian picked her up and sat down with her draped across his lap on the deck's chaise lounge, never breaking their connection. She ran her hands over the contours of his body, mapping the dips and valleys of his muscles. Needing to be skin to skin, Olivia grabbed the hem of his t-shirt and pulled it up. Ian obligingly lifted his hands over his head as Olivia slipped the shirt off and tossed it behind her. Ian captured her lips once again. Coming up for air, Ian stood and situated Olivia flat on the chaise coming down on top of her careful to prop himself up on his elbows so as not to crush her under his weight. Leaning up, Ian began to undo her tunic buttons one at a time revealing a lacy white bra underneath.

"Beautiful," Ian whispered as his lips ran over her burnished skin.

Suddenly impatient, their hands began bumping into each other as they divested themselves of the rest of their clothing, each sighing as their bodies came together. Ian looked into Olivia's soft eyes so that he could imprint their first time on his soul. He held her head between his hands and watched each expression slide across her face as their passion carried them away.

Olivia's eyelids fluttered closed as their satisfied bodies relaxed into the chaise. Trying to regain his equilibrium, Ian turned on his side, bringing Olivia with him until her head rested on his outstretched arm. He gently ran the back of his hand across her cheek. Olivia's eyes slowly slid open, and Ian felt a sense of male pride at the siren's smile she gave him.

"Are you ok?" he quietly asked, still stroking her cheek.

"Perfect," Olivia said turning her head to place a small kiss on his bicep. Olivia arched her back as she stretched out her muscles.

"Ah, ew," Olivia squeaked.

"What's wrong," Ian said startled when she jumped like she'd been pinched.

"Dolce!" Olivia exclaimed, "go lay down."

Ian lifted his head and began to laugh when he saw Dolce licking Olivia's toes. "Do you think he's jealous of all the attention you've been lavishing on me?" he asked as he drew her close for one more kiss.

"Perhaps we should move this inside," Ian said as he sat up. He began picking up their clothes where they had dropped them. They both began to dress, helping each other button and zip their garments closed in between kisses and caresses.

Ian grabbed Olivia for one last hug and said, "I need to put the tools and ladder away."

"I've made enchiladas for dinner," Olivia stated keeping him within the circle of her arms.

"Sounds good," said Ian giving her a kiss on the forehead. "I'll be in, in a minute."

Olivia grabbed her phone and shooed Dolce into the house before her.

Ian was just stepping up on the porch when he heard Olivia yell "Ian," in a panicked voice.

He flew up the steps and almost ripped the door off its hinges trying to get to Olivia. He ran into house with his heart in his throat looking everywhere for danger. She was standing, frozen in the kitchen staring at her phone.

"What's wrong?" Ian questioned, trying to get his breathing under control.

She looked up at him, her cheeks tinged with red, and a mortified look on her face. "Look at this," she said shoving the phone at him in an almost angry gesture.

Ian took the phone not understanding what he was looking at for a moment. When it dawned on him that he was viewing the security app on her phone, he started the video that she had been watching. As he watched himself and Olivia in the throes of passion, he was startled, a little turned on, and a lot humored.

Ian almost dropped the phone as he broke out into laughter. Olivia swatted him on the arm, grabbed the phone, and said, "this isn't funny, we unknowingly made a sex tape."

Ian dropped into one of the dining room chairs holding his stomach belly laughing in hilarity.

"Ian," Olivia said in exasperation, "delete this now!"

Ian put up his hand, mutely asking her to give him a second. He was trying to get enough air in his lungs to answer her.

"That's a first for me," Ian heaved out, still trying to get himself under control. He stood, grabbed Olivia, and wrapped her stiff body up in his arms.

"I should hope so. I can't believe you're laughing about this. It is so embarrassing!" Olivia exclaimed.

"I know, I know," Ian chuckled. "I'll delete it, but can I watch the whole thing first?"

Olivia gave his arm another slap. "No, delete it now!" she repeated.

He let her go, took the phone, and deleted the camera feed.

"Is that all of it? There's no back-up anywhere is there?" Olivia questioned.

"No that's the only one. I didn't have the chance to finish setting it up because somebody distracted me," Ian said, handing her phone back to her and wrapping her up in his arms again.

Olivia laid her head on his chest as Ian ran his hand up and down her back helping her to relax.

"You must admit. It would make a good story for our grandchildren," Ian said.

"We are not telling this story to anybody. You have to promise me," said Olivia as she pulled back to look in his eyes.

"Scouts honor," Ian promised holding up three fingers in a salute.

"That's the girl scout symbol. That doesn't count," Olivia said grinning.

"I promise, my Livvie," Ian said kissing her gently on the lips. "As long as you admit that was hilarious."

"I'm admitting no such thing," she said, "But since we no longer have the video, I might need a do over to remember exactly what happened."

Raising her eyebrows, she smiled a secret smile as she led a very willing Ian down the hall to her bedroom.

Dear Veritas,

I have a neighbor who loves to host dinner parties for other couples in the neighborhood. She has introduced my husband and me to a lot of other families on our street, and for that, I am thankful. However, there have been a couple of times when I've asked for a recipe for one of her dishes and, although she has said she will send it to me, she never does. At one dinner party, I happened to look in the trash and discovered take out boxes from various restaurants and realized the reason I never received any recipes was because many of the dishes were not homemade! My neighbor had even taken credit for making the cuisine. I'm not sure why she feels like she must hide the fact she didn't make some of the dishes, but I wish she would be honest about the fact she will never be sending me the recipes. How do I tell her that I don't care who makes the dinner; it is just a pleasure to spend time with neighbors.

Signed: *Dishing in Dishonesty*

Dear Dishing,

I think you answered your own question. It doesn't matter who does the cooking if the company is pleasant and you are enjoying yourself. I have a question for you. What were you doing rooting around in your neighbor's trash? Just a caution, if she catches you, my guess is that you won't be enjoying many more pleasant dinner parties.

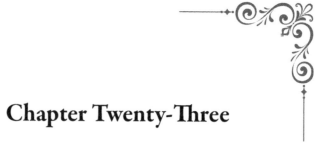

Chapter Twenty-Three

"Ian, it is so good to see you," Adam, the publisher of the *Poulsbo Weekly Gazette* said, shaking Ian's hand and sitting back down in his tufted leather chair behind his heavy oak desk.

The publisher's office was a quintessential gentleman's literary space - all dark woods, leather trimmings, and dim lighting glowing against paneled walls, littered with headlines announcing fires, the " pumpkin in the "Guinness Book of World Records," murder and political commentary.

"Can I get you something to drink?" asked the publisher.

"No thank you," answered Ian sitting down in the chair Adam indicated. "How are you, Adam? It's been a while since we've talked."

Adam relaxed back in his seat. "I'm good. How have you been? Busy, if the rumors of your buying another building downtown are true."

"They are true; escrow will be complete in a few weeks," Ian stated. "So, tell me, how is the column doing? Should I keep writing or should I wrap it up?"

"I have to tell you when we first discussed your writing an advice column, I thought it would be well received, but I was stunned when the new numbers came out," Adam said, raising an eyebrow.

"Good stunned or bad stunned?" Ian asked leaning forward in his seat.

"Definitely good stunned. The reviews have been great, and the number of online hits is amazing. Of course, the mystery of who

JUST A WHISTLE AWAY

is writing the column has boosted the mentions of the articles in literary blogs. You are very popular even if you are unknown and I appreciate you writing more than the six you originally agreed to."

"Does that mean we are good to go, at least for now?" asked Ian.

"Definitely. Are you up for it?"

"I think I am. As long as we continue to disassociate my name with the writing. I prefer to remain anonymous," Ian said.

"At some point, if sales start to droop, we should talk about revealing your identity," Adam said. "But I'm willing to let it lie for now."

"When the time comes, we can talk about it, but then we'd need to renegotiate. I'd prefer to remain a man of mystery," Ian reiterated with a chuckle.

Adam gave Ian a lopsided smile nodding his head. "Do you have anything for me today?"

Ian drew a thumb drive out of his pocket. "Here's the latest."

Adam plugged the thumb drive into his laptop and searched for the file. He read silently as Ian watched for his reaction.

"Perfect," Adam said. "I'm putting it in the next issue."

"Thanks," Ian said as he stood to go. "I'll keep them coming, just promise me you won't give me the credit."

Adam smiled, "Your secret is safe with me," he said.

For now. The words went unspoken in the air between them. It's not that he didn't trust Adam, but people did interesting things for money. If Adam thought outing him would be a way to boost sales, if the column became less popular, he hoped he would speak with him first and not pull the trigger too quickly.

Ian rose and turned toward the door, then quickly turned back around. "I promise I will tell you when and if I'm ready to go public before I mention it to anybody else."

Ian turned back toward the door and made his way out of the office. Instead of going out the front where he would be seen and people would speculate why he was in the newspaper offices, he snuck out the back looking both ways to ascertain if the coast was clear and jumped into his SUV. He laughed at himself for acting all cloak and dagger over a newspaper column as he pointed the truck toward Garrett's place.

He was almost there when his phone rang. Hitting the answer button on the steering wheel, he said, "Ian here."

"Hey man, everybody is here. Where are you?" asked Garrett.

"I'm a couple of minutes out. I didn't realize it was so late."

"You are never late. You do know the rule and that you need to bring the beer. I hope you stopped by the store?" Garrett said.

"I have it covered. I also have a new bottle of scotch since you were almost out last time we gathered at your place," Ian stated, turning into Garrett's driveway. "I'm here. I'll be in, in a minute," Ian said hanging up.

Ian brushed his boots off on the welcome mat, opened the door and walked into the kitchen.

"What did I miss," Ian said by way of greeting.

"We were just discussing the rehearsal dinner plans," Garrett said. "Jacq needs to know the head count. I assume you are in for one?"

Ian paused in the open refrigerator door, turning slightly toward Garrett, he asked, "Is it too late to bring a plus one?"

Behind Ian's back, three sets of eyebrows were raised as Garrett, Donovan and Emmett looked at each other with surprise.

"Ok Ian, spill. Who's the lucky lady?" demanded Donovan.

"Olivia, of course," said Ian putting the beer in the refrigerator.

"There is no "of course" about it," Emmett said emphasizing the "of course" with a wave of his hands. "You've failed to mention that you two were at the point that you would be attending your best friend's wedding together."

"Let me get a scotch, somebody deal the cards and I'll tell you all about it," Ian said taking the crystal tumbler Garrett handed to him.

As the guys sat down to play, Ian filled them in on his dates with Olivia, the run-in with Wayne Hoffman, and the harassment Olivia was experiencing. He left out the personal stories of the sex tape they had managed to unknowingly record and his deepening feelings for Olivia. Given the looks Donovan was giving him, Ian suspected he knew that he was falling hard for Olivia. He wasn't sure anybody missed the fact that Olivia was becoming important to him, but he wasn't ready to admit it.

"Do you want me to look into it?" Donovan asked.

"Look into Olivia?" questioned Ian, looking at him with confusion.

"No, into Wayne," Donovan clarified. "I could also look into Olivia's past to see if there is anything that would trigger the harassment behavior toward her. But I don't want to do that without Olivia's permission."

"You can do that?" Ian asked.

"Of course, I'll just need a few days," Donovan affirmed looking down at his cards.

Ian caught Garrett's surprised look across the table.

"What are you, a private investigator?" Ian questioned, chuckling, not considering for a second Donovan might be something like a super spy.

"No, but I know people," Donovan said enigmatically, not looking up from his cards. "Just get me everything you know about him."

"Um, ok. I'll ask Olivia what she knows. He used to work for Paolo, so they should have quite a bit of information on him," said Ian, still unsure what exactly Donovan was going to do about it.

Ian looked up at Emmett waiting for him to play his next card, but Emmett was looking at Donovan with what, he was sure, was the look on all their faces; a combination of surprise, interest, and confusion.

Realizing the game had stopped, Donovan looked up to see three pairs of eyes staring at him.

"What?" he questioned.

"Well, you kind of surprised us there, pal," Emmett said, "what do you mean you have people?"

"What?" Donovan said again, "I have a friend who is a private investigator. I was going to hand it over to her to see what she could find out. There's no mystery here."

"Um hum," Garrett muttered resuming the game.

"And how do you know a PI?" Ian questioned.

"She's a friend of mine from college. She went into the police force and ended up with her own investigation business," Donovan explained.

"And you call on her often?" Ian questioned, continuing to grill Donovan.

"Ok, why the twenty questions? It's just a friend Ian. Nothing out of the ordinary," Donovan stated looking at his friends.

"Ok, ok, I'll drop it, but you are gone an awful lot with no explanation of where you get off to," Ian said.

Garrett and Emmett's eyes were ping ponging between the two friends as they talked.

"I have investments to buy and sell and that means I need to get eyes on some of them," Donovan said with an edge to his voice. "Are you complaining about covering me at the Longhouse? If you don't want to cover, I can find somebody else."

"No, that's not what I'm saying. I'm happy to be at the Longhouse. Just want to make sure you're safe, happy, and healthy," Ian said with a smile, breaking the tension.

"What would make me happy is winning this game," Donovan said with a look to Emmett.

"No way, super spy, Garrett and I have this one in the bag," Ian quipped.

Donovan shook his head in exasperation. "Just for that, read 'em and weep," said Donovan playing the last trump and securing the game for him and Emmett.

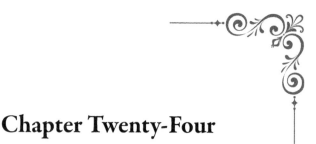

Chapter Twenty-Four

Christopher's jaw dropped as Jacq rounded the corner to model her wedding dress. Each had their cell phones in hand and were FaceTiming with Beth who was home in New York.

"Chris, hold up your phone so I can see too," Beth said, a bit of irritation creeping into her voice.

Christopher juggled his phone and then steadied it to capture a full-length view of Jacq's exquisite dress. Beth squealed in delight as Jacq twirled, providing a 360-degree view of the simple yet elegant creation.

"It's perfect," Beth gushed, "and so, so You!"

The A-line skirt was fitted at Jacq's waist and then gradually widened toward the high-low hem. The hem reached just to her knees in the front of the gown and almost to the floor in the back. The fitted sleeveless bodice and squared neckline showcased Jacq's toned arms and drew attention to her long neck and delicate collarbones. But the showstopping and unexpected aspect of the gown was the five-inch scalloped band of blue forget-me-not silk flowers that ran around the **inside** hem of the dress. Had the dress been full length the silk flowers would have not been visible; but the high-low hem revealed the delicate flowers toward the middle and back of the gown as the inside of the skirt's hem became visible from the front. Somehow the flowers created a perfect balance between classy and flirty.

JUST A WHISTLE AWAY

"Chris, can you get a close-up of the flower detail," Beth ordered more than asked.

Dutifully, Cristopher zoomed in on the delicate silk flowers and Beth gasped, "So lovely! Is each individual flower attached with a tiny yellow pearl?"

"Yes," Jacq replied, "It was a splurge, but I thought that tiny detail would be worth it."

"It is," Christopher breathed, finally finding his voice. "The gown is both sophisticated and elegant and flatters your curves perfectly."

"Thank you," Jacq blushed twirling once again. "And you tried to talk me out of altering my mother's gown," Jacq said, eyeing Christopher and hitching an eyebrow.

"That can't possibly be your mother's dress," Christopher exclaimed, conjuring up in his mind the gaudy image of the poofy-sleeved, lace gown he was horrified Jacq insisted on having altered to wear.

"It is," Jacq assured him. "Well, it is the same satin A-line dress minus the sleeves and minus the mesh overlay of lace and floral appliques. And, of course, I had the hem and neckline altered, and added the band of silk forget-me-nots, but the bones of the dress are indeed my mother's. The dress didn't even need to be altered, it fit me like a glove."

"Well, I'm having a hard time believing what you have on is your mother's wedding dress, but I must say you are breathtaking in it," Christopher conceded.

Beth agreed wholeheartedly. "Garrett will be blown away when he sees you walking down the aisle."

"That's what I was aiming for," Jacq nodded.

"You nailed it," Christopher confirmed with an enthusiastic head bob.

"Okay, let me get a good look at the two of you," Jacq implored. From what I can see, I already know I love the color and neckline of your dress Beth and Christopher's ensemble is perfection. Christopher rolled his eyes and tilted his head in a "but of course" gesture. "Beth, can you position your screen so we can see your entire dress?"

Both Jacq and Christopher looked down at Beth's image on their cellphones. The live-streaming video moved wildly about as Beth adjusted her computer screen and then backed away from it to offer a full-length view.

"I love it!" Jacq exuberantly exclaimed. "I love everything about it. The color is perfection," Jacq went on.

Beth had chosen a magenta-colored, more pink than purple, sleeveless, knee-length fitted gown. The dress had an elegant Bateau neckline running horizontally front to back almost to her shoulder points and across her collarbone. Beth sported a thin navy-blue belt to accentuate her trim waist and to color coordinate with Christopher's navy suit.

Jacq's gaze moved from Beth's image to Christopher and back again. "How did you match the colors so perfectly?" Jacq inquired. "That gorgeous pink is not exactly a common shade."

"It was Chris' idea to have me pick out a dress and then color match his bow tie and pocket square. That was easier said than done, but I finally succeeded at Bergdorf's," Beth triumphantly recalled.

"She popped them in the mail to me and voila," Christopher added with a devilish grin as he unbuttoned and opened his jacket to show off the gorgeous navy tone-on-tone paisley satin lining.

"You both look sensational," Jacq said, her voice cracking and unshed tears welling in her eyes.

"Oh, honey, what's wrong?" Christopher tenderly asked, walking over to Jacq and putting a protective arm around her shoulder.

"Absolutely nothing," Jacq assured her friends. "I just think it is finally hitting me that this is real. Soon I will marry the man of my

JUST A WHISTLE AWAY 173

dreams, and my two best friends will be there at my side to share in the celebration. I am so happy and more than a little excited."

Jacq took a deep breath, switched gears and said, "All right, let's all take a minute to change into something comfy and grab a glass of wine. We e still have a lot to talk about.

"Just give us one more twirl," Beth prevailed upon Jacq. Her beaming friend happily complied.

After a short intermission, the friends reconvened as if the conversation had never been interrupted. Christopher lifted his wine glass in a toast, "To Jacq and Garrett, may we all be around to celebrate your golden wedding anniversary."

"Ahhh," Beth said, "I love that, I was just thinking, here's to getting through the wedding without a hitch."

"Let's drink to both," Jacq said lifting her glass in salute before taking a sip.

The next two hours flew by going over wedding details and discussing pre-wedding events. Beth was flying out to Poulsbo three weeks before the wedding to attend a bridal shower that Nicole was hosting, to attend the bachelorette party that she and Christopher had been planning on the sly, as well as the rehearsal and rehearsal dinner.

"I can't wait to meet Garrett and all your friends in person," Beth said. "I already feel like I know them. Between all the FaceTime calls with you and Garrett and all the stories you've both told about your Poulsbo friends, my time out there should be a blast. I've missed you both so much."

"I love my life out here," Jacq said smiling wistfully at Beth, "but I would love it even more if you were a daily part of it."

"Well, I will be for at least three weeks," Beth assured. "Are you and Garrett positive you want me as a house guest for the three weeks prior to your wedding?"

Christopher interjected with a snarky retort, "Garrett has no idea what he is getting into and there's no way to prepare him for you. But I've already promised him when, not if, he is ready to kick you out I would be happy to lend you my guestroom."

"Now you've given me ample incentive to be on my best behavior," Beth chuckled.

The three friends continued to laugh and carry on, reminiscent of shared times together in New York. Time and distance had only sealed their resolve to connect regularly via technology, but each was looking forward to soon being together in the same room.

"Any other news from the frontier?" Beth teased.

"Hum," Christopher cooed. "Word on the street is that Ian is off the market."

"Oh yeah," Jacq agreed. "Garrett seems to think he has it bad. He's fallen head over heels for our new Doc in town. She's a veterinarian who has captured his heart it seems."

"...and lips and other things," Christopher added.

"Chris," Jacq admonished.

"I call 'em like I see 'em," Christopher countered. "Honestly, he looks like a doe-eyed puppy anytime he is around her or her name comes up in conversation"

"Do you both like her?" Beth queried.

"Yes, very much," Jacq affirmed as Christopher nodded in agreement. "She's intelligent, sweet, and seems to anchor the big guy. Although right now he's like a dog with a bone. Someone is stalking her or at least sending a message that she is not welcome in town."

Jacq and Christopher filled in an appalled Beth about the escalating events that had occurred over the past few weeks.

"My gosh," Beth exclaimed, "I hope they catch the creep soon before anyone gets hurt."

"Yeah, so do we. We'll keep you posted," Christopher promised.

JUST A WHISTLE AWAY 175

Reluctantly, the friends brought their time together to a close. It was late in New York and so they said their goodbyes. They were cheered that their next long get-together would be face-to-face.

Dear Veritas,

Have you ever been in the grocery store trying to make quick work of your shopping and you turn the corner and there sits a cart right in the middle of the aisle? Not only is it in the middle of the aisle, but the shopper is at the opposite end of the lane looking for something. Why didn't they take their cart with them? What is it with people who, if they want to park their cart, can't stay on their side, but must block all other shoppers? Where has the common shopper courtesy gone?

Signed: *Blocked in the Cereal Section*

Dear Blocked,

I know sometimes it seems as if people are thinking more about themselves these days than others. But you never know what the other shopper has been through. Perhaps they had an auto accident that day or they are in the midst of a bad break up. Perhaps they didn't mean to leave the cart in the middle of the aisle, but they just had a really bad day and all they can concentrate on is getting food home to the kids. Some days we all could use some grace. How about helping by simply moving the cart out of the way. Even if the other shopper was truly a rude, insensitive individual, you can at least achieve an unblocked state of mind. Isn't that what really matters?

Chapter Twenty-Five

The large pots of flowers that Ian and Olivia had planted were thriving with bright blooms now reaching up toward the sun and others cascading densely over the sides. Fortunately, no more mishaps had been wrecked upon them and everyone who entered the clinic commented on what a beautiful and cheerful addition they were. Olivia had added one more of the planters to a small landing off the back door of the clinic where she had placed a couple of chairs and a small table that were perfect for the occasional break when she could grab one. There was a small overhang that afforded just the right amount of shade over the seating area, leaving enough cover for a perfect spot where Dolce could hang out with her.

Zio Paolo was joining her this afternoon for what was becoming their regular weekly tea and pastry date. She decided to select something from Lily's and sit outside with him at her little retreat. She had picked up the pastries earlier—an assortment of cookies this time and had steeped a pot of Earl Grey at the clinic. She went outside to carry the things they'd need to the little table ahead of when her zio was expected, wondering if she might catch a glimpse of Ian coming or going today. She needed to keep her promise and fill her uncle in on the slashed tire, but she was also considering whether or not she should tell him about the budding relationship she was having with their charismatic landlord. Part of her wanted to come clean, and part of her wanted to keep it private just a little bit longer.

She still blushed just thinking about the surveillance camera fiasco but couldn't help chuckling about it either.

She pushed the back door open with her hip as her hands were full of cups and plates and things and stepped out onto the landing. As she set the tray on the table, she heard footsteps and turned to see if it was Ian, but it was Heather, the waitress from the bakery, descending the steps from Ian's apartment. Olivia raised her hand in a friendly greeting when Heather looked back over her shoulder and spotted her, but the girl simply turned away after making eye contact. Heather walked through the back entrance to the bakery, smoothing and patting her hair into place as she did so.

Olivia thought it strange that Heather was acting cool toward her, but perhaps she was one of those women who was all business around other women and all charm around men. That said, she couldn't help but feel a little twinge of curiosity about why the girl was coming from Ian's place. Perhaps she was delivering the rent check for Lily or an order or something. While she and Ian hadn't arrived at a point that defined their relationship yet, she felt pretty certain that he wouldn't be dating her if there was anyone else in the picture. He didn't seem like that type of guy, so she wouldn't allow her head to go there.

The clinic bell tinkled in the distance and since she had already closed up and locked the front door, she knew Zio Paolo had arrived. Olivia went back in to greet him and grab the tea and cookies. As usual, he greeted her with a big hug and a kiss on each cheek.

"How's my beautiful niece?" Paolo inquired.

"I'm fine Zio, and very happy you're back in town. I want to hear all about your trip," she responded. "Come on out back and let's get caught up. I'll just grab our tea."

"Let me help you Livvie, what can I carry?"

"Sure, how about bringing that plate of cookies? I've got everything else handled," she said nodding toward the treats.

JUST A WHISTLE AWAY 179

They went outside, sat down, and Olivia poured their tea. Dolce wasn't with her today leaving plenty of room for her zio to stretch out his long legs.

"So, Zio, I want to hear all about your trip."

"Of course, of course cara, but you, first. I'm anxious to know if all is well and if you've had any more problems." He took on a serious look as he saw her briefly look away and her shoulders tense. "What happened?"

"Well, there was another incident I'm afraid. It may or may not be related, but somebody stabbed my tire one night at my house while you were away."

"What? At your house? What the—this is just crazy!" Paolo stood up and ran his hand through his hair. "We've got to call the police this time. I still wonder if Wayne isn't somehow to blame, but this seems a bit extreme even for him. I was thinking about it and maybe it wouldn't hurt to put some fear into him."

"Zio, hold on a second. I asked Ian for help and he came over and installed some video surveillance cameras." Olivia looked down at her hands as she told him so as not to reveal how awkward she felt recounting even this much. "If anyone puts a toe near my place, we'll know who it is and what they're doing. Plus, he's going to have one of his friends look into Wayne. Apparently, his friend Donovan has connections or something. If you still think we need to report it, then that's fine, but I feel confident that Ian is handling things well."

Paolo thought about it a little longer. "Perhaps it's best to see what Ian comes back with. If it is Wayne behind this malicious mischief, it might be best not to tip him off. I'm just worried about it escalating."

"Really Zio, I feel safe enough. Between the video cameras and Dolce, I think I'm fine. I always bring Dolce with me to work now if I know I'm going to be late. And I have both you and Ian looking out for me," she said putting a hand on his shoulder.

"Did I hear my name?" asked Ian, walking up and surprising them. He gave Paolo a pat on the back and then walked over and bent down to give Olivia a kiss on the cheek, appreciating the blush it elicited.

"I was just filling Zio in on the tire incident and the video cams," she explained.

Ian glanced at her with a knowing look punctuated by exaggerated raised eyebrows since his back was to Paolo. Olivia turned away so she could compose her features while Ian looked back at Paolo with a blank face and gave a serious nod.

"Someone has crossed the line and we're going to get to the bottom of it," he assured him.

Paolo offered to get another chair for Ian.

"Thanks, but no. I'm late for an appointment, but I wanted to come say hello when I saw you. I don't think this guy is a huge threat, but I don't like what's gone on at all and I'm serious about putting an end to it," Ian said. "I'm going to talk to my friends about it. This really hasn't become anything big enough for the police to do much, but a few of us angry vets ganged together can be pretty intimidating, no pun intended."

Paolo smiled and nodded. "Okay, you take the lead and let me know what I can do."

Ian shook his hand and turned back to Olivia. "I'll call you later, okay? We've got this."

Olivia smiled and nodded back and said goodbye. She looked at her uncle who just smiled back at her with an "I saw that" look in his eye. "He's a good young man Livvie. I approve," he said.

"Thanks, Zio. I don't really know if anything is going anywhere, but we seem to be hitting it off."

"I'm glad. He's responsible, stable, and he knows how to keep a woman safe. He dresses a little odd, but then, that's the Scot in

JUST A WHISTLE AWAY

him. You know, there's never been a successful fashion designer from Scotland."

Olivia laughed and felt relieved that her uncle was taking it all in stride. "Do me a favor Zio; please don't say anything to Mom and Dad or anyone else for that matter. There's really nothing to tell at this point and you know how anxious Mom is to see me matched up with someone.

"I won't say anything, my lips are sealed," he said making a zipper gesture across his mouth. "You know we all just have your best interests at heart. Would you feel better if you and Dolce came to stay with me for a little while? I can make up the guestroom."

"No, thank you Zio, but really we'll be fine. I know you are always there for me. Now please, tell me all about your trip."

Paolo relaxed and told her about the short cruise he had taken from Seattle to Canada and the fishing trip he went on with a friend when he returned. It had been a great getaway and a nice appetizer for what was going to be a full retirement menu in the near future. He entertained her with greatly exaggerated stories of widows fighting over him on the dance floor, of the cruise ship, and of course, the fishing story of the biggest catch ever that got away.

Olivia filled him in on all the clinic business, a staple of their check-ins, and booked a couple of days with him in the clinic for the following week. She wrapped up the leftover cookies for her uncle and locked up while he went to do something in his office and then came back to walk her out to her car. She gave him a hug and a kiss goodbye and decided to go grocery shopping on her way home. She wanted to stop at the Central Market, her favorite store, and stock up on a few things. She decided to invite Ian over for dinner in the next few days and wanted to have some items on hand that she liked to cook that usually turned out well. Olivia was an Italian girl through and through. While baking beautiful shortbreads was her specialty, she had learned how to make a great sauce and perfect pasta at a fairly young age at her Nona's side. Homemade pasta was always a man pleaser, and she was feeling in the mood to thank the man who was certainly coming through for her. Since he had taken her out on a couple of fun dates, she felt it was her turn to take the lead and plan their next one.

The parking lot at the market was busy, but not packed, so she was able to park fairly close to the front. While she didn't really expect a knife wielding maniac to be hiding behind the flower display ready to sneak out and stab more of her tires, it seemed like a good idea to take precautions and park where she was easily visible.

The Central Market had one of the best cheese counters she'd seen in a long time, so she stocked up on some good pecorino, parmesan and fresh burrata. The produce section was also a dream, piled high with everything a chef could want and she filled her basket with fresh veggies and salad fixings, including several types of mushrooms and a whole basil plant that she decided would be good to go ahead and grow at home. Next, she selected a package of ground beef and another of sausage. She headed over to the wine section getting distracted by a few of the tempting displays along the way. The handmade soaps that you could slice and buy by the pound always got her attention and when she finally finished inhaling them all and selecting the one she wanted, she'd found that she'd spent a good half hour shopping already. She wrapped up the soap and started wheeling toward the wine section when she thought she saw a familiar face across the store. *Was that Wayne*? It looked like him from a distance and the man seemed to be glancing back her way but not long enough to be absolutely sure. Olivia started getting mad and decided she'd had enough. With her cart in front of her as her shield, she decided to wheel right up to him and stare him down. What, if anything, she'd say to him was yet to be determined, but she was

JUST A WHISTLE AWAY 183

done standing by and being harassed. As she began to purposefully head his way, her cell phone chimed with a text.

"Hey lovely, are you home yet?" It was Ian.

"No, I'm at the market. I think Wayne is here."

"Which market, I'll be right there."

Before she could text a reply, her phone rang.

"Hi Ian, I'm at the Central, and you don't need to come over. I'm fine. I was just going over to stand up to him. I don't want him to think I'm scared of him."

"Livvie, please don't do that. I can be there in ten minutes. Make that five. To hell with speed limits."

"Ian no, I'm not even sure it's him. Hold on, I don't see him anymore. If it was him, I think he may have left."

"You're sure you're, okay?

"I'm sure. I was getting mad and was ready to nail him. Whoever it was, he probably felt my wrath from across the store and got out of Dodge," she quipped.

Ian smiled through the phone. "It really isn't something to joke about, but I do admire your spirit," he told her. "Okay, I'm going to be home in about an hour. I can come over if you want me to."

"I'd love to see you, but not tonight. I've got some work to do at home. But what about tomorrow? I was thinking it might be nice to make you dinner."

"And she cooks too? Be still my heart!" Ian said, thumping his chest loud enough for her to hear it over the phone. "Absolutely, yes, just tell me when and what to bring."

"I'll send you a text," she said. "And you don't need to bring anything, just you."

"You have me," he stated as simply as that.

Olivia felt the warmth of his words and didn't know what to say.

"Are you there?" he asked.

"Oh yes, I'm here," she answered. "Thanks Ian, it feels really good to, to have you, you know—here for me."

There was a pause on the other end of the line and then Ian said, "I'm always here for you. Maybe shoot me a text when you get home?"

"I will," she promised. "Bye Ian."

She disconnected and put her phone back in her purse and pushed her cart near where she had seen the man who looked like Wayne. There was nobody around that part of the store, but an abandoned shopping cart was left in the middle of the aisle with a few frozen food items in it. She looked around but couldn't spot anyone who looked like it belonged to them. Olivia went over to the wine section and picked up a couple bottles of Merlot and then checked out, still scanning the store just to be sure. Nothing. Perhaps she was imagining things. Having just talked to Zio about it, it made sense that she might be seeing Wayne around every corner. She raised her hand to the little whistle and rubbed it thoughtfully as she walked toward her car. It gave her comfort, and it reassured her that she had a partner in solving this mystery. If it was Wayne, he'd soon be sorry he harassed her in even the slightest way as she had a feeling Ian wouldn't let him off easy. She loaded her groceries into the car and returned the cart to the cart corral, then got in her car to go home. She made one last scan of the parking lot before turning on the ignition and driving away. It was good to have a champion in her corner, but it was still her responsibility to take care of herself and being alert and aware was the cornerstone of personal safety—so she had been told in her women's safety class back in college.

Olivia had never had a problem with any guy making her feel unsafe before, but she knew women who had. A friend of hers once had a stalker—a guy she had gone out with just one time who fancied them practically engaged. They'd laughed at first but it quickly escalated to something scary. Her friend had to get a protection order, to change her phone number, and eventually she moved away. Olivia knew that these things could seem harmless but weren't always so. That said, it was much more likely that this was really nothing but maliciousness and wouldn't go anywhere bad, but she wasn't going to take any chances. Perhaps she would bring Dolce to work a bit more regularly.

She thought again about her phone call from Ian. "You have me," he'd said. He'd said it in a way that implied much more than just confirming he'd like to come for dinner. Just thinking about it flooded her with warmth and anticipation. "You have me too," she said out loud to herself.

Chapter Twenty-Six

Olivia sat with Ian's head on her lap sifting her fingers through his red hair. She was looking out the window at the gray, drizzly day thinking her garden will love the moisture, but the weather put a damper on what should be a bright summer day. She had spent some time at Garrett's that week looking over the animals and checking on Sadie. The dog was getting older and having pain in her hips. Olivia could tell Garrett worried about her and hated to see her slowing down. She had assured Garrett she had a lot of life left in her and they could manage old age aches and pains. She hated to think about the time when Garrett, Jacq and Nitro would have to say goodbye to the old girl. Losing a member of the family was never easy but was inevitable one day.

Oliva paused her hand when she felt Ian move. Looking down into his slumberous eyes she gave him a soft smile.

"I'm jealous that your hair is softer than mine," Olivia said quietly.

He reached up and tugged on one of her curls. "Maybe, but I continually want to bury my hands in your hair," he demonstrated by reaching up and pulling her head down for a soft kiss.

They had both decided a leisurely Saturday night watching a movie and cuddling on the couch was the best way to unwind from a stressful week. Ian had been juggling the closing of escrow on his new building, writing the next Dear Veritas article, covering for Donovan at the Longhouse as well as participating in "Best Man" duties which he realized consisted of whatever Garrett needed him to do at any time day or night. Although the groom seemed to be calm on the outside, he knew Garrett was fretting on the inside and trying his best to get the farm in order before the wedding and before he whisked Jacq away for their honeymoon.

"Best day ever," Ian sighed closing his eyes as Olivia resumed massaging his scalp.

The old Cary Grant movie "Arsenic and Old Lace" was playing on the TV. The movie was one of Olivia's favorites. She loved the interaction between the Cary Grant character and his beloved aunt. The movie was funny without being campy, but she had seen it so many times she was letting her mind wander from topic to topic enjoying having nothing to do in the moment but letting Ian's hair slide through her fingers.

Jacq and Garrett's wedding was coming up and she had been baking and freezing dozens of cookies that Christopher decided would be perfect for the reception.

Just a few more batches to go, she thought as she sank more deeply into the couch. The day before the wedding she would decorate them with the edible flowers that were her trademark.

"Uncomfortable?" Ian murmured as Olivia shifted her legs underneath him.

"I think my legs went numb fifteen minutes ago," she said. Ian immediately started to sit up until she pushed him back down. "Don't get up," she remarked, "I'm fine."

He looked up at her and said, "I like being here in your house, on your sofa." She smiled down at him.

"Do you know where else I'd like you to be?" Ian asked.

"In my bed," Olivia snarked with one quirked eyebrow.

"Get your mind out of the gutter Livvie. Although now that you mention it, that is a good idea," Ian stated waggling his eyebrows comically. "But what I was going to say is, I'd like to have you beside me at the rehearsal dinner, if you would like to come with me?"

Olivia looked down at him with a small frown, "Hmm, I don't know Ian. You'll be surrounded by family and friends that you've known forever. I'm not sure it's the place for someone they've recently met."

Ian sat up then and swung his legs to the floor. He looked down at her hands as he took them in his. "One, you are not a new face. Our friends love you and I know Jacq and Garrett would be happy that you shared the time with them," he said looking into her eyes. "Second, I'd like you to be there with me. You could meet my family. Well, at least my Mom and Dad as I'm not sure my sisters' flight will arrive in in time."

She did like the way he emphasized *our* friends, but stated, "I was hoping to finish up the cookies that evening."

"I tell you what. The rehearsal begins at four o'clock on Thursday. After the rehearsal we're all headed to Shore's End for dinner. If you want, you can skip the rehearsal and I'll pick you up for dinner a little before five. That way you can work on the cookies and then when we get home, I'll help finish up whatever you need to do," Ian cajoled with a pleading look in his eyes.

Olivia blew out an impatient breath. "OK, but no reneging on the promise to help with the cookies," she said.

Ian smiled and drew her into a hug. "I have no idea how to decorate cookies, but I'm a quick learner," he whispered into her ear. Pulling back, he said, "Thank you. I'd really like for you to meet my family and it will be fun."

Unsure whether she would describe meeting his family as fun, she cuddled up to him and put her head on his shoulder. "It will only be fun if they like me," she quipped.

"They'll love you. I'm sure of it. I just hope you like them," Ian stated. "They can be a bit much at times."

Olivia chuckled. "I'm sure if I can handle you then your family shouldn't be any problem."

"I don't know, they are pretty quirky," Ian said with a serious look on his face.

"And you aren't?" Olivia asked.

"Well, my quirk is cute, theirs can be downright weird sometimes," Ian said.

Olivia just shook her head wondering what she had gotten herself into.

Ian stood beside a fidgeting Garrett waiting for Jacq to make her way down the aisle. The minister was giving Garrett last minute instructions like don't lock your knees or you may faint and don't stand with your hands clasped in front of you as it looks like you need to use the bathroom. He surmised the minister didn't know they had made it through combat and if Garrett could make it through a war without fainting, he certainly could make it through his own wedding. As he waited, he let his mind wander over the wedding venue taking in the flowers and decorations adorning the altar. Christopher had certainly outdone himself, creating a peaceful and beautiful space for the couple to say their vows. Donovan had not arrived, and Ian briefly wondered why he was late.

Ian caught his mom's eye as he scanned the parents sitting in the front row. His parents had arrived yesterday and were staying at a local bed and breakfast for a few days. Garrett's mom had invited them to sit with her during the wedding. They had come to know each other through both their sons' deployments, meeting occasionally during send-off and homecoming ceremonies. The two moms had stuck together each sending the men care packages filled with goodies enough for both. Now the two moms were leaning toward each other, no doubt talking about the wedding, as his dad looked around the venue much like Ian had been doing. Ian chuckled to himself and wondered if his accountant dad was calculating how much the wedding cost and what kind of tax write-off Christopher and Jacq would be entitled to when they filed their returns next year.

Ian brought his attention back to the rehearsal as soon as the music began. He felt Donovan slide into place behind him just as the wedding planner sent Christopher and Beth down the aisle.

"Where have you been?" Ian asked quietly, turning slightly toward the other groomsman.

"Talk later," Donovan stated just as quietly.

Ian nodded and smiled at Beth and Christopher as they peeled off to stand on the other side of Garrett. Christopher was his put together self, wearing a suit that had the look of custom tailoring. Ian was glad he had pulled out one of his dress kilts. It was black wool that he had paired with a white button down and a tweed vest. He had even left his combat boots at home and was sporting black wool socks with black Italian wing tips. Even Garrett was wearing a navy-blue sport coat and khaki slacks, a departure from the jeans and flannel shirt his friend usually saw him in.

Everybody's eyes turned to the back of the aisle as the music changed. Jacq had her arm in Emmett's looking up at him. They were both laughing, looking as if they were sharing a joke. Jacq's smile got bigger as she turned toward Garrett in preparation for her walk down the aisle. She was beautiful in a sage green silk maxi dress that flowed around her body like water. Ian put his hand on Garrett's shoulder, leaned forward and whispered, "You are a blessed man."

Garrett nodded, never taking his eyes off his fiancé. Jacq and Emmett stopped in front of Garrett. Emmett kissed Jacq's cheek and put her hand in Garrett's. The minister intoned, "Who gives this woman to be married to this man?"

"Her family and I do," Emmett answered. Jacq looked back at Emmett with soft eyes and silently mouthed "thank you" acknowledging Emmett's inclusion of her family in the ceremony. Even though they were gone they were not forgotten.

Ian watched as Garrett took hold of Jacq's hand. He could only see Jacq's face, but her love for his best friend was apparent in her tender smile and shining eyes. He could imagine that the same feelings were mirrored on Garrett's face as well. As the minister continued the rehearsal, giving instructions to the wedding party, Ian wondered if anyone would ever look at him the way Jacq looked at Garrett. His thoughts turned to Olivia and his growing feelings of adoration and possessiveness. He had never been in love, but he feared that he was fast falling for the woman who seemed to continually occupy his thoughts.

The rehearsal was over before Ian realized he had missed the last bit of what they were supposed to do. Ian assumed Donovan would fill him in at some point. Donovan had already slipped from Ian's side and was talking with Beth on the other side of the altar. Ian walked toward them catching a bit of their conversation.

"...when you were last in New York," Beth said.

"I haven't been to New York in quite a while," Donovan commented.

Ian walked up to the pair, breaking into the conversation, "I didn't know you spent time in New York?"

They both looked up at Ian's intrusion.

"Not often," Donovan said cryptically.

Ian nodded distractedly. "I'm headed to pick up Olivia. Could you take my parents to the restaurant? We'll meet you there."

"Of course, it will be good to catch up with them," Donovan nodded and excusing himself headed towards Ian's mom and dad.

"I'm sorry, I didn't mean to break up your conversation," Ian said looking at Beth.

"No worries, we were just discussing where we met," Beth said. "When Jacq said Garrett's friend Donovan would be in the wedding, I didn't put two and two together."

"Oh, so you've met before?" Ian asked.

"Yes, briefly. Donovan was doing some work with my company. I work for a large security firm, and Donovan was meeting with my boss. It was quite a while ago, but his face is hard to forget," Beth answered.

Ian was about to ask more questions, but at that moment Donovan and his parents walked up to let him know they were leaving for the restaurant. Ian excused himself from the group, retrieved his phone from his *sporran* and texted Olivia that he would pick her up in a few minutes. A few seconds later he received a thumbs up emoji. Kissing his mom on the cheek he quickly left to go get his girl.

As Ian pulled up to Olivia's cottage, Dolce came tearing around the back of the house barking a warning. When he realized it was Ian, his guard dog bark turned into a friendly yip accompanied by a frantically wagging tail.

"Hey boy, I'm here to pick up Olivia," Ian said scratching him behind his ears.

Dolce gave a quick bark and turned toward the front door. The dog stayed by Ian's side as he made his way to the porch and knocked. Olivia opened the door and smiled at Ian. He blinked slowly at the beauty before him. Olivia had opted to wear a sleeveless sheath dress of peacock blue with white paisley embroidery. Ian didn't know what the material was, but it hugged her curves in all the right places. She wore her hair down in the bouncy curls that he loved to play with.

"You look beautiful," Ian said, softly crowding her so she had to back up into the house.

JUST A WHISTLE AWAY

193

Ian buried his hands in her hair and tipped her head up for his kiss. She rubbed her hands up and down his biceps as they shared a soft and slow embrace. Coming up for air, Ian looked in her eyes and said, "I've been thinking about doing that all day."

Olivia smiled and put her hands around his neck to give him a hug. "I think we need to go before we're late." Ian nodded, reluctantly letting her go.

Placing his hand on her lower back, Ian guided Olivia out of the house and to the car. Opening the passenger door, Olivia scooted in while Ian made sure her skirt wasn't caught in the latch. Rounding the front of the SUV, Ian jumped in and started the engine. Backing out of her driveway, he made his way to the restaurant listening to Olivia's comments about her day and answering questions about the wedding rehearsal.

In a short time, they were pulling up to Shore's End. The restaurant was two stories with its back facing the water. The top floor was a private dining area where the rehearsal dinner was to be held. Floor to ceiling windows allowed diners to enjoy the view of boats and sea life in Liberty Bay. Ian helped Olivia out of the car and reached into the back seat to take out his bag pipe case. Seeing what was in his hand, Olivia gave him a questioning glance.

"A surprise for Garrett and Jacq," he said by way of explanation.

Ian left his instrument with the hostess then he and Olivia were escorted upstairs to the private dining area where friends and family were already assembled. There was much conversation and laughter as wine glasses were filled and clinked together in congratulation toasts. Jacq was the first person to spy the couple at the top of the stairs and walked over to give them a hug. Hanging on to Ian's arm, Jacq exclaimed, "Thank you so much for coming Olivia. I was so happy when Ian said he had asked you to attend with him."

Jacq reached over to squeeze Olivia's hand. "It's hard to believe the wedding is actually here. Some days it seems like the day would never come and then on others the time was flying by, and I didn't think we'd get it all together in time."

"From what I've seen, it will be a beautiful event," Olivia said squeezing Jacq's hand in return.

"You made it," Garrett said, gently moving Jacq out of the way and clasping Ian's hand and bringing him in for a manly hug pat on the back. Garrett turned to Olivia and enveloped her in a hug as well. Drawing back, he said, "Thank you for coming. Ian's parents just remarked that they were looking forward to meeting you."

Olivia blew out a breath. "I'm looking forward to meeting them as well."

"You don't look too sure about that," Garrett said softly.

"Just a little nervous," Olivia whispered back.

"No need. They'll love you," he said looking over Olivia's shoulder. "Get ready, here they come."

They all four looked up as an older woman made her way toward them with an older gentleman that, by the look of him, had to be Ian's dad. "Mom, Dad, I'd like you to meet Olivia. Olivia, this is my mom and dad, Amelia and Shaun," Ian said by way of introduction.

Ian's mom was a slight woman with porcelain skin and chocolate brown hair. His dad looked like an older version of Ian with red hair, shot with silver and piercing blue eyes.

"It is very nice to meet you," Olivia stated shaking hands with them.

Ian's mom encased Olivia's hand with both of hers and gave her a big smile. "It is so good to meet the woman that my son can't stop talking about."

Olivia looked at Ian with raised eyebrows and a smile. "Way to lay it right out there, Mom," Ian said with a sigh.

Olivia and Amelia laughed at his discomfort while Ian's dad looked on with a smile. At that moment Garrett asked everybody to take a seat. Ian escorted Olivia to the end of the table nearest the

JUST A WHISTLE AWAY · 195

stairs and pulled out her chair. Olivia said hello to Nicole who was seated on her other side.

When all the guests were seated, Garrett stood and said, "Thank you all for coming. On behalf of Jacq and me, we couldn't think of anything better than to be surrounded by family and friends. You all have been a big part of our journey as a couple, and I want to make a toast to thank you for your support and love as we found our way toward each other. And I know that support and love will continue throughout our lives. So, I want to toast you. To family and friends."

"To family and friends," all the guests said in unison raising and drinking from their glasses.

Olivia turned to Ian to say something and realized Ian wasn't in his seat. Just as she was about to ask Nicole if she had seen him, Olivia heard the sound of a bagpipe filling with air. She looked to the head of the table where Jacq and Garrett were looking quizzically at the stairs. Soon the sound of the lilting Scottish folk song "Mairi's Wedding" came wafting up the stairwell. Not only did Ian come marching up the steps playing the bagpipes, but closely behind him was another kilted man belting out the refrain.

Step we gaily, on we go
Heel for heel and toe for toe
Arm in arm and row on row
All for Mairi's wedding

Olivia looked around the table watching with wonder as Ian's parents began to sing along and all the guests began stomping their feet and clapping their hands. She had never seen Ian play, but she thought the instrument suited his boisterous spirit as he blew into the reed and tapped his toes in time to the music as his hands flew over the pipe.

As the song ended with a flourish, enthusiastic clapping came from the crowd. Ian and the unknown gentleman took their bows. "This is my good friend Michael. He generously volunteered to accompany me today. If you didn't guess that song was in honor of the bride and groom. May your hands be forever clasped in friendship and your hearts joined forever in love."

Jacq put her hand to her heart and blew a kiss to Ian as Garrett rounded the table and gave his best friend a hug. Michael gave a quick wave and made his way back down the stairs. Ian followed him, and Olivia presumed he was putting away his bagpipes when she heard the sound of a moose in distress as he presumably pushed the air out of the pipe bladder. She wondered what the other diners in the restaurant were thinking right about now.

A few minutes later, Ian collapsed into the seat beside her as the salad course was being served. Olivia bumped her shoulder with his and said, "That was wonderful. I've never known anybody who played the bagpipes."

Ian turned to her and winked. "I'd play them for you anytime."

Olivia laughed shaking her head. "You are a goof."

"But a lovable goof?" Ian asked looking at her with a question in his eyes.

"A very lovable goof," Olivia stated emphatically clasping his hand in hers.

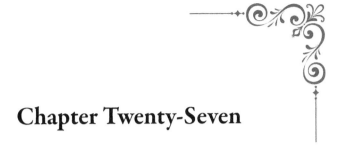

Chapter Twenty-Seven

Jacq awoke to golden light filtering through the sheer curtains and the glorious aroma of coffee. A perfect start to a perfect day, she thought. *Next time I wake up I'll be Mrs. Olsen*, Jacq mused, so happy that her wedding day had finally arrived. She flung on her silk robe and padded down the stairs.

"Here comes the bride," Beth said, from the table in the corner of the room as Jacq entered the kitchen.

Jacq poured herself a mug of coffee leaving room for extra cream. She was in a celebratory mood after all, and took a seat across from Beth. The two old friends looked at each other and grinned ear to ear wordlessly communicating their excitement over the big day.

"Where's Chris?" Jacq asked.

"Outside directing the troops no doubt," Beth said. "He was up before dawn and out at first light, inspecting the venue and by now is driving the wedding coordinator crazy. On the other hand, it's kind of sweet that he wants everything perfect for you."

"He has taken a huge load off me," Jacq divulged. "Two and a half weeks ago he made me promise I wouldn't come into the office or even glance in that direction which is a bit hard to do given that Garrett's property and our events center property border each other. I tried to comply the best I could as I didn't want to ruin any surprises he had in store."

"Well let me tell you, the venue has been transformed since the Thursday rehearsal. But no peeking," Beth instructed.

"I've come this far without peeking. I'm sure I can make it until two o'clock without breaking my promise," Jacq assured Beth.

"What's this about peeking?" Christopher sharply asked as he entered the kitchen from the back door off the deck.

"I haven't, won't, nor will I be tempted to peek," Jacq promised crossing her heart for good measure.

"Glad to hear it," Christopher said, grabbing a cup of coffee and kissing Jacq on the top of her head before taking a seat and joining his friends. "Where is the schedule I had on the table?" Christopher inquired.

"Oh, right here," Beth said, shuffling the pages of the weekly *Gazette,* She had been enjoying an amusing advice column before Jacq made her entrance into the kitchen. "Here ya go," Beth said, pulling the schedule out from beneath the local paper and handing it to Christopher.

Christopher read the highlights aloud. "Brunch will be delivered at 10 am; hair and make-up artists arrive at 11:30 am; at 1:00 pm Emmett will be coming over to dress here with the rest of us; 1:30 pm the photographer will arrive for a few pre-wedding shots; and 2:00 pm is show time!"

"In that case, I'll put on a third pot of coffee," Beth volunteered.

Across town at Ian's flat, Garrett and Ian were working on their second pot of coffee. Garrett had stayed the night, recalling something about not seeing the bride before the ceremony on the wedding day, when the doorbell rang.

"Was Donovan coming over this early?" Garrett inquired.

"I don't think so," Ian replied.

When Ian opened the door, Heather from Lily's bakery stood there with a platter of rolls, croissants, pastries, and fresh-cut fruit.

Ian never saw Heather's coquettish expression directed at him as he had eyes only for the food before him.

"You must be reading my mind," Ian said as he took the tray from Heather. "Thank you."

"Oh, I almost forgot," Heather said as she slowly reached down the top of her blouse and pulled out an envelope. Ian blinked at her seductive retrieval of the envelope that was not lost on him even though he was still half asleep. "I'm supposed to give you this," she added in an alluring voice.

"Umm, thanks," Ian said a bit awkwardly as he took the envelope and retreated from the door with the tray, kicking the door closed.

"That smells fabulous," Garrett said as he walked over to the platter and selected a pastry. "What's in the envelope?" Garrett asked.

"I'm afraid to look," Ian responded, still a bit taken aback by Heather's suggestive performance at the door.

"Allow me," Garrett said taking the envelope from Ian and opening it. "It's a schedule, from Christopher no doubt. If things go as planned, Donovan will be arriving here at noon when we are all to change into our suits. The photographer will be here at 12:45 pm to take some photos before we head over to the venue."

Garrett was surprised by how quickly the morning passed. Before he knew it, 1400 hours was fast approaching, and he and his groomsmen were driving to the wedding site.

The wedding coordinator met their vehicle as they pulled up to the venue and with military efficiency had their boutonnieres pinned on their navy suits in record time.

"Please follow me," she said as she led them to where the minister was waiting. All three dutifully followed her until Ian spotted Olivia.

The site of her in an orange-colored halter dress that flowed around her curves and highlighted her brown eyes stopped Ian in his tracks. For a long minute, he was riveted in place as he took in the vision in front of him. Sensing eyes upon her, Olivia turned and smiled at Ian dressed in his blue suit and looking quite handsome. Without saying a word, Ian walked to Olivia, reaching his hand toward hers. By way of greeting, hand in hand he guided her into the greenhouse out of eyeshot of arriving guests and bustling catering staff. Even before coming to a complete stop, he swung his body around to face hers and his free hand traveled up her bare back to her neck until his fingers caressed her scalp, twisting his fingers around her luxurious brown hair. He pulled her head back exposing more of her cream-colored neck. Gently and slowly at first, he started planting kisses on Olivia's soft skin. When her body responded to his and she inhaled sharply, his kisses became urgent and feverish until his mouth found hers. The citrusy smell of her shampoo and the minty taste of her kisses made him forget where he was and what he should be doing.

Three raps at the door and a loud "Ahem," from Donovan brought Ian back to his senses that had been so completely lost in all that was Olivia. Donovan waited for a discrete few moments before opening the door.

"Good afternoon, Olivia," Donovan said, doing an admirable job pretending he had not interrupted an intimate moment.

Ian leaned his forehead against Olivia's and said, "yes, good afternoon, Olivia."

"Seriously, you're just now getting to that;" Donovan said directing his comment to Ian along with an exasperated expression.

"Hello Donovan," Olivia said smiling sheepishly, her face flushing even more than it had been from Ian's wordless greeting.

Donovan responded to Olivia with a courtly nod in her direction and then turned to Ian. "I do hate interrupting, but the minister requires a witness's signature on the marriage license and that honor is usually reserved for the best man. Plus, Garrett wanted me to tell you that if you delay him for even a second from becoming

Jacq's husband, he will...," Donovan paused, glancing over at Olivia, "well, let's just say you don't want to go there. Not to mention what the wedding coordinator may do to you, and I wouldn't test her if I were you," Donovan added for good measure.

Ian sighed loudly and leaned in toward Olivia. He placed his cheek on hers, the current between them sizzling despite Donovan's dampening effect on their unplanned tryst. "I'll find you after the ceremony," Ian finally whispered softly in her ear. Ian gave Olivia a quick peck on the cheek and then he turned and followed Donovan out the door.

Olivia was grateful for the time alone to compose herself. Ian had a physical effect on her that no one had ever come close to evoking. He was nothing like anyone she had ever dated. He had an irresistible combination of a child-like enthusiasm for adventure; a devil-may-care manner about the man he was and what he wore; a fiercely protective and loyal side; and a touch so gentle it seemed incongruent with his strength. She wondered if growing up with two sisters had cultivated his tender and protective side and his military service intensified his power and athleticism. When he turned his considerable intensity toward her, whatever the situation was, his force and energy made her weak in the knees. She had a growing desire to be near him that she was less and less able to control – it both thrilled her and scared her to death.

Music from a string quartet penetrated Olivia's thoughts and she realized it was time to find a seat for the ceremony.

A dramatic center aisle, wide toward the back and tapering narrower toward the front where the ceremony would be held, was created from two long rows of white billowing lilac bushes in full bloom. The bushes were low to the ground, less than three feet tall Olivia estimated, but the profusion of white fragrant blooms was breathtaking against the green meadow and under an azure cloudless sky.

On both sides of the aisle, large round tables had been set up rather than the traditional rows of chairs. The tables were clad with sage green tablecloths, and each had a white fringed umbrella casting shadows allowing six guests per table to sit in the shade. Each table could accommodate 10 guests but only 6 chairs were arranged at each table so that all seated guests would have an unobscured view of the aisle and a clear view of the ceremony. In the center of each table was an ice bucket containing an open bottle of champagne and a large glass pitcher of minted ice water. The ice cubes were oversized and each one had a colorful flower frozen in its center. A silver tray held six champagne glasses and six water glasses along with a stack of floral cocktail napkins in a caddy to prevent them from blowing away. The final flourish at each table was a glass domed-covered cake plate piled with the shortbread cookies Christopher had asked Olivia to make.

Olivia had topped each cookie with a pressed edible flower or a decorative arrangement of petals or tiny leaves. She had spent half the night getting the powdered sugar and lemon juice to a perfect glue-like consistency, brushing the "sugar glue" onto each cookie, carefully placing a pressed flower on top, and sealing the edges with additional sweet glue. Between the platter of cookies and colorful ice cubes, the array of multicolored flowers was stunning. The arrangement was incredibly inviting, especially on a warm July day, and a delicious way to engage the senses.

Olivia recalled Jacq saying that she wanted an elegant yet relaxed garden party theme for the wedding. The fringed umbrellas blowing in the breeze, the sounds of the string quartet playing contemporary music, the occasional scent of lilacs that perfumed the breeze, and the drinks and cookies guests were already enjoying set just the right tone.

JUST A WHISTLE AWAY   203

Olivia glanced around, trying to decide where to sit when she spotted Nicole and Lia waving at her. She smiled and headed their way.

"We've been saving you a seat," Lia said.

"I don't believe that you've met my husband, Matt."

"Or my husband, Brett," Lia added.

Introductions were made and Olivia noted that they had saved her the best view where the groomsmen would be standing. Matt asked Olivia what she would like to drink and poured a glass of champagne for her.

"We have Olivia to thank for these divine shortbread cookies," Nicole noted.

"They taste as good as they look," Lia said. "Good thing you got here in time to claim a few for yourself," Lia added. "Once the guys figured out that the flowers were meant to be eaten and they tasted delicious, half the platter disappeared in less than five minutes.

Brett and Matt looked at each other sheepishly and Brett said, "They are meant to be eaten, right! We are just doing our part," he insisted.

"Absolutely, Olivia agreed. "And no worries, I think Christopher ordered a dozen per person."

"Then pass them this way," Brett said, and they all laughed.

The music stopped, which drew everyone's attention. Laughter and conversations came to a close at the anticipation of the ceremony beginning. All at once the sound of Pachelbel's *Canon in D major* began and the men filed onto the makeshift altar being led by the minister. When Garrett saw his mother seated at the table closest to the groomsmen, he walked over to her and gave her a kiss on the cheek, squeezed her shoulders, and said something to her that was lost on the breeze to all other ears, but his words caused her to beam.

When Garrett reclaimed his place at the altar, his eyes sought his bride. What he saw instead, headed in his direction, was Christopher with Beth walking arm in arm together down the aisle. Instead of taking up their positions on the left side of the aisle as they did in rehearsal, they both walked directly up to him.

Christopher reached out his hand to shake Garrett's and said, "Congratulations Garrett, I couldn't be happier for you and Jacq. May your love continue to grow stronger with each passing day." Then Christopher stepped aside, and Beth kissed Garrett on the cheek. Beth looked up into Garrett's face and said, "Take good care of our girl. Her heart is in your hands."

Only the groomsmen and those seated at tables closest to the altar could hear what was said to Garrett, but all could see his profound reaction to Christopher and Beth's words. He nodded to each of them, not trusting his words to communicate his feelings, and then gave them each a warm embrace. Then hand in hand, Beth and Christopher walked to their places for the ceremony.

Garrett took a deep breath, moved beyond words by Christopher and Beth's sweet gesture. When he looked up and got his first look at Jacq on Emmett's arm walking down the aisle, time slowed, and the rest of the world blurred. When their eyes met, Garrett was sure he had never seen Jacq's smile look so radiant and Jacq was thinking the same about Garrett's smile that she knew was meant just for her. Their connection and love for each other was palpable.

Anyone, except for Ian, who had been looking at Garrett turned their attention to the object of his sole focus, his lovely bride slowly approaching him. Ian continued to scrutinize Garrett's expression. He had never before seen on the face of his best friend the manifestation of complete love. Ian realized beyond a shadow of a doubt that Garrett had found his soul mate. Until this moment Ian had always scoffed at the overused term. But looking at Garrett, he knew it perfectly fit what Garrett and Jacq had found in each other. Ian wondered and hoped he had found the same in Olivia.

At that thought, Ian's gaze instinctively moved to Olivia. In the same instance, Olivia looked over her left shoulder at Ian and a wide smile spread across her face. Ian felt it once again, that magnetic pull whenever he was in her presence. She undid him with just a look or a kind word.

Ian sensed movement next to him and realized that Garrett was walking down the aisle toward Jacq. That wasn't part of the rehearsal, Ian thought. Two-thirds of the way down the aisle, a grinning Emmett graciously offered Jacq's hand to Garrett and watched the two of them approach the alter hand in hand before he found his seat.

When the minister asked, "Who gives this woman to be married to this man?" Emmett stood and said, "Well, it seems to me that he took that woman not waiting for anyone to give her away. But, for her family and all of us who consider her family, we do!" Laughs and a few cheers erupted, the tone of the celebration had been firmly established.

To say the ceremony was short and sweet was an understatement. It probably took Jacq longer to walk down the long aisle than for the minister to perform the ceremony. Jacq and Garrett had decided to forego traditional vows. Instead, they each chose a quote that summed up their feelings for the other.

Standing under an arch festooned with white lilacs, peonies, roses, and a plethora of various greenery, Garrett quoted from Song of Solomon: "I found the one whom my soul loves."

Jacq replied with a quote by Roy Croft: "I love you, not only for what you are, but for what I am when I am with you."

Jacq handed her bouquet of Wedding Slipper orchids and forget-me-nots to Beth to exchange rings with Garrett. Each in turn exchanged rings stating: "With this ring, I give you my heart and affirm that you dwell in my soul. May my heart be your shelter and my arms be your home."

206   **J. KIMALIE**

After a closing prayer, the minister pronounced them, "Garrett and Jacqueline Olsen, husband and wife" and Garrett wasted no time sealing the deal with a kiss. A very long and passionate kiss. Even Ian raised an eyebrow at the intensity of their exchange. The guests applauded as they rose to their feet.

As the newlywed couple turned to face their guests, Beth handed Jacq her bouquet. At the same time, a waiter appeared with a tray of champagne glasses, handing everyone in the wedding party a bubbling glass of Rose Champagne.

Ian took a step forward and said, "Please, raise your glasses and join me in a traditional Scottish toast to the newly hitched couple." Ian turned and looked at his radiant friends, "May you always live life to the fullest, laugh often, and love eternally." A chorus of "cheers" reinforced the sentiment and champagne glasses were drained.

The string quartet struck up a rousing rendition of "A Million Dreams" from "The Greatest Showman" and rather than a formal recessional, Jacq and Garrett began greeting their guests, starting with hugs for the wedding party.

Guests dressed in bright summer colors clustered together greeting one another as waitstaff circulated, refilling champagne glasses or offering a traditional English cocktail of gin, apple juice, elderflower cordial, and cucumber. Each cocktail was garnished with a brightly colored edible flower.

While guests were enjoying their drinks and circulating among friends, a small army quickly and discreetly rearranged the ceremony area, expanding the small, raised platform where the wedding party had stood into a much larger dance floor. The potted lilacs were repositioned to surround the dance floor with a gap on each of the four sides to allow entry to the area. Tables were likewise moved to surround the dance floor on all four sides.

At the same time the venue was being transformed, a dozen big band musicians were setting up. Some guests noticed the buzzing activity, but most did not. Laughing and chatting guests were focused on the jubilant bride and groom who had moved to a stunning display of garden party food set up outside alongside the greenhouse. Tiered platters tempting guests with a colorful assortment of bitesize appetizers were laid out with artistic flair. Every inch of the tables not covered with food trays was covered in flower petals of every color. There was something to entice everyone: sweet onion and pimiento cheese deviled eggs; asparagus goat cheese and pistachio roll-up bites; grilled balsamic chicken bites; miniature fruit kabobs; small roasted potato halves stuffed with sour cream and caviar; an assortment of crustless finger sandwiches; and the list went on and on.

Ian made his way to Olivia just as quickly as he could. She waited patiently for him as he was interrupted by friends greeting him along the way. When he finally reached her, he took her hand and said, "I am sure that you have never looked lovelier than you do today!" The look in his eyes actually made her blush.

"You look rather handsome yourself," she said as she fussed with his boutonniere, leaving her hand on his chest.

"Sorry I didn't have time before the wedding to properly greet you," Ian said apologetically.

Olivia grinned and said, "Oh trust me, my lips still feel the tingle of being properly greeted. In fact, one of my favorite quotes is what Ingrid Bergman said, 'A kiss is a lovely trick designed by nature to stop speech when words become superfluous.'"

Ian took the quote as an invitation to give her a kiss and did he ever! One to rival the kiss Garrett had given Jacq at the altar. When they finally pulled away from each other, he raised his head and caught movement out of the corner of his eye. His mom, dad, and two sisters were standing just a few yards away having witnessed the show Ian and Olivia had unwittingly put on for them and anyone else looking in their direction. The expressions on the faces of his family ranged from shock to amusement.

Olivia started to turn her head to see what had captured his attention when Ian put a finger on her chin and gently turned her gaze back to him. Smiling down at her he said, "Take a deep breath, my family is standing behind you. Prepare yourself to meet my sisters."

Olivia gasped and then gulped in air causing a cute little hiccup to escape from her mouth. She had never felt so self-conscious in her life. She was guessing that his family had just watched their exchange and she was thoroughly mortified.

"Ready?" Ian said with a twinkle in his eye.

"Do I have a choice?" Olivia said in a pleading tone.

By way of an answer, Ian took her hand, and they walked over to his family. "Mom, Dad, you've already met Olivia. Blair, Lucy, I would like to introduce you to Olivia, my..." he paused as he was going to say date, but given the length and voracity of their kiss, he amended it to "someone very special to me." Everyone seemed to exhale at the same time.

"It's nice to finally meet the entire McKay family," Olivia said, her face still a fairly bright shade of red. "I met your folks at the rehearsal dinner," Olivia added, directing her comments to Ian's sisters.

"Aye, nice to see you again," said Ian's dad, adding a wink for good measure. Everyone added their greetings and then Ian suggested that they head toward the greenhouse where most of the guests had congregated.

The photographer walked over and asked the group if she could borrow Ian for a few photos. "Of course," Ian said perfunctorily as he squeezed Olivia's hand before releasing it to follow the photographer.

JUST A WHISTLE AWAY   209

Ian's mother turned toward Olivia and diplomatically said, "Ian hasn't told us much about you and I would love to learn more about your background." What she could have said was, Ian had never mentioned you before the rehearsal dinner and clearly, you've known each other for a while. But her graciousness would have never allowed her to be so brash.

By the time Ian returned to the group, Olivia had completely charmed his family with her candidness, sincerity, and humorous retelling of their first date. It didn't hurt that all of them knew her Zio Paolo, who was universally liked, that fact scoring her bonus points in their estimation.

"I've come to rescue Olivia from the grand inquisition and hopefully before you've all had a chance to bore her with stories from my childhood," Ian said with a crooked grin. "We'll catch up with you all later, but I've gotta eat something before I startle unwitting guests by swiping hors d'oeuvres off their plates." As if on cue, Donovan walked up to greet Ian's family and Ian swiped some sort of mini roll-up sandwich off his plate as he guided Olivia to the buffet.

Jacq saw Olivia and took Garrett's arm and they made their way to her. "Thank you for baking all those gorgeous and delicious cookies. Together on a plate, they look like a miniature flower garden," Jacq gushed. "I can't tell you how many guests have thanked us for the pre-wedding treats and wanted to know where we got them. If you ever want to switch careers, your cookies would be an instant hit."

"I was happy to add a little somethin', somethin' to your special day," Olivia responded. "Your attention to detail has created a magical event. The weather is perfect, the setting is perfect, and your dress is perfection," Olivia stated with real admiration.

Garrett, who had his arm around Jacq's waist gave her a squeeze and said, "And the woman wearing the dress could not be more perfect for me!"

The reverberation of four stringed instruments holding out a particularly long note ended in unison. Two beats later a saxophone broke the silence with the first energetic notes of "In the Mood," the big band-era jazz standard popularized by Glenn Miller, signifying that the celebration had just turned into a party. "Excuse us Olivia, but that's my cue," Garrett said as he swept Jacq off her feet and carried her to the dance floor. By the time she was upright, Garrett was leading her in a swing with a trumpet and trombone adding their accent riffs to the lively tune. Their exuberance drew others to the dance floor and with a wave of Jacq's free hand, she invited everyone to join them. Next on the floor were Donovan and Beth, followed by a rush of guests buoyed by the music and pure joy of the moment.

Christopher noted that Olivia was standing alone, and Ian was nowhere in sight. He walked up to her and asked, "Do you by chance know the Lindy Hop?" With a note of apprehension in her voice, she said, "I know the first eight counts and after that I usually just wing it."

"Close enough for me," Christopher said as he offered Olivia an outstretched arm, "shall we?"

Olivia looked around and not seeing Ian she said, "Why not?"

A few minutes earlier, Ian had popped a meatball in his month slathered with raspberry barbeque sauce. The wedding hostess rounded the corner in time to see a dollop of sauce land on his lapel. "Come with me," she ordered with such authority he fell in line behind her. Ian was raising a napkin to his lapel when the hostess commanded, "Dab don't rub. Here, allow me," she hurriedly went on. She dunked a napkin into a glass of abandoned water and dabbed at the offending spot, cleaning it the best she could. "Let me reposition your boutonniere just a little higher and no one will ever know."

"Umm, thanks," Ian said, feeling like a schoolboy having just been reprimanded. Ian returned to the abandoned buffet and filled two plates with food, deliberately avoiding the meatballs. He wasn't sure if Olivia had snagged some food and he didn't want her missing out.

His mom waved him to a table his family had claimed, and he put the plate down and took a seat. His mother said, "Olivia is delightful and very attractive. Aren't you a little concerned she's dancing with that dashing gentleman? The minute you walked off, he swooped in and escorted her to the dance floor."

Ian looked up to see what "dashing gentleman" had absconded with his date and relaxed when he saw it was Christopher.

"No, I'm not worried at all Mother, I'll get my turn on the floor with her. Right now, I'm just happy to have a moment to eat." Ian felt no need to explain that he was closer to Christopher's type than Olivia.

While he ate, Ian watched Olivia with admiration. The delicate chiffon fabric of her dress draped along her curves and flowed around her legs when Christopher twirled her, highlighting her graceful movements. She often reminded him of a 1940s pin-up girl with all the sex appeal and glamour of a model from that era.

"How long are you going to let him dance with her without cutting in?" His mother inquired.

"Until the first slow song or when I'm finished eating whichever comes first," Ian replied.

"I wouldn't wait too long dear; she looks like she is having a wonderful time."

Ian smiled; she did look like Olivia was having a wonderful time. She threw her head back and laughed as Christopher executed a spin on his heels and didn't miss a beat reconnecting with her outstretched hand and leading her into a lindy turn. When she spotted Ian, she gave him a wave and a little shoulder shimmy. Ian raised his eyebrows twice and puckered his lips together unleashing a low wolf-whistle. She must have heard it because it earned Ian another flirty shimmy, her brown eyes boring into his.

Christopher and Olivia stayed on the dance floor for one additional song and then Christopher escorted her to the table where Ian and his mother were sitting. He bowed regally before Olivia, thanking her for the dances, and winked at Ian as he went in search of his next dance partner.

Olivia was happy to sit down, catch her breath and have a bite to eat. Only one song later, the band began a slow version of "Moonlight Serenade" and Ian turned to Olivia indicating the dance floor with a nod of his head in that direction. She smiled and they both stood and made their way to the floor.

Couples flowed on and off the dance floor with the music's change in tempo. As they were exiting the dance floor, Ian's father and Blair, Ian's older sister, walked past Ian and Olivia. Ian's sister gave Ian a stealthy wink and said, "Brother, you owe me a dance later." Ian knew that was "sister code" for I want all the scoops on your "special someone." The proverbial cat was out of the bag, Ian thought. As far as Ian was concerned, he was comfortable introducing his family to Olivia as she had indeed become incredibly special to him; he just hoped that Olivia felt the same way about their relationship being public. He hadn't intended to keep his deepening relationship with Olivia a secret from his family or friends. He had just enjoyed having her all to himself.

Emmett, Donovan, and Christopher converged on a waiter holding a platter of drinks and sat down together at the nearest table.

"He has it bad," Emmett said matter-of-factly as he was looking at the dance floor.

"Who?" Donovan said, "Garrett or Ian?"

After a beat, Emmett and Christopher said in unison, "Both."

JUST A WHISTLE AWAY

Garrett and his bride were on a crowded dance floor, but they were clearly lost in their own blissful world. Both looked happier than their friends had ever seen them look.

Ian and Olivia also appeared to be in their own universe. Olivia's head was resting on Ian's chest and for once the big guy had his eyes and mouth shut. While a good dancer, Ian was content to hold Olivia and just sway with the music.

Emmett, sensing his friend's change in demeanor said, "What is it?" Donovan pushed the cell phone toward Emmett and said, "I'm pretty sure someone is sitting in a car watching someone or something with binoculars."

Emmett studied the photo and said, "Looks like someone is in the car all right but given the shadows it's just a blurry head. I can't even make out if it's a man or a woman."

"I'm going to go find out who it is," Donovan said. "If it's Olivia's stalker, this is a chance to put an end to the nonsense. Emmett, do you have your cell phone?" Emmett reached into his pocket and pulled out his cell phone.

"If something nefarious is going on, the person is likely to drive away." Donovan continued, "So, what I would like you to do is walk between the office and the greenhouse to get well in front of the car. If the car pulls away as I'm walking toward it, get a picture of the car and license plate as it passes. Walk casually. I'll give you a head start so you can get into position."

"Ten-four," Emmett said as he stood and walked diagonally toward the buildings and his ambush location.

Donovan gave Emmett a two-minute head start. Then the band ended the slow dance song and struck up a lively tune. Donovan used the commotion of people exiting and entering the dance floor to cover his approach toward the vehicle. As there were no buildings or large trees between him and the street, as soon as Donovan passed the tables on the other side of the dance floor, he planned to head directly to the vehicle. As luck would have it, Beth and Nicole were chatting and standing next to the table that would serve as Donovan's last element of concealment before he would be out in the open. He paused when he reached them and grabbed Beth's hand stating, "I need to borrow Beth for a moment."

"Ohhh kay," Nicole said exaggerating the word, a little stunned by Donovan's tone which seemed to be all business.

Donovan said to a startled Beth, "As we walk, I want you to look at me as if I'm the most intriguing and handsome man here at the wedding."

Not a stretch, Beth thought as she looked up at Donovan who was intriguing in a mysterious way and *was* the most handsome man at the wedding.

"I'm trying to get close to a car parked on the street about 125 yards from here. So, in a minute, I'm going to stop, turn toward you, and I'd like you to turn toward me. I'm going to kiss you on the cheek. I want it to look like we stepped away from the crowd for a romantic moment alone."

Beth wasn't sure if he was serious or not. If this was a pickup strategy it was a new one for her, but she was willing to play along at least to see where this was going.

Donovan abruptly stopped and pulled Beth close to him. He planted a chaste kiss on her cheek but realized as he did it, he was facing away from the street. So, he switched to the other side of her face and kissed her lower on the neck so he could keep an eye on the car.

At this point, Beth didn't know what to think except that his lips were very soft, and his hands were warm and large.

"Okay, let's keep walking slowly toward the street, keep looking up at me as we walk."

It was like he was calmly directing a movie, Beth thought.

JUST A WHISTLE AWAY   215

About four steps later, Donovan released her hand and started running toward the street. While running, he lifted his cell phone and clicked off a series of photos.

Oh darn, and I was just starting to like this movie, Beth thought.

Donovan had started running the second he heard the car's engine come to life. His little ruse with Beth bought him several yards he was sure, but not a sufficient amount to get close enough to the car to see who was driving. The car pulled away from the curb, and to Donovan's disappointment, executed a U-turn and sped away. Donovan still hadn't been able to identify the driver, but he did notice a round faded yellow sticker with a black peace sign on the right bumper of the car. Once the car was out of sight, Donovan stopped and looked at the photos while waiting for Emmett to trot up to him. Unfortunately, the blurry photos didn't supply any additional information on the make or model of the car but did confirm the bumper sticker.

"It was a good plan, it just didn't come together," Emmett said glumly.

"Well, at least we know it was someone who had something to hide given the way they peeled out of here. The person drives a mid-sized sedan with a peace sign bumper sticker. I think the car was dark blue," Donovan said.

"Roger that," Emmett confirmed.

"Did you get the make?" Donovan asked hopefully.

"No, you were closer to the car than I was," Emmett remarked. "But whoever that was they know we saw them watching. Do you think it was Olivia's harasser?'

"I think it is a good bet," Donovan said. "Who else would it be?"

The men walked over to where Donovan had left a perplexed Beth standing. She stood watching them with a quizzical expression on her face. Donovan placed his hand on the small of her back steering her back to the party. Donovan and Emmett filled her in on the situation as they all made their way back to the celebration.

The party was in full swing, literally and figuratively. The dance floor was hopping, and Ian need not have worried about missing out on food. The waitstaff was circulating with trays of delicious tidbits and drink offerings. Laughter and conversations competed with the band. The cacophony of voices and music was exuberant.

The rest of the afternoon Donovan and Emmett kept an eye out for a dark blue sedan but didn't really expect the person to return. The guys would inform Ian, Christopher, and Olivia about the uninvited interloper after the reception. Garrett and Jacq would be informed of the situation once they returned from their honeymoon but now was not the time. Now was the time to celebrate with their friends.

Olivia had never been with a group of people who liked to dance so much and to her surprise most guests were really good dancers. She might have to take a lesson or two to brush up on her skills for future events.

By the time dessert was served, mixed berry shortcake topped with a generously sized ice cream ball garnished with a sprinkling of colorful flower petals, most guests were ready for a well-earned break from the dance floor. Only the most resolute and aerobically fit danced the set played during dessert.

Garrett and a radiant Jacq were making the rounds thanking guests for coming. Occasionally, one of them would pull someone aside for a private word. Jacq and Emmett had their foreheads together and each looked like they wiped a tear from their eyes although they smiled throughout their intimate conversation.

While Jacq was engaged in conversation with Emmett, Garrett had corralled Donovan and Ian. Their conversation ended with handshakes, a one-sided hug, and a slap on the back. Their close bond of brotherhood was undeniable.

JUST A WHISTLE AWAY

217

After saying goodbye to Patricia, Garrett's mom, the newlyweds sought out Beth and Christopher. Jacq threw her arms out wide and the three came together in a group hug. "Thank you so much for being here for me and for all the planning you took off my shoulders. The day could not have been more perfect. The theme of the event was carried through with exquisite details as I knew it would be," Jacq said looking toward Christopher. He flashed her his best "but of course" expression. "It allowed me to just enjoy the day, but I knew you two were working behind the scenes to make sure things were perfect. We can't thank you enough," Jacq said. Garrett added his own hugs and words of thanks.

Christopher said, "We have one more surprise before you go." In response to the quizzical look on Jacq's face, Christopher added, "You don't think we were going to let you leave in a less dramatic fashion than your entrance do you!" Christopher turned to the wedding hostess and twirled his index finger in the air three times giving her the preplanned signal. The hostess nodded and spoke into her cell phone. The waitstaff began circulating among the guests handing out cones full of colorful flower pedals. "Wait for it," Christopher said. About that time, an open-air carriage pulled by two white horses came into view from behind the barn to the delight of everyone.

"Our gift to you two," Beth said. "We wanted to bring a little of New York to you," Beth smiled.

"It's not a ride through Central Park, but it is a great photo opportunity," Christopher quipped.

The carriage was decorated with garlands of colorful flowers and as Jacq and Garrett left, the party guests showered them with a blizzard of living confetti to punctuate their exit.

Christopher flopped down into a chair and expelled a loud breath. Flopping anywhere was not Christopher's style, so Beth knew he was exhausted.

218   J. KIMALIE

"You did good Chris, I've never seen Jacq look so happy," Beth exclaimed as she took a seat next to Christopher.

"I'm just glad it's over and it came off as planned."

Guests were saying their goodbyes, gathering up their personal belongings, and heading toward their vehicles. Donovan had rounded up Emmett, Ian, and Olivia and they were heading directly toward Christopher and Beth.

They all took a seat around the table and the jovial tone of the day turned to business as Donovan succinctly recounted the disturbing events surrounding the mystery driver. During Donovan's briefing, Ian's jaw tensed, and he put a protective arm around Olivia. Olivia's hand went to the spot where the whistle normally hung on her chest. She had not worn it today because it didn't really compliment the lines or flow of her dress. Fashion be damned, she resolved to put it back on and not take it off until the creep was caught.

"We don't know for sure that the person is Olivia's harasser, but I think there is a pretty good chance that it was," Donovan said.

In a low menacing voice Ian said, "Next time I see that worm, I may just choke the life out of him."

"Who?" Beth asked. "Today's the first time I'm hearing about any of this."

Olivia explained about Wayne, the accountant who had been caught stealing from the clinic, and his subsequent termination.

"We don't know if it's him," Donovan said reasonably. "I'll find out if he has more than one car registered to him. But I don't recall his vehicle being a dark blue sedan. I just think we all need to be hyper-vigilant and keep an eye out for a dark blue car parked in the vicinity of the clinic or following anyone – especially you Olivia," Donovan added, looking at her with concern. "Now that the perp knows we've seen the vehicle, they may switch it out for another ride. So, keep an eye out for any vehicle that keeps showing up."

Donovan took a deep breath and continued to address the group, "I didn't mean to end this happy day on a negative note, but I felt it was important to all be on the same page."

"You did the right thing in telling us," Ian said flatly; all heads nodded in agreement.

"Well, I'm not letting you out of my sight tonight," Ian said looking at Olivia.

"Like that wouldn't have happened anyway," Emmett stated with a knowing smile, attempting to lighten the mood.

"Darn straight," Ian quipped back, taking Emmett's cue to ease tensions. "I saw how you danced with my date, and I knew then and there I needed to book her dance card for the rest of the evening." The look that Ian and Emmett gave each other drew chuckles from everyone. On that note, the friends bid each other a good evening.

Dear Veritas,

My manager is lame. He is this old guy who has to be fifty plus. He thought a pivot table was

an actual table with a flip top. Just last week at a team meeting he thought AI was an audit

inquiry. He is technically incompetent and doesn't deserve his job. How can I show his boss I'd be a better man for the manager position?

Signed: *Out With the Old and in With the New*

Dear Out,

As in, you may want to get out of a hierarchical organization. To be fair, since I don't know enough about your manager and his role, he may indeed be lame and incompetent. But don't confuse lack of knowledge in one area with failure in all other areas of his role. Depending on his job, other skills may be more important to a manager role.

Perhaps he hired you to bring needed tech skills to the team. One of my oldest and wisest friends uses about 2% of his iPhone capability. But when I have kept my mouth shut and listened to his successes, failures, and insights over the years, I have learned much from him.

Perhaps you need to judge your manager on the managerial skills that I assume earned him his

JUST A WHISTLE AWAY

job. If he is a good manager, identify what makes him good and learn from him. If he is not a

good manager, identify those things you would never do as a manager – you can still learn from

him.

I can't help but wonder if your managerial experience is as developed as your technical skills. If

this is the case, rather than trying to bump someone out of their job, why not go find a better one for yourself?

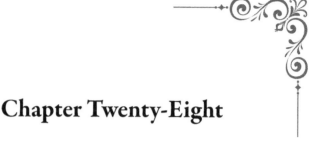

Chapter Twenty-Eight

Paolo de Luca walked purposely toward the door of the Longhouse. Donovan had left him a voicemail asking him to stop by anytime this afternoon to have a conversation about the strange mishaps that had been plaguing his niece. While Paolo didn't know Donovan well, he knew he was Ian's very close friend and he always had a good impression of the man. Paolo always trusted his instincts about people as they rarely failed him. In fact, other than Wayne Hoffman, he couldn't remember a time when they ever led him far from the mark. He typically didn't talk about people to others unless he knew them very well, but if Donovan said he might be able to help, then he would happily answer any questions put to him.

The pub was not very busy, but it was only about 2:30 PM in the afternoon and one wouldn't expect it to be. Paolo saw Donovan sitting at a table off in a corner going over paperwork of some kind. He looked deep in thought, so Paolo greeted Donovan as he approached so as not to startle him.

"Dr. Paolo, thanks for stopping by," Donovan said and got up to pull out a chair for his guest. "What can I get you? A cold beer or glass of wine? "

"I'd love a glass of Chianti if you have it," answered Paolo, taking a seat.

JUST A WHISTLE AWAY

"You've got it," responded Donovan who went behind the bar to serve it himself, returning a few minutes later. "So, are you enjoying retirement?"

"I am, I am, but I'm still working a little bit now and then to help out. I've been sleeping in and fishing and doing what men my age do," Paolo answered with a smile.

Donovan nodded and tilted his head slightly, "You looked to be quite the dancer at the wedding. In fact, I'd guess you've taken lessons."

Paolo smiled and replied, "I don't know why so many men are afraid to dance; it's a great way to be popular with the ladies."

Donovan nodded and added, "Women make our lives more challenging, but a lot more fun. On another note, I hear you and your niece met someone who wasn't so fun to deal with."

"Indeed. I understand that's what you wanted to talk to me about today," invited Paolo taking another sip of the Chianti.

"Thank you, yes," continued Donovan. "Ian told me about the problems the clinic and your niece have been having. Apparently, you had some trouble with your former accountant that might possibly be related? Do you mind telling me about him?"

"His name is Wayne Hoffman. There is really nothing that points specifically to him as our culprit, but there isn't anything that points to anyone in particular," explained Paolo. "That said, things seem to have escalated from stupid pranks to nasty incidents and we just can't ignore them anymore."

"Why don't you tell me about him for starters?"

"Well, as you know, he was my accountant. I hired him a few years ago when my previous accountant retired. He seemed like a nice enough guy when I met him." Paolo ran his hand through his thick gray hair and frowned.

"How did you find him?" inquired Donovan.

J. KIMALIE

"Actually, he found me. I was just about to go looking for someone when he stopped by and asked if I had a bulletin board within customer view where he could post a flyer. He told me he was new in town and starting a business. He seemed like a nice young man, and I know how hard it is trying to get a new business launched. I did call a couple of his clients whose names he gave me. They were back east somewhere and they seemed happy with his services. He offered me a good rate and I needed someone right away, so I went with it. He always kept in touch, got tax forms in on time, didn't seem to mind that I gave him unsorted piles of notes and receipts. He just shook his head and teased me every time and said he'd sort it all out for me."

Donovan looked up from the notes he was taking, encouraging the man to continue.

"Since Livvie was taking over my business, she was reviewing the books. She noticed that our revenues were down a little the previous two years, but I thought that was because of supply cost increases during COVID and our reduced windows for seeing patients. Nothing extreme. I'm not particularly good with computers you know, and I had no reason to doubt the work Wayne was doing. But Olivia is very sharp, and she did a spot audit and found discrepancies. She dug deeper and brought in a CPA to do a review and we discovered that Wayne had been regularly skimming a bit here and there. Not a huge amount, but it added up. I was shocked, of course, and disappointed. After all, I hired the guy, but Livvie was angry. She reported it. It was not enough to trigger jail time, and I just wanted it over and behind me, so I didn't pursue it as far as I could have, but I didn't want anyone else to get taken advantage of. I don't know what happened beyond our case, but he lost his license, got a warning, and has to pay me back. That's about all I know. He didn't strike me as the type of guy to get revenge, but then again, he didn't strike me as the type of guy to cheat me either. He's the only person we can think of that might have a beef with us."

"Did you ever go to his office or run into any of his other clients?"

"No, he always met with me at the clinic after hours. I don't know if he has an office or works from home. I always mailed his check to a PO box."

"Did you ever run into him around town or see him with anyone?"

"No, I never did. I never thought about it but now that you ask, that is kind of strange as Poulsbo isn't a very big town."

Donovan nodded thoughtfully and then asked if Paolo remembered the name of the police officer that investigated the charges."

"Daniel Parker. I don't know if he had anyone helping him or not, but he looked into it and kept in touch with us. Terrific guy. He's got a huge Great Dane called Alfie that I've taken care of for years. Wonderful dogs Great Danes. They look tough but are really just big babies." Paolo spread his hands apart wide punctuating the comment.

"They are, aren't they?" Donovan grinned in return. "Okay, that's really all I can think to ask right now. Ian's asked me to help him investigate Wayne just as a precaution."

Paolo looked at him intently. "So how is it you are able to help with this? Do you do detective work out of the back of your bar?"

Donovan shook his head and responded, "No, nothing like that. You hear a lot and meet a lot of people in a place like mine. I have a friend or two that I can ask to give us a hand. Ian is like a brother and I'd do anything to help him. He seems pretty fond of your niece from what I can tell."

Paolo gave him a sage look and said, "Oh yes, I can see a bit of fondness on both sides of that coin."

Donovan raised his glass in a silent toast, clearly approving of the concept and Paolo met the offer with a clink of his glass. Both men downed the rest of their beverages and Paolo got up and offered his hand which Donovan took in a firm clasp.

"Thanks for your help, Donovan and for the Chianti."

"My pleasure sir, and I'm sure Ian will get to the bottom of this. He's very good at these kinds of things."

"I'm sure he is," the older gentleman responded and walked out.

Donovan looked at his notes again and pondered the story. "So, Mr. Hoffman, what else might you be up to?" he said aloud to himself, punching a number into his cellphone. He then spent the next few hours making calls, working contacts, and calling in favors to quickly pull together background on David Wayne Hoffman.

Ian's phone buzzed with a text just as he was headed out the door to meet with one of his tenants. Donovan sent him a thumbs up emoji and asked when he could meet. He texted back that he'd see him in an hour or so. He'd just asked him a couple of days ago to look into Wayne so he wasn't sure that was the subject, but he was hopeful. The sooner he could solve this problem for Olivia the better. While he had only been dating her for a few months, he already felt very protective of her. Ian wished he could just be there to step in and deal with things the next time something happened, and he had a feeling there would be a next time. But the events always seemed to occur when he wasn't close by. He was hoping that Wayne was the source of the problem since it would be an easy remedy. If not today, he'd have the info on him soon enough. Ian didn't know how Donovan did it, but he usually worked some magic quickly. It was just sort of understood that although they were very close, there were things about Donovan's life that you didn't ask about, but he was clearly well connected.

JUST A WHISTLE AWAY 227

After meeting with his tenant and discussing some electrical upgrades that needed to be made to the space he was renting, Ian headed over to the Longhouse. It was a nice day and he enjoyed taking the bike out and getting some fresh air. It was invigorating and relaxing at the same time. He parked in the back and went in the delivery door guessing that he'd find Donovan in his office.

"Hawk, how's it goin'?" They did the shoulder lean, half hug thing that guys who are like brothers do, and then sat down on each side of Donovan's office desk. Ian took off his leather jacket and draped it over the back of his chair, revealing a tight black t-shirt that sported a red Jolly Roger emblem.

Donovan opened a drawer and took out a manila envelope and handed it over to Ian. "Here's everything we could find on Wayne. Not a lot. He's not someone I'd want to be friends with, but he's not the stuff criminal masterminds are made of. By the way, Wayne's actually his middle name. He started going by it when he moved out here."

Ian pulled a clipped bundle of papers out of the envelope and started to flip through them.

Donovan summarized it for him. "David Wayne Hoffman. Came from a fairly well-off East coast family so he had a good start in life but he never applied himself. You know the story. Parents still alive. One sister, younger. Got tossed out of a couple of schools along the way for missing classes, cheating, and just screwing up in general but squeaked by and graduated from some online college with a business degree. Went from job to job, girl to girl. Always seemed to take a little extra from each one than was his due but never enough to bring charges. Somehow landed here and upped his game a little with Dr. Paolo. No history of stalking, no history of complaints of the nature of Olivia's tormentor, just a lazy ass loose producer who thinks people owe him an easy life. All the family and personal details are in there. I don't think he's your creep, but then again, they all gotta start somewhere."

Ian frowned and considered what Donovan had told him. "I think I'll pay him a visit just to be sure."

"Do you want company?"

"No, not yet. I just want to make sure if he's the guy he gets the message; and if he's not, that he doesn't get the idea to ever get started."

"Sounds like a plan. Nothing new has happened, right?"

Ian shook his head. "Nope. But I don't think this is over."

Donovan reached across the desk and bumped Ian's shoulder with his fist. "Just let me know if there's anything more you need."

"I will, thanks. And thanks for taking care of this. You really pulled it together fast for me." Donovan smiled his enigmatic smile and said nothing. "There's something special about this girl, Hawk. I don't want anything to happen to her."

"I know," Donovan said. "I'm with you."

By the time Ian got back to his apartment the clinic had closed for the day and Olivia had left. He had been debating whether or not to go over the packet of info with her first but decided just to deal with it on his own. As he told his buddy, a little friendly visit was called for regardless of whether Wayne was their man. Ian went upstairs to have a cold Guinness and give the packet a thorough review. There was still plenty of time to follow up today if he felt like it. A small pink box was waiting for him on the step in front of his door, tied up with a polka dotted black and white ribbon. He pulled a small note from under the ribbon, curious to see what it said. "We had some extras, and I know they're your favorites. Have a nice day!" It was signed by Heather, the waitress from the bakery downstairs. The dot over the "i" in "nice" was made to look like a daisy. Inside the box were about a dozen ginger cookies. She was right, they were his favorites. She must have noticed that he bought them most often when he stopped by for a treat. Ian was used to women flirting with him, so this didn't seem so unusual, but while she seemed pleasant enough, she'd been a little more friendly lately than felt right. While casual flirting was something Ian always enjoyed, he hadn't really felt like partaking in it with anyone but Olivia since he had first met her. He also didn't want to give any false hopes or create any friction with someone who worked for one of his tenants. He decided to wait a day before stopping by to thank her and to nicely tell her that he was watching what he ate so as not to encourage a repeat of the gift, or any other attention for that matter.

He poured a chilled glass full of Guinness, plopped on the sofa and ignored his laptop that was an open reminder he had a deadline to meet. Instead, he perused the file once again that Donovan had given him. Nothing noteworthy stood out and it was just as his friend had summarized.

Ian decided there was no time like the present, so he'd swing by the address in the file and see if Wayne was home. It didn't need to be much of a conversation—just a brief chat to clarify that Olivia had friends in her corner and was not to be messed with. He finished his beer, locked up, and decided to take the motorcycle out for one more spin today. The sun would be setting before long and it promised to be a nice ride. Ian recognized the general location of Wayne's address and knew it to be an older, boring apartment complex off the main drag headed back toward Silverdale. He could be there in ten minutes or less. He swung his bare leg over the seat of his bike, put back on his helmet and leather jacket, and headed south. Just as he turned into the parking area of the apartment complex, he saw Wayne unloading some boxes out of the trunk of his car. Wayne briefly looked up when he heard the loud sound of the motorcycle and then turned his attention back to the boxes. Ian parked his bike, removed his jacket, and walked over to the man.

"Need some help with that?" Ian asked.

"No, I'm good," Wayne replied.

"That's not what I hear," Ian responded.

Wayne dropped the box he was lifting back into the trunk and turned to face Ian. "Excuse me?"

"I said, I haven't heard that you're particularly good." Ian said. "Actually, I hear you're not a good guy at all."

"Well, you heard wrong." Wayne spat out. "Hey, I know you, I've seen you around," he added in smug voice, his lip curling slightly. "Your name is Ian and you're just some bartender. You're kind of memorable," he added looking directly at Ian's kilt and chuckling at his own quip.

Ian crossed his arms over his broad chest, causing his muscles to bulge. Ian's guns were the envy of many a man at the gym he frequented. "Is that so?" he asked with a confident grin. "Do you want to elaborate on that for me, David?"

A worried look crossed Wayne's face and he coughed a little. "No man, just joking. We don't know each other, and I don't know why you called me that or why you're harassing me."

"Harassing you? No, that's not what I'm doing. In fact, I'm just paying you a friendly visit to make sure you know how wrong it is to harass anyone. Especially ladies. Or older gentlemen."

"Why would you say that to me? I don't do that. I don't hang out with seniors. I don't bother ladies. I'm a professional businessman so clearly you have the wrong guy."

"Oh, do I? You lost your license so I'm not sure why you are calling yourself a professional. Aren't you David Wayne Hoffman, 34 years old from Westfield, Rhode Island? The same David Hoffman who got tossed from several boarding schools and who ripped off my favorite vet right before he retired? And might you also be the creep who's been harassing his niece just because she discovered and reported your little skimming operation?" Ian didn't unfold his arms;

JUST A WHISTLE AWAY 231

he just lifted his chin slightly which was enough to cause Wayne to take a step back.

"I made one mistake and I'm making it right," he declared. "I was stupid, but I'm not stupid enough to harass anyone. I'm not a creep and you have no right to come accuse me of anything."

Ian just stared at him for a few minutes, letting him stew in the uncomfortable silence.

"I mean it man, I haven't bothered no one."

"Anyone," Ian replied correcting his grammar.

"What?" Wayne uttered, confused.

"The correct term is 'anyone' and yes you have. You've bothered me. If you mess with them, you're messing with me. I don't want to see you anywhere near either of my friends. I don't want to see you period. And if I find out you have any direct tie to anything bad that happens to them from this day forward, well, I would take that insult very personally." Ian snarled a little as he ended his speech.

"You have no right to come and threaten me." Wayne looked nervously around to see if anyone else was near, but they were still alone in the parking lot. "I have half a mind to call the police."

Ian nodded and calmly replied, "That's not a bad idea. Why don't we give Dan Parker a call. I understand he knows you quite well. Maybe you'd like to phone a friend too, just to make you feel supported."

Wayne started to panic. *Who is this guy?* "You don't have anything to worry about from me," Wayne assured him. "I'm not planning to get into any trouble with no one. I mean anyone."

"That's smart," Ian said. "You shouldn't. And you especially don't want to get into any trouble with me."

On that note Ian turned around and walked casually back to his bike. He took his time putting on his jacket and adjusting his helmet. When he glanced over and saw that Wayne was still looking at him, he made the two fingered gesture to his eyes indicating that he'd be watching him. Wayne quickly closed his trunk and scrambled up the stairs to his apartment leaving whatever he was originally unloading back in his car.

"Bloody little weasel" Ian said to himself just before he started his engine. He lifted his face briefly to the sky enjoying the feel of the last few rays of sun, and then sped away. He was just in time to enjoy the gorgeous sunset that was blooming before him as he rode home.

Dear Veritas,

I don't know about you, but I'm starting to get very upset by all the stories I hear about porch pirates these days. A person ought to be able to expect that a package delivered to their home could be left safely without some delinquent coming along and stealing it. In my neighborhood alone there have been at least three such thefts in the past month.

Last week as I was driving home, I noticed a car that I'd never seen in our area driving around slowly. It stopped in front of my neighbor's house and a sketchy looking guy got out and grabbed a big package from the front porch, put it in his trunk and drove right off.

I guess that was the straw that broke the camel's back so to speak so I turned around and followed him. I got right up close too so he could worry about what he'd done. He sped up a little and started taking some evasive turns, but I stayed with him. He finally pulled into a strip mall, parked, and sprinted away before I could tell where he'd gone to hide. I called the police who arrived about 5 minutes later. Okay, here's where things get awkward.

The officer told me I should have just called in the plate number and not followed. I get it, but as I said, enough was enough. I was told to wait in my car and he went to see if he could find the guy I described. Coincidentally, the officer got another call to the same strip mall with a complaint from someone who reported being scared because they were being followed. It was the same guy. Turned out that he had been in my neighborhood picking up a package of items that was left by my neighbor as a donation for the thrift shop that was located in the strip mall.

Naturally, I'm embarrassed, but in my defense, I felt it was time to take a stand. If we each don't step up to make our neighborhoods safer, how are things ever going to change?

Signed: Guilty, But Not Guilty

Dear Guilty,

Or is it not guilty, that is the question, right? I'm hardly in a position to judge since I agree that these porch thefts are frustrating and wrong. But there is a big lesson in your story about judging things by appearance isn't there, and I think at the end of the day you must admit you were guilty of not using your best judgement. So, I say you are indeed both guilty and not guilty—guilty for not doing what the officer said you should have done in the first place, but not guilty of looking the other way and failing to step up. Clearly you were trying to be a good neighbor.

Chapter Twenty-Nine

Dolce finished licking up the crumbs from the dog bone Olivia had given him after she'd tidied up the clinic. There was a cleaning crew coming in the next day and she wanted to make sure everything was put away so they could access all the areas they needed to clean and get in and out in a timely fashion.

"Did you enjoy that buddy?" she asked, knowing full well how much the dog loved getting a surprise treat.

Dolce executed a big doggy yawn and lay down for a little nap, resting his big head on his paws. Olivia turned to her files and decided that she could plow through them in less than an hour. It was a Friday night, and it would be so nice to have the weekend free without any work left to complete. The clinic kennels were empty and Zio was on call as the relief vet, so she'd be able to do whatever she felt like.

Ian had suggested she stop by the Longhouse after she wrapped up, and she was planning to invite him over for dinner the next evening. Everything had been going so well between them that she found herself smiling just thinking about him. Olivia didn't trust men easily. One outcome from not having many relationships was that she had never really had her heart broken and stomped on before. She'd seen it happen to enough friends, however, and had experienced more than enough beginning relationships where guys had told her they could hardly wait to see her again and then never followed through. Ian was a refreshing change. He certainly defied the definition of "typical guy" in almost every way, but in the few months she'd known him, he was claiming more and more space in her heart. It felt both natural and exciting and, just maybe, he was someone she could go the distance with.

The files weren't getting sorted with her thoughts focused on Ian, so Olivia turned her attention back to the task at hand. By the time she was more than halfway through, the overhead light flickered and went out.

"No, not tonight," she sighed out loud, wondering where the replacement bulbs were kept. She dug through the supply cabinet and located the right size bulb, but she looked everywhere for a device that extended up to the high ceiling socket that would enable her to replace it, but to no avail. If she didn't get this taken care of tonight, it would be a problem for the cleaning crew. She moved to the part of the office that still had sufficient light to finish up with the files and shot a text off to Ian. Just as she was putting the last patient file away, she got a reply to her text.

"Hi beautiful! Wish I could be there to take care of this for you, but the place is hoppin' and I can't get away. You can go up to my apartment and get the telescoping bulb changer out of the utility closet if you need it done right away. Otherwise, I can take care of it for you tomorrow."

Already resolved to finish things up tonight, she shot back her reply, "I do need to take care of it now as the cleaning crew may come in early tomorrow, so thanks. How do I get into the apartment?"

"There's a hidden key inside the mouth of the gargoyle plaque on the wall going up the stairs."

"What, not under the mat or flowerpot like normal people?"

"Nope, your guy is anything but predictable. Will I see you later?"

"Maybe. I'd hate to be predictable," she responded with a wink emoji and set down her phone.

JUST A WHISTLE AWAY

Olivia stepped outside and scanned the back area of the building since everyone normally around the place had left for the night. Ever since the rock throwing incident, she'd been on alert and always checked before she stepped out of the building after hours alone. Since she was just doing a quick dash upstairs, she didn't bother to bring Dolce or her phone so she didn't hear the chime of another incoming text.

Ian had been so busy when he answered Olivia's text that he hadn't thought twice about telling her to go into his apartment until after he'd done it. Now he was wondering if he had left the Dear Veritas out on his desk in plain view or picked them up after working on them earlier. He couldn't remember. He wasn't quite ready to come clean about his side gig with anyone yet, even Olivia. He wasn't completely sure why as he enjoyed the project, but it felt a bit rewarding to be anonymous. A guy could have a few secrets when they didn't hurt anyone. In fact, a little mystique came across as sexy as had been proven time and time again by the way women were drawn to Donovan.

The more he thought about it, the more sure he was that he'd left everything out. In a panic, Ian sent another text to Olivia, "Hey, on second thought, please wait. I'd rather do this for you myself. I can take care of it when I get home tonight. I don't care if it's late."

Olivia looked at the ugly little gargoyle face plaque hanging high on the wall midway up the stairs to the apartment and wrinkled her nose as she tentatively reached two fingers into the grimacing mouth. There were cobwebs around the gaping hole indicating the hiding place hadn't been breached in a while. She had to reach up on her toes to access it as it was high enough that an average person couldn't see into the space. Leave it to Ian to have a hiding place like this. Grabbing the key, she climbed the rest of the stairs and fit the key into the lock and went in. It felt a little strange being in Ian's home without him there for the first time. It was neither neat and tidy nor in complete disarray. It simply had that lived-in look. She easily found the utility closet and bulb changer. She tested it first to figure out how to extend the telescoping feature and accidentally bumped a little pile of papers off the corner of the counter when she backed up to give herself more space. Bending down to pick them up, she couldn't help but notice a little pink note that was written in a girlish script with a flower scribbled around the dot to an "i". It was from Heather, the waitress at the bakery downstairs who always acted so cool to her. Apparently, she had brought some treats to Ian. Why would he bother to keep the note?

She recalled seeing Heather leaving his apartment in the past but hadn't thought anything of it. Could something possibly have been going on between them? No, Ian would have said something. He would never have gotten intimate with her if there was someone else in the picture. Crazy anyway to think he and Heather would have any kind of romantic involvement. She certainly didn't seem like his type and why would he get himself even casually involved with two women who worked in his building? It didn't make sense. Besides, everyone said what a great guy Ian is, and she felt like the only woman in the world when she was with him, especially when he held her in his strong, capable arms. Olivia shrugged it off as a silly moment of doubt as she finished gathering up the spilled pages and set them back in a tidy stack. She grabbed the bulb changer and locked up and returned the key back in its hidey hole on the way down.

Back in the clinic, she gave Dolce a pat on the head and completed the task of changing the light bulb. She noticed as she walked back toward the door that she had a text and checked her phone, discovering that she had missed a message from Ian earlier. He had texted back shortly after she'd first reached out with another reply asking her not to go in his apartment after all. That seemed strange. Could he possibly have been worried she'd see something she shouldn't? Were there more notes lying around than the one she'd accidentally discovered? Something didn't feel right about this. She had been about to return the bulb changer to his apartment, but now she felt weird about going back inside. Doubting Ian felt wrong. Going in again after seeing a request for her to wait felt wrong. Finding that stupid pink note was starting to feel really wrong. Olivia reminded herself that she was a grown woman, and she knew by now to trust her gut. Her instinct up until this moment was to trust Ian and even now she felt guilty about having a hint of doubt. She decided not to go back in, but to swing by the Longhouse as planned and explain what happened when she saw him. If he wanted to elaborate on why he told her not to go in, he would. She decided there really wasn't any need to call out the note as there could be dozens of reasons why it was there, and it was not really any of her business. She wanted this relationship to be built on a foundation of trust. They would be having a conversation in the future, however, about what dating each other really meant in the way of commitments.

She bolted the clinic door and secured Dolce in the back of the car. It was around 4:30 PM and her stomach was growling. She decided it was a mild evening and she'd get a quick bite at the Longhouse and then head home. Dolce would be fine napping in the car.

It seemed as if everyone in town had come to the Longhouse for an early dinner or to have something to drink to cap off the end of the work week. Every table was full and there was a group of people hanging out by the door hoping to snag a table when one opened up. The music was blaring, and the general atmosphere was festive. Ian was bustling between helping to pour drinks behind the bar, clearing tables, and being as attentive as he could to everyone who wanted a word with him. Donovan was due back tomorrow and as far as Ian was concerned, it couldn't come soon enough. He had his Veritas column to finish, some repairs that had to be done in two of his rental units over the weekend, and he wanted to spend some quality time with Olivia. He enjoyed helping out at the bar, but with a new rental property coming on board and his deepening feelings for a certain curvy vet, he was considering talking to Donovan about hiring someone who could help fill in as manager when Donovan was away to free him up for other things.

He hadn't heard back from Olivia, so he assumed he'd be taking care of her light bulb problem tonight. He looked forward to anything that brought a smile to those luscious lips of hers and he grinned just thinking about how she might decide to thank him. Maybe it was time to confide in her about his little advice column gig. It might be nice to finally tell someone about it and to let her know that she was the one he wanted to share his secrets with, not that he really had all that many. He trusted her completely and was sure she wouldn't say anything until he was ready to go public.

He was also fairly confident that their creeper problem had been resolved after his little face to face with Wayne. Nothing else had happened and he was anxious to spend more time together without worrying about her when he wasn't near. He supposed worrying about someone you loved was a natural thing to do anyway. Wait, did he actually just think the "L word" in his mind? Did he love Olivia?

"Hey Gams, wakey wakey." Emmett was occupying a seat at the end of the bar and interrupted his thoughts. "How about another cold one down at this end?"

"You got it Crank," Ian piped back using Emmett's old army call sign. He grabbed a glass and pulled a Mack n Jack from the tap, topping it with just the right amount of foam. "Here you go. More than one tonight. Living large I see."

JUST A WHISTLE AWAY

Emmett sipped the foam off the top and smacked his lips, raising the glass to Ian. "Someone's gotta stop by while Donovan's gone and make sure you're acting responsibly in his absence," he joked. "Besides, I haven't seen you for a while and just wanted to say hello."

"I've missed you too man," Ian replied. "I've missed our cards too. We're due a rematch as I recall. Hope the fact that Garrett's married now won't put a damper on our rook games."

"Hardly, you've seen how busy Jacq always is. I'm sure we'll have plenty of time for cards once they've both caught up from all the wedding business. Did anything more come of that car Donovan chased?"

"Not yet. Everything's been pretty quiet lately. I actually had a little man to man talk with the guy we think may have been behind the crap that's been going on anyway. I gave him a little friendly advice if you know what I mean." Ian raised his eyebrows just a tad to punctuate the comment.

"Oh, I know what you mean," Emmett nodded. "Course, you did keep things cool, right? You don't know for sure if this is the guy or it wouldn't have been so friendly, I take it."

"Correct. Gotta admit though, he's the kind of guy you want to punch in the gut anyway. You know the type."

Emmett chuckled as he certainly did know the type. "I've had to tune up a couple of losers back in my day too. Let me know if you need any more help with that." He downed the rest of his beer and clapped Ian on the back. "Good seeing you, Gams. I need to make my report about the animals to Garrett since he and Jacq have returned. Say hi to your pretty lady for me."

"I will. In fact, I'll give her a hug for you."

"You do that. Oh, by the way, I thought of you when I read that advice column a couple weeks ago."

"What do you mean?" Ian asked, trying to mask any emotion in his voice.

"It seemed to be a young person's complaint and that lady advice giver wrote sort of a 'time to grow up' reply that sounded like you. Maybe she's been picking up her advice from eavesdropping on bartenders." Emmett chuckled at his own joke and left with a wave while Ian cleared his glass and swiped the counter clean in one fluid movement. He always enjoyed bantering with Emmett and felt bad he hadn't seen much of him lately, but he reminded himself to be careful. Emmett picked up on things that nobody else could. Noticing that two of the tables in the back of the bar were emptying out, he hurried over to clear them and wipe them down as well since he knew there would be people anxious to sit down.

Ian was so focused on getting the work done swiftly that he didn't realize someone had come up right behind him until he felt a tap on the back.

"Ian, I'm so glad I caught you! I was hoping you might be here tonight." Heather, from the bakery, was smiling up at him, her head coquettishly tilted to one side. She had a short little light pink schoolgirl type skirt on with a lacy trimmed halter top and a matching cropped white eyelet lace jacket. She looked all of 18 in the outfit, if that.

"Hi Heather, are you and your friends looking for a seat? I've just cleared this table," he responded.

"I'm waiting for my best girlfriend to join me. Will you let me sit here now while I wait for her?" she asked in sort of a flirty, pleading voice, pursing her bright pink lips. Clearly, pink was her favorite lipstick color as she always had it on.

"Of course," Ian answered, pulling out a tall bar chair for her like the gentleman he was.

She walked around him and set her sparkly, bejeweled clutch on the table and scanned the crowd. In the distance, she noticed Olivia had entered and was standing just inside the door, surveying the room.

"It's so nice of you to give me special privileges!" She threw her arms around Ian and kissed him full on the lips, running one of her hands up through the back of his thick hair.

Ian was so stunned he didn't know what to do for a minute and froze. He then untangled himself from her arms and took a step back, "Whoa girl, no need to thank me. Anyone is free to sit down wherever they want. You're very nice, but please, someone might get the wrong idea."

Heather giggled, threw her arms around him again replying, "Oh, I'm not worried anyone is going to get the wrong idea about me. What man wouldn't enjoy being thanked that way?"

Ian looked at her with a confused expression as he grabbed her arms again to free himself. "Hey, no harm done, but a lot of men might not take it as a joke. Just be careful, okay? I'll have someone bring you a menu."

Heather scanned the room again and smiled, refusing to let go. "Okay then, relax already. I won't tell anyone you don't like women flirting with you. Some men like to always be the one in charge in public," she teased and giggled again.

When Olivia opened the door to the Longhouse, she was surprised that it was as busy as it was. She knew Ian was in here somewhere and she thought she'd look for a place to sit in the back where she could grab a burger and wait for things to calm down a bit, hoping Ian could join her. She scanned the room and spotted Ian talking to what looked from the back to be a teenage girl. She raised her hand to wave and get his attention only to immediately lower it as she watched a shocking scene unfold before her eyes. It wasn't a teenage girl, it was Heather, dressed like a teeny bopper. She could see that now as Ian moved out of her way and guided her to her seat and then they were kissing madly—the kind where her hands were tangled in his hair. She was practically climbing him!

Olivia couldn't believe what she was seeing, and she felt the tears well up in her eyes. Without thinking, she stalked forward and in a furious voice said, "What are you doing?"

Ian yanked Heather's arms from around his neck and put some distance between them all the time looking at Olivia's horrified face.

"This isn't what it looks like," Ian said.

Heather turned and smirked at Olivia. "I was just thanking Ian for everything he's done for me."

Ian said, "Heather you need to leave," in a low voice.

"Don't bother," Olivia said. "I'll go" and she turned and rushed out of the pub without looking back. How could he? And in front of everyone. How could he do that to her? Now the text he'd sent made sense. He didn't want her to find any notes or other evidence of his relationship with Heather in his apartment.

"Olivia, wait," Ian shouted.

Not looking back, Olivia started the car and drove off. She looked in the rearview mirror to see Ian standing outside the Longhouse with his hands in fists by his side. Olivia took a breath and thought again about the time she saw Heather leaving Ian's place. She remembered now how the girl had been adjusting her clothes and hair as if she needed to put it back in place before returning to work. How could she have missed this sign and been so stupid? How could Ian have done this to her? Just then her phone rang, and wouldn't you know, it was from Ian. She let it roll to voice mail. Then her phone pinged with a text. "Please Olivia, will you slow down and talk to me?"

Olivia took another deep breath and wiped away the tears she hadn't been able to hold back. She caught herself rubbing the little silver whistle dangling from her neck. She was tempted to take it off, but it had become part of her. Something else she'd have to think

JUST A WHISTLE AWAY   245

about as she headed toward home. She could see the anxious look on Dolce's face in the rear-view mirror. "It's okay boy, just a little hiccup. I'll be fine." Dogs were so intuitive and definitely more trustworthy than men. In fact, she didn't know why some women referred to men as dogs. Dogs were always there for you; they never lied and they never cheated.

It was bad enough that Ian had made a fool of her this way, but what hurt just as much was discovering what poor judgement she had used in trusting him to the degree she had. He had seemed so genuine. He seemed so safe. She realized in her anger that she was driving a little faster than she should be and she slowed back down. No two-timing man was worth a speeding ticket to boot. Before she knew it, she was at the turn-off that led home. She was about to make the left turn and then reconsidered and pulled off to the side. She always had an emergency change of clothes in the car as well as extra supplies for Dolce. As a vet, you never knew when you might have to spend the night unexpectedly with a patient.

Going home had seemed like such a comforting thought when she first left the Longhouse, but now, she wanted to be somewhere alone where there were no memories of intimate time spent with Ian. She needed to think without interruption.

"How 'bout it Dolce, shall we get out of town?" Decision made, she forwarded her emergency clinic calls to her service which would contact Zio, and pulled back onto the road headed straight north, leaving the cottage and Ian behind.

Chapter Thirty

Olivia drove the winding road not seeing the scenery racing by the windows. In her mind's eye she was back at the Longhouse watching Ian and Heather embrace. She had been sure Ian wasn't the type of guy to two-time her, but she was so shocked by what she saw. Once again, she recounted the things that had happened over the last months now making sense in light of the behavior she witnessed; Heather coming down the stairs of Ian's apartment, the note she found inside his apartment and now the embrace.

Was she crazy? she asked herself, *and potentially misinterpreting what was going on? Or has Ian moved on and he just hasn't told me yet?*

Just as she was rounding the last curve that would take her onto the highway her phone chimed. Glancing at the screen, she saw again that it was Ian. She didn't want to stop to answer it. She didn't want to do much of anything but get out of Poulsbo to clear her head. She knew she needed to reach out to him, and she would, at some point.

Dolce sat up, his eyes scanning back and forth from the scenery to Olivia, looking as confused as Olivia felt. Dolce knew Olivia was upset and wasn't quite sure how to handle the emotions.

Up ahead Olivia saw a sign for Port Townsend. She hadn't even realized she was heading north. Port Townsend would be a good place to stop and try to get her hectic thoughts in order. She couldn't wander around aimlessly. She needed a plan so she took the Highway 19 exit thinking the hour-long drive would give her some time to contemplate her situation. However, all through the drive she found her thoughts ping-ponging between her moments with Ian and the last picture she saw of him embracing another woman. She knew if she let them, the tears would come, but she didn't want to risk obscured vision, so she sucked in a huge breath and kept going. Ugh, she needed to talk to Ian. There had to be a good explanation, but first she needed a cup of coffee, a bathroom break and to stretch her legs, and maybe a good cry to release some of the tension.

Ian's brow furrowed as Olivia's phone went to voice mail. He needed to talk with her after that scene at the Longhouse, but it seemed she was intent on ignoring him.

He was still so irritated with Heather. As he made his way to his apartment stairs there she was again standing in his way. She seemed to have developed a habit of turning up at his place to either bring him pastries or ask him for a favor. He had thought their meetings were harmless until this afternoon. Ian had enough of an ego to know that women found him attractive, and he knew from prior meetings Heather liked him. But he had never encouraged her, and he had thought that was enough for her to get the message that he wasn't interested. Apparently not. Heather had stopped him at the bottom of the stairs, asking if she could talk with him for a moment. Ian had stopped, curious as to what she was going to say. Instead of saying anything she had launched herself at him, forcing him to catch her. The next thing he knew her lips were once again glued to his. He grabbed her arms and pried her off his chest.

"What the hell are you doing?" he had all but shouted at her, wiping his lips with the back of his hand.

"I was kissing you. If you didn't recognize it then apparently, I was doing it wrong," Heather said with, what Ian thought she believed was, a seductive pout to her lips.

"Yes, well, your advances are unwanted and unwelcomed," Ian said with a scowl. "I thought I made that clear at the Longhouse. Have I ever led you to believe there was anything between us?"

"You were always happy for my visits and, I know, you came into the coffee shop mostly to see me," she stated as she flipped her hair behind her shoulder and placed her hands on her hips. "You can't fool me, Ian. I know you've been watching me."

Was this woman bat-shit crazy? Ian thought to himself. *She had always seemed sane when she waited on him.* "Look Heather, if anything I did gave you the wrong impression, I'm sorry. But you and I," Ian said waving his hand between the two of them, "will never happen."

Heather looked at him through slitted, furious eyes. "It's because of her, isn't it?" she hissed.

"Who are you talking about?" Ian asked, although he knew full well who she was talking about. Ian backed up a couple of steps to put him in a better position to defend himself. The woman had gone from seductress to witch in two point three seconds and it was making the hair on the nape of his neck stand up and take notice.

"The woman who spends all day shoveling animal shit," Heather said with a sneer. "She's not right for you, you know. I can be what you need better than she can!" Heather emphasized her words with a thumb pointed toward her chest moving toward him.

"Look," Ian said backing up holding his hands out in front of him. "I'm in love with Olivia, she's an amazing woman and I'm not interested in you or anyone else. She's it for me."

Heather continued to stalk toward him invading his personal space. Ian stood his ground wondering what she was going to do next.

"You want me, I know it," Heather practically screamed at him.

"You're wrong," Ian said calmly. All his senses were trained on the woman, his body tense and ready for battle.

Heather's hand came up and swung toward his face. He grabbed her wrist before it could connect with his cheek. "Enough," Ian said in a stern voice. "Do I need to call the cops?"

Breathing heavily, Heather yanked her wrist out of Ian's hold. Her cheeks were flushed, and her eyes shot angry darts at him. "You can deny it all you want. But someday you'll come crawling back to me," Heather stated ominously, then she spun away and stomped off.

Ian just stood there letting the adrenaline drain from his mind and body. He needed to speak with Olivia.

Olivia drove into the parking lot of Fort Warden State Park. She had stopped at a java hut for a mocha where they had spoiled Dolce with a pup cup. Now the dog was ready to get out and stretch his legs. Hooking the leash to Dolce's harness, Olivia got her coffee, walked around the front of the car, opened the door, shooing Dolce out, and walked toward the beach. She let her dog sniff every bush and tree as they ambled along the trail. She had purposely left her phone in the car needing to order her thoughts before she called Ian back. Finding the off-leash area, she let Dolce go and the dog took off for the water's edge with his tail waving like a flag. Olivia's lips quirked up taking pleasure in Dolce's antics. Very soon however, thoughts of Ian crowded in making the small smile disappear from her face.

She turned her face up to the wind and let the tears escape. It was horrible to realize she loved Ian only to be confronted by what looked like infidelity. Sensing Olivia's distress, Dolce was making a beeline back toward her. Wiping her eyes with a napkin, she reached down and placed her hand on Dolce's head, letting the dog ground her emotions. Leashing Dolce back up she made her way to the car ready to confront Ian.

Ian was backing his motorcycle out of the garage when he felt his phone vibrate against his leg. He fished it out of his pocket relieved to see it was Olivia.

"Hey Liv, I'm glad you called, I was getting worried," Ian said. "Where'd you go?

"I'm in Port Townsend at the moment," she said with a hitch in her breathing.

Ian frowned irritated, "What's in Port Townsend? Look it doesn't matter, I need to talk to you.'" he asked.

"I...," she started then stopped. "Ian, be straight with me. Are you seeing somebody else?" Olivia questioned softly.

"What?" Ian said incredulously. "I know what you saw looked bad, but no I am not seeing anyone else. Why didn't you stay and talk to me?"

When she didn't respond Ian continued "God Livvie, of course I'm not seeing somebody else," taking his phone from his ear, looking at the screen as if he could will her back to him.

"You can't deny you were in an embrace with another woman," she said with a wobble in her voice.

"Olivia, listen to me. I've been accosted by Heather twice now today. I'm not sure what I should do about it. Part of me wants to turn her over to the police for assault and part of me wants to forget it ever happened," he said.

"Tell me what happened from the beginning," Olivia replied.

"I had pulled a chair out for her to sit down, and the damn woman threw herself at me. I've never had anything like that happen to me before. Later when I came home, worried about you, she showed up again. This time when I rejected her, she tried to slap me and threatened me," Ian exclaimed running his hand through his hair.

"I'm sorry Ian, I guess I should have come to your rescue rather than yell at you and run," Olivia sighed.

JUST A WHISTLE AWAY   251

"But instead, what? You were cursing me thinking I was cheating on you," Ian stated in a flat voice.

"I really am sorry if I handled it wrong. I didn't know what to think between seeing you with another woman in your arms and piecing together other things I had noticed. I think we need to have a face-to-face conversation. I'll call you soon," Olivia stated.

"Yeah, that sounds good," Ian sighed. "I'm headed to Garrett's right now. Let me know when you are back in town and ready to talk."

They said their good-byes and Ian stuck his phone back in his pocket. He looked toward his motorcycle not really seeing it. *What did it say about a relationship that the woman you had just realized you were in love with didn't trust you?* Ian questioned to himself, but at least he knew Olivia was safe.

Sighing, he swung his leg over his bike, kicked the starter and pointed the wheel toward Garrett's. All the way to the farm he thought of Olivia, trying to understand why she would jump to such a horrible conclusion. Pulling his bike up to the garage, he took off his helmet and sat for a moment getting his thoughts in order. Garrett found him there staring at the helmet in his hands.

"Hey, I thought I heard your bike," said Garrett.

Ian looked up. His face creased in a frown.

What's going on?" Garrett questioned as his friend sat there silently.

Ian looked back down at his helmet. "This has been a shitty day," Ian muttered.

"Come in the house. I could use a break and a beer," Garrett said.

Ian dismounted and followed Garrett into the house. The house smelled like cinnamon and sugar. On any other day, Ian would go in search of whatever goody Jacq had cooked up, but today he couldn't bring himself to care.

Garrett handed him a finger of scotch and led the way onto the back deck. The two friends made themselves comfortable on navy upholstered lounge chairs, clicked the beer bottle and the scotch glass in solidarity, and took a drink.

After a few seconds of silence, Garrett asked, "Are you going to tell me what happened?"

"Olivia doesn't trust me," Ian blurted out.

Garrett looked at him with a frown, "What do you mean and how do you know?"

"She thought I was cheating on her."

Garrett's eyebrows winged up. "Ok, start at the beginning because I think I'm missing something."

Ian sighed, looking out at the stand of trees in the distance. "I was bussing tables at the Longhouse when Heather, a waitress at Lily's bakery, threw herself at me. She said she was thanking me for getting her a table, but the smack she gave me on the lips felt like more than a simple thank you. Then later when I got home to go in search of Olivia, I was going up to my apartment and there she was again. Before I knew it, I had an armful of woman who had me in another lip-lock."

Garrett just stared at him. "You're telling me that this woman Heather threw herself at you and kissed you. Not once, but twice?"

"Exactly," Ian said.

"Does this happen to you often?" Garrett asked with a smirk.

"Not funny. You know it doesn't," Ian said appreciating the fact Garrett was trying to lighten the mood.

"I pushed her away both times," Ian said continuing the story. "She said she knew I wanted her and then when I denied it, she tried to slap me. I swear Garrett there was a look in her eye that was downright scary. I'd never hurt a woman, but if she had gotten violent, I'm not sure what I would have done."

"What does this have to do with Olivia?" questioned Garrett.

JUST A WHISTLE AWAY

"She saw the part where Heather kissed me at the Longhouse and then she left town," Ian said matter-of-factly. "She called me and accused me of having another woman in my life."

"I can see her point of view. If I saw Jacq in the arms of another man, I might question what was happening."

"Yes, but wouldn't you have taken Jacq aside right there to discuss what you saw and not left thinking she was cheating on you?" Ian asked.

"But I've known Jacq for a long while now. Your relationship with Olivia is fairly new. I get that you're hurt, and you think that she doesn't trust you, but I think it is more like she was shocked and didn't know what to do," Garrett proffered.

"Maybe," Ian said grudgingly.

"I think what you have to ask yourself is...is Olivia important enough to work through this?" Garrett said looking at Ian.

"I love her," Ian said softly.

"Woohoo, Ian's in love," Garrett said with a chuckle socking Ian in the arm.

Ian pushed him back with a scowl on his face. "I thought you were a grown man," Ian said, disgruntled.

Garrett smiled at the frown on Ian's face. "Just talk it out with her. I'm sure right about now she's feeling remorseful and beating herself up for running away."

"Maybe," Ian took another sip of his scotch.

"I know I'm right," Garrett said. "I've learned a few things being married to Jacq and one of them is that our women hurt when we hurt, and Olivia knows that she hurt you."

Ian gave Garrett the side eye. "When did you become a relationship guru?"

"Oh, Ian my man. You don't know the half of what I know about relationships. I should be the one writing the Dear Veritas columns in the newspaper. I could give much better advice than the knucklehead writing the column," Garrett stated with a smile.

"You are so full of shit," Ian grumped.

Garrett just laughed in response.

Dear Veritas,

I'm a fairly new bride and my mother-in-law is a strong personality, but a lovely person. I want to have a great relationship with her but there is a problem that I just can't seem to solve. I'm highly allergic to certain fragrances and the perfume she wears affects me past the extreme limit of my tolerance. She insists on wrapping me up in a big bear hug every time she greets me, and I suffer. She always wants to ride in the car with my husband and me to go to family events, and I suffer. She often sits next to me at the table when we're dining, and again, I suffer.

If my sneezing and swollen eyes weren't obvious enough that something is terribly wrong, you'd think my polite explanations about my allergies would be enough to curb her excessive use of "her signature fragrance," but no. She just laughs and says, "Oh my poor darling."

I love my new husband, but he's a momma's boy and he doesn't want to hurt her feelings. He thinks I'll get used to it in time. Allergies don't work that way. I'm at a point where I'm starting to make excuses and bowing out of family events to avoid her and it's becoming awkward. Please advise as I don't want to create a problem for my family, but a girl's got to breathe!

Signed: Breathless on Bainbridge

Dear Breathless,

I'm sorry to hear that you're suffering and yes, you've got to breathe. Perhaps what you refer to as "polite explanations" is just a bit too subtle for your new mother-in-law? I'm not encouraging you to be rude, but I do think you need to be very direct. Explain to her that this is a real health issue. If you have doctor orders about your condition, use that to help emphasize the importance of avoiding exposure to strong fragrances.

Your new husband may be a momma's boy, but I'm sure he loves you very much. Sit down together and make sure he understands that this is a serious health matter for you. He needs to know that if you can't catch a break, you won't be able to catch your breath. Nobody would choose to go anywhere where they can't breathe. He should support you on this and talk to his mom.

Chapter Thirty-One

Ian's explanation kept repeating itself over and over in Olivia's mind like a looped song at a dance club. No matter how many times she reflected on it, the sound of disappointment in his voice never changed. He was disappointed in her for not giving him the benefit of the doubt and for running away. Her emotions had run a triathlon in the last four hours. First leg, her blinding pain and hurt at seeing this man she had developed feelings for enfolded in another woman's embrace. Second leg, a detailed review of all the signs of involvement with Heather that she had dismissed because, unlike what his tone had accused her of, she trusted him. And finally, the big one, the realization that she didn't just have growing feelings for Ian, she was actually falling in love with him. Although he had denied anything going on with Heather, she still didn't feel that she could dismiss what she saw even though she had apologized for it.

Ian wasn't aware of the less overt signs she had factored in that had tipped the scales in taking her to a place of distrust. Why had he panicked after he had first told her to go in his apartment if he hadn't realized she might see something she shouldn't? She needed to calmly discuss all of this with him. She hated that she kept flipping between questioning his integrity and doubting her own judgment, and yet, just earlier she had told herself to trust her gut. Right now, her gut was as confused as her mind which was trying to logically sort through all the evidence.

The miles were cruising by, the stars were becoming visible, and she was getting closer to home. She needed to decide how to move forward. She both wanted to see Ian and dreaded it. She was tired, emotional, and felt very much alone. Talking to somebody about this would be a relief, but whom? She loved Zio, but this wasn't the kind of thing you talked to your uncle about. Besides, if he thought Ian had cheated on her, he'd probably go find and fillet him. This was a time when a girl needed a close sister or her best girlfriend, but in truth, Olivia didn't have either one. Sure, she had plenty of out-of-town friends from college, from past work, and from activities like her trivia night, but nobody she really ever confided in. She had been so busy and invested in her career that she never spent enough time to get close enough to anyone to develop that kind of friendship.

Moving to Washington had been good for Olivia in many ways, one of which was that she was beginning to take more chances and get to know people outside of her work. She admired the deep, close and supportive friendships she saw among the people she was getting to know and wanted that for herself. Thinking about it further, she knew who she felt most comfortable reaching out to. She dialed Jacq and was relieved when her call was answered on the second ring.

"Olivia, how wonderful to hear from you!" Jacq exclaimed.

"Hi Jacq, I hope I'm not interrupting anything. You must be so busy since you've come back from your honeymoon. I hope it was wonderful," Olivia offered.

"It was that and more," Jacq replied, "I'll tell you all about it when we get together. I think we're due a repeat coffee break."

"Yes, I'd like that too," Olivia said, "But I'm wondering if you might have time to get together just the two of us sometime sooner. I sort of need someone to talk to and it's, well, rather private."

"Olivia, is something wrong? Of course, I'll be there for you."

"Well, yes, but I'm not in danger or anything—not more of the stalker stuff. This is, well, something personal. It's about me and Ian," she said hesitantly.

"Okay, let's talk." Jacq could tell from Olivia's shaky voice that this needed to happen sooner rather than later. "I'm actually free tonight if you want to get together."

"That would be great," Olivia replied with relief evident in her voice. "Where can we meet? I'd prefer not to meet at either of our homes, so we don't get interrupted."

"I understand. I know just the place. Do you know where Liberty Bay Books is located? It's right in downtown Poulsbo."

"Yes, I've never been inside, but I've seen it."

"Let's meet there. They have a little bistro in the back that stays open late where we can grab coffee and have a private chat. Besides, there's something so cozy and comforting about being surrounded by books," Jacq suggested.

"I agree, that sounds perfect. I'm in the car and on my way back to town. I can drop Dolce off and meet you in an hour if that works?"

"That works perfectly. I'll see you soon," Jacq said encouragingly. She hung up and wondered to herself what could be going on. She had heard Ian's bike pull up to the house earlier and knew he was talking to Garrett. Something was up and clearly Olivia was hurting and needed someone to be there for her. While they didn't know each other all that well, she had taken an instant liking to the woman and had been around her enough to consider her a solid, responsible, professional person and a new friend. She actually felt it was a compliment that Olivia had turned to her when she needed someone to confide in.

Olivia made it to the bookstore first after dropping Dolce off at home and freshening up after the tumultuous day. She had always been curious about the little bookshop that had clearly been there for years with its tall ornately topped steeple and warm, spicy colors. She followed the rich smell of espresso to the back of the building where she snagged two chairs that afforded the most privacy, took off her denim jacket, and waited for Jacq. She didn't have to wait long. Minutes later she stood up to greet her new friend only to find herself wrapped in a big, secure, "I've got you" girl hug that triggered a flow of tears that she thought had been corralled for the day.

"I'm here for you," Jacq said quietly. "First, I'm going to get you something warm to drink. Then you are going to tell me everything you need to tell me and it's not going to leave this shop. So, what would you like me to get you? A latte?"

Olivia sunk back into the chair and felt the first level of weight lift off her shoulders. She was no longer alone. "Yes, a latte would be great. Nonfat milk. Just a splash of vanilla please. Jacq, I'm..."

"Shh, no need," Jacq reassured her. "We've all been there. Just give me a couple minutes." And with that, she left Olivia to collect herself while she went to conduct business with the barista.

Jacq returned with two giant steaming beverages and set them on the table. She pulled up a chair, took her time removing her sweater, organizing her purse and stirring her mug, allowing Olivia to begin when she was ready.

Olivia wasn't used to talking to people about something as emotionally charged as her feelings about Ian and all that was going on. She was normally so forthcoming and direct about all things business and normal social interaction, but this was foreign territory. That said, the need to talk about it had been strong and her instincts had pointed her toward this lovely, caring woman who had responded so quickly.

JUST A WHISTLE AWAY

"Jacq, thank you again. I do want to hear about your trip and how you're doing. I feel so bad about dragging you out at night and asking for your help right after you got back," she offered apologetically and cupped both her hands around the warm, comforting latte like it was a lifeline.

A hand reached over and patted her arm. "We've got plenty of time later for that story. I'm so glad I can be here with you now. Tell me what's wrong. Let me help if I can," she offered earnestly.

Olivia smiled a little shyly and sighed. "I feel a little weird talking to you about this because you are close friends with Ian, but that's probably why you are the right person to talk to, along with the fact that I just feel like I can trust you. That, and because I need a woman's perspective," she began. She then proceeded to tell Jacq everything, beginning with her interactions with Heather. She told her about the things that happened along the way that made her pause and wonder but not really doubt Ian's integrity, until now. By the time she got to the point in her story where she witnessed Heather and Ian kissing at the Longhouse, she couldn't hold her tears completely at bay and a couple trickled slowly down her cheeks.

Jacq automatically dug into her purse and produced a tissue, one of those thick, pretty ones that had a beautiful floral design. Olivia graciously accepted it, patted away the tears, and continued with her story. After she summarized the phone conversation and Ian's explanation about Heather throwing herself at him, she explained how she could hear in Ian's voice his disappointment in her lack of trust, her voice breaking a little as she spoke. She recovered again and then recounted how she had apologized to Ian for the way she confronted him at the Longhouse, running out of the bar and assuming the worst.

"The thing is," she added, "I couldn't see anything other than what was right before my eyes. It wasn't a simple kiss like from a friend; it looked like a full-blown lovers' lip lock. I was already planning on asking him why he didn't want me going into his apartment after saying it was fine. Why so mysterious—and then my accidentally finding a note from the woman I later saw kissing him. Since I'm laying it all out for you, I have to admit that I never would have thought this could happen with Ian. Not only has my gut told me all along that I could trust him, but I realized when this hit me so hard that my feelings for him have grown even deeper than I imagined."

She paused and looked down at her coffee, reflecting on what she had said. She looked back up and directly into Jacq's eyes. "I realized just today that I'm falling in love with him. And now I don't know if I've blown the whole thing by questioning his actions, or if when I add everything up he really is somebody that I can't trust with my heart. He only knows I saw him at the Longhouse. He doesn't know that there is more to why I reacted the way I did. I must admit that I'm confused and hurt and no matter what Ian did or didn't do, I end up blaming myself for being in this state."

The sound of steam from the espresso machine hissed loudly in the background. People chatted over coffee and pastries and milled around the shelves behind them. It was the perfect curtain of background noise and activity that made their conversation feel private and yet grounded in the normalcy of everyday activity. Olivia graciously accepted the entire little package of tissues that was slid across the table toward her. Jacq had listened to everything without interruption, nodding at all the right moments and absorbing the information free of judgment. Olivia was anxious to hear what she thought of it all.

Jacq slowly exhaled and shook her head in disbelief. "I'm so sorry this has happened to you," her friend began. "For what it's worth, I think you are both hurting and a bit confused. I saw that Ian was over at the house visiting Garrett, so I assume he also needed someone to talk to. I think that's a good sign and Garrett will not steer him wrong." Jacq took another sip of her coffee to allow Olivia time to reflect on that for a moment.

"First of all, no need to blame yourself for how you're feeling or for being in this situation. There are pieces of the puzzle that don't seem to fit and I think you need answers. Second, if Ian was dating anyone other than you, I'm certainly not aware of it and I think I would be. In fact, I've known him now for almost two years and while he has always been outgoing and a little flirty with the ladies while on shift at the Longhouse, I've never heard of him dating anyone seriously and I've never seen him putting on PDAs. You're the first woman I've ever actually seen him act serious about. And while I don't have any tangible information, I really doubt that he would have anything going with anyone else at the same time. I don't know Heather, although I think I have seen her around and know who you're talking about now that you've described her, but I must say, she doesn't seem at all like somebody Ian would be interested in or ask out. I know that people generally think most men enjoy playing the field, but the truth is Garrett and Ian and their little circle of buddies are pretty solid, decent guys. If Ian was a player, I think Garrett would have mentioned it to me or I would have become aware of it by now."

Olivia was listening intently, and a look of hope flickered across her face. "Do you think I jumped the gun?" she asked.

"No, not under the circumstances," Jacq replied. "You've seen what you've seen and of course you are going to think twice about what it means. I think when you sit down and explain to Ian why you reacted the way you did, he will understand better. If he can't put himself in your shoes and accept that you had total trust in him up until you were blindsided the way you were, well, maybe he's not ready to be in a serious relationship. Communication and being willing to risk being fully honest about your feelings is the key in a healthy relationship. When are you going to talk with him?"

"I'm supposed to reach out tonight now that I'm back. Talking to you has helped. I haven't really ever had a friend to confide in this way. Actually, I haven't ever had a reason for a conversation like this." Olivia's face blushed slightly as she added, "I've never been in a romantic relationship that felt this way. I must be the only woman in her thirties who never once thought I was really in love. I needed to talk about it. I think I needed to say it to someone out loud first, to someone I could trust. I know we haven't been friends for very long..."

"I trust you too," Jacq said seriously. "I also know we're going to be there for each other in the future, so let's not worry about thanking each other. I'm lucky to have you as a friend and I know it."

The two women leaned together and hugged for dear life across their chairs in that way that only woman do, cementing their bond of friendship. Olivia felt reinforced, validated, and loved. She got more than she hoped for and exactly what she needed from Jacq.

"Okay then, I won't say "thank you" because you clearly know how I appreciate this, but I can say that I'm feeling so much better, and it has helped so much, your being here for me. I think now I could use a little alone time to process and recover before I see Ian. It will be good to talk to him and figure things out regardless of the outcome. How about I follow up with you after that?"

"I was hoping you would," Jacq replied warmly. Let's walk out together."

The two women returned their cups to the dish bin and walked outside together. They crossed the street and paused under a tall, red, antique iron street clock.

"Oh my gosh, look at the time," Olivia exclaimed. "I've kept you much longer than I realized."

"Not at all," Jacq assured her. "Don't get me wrong, it was great having several weeks alone with Garrett, but it's good to get together

JUST A WHISTLE AWAY   265

with a girlfriend even though the circumstances are what they are. Let's make this shop 'our spot' and get together again soon."

"You're on," Olivia replied with a positive note. The women hugged again and went back to their cars. Olivia's step was a bit lighter, and she felt another layer of weight removed from her shoulders. Jacq was right. If Ian couldn't explain his actions and understand why she felt so hurt after she recounted her side of this story, well then, maybe he isn't ready for a committed relationship, or maybe he's just not the man for her. She knew this was a sensible way to look at things, but the possibility of going their separate ways ripped at her heart.

She sent Ian a brief text to tell him she was back in town, but too spent to talk tonight and would be in touch tomorrow.

Dear Veritas,

I've been seeing a woman for about two years now and thought for sure that she was the one. We seemed to click from the day we met and lately we had started having conversations about what a future together might look like. About the time I had saved enough money for an engagement ring, I sensed something in our relationship had changed. It's a subtle shift but a definite one on her part. Lately she has been too busy to get together as often as usual. Excuses run from she's swamped at work to she needs to be there for a friend in crisis. I understand that what I referred to as excuses can be legitimate; however, it is more than that – she seems to be pulling away from me physically and emotionally. Whatever the reason, should I go forward with popping the question to let her know I am totally committed to our relationship or wait to see if she is second guessing a future with me?

Signed: *A Ring in Hand but Not Going as Planned*

Dear Ready with the Ring,

I can guarantee that wracking your brain over what you may have or have not done to cause the shift in the relationship is not helpful. You'll just beat yourself up trying to figure it out and probably won't come to the right conclusion.

You have got to talk to her. Tell her honestly how you feel and what you have been sensing regarding the change in her behavior toward you. Everyone says that open and honest communication is key to any healthy relationship. I have no doubt that's true, but starting a conversation fearing you may hear something that will break your heart is easier said than done. Do it anyway, you've got to know where you stand before you know where the ring should land.

Chapter Thirty-Two

Ian sat at his computer looking over the Dear Veritas letters that had come in from the week before. Reflecting on the encounters with Heather and the chaos they caused in his and Olivia's relationship, he couldn't get into the frame of mind to provide somebody else advice when he was struggling with his own life challenges. He had picked out a couple of likely candidates but couldn't summon the energy to start writing. Heaving a huge sigh, he rose from his desk chair and made his way to the kitchen. Opening the refrigerator door, Ian stood staring at the contents, not really seeing the condiments and left-over containers that filled the shelves. After about a minute of quiet refrigerator contemplation, he shut the door, walked over to the fireplace, flipped the switch and watched the flames begin to dance along the logs. Next, he walked to the window and looked out at the rain that was splashing down on the asphalt, wishing the weather was better for a bike ride.

Ian was in a funk, his thoughts swirling between Olivia, Heather, the stalker, Dear Veritas, his Longhouse schedule, and other miscellaneous subjects. Around and around his mind went, reaching no conclusions on anything, just a lot of random musings as the rain slowly tapered off. Just as he was thinking he would go to the Longhouse to see if Donovan was up for a beer, his phone rang. Walking to the kitchen counter, Ian saw Olivia was calling. He debated whether to pick it up as he really wanted to be more settled in his thoughts when he talked with her, but also wanted to make sure she was ok and didn't need his help.

Picking up the phone, he said, "Hey Liv," with no inflection in his voice.

"Hey," Olivia responded. Ian realized even though he still wasn't over the hurt of her assumptions about him, it was a relief to hear her voice.

"I was hoping you were free sometime this week so we could talk," Olivia said hesitantly as if she was afraid Ian would turn her down.

"Of course, I'm at the Longhouse tonight, but tomorrow evening works or later in the week."

"How about tomorrow? Do you mind meeting me at the lighthouse?" Olivia asked.

"No, what time?" Ian said running his hand through his hair and mourning the fact that their conversation was so stilted.

"About 4 o'clock. Is that too early?" she said.

"No that works. I'll see you then," Ian said wanting to get off the phone and really needing that beer he was contemplating before she called.

"Great," Olivia said trying to infuse some cheer into her voice. "And Ian," Olivia prodded.

"Yeah," Ian prompted.

"I've missed you," she stated with catch in her voice.

"And I, you. I'll see you tomorrow," Ian said reluctant to hang up now that it was time to say goodbye. He knew Olivia was still on the line, it seemed they were both reluctant to end the conversation. "Bye Liv," he said quietly. He heard her soft goodbye as he slowly cut their connection.

The next afternoon, Ian snatched his keys off the console as he headed out the door. It had been a busy day which had kept his mind off the upcoming meeting with Olivia. Old Mrs. Kinney had asked him to come over to look at her washer. Appliance repair was not something he did for most of his renters, but he had known Mrs. Kinney for a long time now and he enjoyed her company. She was a widow and had moved to Poulsbo to be near her daughter. As it happened, her daughter lived on the same street as Ian's rental and fortuitously the house was vacant when Mrs. Kinney was in need. Ever since her move-in date, Ian had become her friend, her handy-man, and her confidant. They had spilled secrets, shared stories, and told jokes to each other over copious amounts of tea – Mrs. Kinney's drink of choice. And Mrs. Kinney liked his kilts and t-shirts which showed her good taste as far as Ian was concerned.

Catching site of himself in the mirror on his way out, Ian thought Mrs. Kinney would wonder at his current outfit. He was dressed all in black, black cargo pants, black t-shirt and black boots. He looked like he was dressed for mourning or combat and wondered which one was appropriate for his meeting with Olivia.

Driving to their rendezvous point, Ian tried to parse through his feelings. There was excitement to see Olivia again. It had only been a few days, but it seemed like forever. He was still a bit hurt over her accusations, but he was also sad that now there was a wrinkle in their relationship that they would either have to work out or let it fester and ruin what they had built. Cry. Forgive. Learn. Move on. Those were the words his mother always said when he had his heart broken or had been marked by unkind words when he was a young man. For the most part they had worked, and Ian decided he would make them work in this instance as well.

As he pulled in the parking lot, he spied Olivia's vehicle and parked in the adjoining space. For a moment he was worried that she was out alone with the stalker still at large, until he spotted her standing on a berm looking out to sea. Sadness and loneliness radiated from her stiff posture. In contrast, the other beach goers ran and yelled, playing games in the sand. Ian took a deep breath and approached her, loving the way the wind picked up her curls and tossed them willy-nilly.

He sidled up next to her, not saying anything, but mimicking her stance looking out toward the water.

Not turning her head, she said, "Thank you for meeting me here."

"I was glad you called," Ian stated.

It was all Olivia could do not to wrap her arms around him, lay her cheek against his heart and beg him to forgive her even though there was much he needed to explain. She was not sure the gesture would be welcome, so she stood where she was soaking up his presence beside her.

"I....," Olivia began.

"Can....," Ian said at the same time. After a pause, "You go ahead," he said, finally angling his body towards hers.

She turned facing him and said, "I am sorry I didn't give you the chance to explain. Will you share with me again what happened with Heather?"

Olivia hadn't yet looked at him. Her eyes were fixed on where the collar of his t-shirt met his throat. Not being able to stand it, Ian reached for Olivia's hand and prompted her to begin walking down the small hill to the lighthouse. He pulled her down next to him on the bench where they had spent a happier time talking on their first date. They sat that way for a few minutes with Ian gathering his thoughts and Olivia wondering if this was it and Ian was about to tell her they had no future together.

"I have to tell you Olivia, I was blindsided by how little faith you seem to have in me," Ian uttered. Olivia went to say something, but he squeezed her hand gently, mutely asking for silence. "But in the scheme of things we haven't known each other that long and I tried to put myself in your shoes to try and figure out how I would feel if I saw you with another man in your arms. I can tell you I would have hated it. And I would like to think I would have confronted the two of you right there and demanded an explanation, but I don't want to armchair quarterback the situation. However, I do wish you would have given me a chance to explain."

"I know. I wish that too. But looking back I was shocked, and a crowded bar wasn't the place to be confrontational. I saw the man I'm falling in love within another woman's arms and all I could think about was how angry it made me, and getting away from the situation," Olivia said quietly. "There were other things besides just seeing you with Heather that made me suspicious and there is the fact that I've never felt like this with any other man, and these new feelings make me nervous."

"What other things?" questioned Ian with a furrowed brow, trying not to focus on the fact that she had just said she was falling in love with him.

"There were a couple of times I saw Heather coming from your apartment very noticeably adjusting her hair and clothing. And remember when I asked you if you had a light bulb changer? There was a note from Heather on your entry table. I wouldn't have thought anything about it except for afterward you seemed concerned that I was in your apartment. Add that to seeing you in Heather's arms, it all seemed to point to the two of you having some kind of relationship."

Ian heaved a big sigh and turned to her with a small smile on his face. Looking into his eyes, Olivia noticed the shadows of doubt lurking there and mentally kicked herself for being the one to have put them there.

"It's obvious this is a big misunderstanding. Heather accosted me twice that day," Ian stated. Olivia stiffened beside him.

JUST A WHISTLE AWAY

"What you saw in the Longhouse was her thanking me in an inappropriate way for holding a table for her and her friend. I wasn't holding the table. I had just cleared it so somebody else could sit down. It seemed uncomfortable, but stupid and innocent enough. However, she was at the apartment when I got home, and I swear Livvie she was a different person." He explained the feeling of being unsafe and how her demeanor had changed from flirty to repulsive in a matter of seconds. "She explained that she was the woman for me and when I disagreed, she became combative. I finally got her to leave, but not before she maligned you and me both."

"Me, what did I have to do with it?" Oliva said incredulously.

"In her mind, you are the one keeping her and me apart," Ian remarked.

"That's creepy," Olivia said in dismay.

"As far as keeping you out of my apartment. You have to promise what I'm going to tell you will be kept between the two of us," Ian said emphatically.

"Promise," Olivia said just as seriously.

"I'm Dear Veritas," Ian said. Olivia just blinked at him.

"What do you mean you're Dear Veritas?" Olivia asked looking at him quizzically.

"You know the column in the newspaper. I'm the author," Ian stated. "I realized when I told you where the key was to my apartment, I had left the drafts of my latest Dear Veritas letters on my desk. I didn't want you to see them."

"You're really Dear Veritas?" Olivia said, still questioning his statement.

"Is it so hard to believe?" Ian asked, a little offended.

"No, not at all, but you'll have to give me a minute because that is the last thing I thought you were going to say," Olivia gave a small laugh in relief.

"But Livvie, you have to know that I would not play with your feelings. If I thought we weren't working, I would tell you straight up," Ian declared. He was so earnest, how could she do anything, but believe him.

"I believe you. I think I realized it even before I went running off to Port Townsend, but I had built up all this evidence in my mind," Olivia acknowledged. She reached up and gently removed the hair that had blown into his eyes.

"Forgive me?" Olivia whispered, a single tear running down her cheek.

He gripped her upraised hand and leaned his head into it while at the same time tugged her forward pressing their foreheads together. "Yes, always, and I love you, Olivia. In fact, to be honest, I don't think I can live without you anymore."

Olivia sighed and without hesitation responded, "I love you too."

Olivia closed her eyes and felt Ian gently kiss the tear from her cheek. He placed butterfly kisses on each eye and went in for a deeper kiss on her lips. When they both came up for air, they smiled at each other each relieved for having expressed what their hearts had known.

After spending some time content in each other's arms, Olivia started to laugh. "I can't believe you are Dear Veritas," she said shaking her head. "Someday you have to tell me how you became the speaker of truth in Poulsbo."

"It is a long story, but right now I just want to celebrate the fact you are back in my arms," Ian declared hugging her tight as they both turned to watch the sun's reflection on the water.

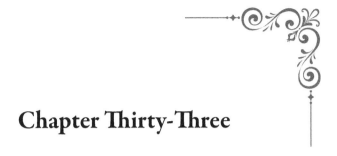

Chapter Thirty-Three

Olivia felt a soft nuzzle against her cheek and smiled before she opened her eyes to wish Ian a good morning after what had been a very good night.

"Good morning handsome," she said after a quick yawn only to turn over and find herself looking into Dolce's big brown eyes. She chuckled and draped one arm around her pet and pulled him into a big hug. "Where's Ian?"

Dolce looked at her with his head tilted a little to one side and then jumped off the bed and trotted out of the room. Olivia sat up and saw a note on top of the pillow next to her. "Good morning sweetheart! I had to go take care of some business and you looked too peaceful to wake. I'll call you later." It was signed with a big, scribbled heart that had googly eyes and an arrow through it making her laugh out loud again.

Reconciling their problems had led to a sense of ease, a cozy evening and a tender night together. She wished that Ian didn't have to leave as he did and that she didn't have to be at the clinic today so they could have spent the whole morning in bed celebrating their reunion, but duty called. She sent Ian a heart emoji text back, so he knew she found his note and then got up to feed Dolce, shower, and get to work. Today was a "leave Dolce with the neighbor day" as she had house calls to make in the afternoon, so she packed a change of clothes, just in case things got messy as they often did in her line of work and grabbed an extra pair of colorful plaid Wellies for good measure.

After dropping Dolce off, she had just enough time to stop at a drive through espresso stand to order a latte, and a savory pastry for breakfast on her way into the clinic. She was now avoiding Lily's bakery because she just didn't want to run into Heather if she could help it. Too bad as she liked giving Lily the business, but not enough to invite any further misunderstandings or drama with her lunatic waitress.

Zio had closed up the clinic the night before and she reviewed the patient files that he had already pulled for her to make sure she was up to speed and ready for today. There was a note that said he'd added a house call at the end of the day for a new client, Don Smith, and hoped it wouldn't keep her too late. It was for an older horse named "Boomer" with an eye infection that needed to be examined and have something prescribed for it, assuming it was all straightforward. Zio had jotted down on a sticky note the address and a comment that the horse was being boarded at an older woman's home (not the owner) and that she should just go directly back to the barn and get started. Smith would either be waiting or meet her there sometime close to 5:30 PM. She grabbed the sticky note and shoved it into her purse. Okay, it looked like the day was going to be a little longer than she'd thought, so best get to it. It was worth it to get a new client as she was glad for the business.

She selected a soft, soothing acoustic playlist for the clinic music system today that had a cheerful but comforting mood that always put her patients and clients at ease. Then she put on a pot of coffee, even though she'd already had a latte, since she was craving another cup. She had just a few minutes to down it before her first appointment at 9:00 AM, a very lively fox terrier with a long complicated registered name that everyone just called Freddy. He needed an exam and official paperwork before heading off to a dog show across the border in Canada. It was a fairly light morning and she hoped to have time to go through the final list of resumes for some part-time assistants she was looking forward to finally bringing on. She loved to help younger people who had a passion for animals get their start and hoped to give them the same leg up in the business that she had once been fortunate enough to receive back when she first worked at a shelter.

She looked at the clock and saw that she had about 15 more minutes to enjoy her coffee and the newspaper before it was time to unlock the clinic door. Glancing at the paper, she smiled looking with a new level of interest at the Dear Veritas column, still hardly believing that Ian was the author. She never would have guessed and wondered if his friends had any inkling. Before she could find the anticipated section, however, she heard a couple of excited barks and decided to open the door early for her first client of the day.

The morning appointments all went well and as hoped, Olivia had enough time to take one more look at resumes and select her top three candidates to possibly interview sometime next week. Now that she and Ian were officially together, she liked the idea of having extra help so that she would have more time to spend with him. She heard the tone of a text coming in and checked her phone, thinking it might be from Ian, given that she was just thinking of him. It was a cute little dog face "selfie" style shot that her neighbor took of Dolce. She responded with a "loved it" tag and checked the rest of her mail. It was after lunch and time to lock up the clinic and head to her offsite appointments. With a little luck, they'd go as well as the earlier appointments did and she'd be done in time to eat dinner at a reasonable time, perhaps even with Ian.

Since it was on her mind and she hadn't gotten a call from him yet, she decided to text Ian again to let him know she had a full day and suggested that they meet at the clinic around 7:00 PM and come up with a dinner plan together. She locked up the clinic and

278   **J. KIMALIE**

headed off to make her rounds. Her first stop was a pregnant sow that, according to her owner, had been "a little testy and off her feed lately." Nothing unusual about that since she was so close to giving birth. Olivia donned her older, army green Wellies for the first visit since she knew she'd be mucking through the pig sty to see her patient.

Three hours, one sow, twin calves, and a mule with a pulled tendon later, Olivia checked her watch and saw that she had just enough time to make it to the barn where her new client's horse Boomer was waiting. It had been a long day, but her mood was still light and she was looking forward to seeing Ian later. He had texted back a happy face, glass of wine, kiss and heart emoji combo that said everything she had hoped to hear. Hopefully, her last appointment would be a fast and easy one and she'd be back at the clinic in no time.

She retrieved the sticky note and entered the destination into her GPS system. The address was a little further out than she realized and situated down a long, overgrown gravel road outside of Kingston. She pulled up to a tired-looking two story with a sagging front gutter and overgrown rhododendrons. The curtains were all closed, and it didn't look as if anyone was home. There was a late model blue sedan with a faded sticker on the back parked under a carport, and she could see an old barn far off across a field that she assumed was where she'd find Boomer. She parked her car, pocketed her keys, and stashed her purse in the trunk exchanging it for her medical bag and a clipboard that had the new client paperwork ready to be completed.

She looked around one more time and still didn't see anyone who appeared to be waiting for her so she ducked through the gap in the barbed wire fence, something she didn't favor for a place that boarded horses, and walked purposefully toward the barn. It looked sturdy enough, although the wood had silvered with age and the entrance door was listing a bit to the right on its rusted hinges.

The latch on the main entrance gate was not secured so she grabbed the handle and pulled the door open to reveal a fairly large space with odds and ends piled on both sides as if it was primarily used for storage, leaving a pathway that led to the back where she assumed the stalls must be. It seemed odd that she didn't hear any of the sounds that horses normally made when someone entered their space, but perhaps the animals were in a pen or something or outside of their stalls.

"Hello," she called in a friendly voice. "It's Dr. de Luca. Is anyone here?"

No answer. Olivia followed the pathway to the back of the barn and saw a solid closed sliding door with a typical lift and slide mechanism on it that suggested a stall where she'd find her patient. She set down her bag, opened the latch, and slid the door open only to reveal an empty stall that smelled a bit stale and moldy as if it hadn't been occupied in some time. It had a dutch door on the outside wall that was closed, blocking out most of the light. *That's strange*, she thought to herself but didn't get any further when she felt a solid and painful whack across her upper back, knocking the wind out of her and propelling her forward and down onto the old straw on the stall floor. The last thing she remembered before blacking out was the sound of the barn door sliding closed and the latch clicking into place.

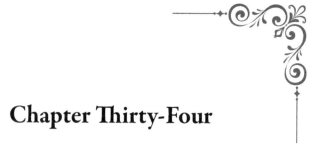

Chapter Thirty-Four

Before sunup on the same day, Donovan arrived at the Longhouse as was his custom. His east coast dealings put him at a three-hour disadvantage at the start of the business day. He compensated by starting his workday no later than 5:00 AM. He really didn't mind getting up so early, even as a boy he had only needed five or six hours of sleep each night to operate at peak effectiveness. The Longhouse opened to customers at 11:30 AM with the kitchen staff arriving earlier to prep for the lunch crowd. The schedule usually allowed Donovan to work a full half day uninterrupted. When he was in his office working behind a closed door, his staff knew he preferred not to be interrupted unless there was an emergency they could not handle themselves. Donovan took great pains to hire and retain a competent team, so he was free to undertake other pursuits.

When Donovan was in town, he normally ate before the lunch crowd converged on the place. He was then available to help with the lunch rush. People in town who knew him knew that he owned the Longhouse. But no drop-in customer from out of town would have guessed it by the way he bused dishes, fetched drink orders and kept the floor free of litter. Donovan had an uncanny way of blending into an environment without notice unless he wanted to project an air of authority and then he was impossible to ignore. Donovan never raised his voice or overreacted to situations. Yet when a situation called for someone to deescalate things or take matters into hand,

JUST A WHISTLE AWAY

like when someone had too much to drink and was becoming obnoxious or threatening, Donovan would politely engage the offender and ask them to step outside. His calm demeanor was disarming yet his self-assurance projected that he could handle what anyone might throw at him. Something difficult to define about Donovan's bearing kept most people in check. Those who tested his mental or physical capabilities attempting to get the upper hand, did so only once.

With rare exception, Tuesday's lunch rush was more like a lunch trickle and this Tuesday was true to form. Realizing that the day was predictably slower than most other weekdays, Donovan took his time eating while he read a copy of the Weekly Gazette at a booth by the window. Donovan never missed the weekly Dear Veritas column. The column itself was often entertaining but the discussions and debates it prompted among his customers and among his friends at their weekly card game were equally, if not more, entertaining.

Two grandmotherly looking women selected the booth next to the one Donovan was inhabiting. Before their lunch order had been taken, one of the ladies launched into an update of her "brilliant" and "talented" grandchildren. In his mind, Donovan had labeled the bragging grandmother as "paisley lady" given the fabric of her blouse. Paisley lady had her back to Donovan, but he could see her friend's expression of blasé indifference to paisley lady's enthusiastic narrative of the latest antics of her three grandchildren. When Lia, their waitress, came to take their lunch order, navy lady, the label Donovan had assigned to paisley lady's companion given the color of her blouse, looked relieved. Lunch order taken, navy lady asserted herself and took control of the conversation.

Navy lady's voice was nasal and shrill. *Nails on a chalkboard*, Donovan thought as he tried to tune her out and refocus on the weekly paper.

Donovan had done an admirable job tuning out the ladies in the next booth throughout his lunch until he heard the name "Ian" uttered. The only Ian he knew in town was his good friend Ian McKay. Donovan refocused on what the women were talking about sorry to have missed the context of why the name Ian had been brought up.

"So maybe it won't be too long until I have some grandchildren to spoil," Navy lady gushed.

Can't be the Ian I know Donovan thought. Ian had always been a bit of a flirt, but he was a one-woman man. It was clear to anyone who knew Ian that Olivia had quickly become the focus of his amorous attention. In fact, Olivia had captured Ian's heart like no one ever had before. Donovan mused that his friend, in spite of his dubious fashion sense, had landed a woman as good for him as he was for her.

Donovan finished his paper and bused his own dishes. He went behind the bar and started to take inventory of what needed to be restocked before the happy hour rush. He was collecting near-empty bottles, and as he stood, a reflection in the big mirror behind the bar caught his attention. A blue sedan with a yellow peace sign bumper sticker was pulling out of the parking lot. It was the same car he had seen at the wedding; he was certain. He hastily unloaded the bottles he had been gathering into the sink. Before the clinking and clanging noises of the bottles had subsided Donovan had bolted to the door. The blue car was accelerating away and once again, he could not make out the driver or the license plate number. However, he did see that someone was sitting in the front passenger seat so two people were in the vehicle.

He scanned the room to see who had left. The two women who had occupied the booth next to him were gone. *Could it have been them in the blue sedan*, Donovan wondered. Donovan checked with the waitstaff and no one had noticed the car, or cars the paisley lady and navy lady had left in, nor had they recognized the women as regulars. Lia thought navy lady looked somewhat familiar but couldn't say from where. No one on staff knew the names of the women or the owner of the blue sedan, but he was determined to find out.

Chapter Thirty-Five

Donovan's brow furrowed as he mentally began formulating a list of how to track down the owner of the blue sedan with the yellow round peace sign bumper sticker. Unfortunately, the ladies who had left the Longhouse about the time the car pulled away from the parking lot had paid cash so there was no credit card information to track. His next thought was to contact local auto shop mechanics to see if anyone remembered working on a car with a peace sign bumper sticker. Without the license plate number his options of identifying the car's owner were definitely hampered. Donovan was pondering other options as he wandered over to the booth where the women had been seated. Perhaps they had left a clue—a matchbook from a local establishment, a receipt, or something else that may have fallen from a pocket or a purse. He doubted he could be so lucky, but it was worth checking out.

A glance toward the booth informed Donovan that Lia had already bused the table and no trash was visible on the ground near the booth. Donovan was about to search the bus bins when he noticed a piece of dark cloth, the same color as the booth fabric, wedged in the crack of the booth where the seat and back met. He freed the fabric and discovered it was a lightweight black scarf. Donovan held up the scarf to examine it more closely using the natural light streaming in from the windows. While the scarf was made of chiffon fabric that draped like silk it didn't quite feel like silk to Donovan's touch. Sure enough, a little white tag identified the fabric as 100% polyester. The scarf was common, void of any decoration, and probably impossible to track, he thought, not feeling defeated but a little disappointed. As he lowered the scarf, movement outside the window caught his eye. I guess today is my lucky day after all he thought, a slight smile forming at the corners of his mouth. The blue sedan driven by navy lady had just pulled up to an open parking space near the Longhouse's front door. Navy lady smiled when she saw Donovan through the window holding the scarf. Before she had come through the door, Donovan had memorized her license plate, the face of her companion who had remained in the car, and every detail of navy lady's features.

"I presume this is yours," Donovan said as navy lady approached him reaching out her hand for the scarf.

"It is, thank you," navy lady said as she took the scarf from Donovan and looped it around her neck. "Where did you find it?" she inquired.

"In the booth, tucked into the seat back. Because it is the same color as the booth and was half hidden it was hard to see," Donovan informed her. "May I ask you a question?" Donovan went on.

Navy lady nodded her head affirmatively raising an eyebrow in surprise.

"I know I saw your car at a wedding the Saturday before last, but I don't remember meeting you there, how do you know Garrett and Jacq?" Donovan asked.

If navy lady was an actress, she was a very good one Donovan thought as she looked totally, and genuinely, confused.

Navy lady said with some defensiveness creeping into her voice, "I don't know who you're talking about, and I definitely wasn't at their wedding. I haven't been to a wedding in years."

"I thought for sure I saw your car there," Donovan pressed. Hoping to jog her memory he added, "The wedding was on the eleventh."

"Well then it couldn't have been me," she stated with a note of triumph in her tone. "I took the train to Portland that weekend to visit my cousin."

"I'm positive it was your car I saw," said Donovan. "Would someone else have been driving your car that weekend?"

Navy lady's expression had turned from confusion to irritation. "Well, sometimes my daughter borrows my car, she has my extra set of keys. But she didn't mention using my car while I was away."

Donovan wasn't sure if her irritated expression was aimed at him or intended for her daughter. Either way, he decided to get to the point. "What's your daughter's name?" he casually asked. Donovan's casual tone did not set navy lady at ease. Her expression morphed again from irritation to suspicion. Donovan stuck out his hand and said, "I'm Donovan by the way," giving her his best disarming smile.

After a beat, navy lady shook his hand and said, "I'm Virginia and my daughter is Heather, Heather Jorgenson."

Sensing he was not going to get any additional useful information from the increasingly suspicious woman, he said, "perhaps it was not your car I saw at the wedding after all. Well, Virginia, it was nice meeting you and I'm glad that you're reunited with your scarf."

Already turning toward the door, Virginia mumbled, "Nice meeting you."

Donovan looked out the window watching the blue sedan with its telltale bumper sticker until it turned the corner and disappeared. Heather Jorgenson didn't mean anything to him but perhaps it would to one of his friends. Either way, he was closing in on Olivia's harasser, his intuition about such things was never wrong.

Donovan went to his office and jotted down some notes: the license plate of the blue sedan, the names of Virginia and Heather Jorgenson, and the physical descriptions of Virginia and the passenger in her car. Then he picked up his phone.

JUST A WHISTLE AWAY 287

After several rings, Ian's voice invited the caller to leave a message. It was late afternoon when Ian returned Donovan's call.

Without preamble, Donovan asked, "Do you know a woman by the name of Heather Jorgenson?"

"Yes," Ian responded with a questioning note in his voice.

The pieces are falling into place, Donovan thought wondering to himself, not for the first time, if luck or tenacity was more important to solving a case. Luckily, he didn't have to choose one over the other.

Donovan didn't ask Ian how he knew Heather Jorgenson, instead he launched into a quick but comprehensive account of how he had come to learn her name and her mother's name, the owner of the blue sedan.

Ian listened intently and with growing concern as Donovan recounted what he had discovered. From experience, Ian knew not to interrupt Donovan as the most expedient way to learn what Donovan knew was to keep his mouth closed and listen. That was easier said than done as Ian's stomach began to roil as his mind was churning through the possible ramifications of what Donovan was sharing.

It took a moment before Ian realized that Donovan had stopped talking and there was silence between them on the call. Ian had no questions for Donovan because he knew his friend had succinctly shared all that he knew of the situation. Ian had always appreciated that "down to business" quality in Donovan even if it came off a bit clinical at times.

Ian found his voice through his growing concern for what Heather might do if she ran into Olivia. Ian quickly filled Donovan in on who Heather Jorgenson was and her recent erratic behavior. Maybe Heather's behavior was not so recent after all as Heather was likely Olivia's tormentor. Donovan had come to the same conclusion as Ian filled him in on Heather's obsession with Ian. On any other day, a woman's obsession with Ian would have been fodder for a joke or two. But today, the fear Donovan could hear in Ian's voice had vanquished such thoughts.

"I've got to get to Olivia," Ian said, the tone of his voice resolute. "If anything happened to her, I don't think I could..." the rest of his thought tailed off.

"Where is she now? Donovan asked.

"I don't know," Ian said flatly, a rising panic crushing against his soul. All that mattered to him now was reaching Olivia.

"I'm going straight to her work," Ian said. "Can you call Paolo and see if he knows where she is?" Ian asked Donovan.

"I'm on it," Donovan replied without hesitation. "If I find her, I'll give you a call."

The friends rang off, nothing more to be said at the moment, yet a volume of words wrapped in worry were left unsaid.

Chapter Thirty-Six

When Olivia came to, it was dark with only a little bit of twilight making its way through the gaps in the old planks that surrounded the musty room. She felt a terrible ache in her upper back and winced as she tried to get up. She sat back down and rubbed her back as best she could, given the pain was centered somewhere between and slightly below her shoulder blades, *What the hell had happened?* She remembered coming to the barn and looking for a horse called Boomer. She remembered a searing pain, loss of breath, and falling down, then lights out. Staying calm, she began to flex, one body part at a time, and take stock of what happened to her. Nothing felt broken but her back severely ached and she felt a jolt of pain when she breathed deeply. She scooted on her rump near a wall and used it for support as she slowly managed to stand up, despite the excruciating pain.

A couple of careful steps got her to the sliding barn door which was shut and firmly locked in place. "Hello, is anyone there?" she called out loudly only to gasp and wrap her arms around herself in an attempt to stave off the pain that the effort of yelling created. Had she sustained some internal damage? Now she began to panic. She checked her pockets and tried to look around frantically for her phone, her eyes adjusting a little to the very dim light, but to no avail. She must have left it behind in the car with her purse. *What was happening? Who would do this to me?* She listened carefully, hopeful for some sign that someone was there to help, but nothing. Just the sounds of the old barn creaking in the slight breeze, the birds making their last rounds of the night, and the warmup notes of a frog symphony in the distance where there was probably a pond or water source. Olivia had never felt so utterly abandoned and alone.

Knowing that calling out again would only intensify the pain, Olivia started talking to anyone who might possibly be able to hear her. "This is not funny. Please let me out. I'm sure you didn't mean to hurt me, but I can tell that I've been injured. Please, I need to get to a doctor." Again, nothing. Olivia did wear a watch with a sweep second hand that she used for taking pulses of her patients. Fortunately, it had the kind of markings that were visible at night with a little light, so she turned it toward the faint beams that penetrated the outer barn walls to reveal that it was about 8:30. That was good. By now, Ian would have been looking for her, but he thought of course she'd be at the clinic. He wouldn't know she was here, and he would wonder why she hadn't called him to let him know why she was late. Being Ian, he'd try to figure out where she was and why she hadn't checked in. But she had no idea how he'd find her here. The appointment hadn't even been entered into their records system. *Why did I have to take the sticky note with me?* Zio had just scribbled the instructions down at the end of the day and probably wouldn't remember the address assuming Ian could even reach him, as he had gone with some buddies on another overnight fishing trip.

Moving around slowly was loosening her up and helping a little with the pain in her back, but any fast movement punished her with a jolt of agony. She tried to reach far enough back to check herself out, but the movement was too awkward and uncomfortable to do her any good. She walked slowly around the dark stall trying to assess what she could possibly do to improve her situation. There really was nothing to work with and no obvious chance of escape. Nor did there appear to be anything she could use to defend herself should the need arise. All she could do was try to make herself as comfortable as possible and be thankful it wasn't a time of year when it could get dangerously cold. A chill, however, was beginning to settle in. She used her Wellies to slowly push as much of the straw as she could into a pile up against the corner of the room in some semblance of a place to sit. She very carefully eased her jacket off, paying the price for the movement to free her arms. Olivia figured she could huddle under the jacket in the corner where she had slowly backed herself down against the joined walls offering some degree of support.

Think Olivia, think. There's got to be something more you can do, she admonished herself.

Olivia slowly rotated her torso to the right and then the left, and carefully pushed back against the wall, trying to evaluate as best she could how badly she was injured. She ran her hands expertly up the front of her ribs to at least assess if there was damage where she could reach. She was fairly sure nothing was broken but she might have cracked something in her back. With luck, she had only sustained soft tissue damage from the hard blow and, while painful, would be okay. She couldn't chance that she was wrong, however, and despite being willing to withstand some pain to pursue an escape should she even think of something, it probably wasn't worth the risk.

She experimented with pressure points to see if she could ease the painful consequence of projecting her voice to call out. But every time she took a deep breath to do so, it caused her to double over. Yelling for help didn't make sense unless she had reason to believe someone could hear her. Once again, her thoughts turned to who could have possibly done this to her. *Could this be that creeper Wayne?* She had felt safe ever since Ian told her he was pretty confident Wayne was dealt with. In fact, she hadn't been constantly looking over her shoulder when she went out alone for weeks now. She'd even stopped bringing Dolce with her to work every day.

Oh my gosh, Dolce—what was her neighbor thinking? She'd never left Dolce there this late without checking in.

Olivia didn't rattle easily, but between the pain and the realization that someone had intended to hurt and abandon her, or possibly even return to hurt her again, the tears began to well in her eyes. She wanted Dolce next to her and Ian's strong arms around her making her feel safe. She wanted Zio reassuring her that everything was going to be alright. She wanted the nightmare to stop. She wanted Ian. Oh, how she wanted Ian.

Just as the tears were about to begin flowing freely down her face, she heard the whisp of a noise in the air. It sounded like the growl of a motorcycle in the distance. Could it be Ian, or was her mind playing tricks on her? The sound grew a little louder, but she couldn't tell how far away it originated. Seconds later it was gone. Now the tears did break loose. And then it happened—she thought she could hear the faint sound of someone calling her name. Was she imagining it? She listened closely. It did sound as if someone was calling out in the distance. She tried to get up but couldn't. She tried to call out, but the effort was too painful. She must have sustained some damage to her ribs that was constricting use of her lungs. "Olivia," she heard again, this time a little louder. "Livvie, are you here?"

"Yes, I'm here," she sobbed mournfully to herself, frustrated that she couldn't project her voice any louder. And then she paused and remembered. She reached beneath her neckline and retrieved the old silver whistle. Elation filled her heart as she raised it to her lips and blew. It was the most beautiful sound she had ever heard, and she blew, and she blew, and she blew.

Chapter Thirty-Seven

Olivia's eyes were shut tight as she focused everything she had on blowing the little vintage whistle over and over. If only she had the strength to blow it louder, but she didn't. What if he couldn't hear her? What if she hadn't really heard his voice after all? Perhaps it was just some trick that being cold, thirsty, injured, and afraid was playing on her mind. And then, just as she was about to give up, she felt his warm hands on each side of her face and she stopped blowing, not daring to open her eyes in case she was hallucinating.

"Livvie, sweetheart, it's okay. I'm right here." Ian tenderly cradled her face and planted a gentle kiss on her forehead. "You're okay baby, open your eyes."

Olivia opened her eyes and blinked through the tears until his face came into focus. "You found me," she whispered, lifting her arm to shield her eyes from the bright light of the flashlight he held, even though he wasn't shining it directly at her.

"Of course, I found you. Are you okay? Let me lift you up," he said, the relief evident in his tone, as he set down the flashlight.

"No!" She exclaimed, pushing him away and holding a flattened hand up in front her in a "halt" position.

Ian's face took on a look of confusion. "What's wrong sweetheart?"

"Cold. So cold. And I'm injured—most likely a cracked rib. If you try to lift me, it could hurt me more. I need you to just help support me as I get up," she directed him.

"Please, don't get up then. Just stay put Livvie; let me call for an aid car. I need to also let the police know you've been found. We'll get you out of here soon," he assured her as he madly stripped off his thick leather jacket and draped it around her shoulders.

Olivia sighed as it infused her with the warmth from his body and nodded.

Ian whipped his cell phone out and hit redial. "Hawk, I'm with her. She's where we thought. No, she's been hurt. Call the EMT's and the detective for me please. I'll see you as soon as you get here." He reached over and lifted her hair as he tenderly adjusted his jacket so it covered her better. "Okay, they are on their way and will be here soon. Oh, my sweet Livvie, what else do you need me to do until they get here?"

"I want out of this stall. Please, just give me your arm so I can get up," she said raising her voice slightly and wincing as a consequence.

"Liv, I don't think you should move until you get checked out," he responded hesitantly.

Olivia gave him a determined look and said, "I'm a doctor and I checked myself over. Ian, trust me."

He wanted to remind her that she wasn't that kind of doctor, and while he didn't like it, he knew that she probably did have a good handle on what her condition was so he blew a little puff of air out and said, "Okay, but I really wish— "

"Ian, just stand close to me and let me grab your arm. As I rise, gradually raise it along with me to help me up." She scootched herself into position and took a couple of deep breaths and nodded. Ian did as she asked, trying not to lose it as he saw her fight through the pain as they hauled her up on her feet.

She took another deep breath and slowly let it out. "This feels so much better. Now, please help me out of this stall."

"You don't want me to carry you?" he asked again.

"No, it's better if I stand as straight as possible." She clung to his arm and slowly, stiffly walked out of the planked prison, following the light that he was now shining out into the barn. Just outside the stall door she saw a short, flat metal scoop shovel, the kind with a big metal base used for cleaning stalls, lying to the side. She pointed to it and said, "That must have been what he knocked me down with." Her vet kit was laying there too, just where she'd left it.

"Did you see who did this to you?" Ian asked.

"No, they hit me from behind. Ian, can you please, bring my kit. Open the outside pocket and grab an ace bandage—the widest one you see."

Ian was still cursing to himself just thinking of what the shovel had been used for as he grabbed her kit and dug the bandage out. "Okay, what can I do?" She gingerly started to ease out of his jacket. "Here, let me do that for you he said," carefully lifting it off her.

"Mine too," she nodded toward her own which was sort of tucked all around her front. "Then my shirt. And no witty comments please as it hurts terribly to laugh."

He made a zipping motion across his mouth and continued to gently remove her garments, trying not to show a reaction when he saw the horrible bruises that were blooming on her back and wrapping around her rib cage. She smiled a little as he couldn't hide the look in his eyes.

"I know, it can't be pretty." She shivered a little from the cold. "Just tell me, am I bleeding anywhere back there?"

"No, it doesn't look like the blow broke your skin," he replied, withholding comment on the color her skin was already turning.

"Okay, that's good. Now let's get this done. I need you to take the bandage and wrap it firmly around me where I point. I need to be well braced." She indicated the area where he needed to start, her voice taking on a leader's tone. It reassured him that she did know what was best for her right now.

Ian deftly unrolled the bandage and pinched the little metal clamps between his lips. He carefully began wrapping it around her torso, checking with her to make sure the tension was right until the job was done and the brace was secured. Then he got her dressed again and the blessedly warm jacket back around her. "Better?" he asked.

"So much better," she sighed. "You'd make a good vet tech if you ever get tired of giving advice to the lovelorn."

Ian grinned and caught himself right before he hugged her.

"Let's get to my car. I've got water there and that's the next thing I need," she added.

"Okay, you're sure you're good to walk that far? It's not exactly close," he asked with concern.

"Yes, please Ian. I'm better now that I'm braced up. The further I get away from this creepy barn, the better. We'll go slowly," she reassured him.

They walked to the barn door and Ian looked out wondering where the troops were. It seemed like forever, but in truth, he'd only been there about 15 minutes and this place was not exactly close to town.

"How'd you find me?" Olivia asked. "I knew you would, but how did you? I'm pretty sure I had my phone turned off."

They slowly made their way toward the car and Ian knew the distraction of telling the story would be helpful to her. "Well, I got some information that concerned me and I tried to reach you. When you didn't answer my texts or calls, I naturally went looking for you. You weren't at the clinic, and you weren't home, so I called in the expert."

"Hawk?" she asked.

"Yep, Hawk. He has ways of finding people."

"Even with phones off? But wait, why did you think I needed finding that early? I thought we agreed that Wayne wasn't really a problem anymore. What tipped you off about him?"

Ian stopped and looked at her with a strange look on his face, his voice breaking. "Liv, it wasn't Wayne. It's my fault this happened to you."

"I don't understand." She looked at him confused and asked, "How could this possibly be your fault. Who did this to me?"

Ian swallowed and gently rubbed her arm. "We think it was Heather. At least, it certainly appears to be her. She has some sort of psycho crush on me and blames you for getting in her way. This is her mom's place. I don't know how she lured you out here, but you can explain that to us later. The police are looking for her now."

Olivia couldn't believe what she was hearing. "I can't believe she did this to me. I thought I was safe and things were back to normal. I stopped taking Dolce everywhere with me. Oh my gosh, Dolce!"

"Dolce's fine, he's still with your neighbor and he said he could stay with him as long as you needed, even overnight."

She winced and said, "Thank heavens she didn't try to hurt Dolce."

Just as they started to take a few more steps toward the house, the sound of a siren could be heard approaching from a distance. Before it closed in, a black Range Rover came tearing up the overgrown, bumpy driveway and slid to a smart stop. Donovan leaped out and booked it toward them. He put one hand on a post and vaulted the barbed wire fence like it was a pony jump. He met them before they made it all the way back across the field, going directly to Olivia's unsupported side offering her his arm for additional support.

"Olivia, you okay?" He asked with concern.

"Boy, this is quite the escort I'm receiving," she quipped, sucking in her breath as punishment for laughing even a little. "Yes, I'm a bit shaken and pretty sore, but I think I'm okay."

Donovan looked at her and said, "Whatever you need. We've got you."

"Thanks, I don't know what I would do..."

He interrupted her with, "Shh, you're one of us. We've got you always."

Olivia's eyes sparkled as the tears filled them once again. "I have no words. Just gratitude. I don't know how you did it, but I know you're the one that figured out where I was."

Donovan smiled at her and added, "It looks like your chariot has arrived," nodding toward the aid car pulling up alongside his SUV. Two EMT's jumped out and started sprinting toward them. Donovan reached out and took her vet kit that was still hanging by its strap over Ian's shoulder and said he'd go make some calls and meet them back at the aid car. He was only two steps past them when his phone rang and he spoke to someone in a hushed voice as he moved toward the fence.

The EMT's ducked through the barbed wires and were at her side directing Ian to step away and let them take over. He looked at Olivia and she smiled and nodded to him. "I'll be fine, really. Let them do their jobs. Don't worry, I'm in good hands."

Ian kissed her softly on the forehead and walked to catch up with Donovan. He kept one eye on Olivia and her EMT's as Donovan gave him the information he asked for.

"I don't know the details yet, but the deputies think that they have located Heather," said Donovan. "Detective Parker is overseeing the investigation and he'll loop us in when they've got something. Garrett is in touch with his mountain rescue buddies and they are going to get word to Dr. Paolo. Garrett is standing by to do whatever we need him to do."

Ian nodded solemnly. "That's good. Heather Jorgenson is going to wish she never met me."

JUST A WHISTLE AWAY

299

One of the medics had gone to the aid car and was rolling a gurney out to the field, stopping to cut through the wires along the way. A patrol car was approaching them up the driveway, lights flashing but no siren. "I'll go tell them what we know," Donovan said. "You go be with your lady."

Ian hurried over to her side as the medics eased her onto the gurney. She had a blood pressure cuff on her arm, a warming blanket wrapped around her and a water bottle in her other hand. She was already looking a bit better. "How are you doing honey?" Ian asked tenderly.

"Just peachy. These two are insisting they take me into the urgent care clinic even though I told them I've checked myself out and will be fine," she added.

The female EMT whose name tag read "Willard" grinned as she tightened the strap securing Olivia to the gurney. "Doctors of all kinds do make the most challenging patients," she declared.

"You only say that since you've probably never had to deal with an angry long horned bull with a bad ear infection," Olivia retorted.

"Yep, she's doing better," Ian reassured them. "I still vote for listening to your medics. After all, they came all the way out here on a Friday night," he added taking her hand as he walked alongside them wheeling her toward the aid car.

Olivia reached into her jacket pocket and found her keys and handed them to Ian. "Can you get my phone and purse and follow me there?" she asked.

"No way are you going without me, right?!" he proclaimed looking at the EMT's.

Willard smiled again and said, "You are welcome to ride back with us."

"Damn right," Ian added and said he'd go grab her gear and be right back.

"He seems to be pretty devoted to you," Willard commented. "Isn't he the guy that works at the Longhouse?"

"He helps his friend out there and works at a dozen other jobs," Olivia replied. "His talents and energy seem to have no limit."

A sheriff approached her with Donovan walking alongside. "Mam, I'm sorry about the day you're having. I'm Sheriff Avery and I'd like to ask you a couple of initial questions before they take you away so I can start looking into this." He nodded toward the other EMT and said, "He said that would be fine. Mr. Hawk has filled me in on some of it. I understand you were attacked in the barn?"

"Yes, I was called out to a vet appointment for a horse. My uncle took the call. Not a former client. Nobody was here and I was instructed to head out to the barn where they'd meet me. When I got there, no horse, no client. Before I knew it, I was struck hard across my back, I think with a shovel, and locked in the stall. I had the wind knocked out of me and I passed out for a while." She tightened her mouth and shook her head. "That's really all I know."

"Okay, that's enough for now," he said, jotting it down. "I'll catch up with you later after you've seen the doctor. He nodded to the EMTs and they began to load her into the aid car.

Ian was back, climbing up into the vehicle behind her and pulling down the metal jump seat that Willard pointed to indicating where he should sit. "I left your keys with Hawk. He's going to finish up here with the police and make sure your car and my bike get brought back." He lifted her purse up for her to see and added, "Just as you asked."

Willard disconnected the blood pressure cuff and unbuttoned the top of Olivia's shirt to listen to her heart one more time. She lifted the slightly tarnished silver whistle and moved it aside. "Beautiful," she exclaimed. "I've never seen anyone wearing one of these before."

"A gift from him," Olivia told her, nodding in Ian's direction.

"Keeper," the responder coughed theatrically into her arm.

Ian turned away, pretending he didn't hear, but his big smile wrapped around his face and the ladies couldn't miss it.

"Tell me more about why this happened," Olivia said to Ian, yawning. "I'm feeling so tired, but I want to know."

"We gave you a little something very mild for the pain," the EMT told her. "Nothing that will prevent the emergency room doc from seeing what he needs to see, but enough to help us get you there without causing you too much discomfort. It does make you drowsy. We didn't find anything terribly concerning, but of course, you'll need some tests and x-rays to be sure. You've probably got a cracked rib or two, just as you said."

Before Ian could say anything more, she had drifted off to sleep.

It was nearly midnight by the time the emergency room care doctor released Olivia with the proviso that someone spend the next 24 hours monitoring her. Ian, of course, had claimed that assignment and he carried the bag of supplies they sent home that she'd need along with several pages of instructions. Olivia felt better after the stronger painkillers kicked in, hugging the little pillow they gave her to use to support her core now that the ace bandage was removed. It also helped having had something to eat and a chance to text her neighbor and confirm that Dolce was fine staying with him until the next day.

Hawk had contacted Ian and let him know that they had picked up Heather, and they'd be checking her fingerprints for a match to those from the shovel. She hadn't admitted anything yet, but they were getting a pretty good idea of what was going on. As it turned out, she had been in therapy for some time and had stopped taking her medication. According to his inquiries, Ian wasn't the first guy she'd sort of lost it over, but after taking things to a new extreme, he would probably be her last.

As the nurse rolled Olivia's wheelchair with Ian walking alongside out to the building entrance, they saw Garrett and Jacq standing right in front next to their SUV waiting to pick them up. Olivia waved and apologized at how late it was for them to be doing her a favor.

Jacq bent down and kissed her on the cheek and said, "Don't be silly, there's never a bad time to help a good friend."

Garrett gave Ian a hearty sideways man hug and then came over and kissed Olivia's other cheek. "Let's get you safely home, shall we? It sounds like you've had quite the day. I'm so glad they let you leave."

"Me too," Olivia sighed. "I'm actually very lucky, all things considered. You wouldn't believe the bruises. Two cracked ribs and some severe contusions, but nothing that won't heal completely. It could have been so much worse. It could easily have damaged my lungs, or..."

Ian helped Olivia into the car and went around to get in the other side as Jack reached out and gently put her hand on her friend's shoulders. "Thank God it wasn't. We're here to help you recover in any way we can."

Olivia reached up and patted Jacq on her arm. "I'm also lucky to have all of you. I never thought I'd need to rely on friends like this. Do you know if anyone has reached my zio yet?" Jacq shut the door and climbed in the front next to Garrett.

Garrett nodded as he started the car and pulled out of the pick-up zone. "Yes, we got word to him about what happened and that you're beat up a bit but alright. He knows you are going home, and he'll meet you there tomorrow. He left instructions to tell you to be a good patient and don't act like a doctor until you're back at work. His words, not mine," he added apologetically.

JUST A WHISTLE AWAY 303

"Hmm, that sounds like Zio." Olivia countered. "As if he's ever demonstrated himself that it's an easy thing to do."

"Cut Dr. P some slack Livvie, after all, he's going to have to miss a few late summer fishing trips filling in for you while you heal," reminded Ian.

"Good point," she offered. "I tease him, but he knows I love him. I hope you all know I love you too." She turned and looked at Ian, her eyes watering once again.

Ian looked back at her with eyes filled with emotion. She blushed as she looked at him. Jacq threw a "We love you too!" over her shoulder and strategically turned on some music and said something to Garrett about needing to stop at a 24-hour market on the way home. Olivia reached out and took hold of Ian's hand and massaged it lightly with her fingers. She fingered the little whistle with her other hand and her eyes told him everything that was in her heart.

"I love you too," he mouthed silently to her.

Chapter Thirty-Eight

Ian lounged with his legs outstretched, ankles crossed and arms resting on his belly. He had been nursing a Guinness for about a half an hour waiting for his friends to arrive at the Longhouse. He had chosen a semi-private corner table for the conversation he had decided to have with his mates. He thought back over his confession to Olivia about Dear Veritas as he watched Donovan's new bartender mix drinks. It was time to come clean. He felt a little guilty that he had told Olivia before the guys, but it was kind of nice to share a secret that he had been keeping for some time.

It was early enough in the evening that the Longhouse wasn't crowded. Just a few regulars hanging out at the bar. The front door opened, and Emmett walked in just as Donovan came from the back office. Emmett walked directly to the table Ian occupied, but Donovan took a detour toward the bar, no doubt, ordering drinks for the group. Ian straightened up in his seat as Emmett grabbed a nearby chair.

"How come we are meeting here instead of at Garrett's?" asked Emmett, sitting down and making himself comfortable.

"I figured Garrett would appreciate a night off," Ian said. "Plus, Donovan was going to be late if he needed to drive out to Garrett's, so I thought we would bring the party to him and save him some time."

"Works for me," Emmett replied, reaching for a menu.

JUST A WHISTLE AWAY   305

"Don't you have the menu memorized by now?" Ian asked, taking a sip of his stout.

"You never know when Donovan is going to take my suggestion and put a tuna melt on the menu."

Ian snorted. "Donovan hates tuna, so good luck talking him into putting it on the menu."

"Tuna is never going on the menu," Donovan stated coming up behind Emmett.

"I'll have a turkey sandwich then," Emmett said looking up at Donovan.

"I already ordered it for you," Donovan said. "I also assumed you wanted potato chips instead of fries." Donovan looked at Emmett with one eyebrow raised as if to say *did I get it right*?

"Excellent," Emmett exclaimed.

"How's Olivia?" Donovan asked Ian.

"Also excellent," Ian said smiling into his beer "She seems to be recovering well and her cracked ribs are almost fully healed."

Emmett and Donovan exchanged a glance of relief that Ian and Olivia had survived their ordeal. Their friend had not been his usual gregarious self during the search for Olivia's tormentor.

Garrett picked that moment to walk in the door.

Ian raised his hand to get Garrett's attention. Garrett waved back and made his way to the table.

Garrett sat down, grabbed a frosty mug and poured himself an IPA from the pitcher Donovan had set on the table. Taking a few big swallows, he hummed in contentment while settling back in his seat.

"It's good to see everybody," Garrett said looking around the table. "Why are we here?"

Emmett chuckled. "I asked the same thing. Our kilted friend over there," Emmett nodded at Ian, "decided you needed a break from hosting duties."

Garrett shrugged. "Sounds good. What's for dinner?" he asked, looking at Donovan.

"I've told the kitchen you're all here. Dinner should be out in a minute," Donovan said looking toward the bar.

Ian leaned forward in his chair saying, "I wanted to thank you for finding who was harassing Olivia. I sleep better at night knowing Heather has been taken care of."

Donovan acknowledged Ian's thanks by raising his glass and taking a sip. "She is a troubled soul but getting the help she needs," Donovan said, remembering his interactions with Heather.

Ian nodded. "I also have some news that I'd like to keep quiet for now."

"We already know you are going to marry Olivia," Emmett said matter-of-factly.

Ian coughed practically spitting out the sip of Guinness he'd just taken. "That is not what I was going to say," Ian almost shouted.

Emmett grinned unrepentant. "Oh, come on. Tell us how you're going to propose."

The guys at the table chuckled as Ian looked around as if to say, "*can you believe this guy?*"

"Maybe the big announcement is he has decided to stop wearing kilts," Garrett said with a grin.

"Or maybe," Donovan chimed in, "He is turning over a new leaf and going to wear only plain T's from now on."

Ian puffed out his chest which was adorned with **Shit Show Supervisor** in big white letters on a navy background. "Read this," Ian said pointing at his chest and making a circle around the words with his finger. "This is what I'm feeling about now."

They all laughed as a couple of pizzas, hot wings, potato chips, and Emmett's turkey sandwich were delivered to the table.

As they all settled down with their plates full of food, Ian said, "Seriously, there is something I want to talk to you all about."

JUST A WHISTLE AWAY 307

"This sounds serious," Donovan said putting down the slice of pizza before he took a bite.

"Not serious. Not really. It just may surprise you," Ian stated, looking around the table.

"Out with it," Garrett remarked popping a chip into his mouth.

"As you know I do a lot of odd jobs to keep myself occupied," Ian paused. "You have to promise me you won't tell anybody what I'm about to tell you."

"Can I tell Jacq?" Garrett asked. "I don't feel right keeping secrets from her."

"Yes, you can tell Jacq, but ask her to keep my confidence." Ian said.

Garrett nodded.

"Do you remember the announcement, about a year ago, that the person who wrote the advice column in the newspaper retired?" Ian asked.

"Her name was Shirley or Susan or something like that," Emmett remarked.

Ian nodded his head. "Her name was Shirley. At that time, the editor of the Gazette asked if I could take her place temporarily. I agreed and Dear Veritas was born."

Ian looked around the table expectantly at his friends' faces. All at the same time, each man reached for his wallet. Emmett held out his hand as Donovan and Garrett, both passed him a twenty.

"I knew it," Emmett crowed as Ian looked around in confusion. "I knew you were Dear Veritas."

"You guys were betting on the fact I was the author?" Ian asked incredulously.

"Yep," Donovan stated. "But apparently Emmett knows you better than we do."

Ian turned to Emmett. "How'd you know?"

"I'm just a very perceptive man," Emmett said smiling.

"Well, we know that's not true," Garrett said with a smirk. "Tell us how you really knew."

"Hey now," Emmett replied. "The column just sounded like his humorous, snarky self and...." Emmett paused for effect. "I saw a rough draft he was editing in his truck when we were doing some work over at Garrett's."

"You read my work?" Ian exclaimed.

"I didn't read it exactly. It was right there on the truck seat. I was looking for a screwdriver and I happened to see a few lines and recognized what it was," Emmett said. "I was wondering when you were going to come clean."

"How did he rope you all into his sucker bet?" Ian asked the other two.

"You remember the serious one you wrote about the soldier back from duty?" Donovan asked.

Ian nodded.

"Emmett said that it sounded like some advice he heard you give somebody once and he thought it was you writing the column. He had pointed out other things as well like quotes you sometimes use. It seemed feasible," Donovan shrugged. "However, I didn't think you had the time to pursue yet another career, so I bet against you."

"I didn't think you could write," Garrett said with a laugh when Ian tried to push him out of his chair. "You never wrote letters to your family when we were overseas, but rather called. Wasn't sure you knew what a pen was for."

"Really," Donovan said. "The column is good and quite popular. Why do you want to keep it under wraps?"

"At first it was just something I was going to do temporarily but found that I liked it. I try to answer most of the letters. Obviously, not all of them get published nor do I want them to be. Probably at some point my editor may want me to out myself to boost sales. I'm not sure whether it will boost sales or make them dry up. Either way,

JUST A WHISTLE AWAY

I think it will change how people look at the column and maybe even look at me," Ian said with a shrug.

"You have friends and family in this town. I think they will love that one of their own is giving advice. And if they don't, who cares. It doesn't take away from the success of the column," Donovan said pragmatically.

"I still want to know how you are going to propose to Olivia," Emmett piped up changing the subject.

"Get your own love life dude," Ian said, throwing his napkin at Emmett.

Emmett tossed it back good naturedly. "I've already been bitten by the love bug twice. Three may not be in the cards."

"What are we, in a 60's time warp? Who says "love bug" these days?" Garrett asked, smiling at Emmett.

"Ok kids," Donovan said, getting up and clapping his hands. "This conversation is all very fascinating, but I have to get back to work. Ian, your secret is safe with me." Donovan gave the guys a two-finger salute as he turned to leave.

"How much you want to bet Donovan is a spy?" asked Emmett quietly.

"I'm not going to take that bet," Garrett said, "Because I think you might be right."

The three nodded as they watched Donovan saunter to his office and close the door.

Chapter Thirty-Nine

Ian's favorite season had always been Fall. He loved the cooler temperatures and bright oranges, yellows and reds of fall foliage that emerged early in the season at higher elevations before cascading down mountains and hills until the colors kissed the coast. The "Evergreen State" has a surprising diversity of deciduous trees that pop in color and appear to be lit from within against the velvety backdrop of evergreen trees that give the state of Washington its nickname. The contrast of greens and the colors that are opposite of each other on the color wheel seemed to amplify the visual effect of fall color in the Pacific Northwest.

Every year, Ian relished the cool sunny days of fall that soon give way to cold and wet days of winter. He always made more time for hiking in the fall to soak in the unique and fleeting sights, sounds, smells, and increased animal activity that distinguished fall. Ian delighted in the fact that Olivia shared his enthusiasm for the season and would juggle her schedule to accompany him on as many hikes as possible.

The current weekend had been grey and off-and-on drizzly, so Ian and Olivia had made a pot of soup at her place, lit a fire, and checked the weather forecast for the next sunny day. The following Saturday was expected to be cool, clear and sunny. Olivia suggested that they go on another glass orb hunt which was exactly what Ian had been planning unbeknownst to Olivia. The fact that Olivia

JUST A WHISTLE AWAY   311

suggested the hunt before he had fit perfectly with Ian's clandestine plan that had been a couple of months in the making.

The seven-day weather forecast for Saturday changed as it grew closer to the day. Sunny skies was still forecasted for the afternoon, but the morning started with fog that was due to burn off by noon.

Ian pulled in Olivia's driveway. Dolce barked a welcome and scrambled to greet Ian at the driver's door. Ian stepped out of his vehicle and rewarded Dolce's exuberance with a vigorous ear scratching and back rub.

"Let's go find her," Ian said aloud as he and Dolce headed for the front door. Olivia was in the kitchen filling a thermos with coffee and shouted a greeting when she heard the door open. Ian entered the kitchen and marveled that the beautiful woman before him had so completely filled his heart. For a moment he thought, *she completes me*. Horrified, Ian banished from his mind the platitude that used to make him gag whenever he heard it uttered. He would rather be battered and deep fried than admit to anyone that the phrase had crossed his mind. Though, he did have to admit to himself that she did completely fill the spaces in his heart that he hadn't known were hollow until he'd met her. *Oh crap*, Ian thought to himself, *maybe she does complete me.*

"What's that look on your face?" Olivia inquired as she approached Ian and leaned into him planting a welcome kiss on his lips. "It looked like you had smelled something vile the way you scrunched up your nose and wrinkled your face," Olivia added.

"I was just thinking that...oh, it doesn't matter," Ian hurriedly, said. "Are you ready to go?" He asked, desperately wanting to change the topic. *Today, of all days, is not the time for me to turn into an emotional basket case*, Ian thought. *I'm already a bundle of nerves.*

"Yep, I am," Olivia said as she zipped the thermos into her backpack and gave Dolce a quick rub goodbye.

312 J. KIMALIE

Ian was grateful that Olivia was in a chatty mood as they drove to the trail head. Her recap of the latest pet emergency at work allowed Ian's mind to focus on how he wanted the day to go. He wanted the day to be perfect, and for that to happen a number of details had to come together.

A month ago, Ian had commissioned a very special glass orb that was intended for Olivia to find. *What if she walks right by it,* Ian wondered to himself, *then what?* Ian thought that he had planned for most contingencies, but what if she simply walked past it? *Do these things ever go as planned*, Ian worried.

Before Ian could mentally rifle through an even longer list of doomsday possibilities how the day could be ruined, they had arrived at the trail head.

"Isn't this the same trail we hiked on our second date?" Olivia asked, a smile curving up from her lips.

"It is," Ian replied. "But is looks completely different in the fall," He added.

Ian parked his vehicle between a beat up, dirt-caked Subaru and an improbably clean new Toyota Highlander that looked like it had come directly from the dealership. The contrast of the two vehicles had him reflecting on the differences between Olivia and himself. Ian was wearing his favorite wool kilt, which was not exactly thread bare but was clearly well worn, along with his broken-in hiking boots that he had attempted, but failed, to shine up for the occasion. Olivia on the other hand looked like an ad for Patagonia with a purple pair of hiking tights that accentuated her body's curves, a light grey, form-fitting, thermal, zip-neck top, and her most recent investment of Renegade hiking boots with purple wool socks folded down around the cuffs. Her thick brunette hair pulled back in a high ponytail exposed a very kissable part of her neck that Ian couldn't resist claiming with his lips.

Olivia relaxed into Ian's warm embrace and tilted her head inviting Ian to explore. Ian's hand automatically moved up to the zipper at her throat which he slowly pulled down. The zipper slid easily down but then abruptly stopped at the top of her cleavage where the antique whistle she wore laid nestled against her skin. Ian looked down to see what was impeding his progress and realized that the zipper stopped at her sternum as the top was not the style that unzipped to the waist.

"We don't have to go on a hike," Olivia whispered suggestively in his ear.

"If you were wearing an easier top to open, I would have forgotten all about the hike," Ian grinned and then planted a firm kiss on her lips.

"Darn, I just purchased this pullover—such a waste as I will probably never wear it again in your presence," Olivia grinned back at him with a come hither look on her face that Ian always found hard to resist.

Ian sighed loudly and took Olivia's hand, "Come on, we can't waste a perfectly stunning fall day."

"Wasting it is not what I had in mind!" Olivia said as Ian pulled her toward their destination.

After using a log at the trail head to help stretch, the pair started up the path. The morning's fog had left droplets of moisture on everything, most of which had not yet evaporated. When the sun's rays filtered through the tree canopy the tiny beads of water sparkled like glitter. The effect was nothing less than enchanting. The newly fallen leaves on the ground crunched under their boots. The path of fall colors looked as if an impressionist artist had beautifully blended an array of golden browns to fiery reds highlighted with all known shades of yellow and orange. The air smelled fresh as it was too early in the season for the aroma of decaying leaves.

"Now I see why fall is your favorite season," Olivia said to Ian as they paused to take in the magical view.

"Aye," Ian responded. "And I am also rather fond of sharing a glass of wine in front of the fire with a sassy someone I adore." The rekindled desire in his eyes was unmistakable.

Olivia blushed when she met his gaze as she remembered the picnic dinner she had laid out for them the week before. She had created a cocoon of blankets and pillows on the floor near the fire and the evening had gone exactly as she fantasized it might except for the fact that the food went untouched until well after the embers of the flames had completely died out.

The heat of the moment was interrupted as two hikers approached from further up the path. They grunted a hello as they passed. Olivia and Ian returned the greeting and resumed their leisurely pace chatting, laughing, and stopping when something interesting caught their eye.

Ian was the first to notice the most gigantic banana slug either one of them had ever seen. The slimy yellow creature with black spots on its tail had to be nearly 10 inches long.

"Doctor, tell me something I might not know about a banana slug," Ian challenged with a glint of mischief in his eyes.

"Did you know that the banana slug is the mascot for the University of California, Santa Cruz?" Olivia retorted, pleased with herself for producing the obscure fact.

"I did not," Ian replied with a chuckle. "I was expecting more of a biological related fact from a veterinarian."

"Well, in addition to converting leaves and fungi into rich soil which you probably already knew, banana slugs consume berries, excreting the seeds which supports plant germination. Apparently, slug excrement is not very tasty to rodents, so they avoid eating the seeds," Olivia concluded.

"Can't fault rodents for that," Ian grimaced.

JUST A WHISTLE AWAY 315

They passed the slug unmolested and continued their hike. As they came upon a wooden bridge over a small creek, they noticed several boards had been replaced. The new boards had not yet taken on the greenish tint of invading moss.

"Looks like the Boy Scouts have been at it again," Ian said. "They often do projects that improve the walkability of this trail."

"Why is that?" Olivia inquired.

"In order to become an Eagle Scout, you have to do a service project. It's to demonstrate a scout's commitment to making a positive impact on the world and to demonstrate leadership of others while performing a project for the benefit of their community."

"How do you know so much about scouting?" Olivia asked. "Were you a scout?"

"Indeed, I was, scout's honor," Ian replied with a grin, demonstrating the Scout's three-finger salute.

"I love a man in uniform," Olivia breathed dreamily. "And in a kilt," she added eyeing Ian's muscled legs.

"What else don't I know about you?" Olivia questioned.

"Well, let's see," Ian paused, contemplating his next words.

Olivia noted the twinkle that suddenly came to Ian's eyes that gave him away before he told a joke or spun an outlandish tale.

"I earned eleven Boy Scout badges before sports became more of a passion and increasingly took more of my free time. Most of the badges I earned were for outdoor activities: hiking, camping, pioneering, fishing...that sort of thing. But my most treasured badge was for gallantry."

Upon hearing "gallantry," it was all Garrett could do not to harrumph out loud and reveal himself and his hiding place. Ian had entrusted his friend with placing the orb for Olivia to find and ensuring that no one else discovered it first. Olivia didn't know that gallantry was not a scout badge, but Garrett did. Garrett steeled

316   **J. KIMALIE**

himself not to laugh out loud with whatever next came out of Ian's mouth.

"How did you earn that badge?" Olivia inquired.

"According to Emmett, I deserved it for managing, at least once in my life, to bow in a kilt without mooning the audience standing behind me. He even made up a special scout badge just for me. As far as I know, it's the only gallantry badge in existence," Ian said with exaggerated bravado.

An audible choked chuckle escaped Garrett's lips as he remembered the night that Emmett arrived at their weekly rook game dressed in his old scout leader uniform and with much fanfare presented Ian with the custom-made badge. The little ceremony occurred shortly after the group had attended their friend's wedding and Ian had unintentionally mooned the grandmother of the bride when he bent to retrieve a dropped ring from the ground.

Thankfully, the noise Garrett made was completely drowned out by Olivia's hearty laugh. She had heard of the mooning incident which was legendary amongst Ian's friends and the story was repeated and probably embellished every time Ian gave someone else a show while wearing a kilt. Now Olivia understood a comment Emmett had made under his breath about taking back the badge the first time Olivia had been flashed by Ian.

Ian and Olivia had passed Garrett's hiding place, neither one noticing him crouched behind a nurse log with several saplings growing from it forming a shield. Garrett readied himself for what he knew would come next.

Olivia exclaimed, "Look!" as she bent down to retrieve a red orb peeking out from a pile of pine needles and cones. It wasn't until she stood up and brushed it off that she noticed it was heart shaped and the two halves were held together by a band of elastic.

"I think it opens," Olivia exclaimed.

"Then you should open it," Ian encouraged.

JUST A WHISTLE AWAY

317

Carefully Olivia removed the band and opened the red semi-translucent glass heart which revealed a leather pouch inside. Excitedly, she extracted the pouch and handed Ian the two glass halves. As Olivia was untying the strings on the pouch, Ian silently dropped to one knee. Olivia tipped the pouch and an exquisite platinum band channel set with sparkling diamonds dropped into the palm of her hand. Tears began to well in her eyes even before she registered that Ian had lifted the ring from her palm and was slipping it onto her ring finger. She looked down at Ian, who had grasped both of her hands in his, and he asked the question she was not sure she would ever hear, "Olivia de Luca, will you marry me and allow me the chance to make you as happy as you make me?" Olivia dropped down on both knees, threw her arms around Ian's neck and responded affirmatively with a passionate kiss that Ian knew he would never, ever, forget.

Garrett knew he must have a goofy grin plastered on his face. He was just so happy that his friend had found his mate. He was confident that Olivia would be as good for Ian as Jacq was for him. Garrett's hiding place had provided the perfect angle to capture photos of the whole exchange. Now, he just had to slip away unnoticed so as not to break the spell that the newly engaged couple were enjoying.

Back at his vehicle, Garrett texted the series of photos to Jacq who was waiting at a poster print shop. Phase 1 of the mission had gone off perfectly, now Jacq and Christopher were in charge of ensuring things went off as planned in Phase 2 of the engagement mission.

While Olivia and Ian were leisurely celebrating their engagement with champagne and chocolate covered strawberries that Garrett had hidden in an ice chest behind a specific rock per Ian's copious instructions, a flurry of activity was taking place in the Victorian greenhouse at Heirloom Farm.

All the details of a surprise engagement party, at least it was to be a surprise for Olivia, were coming together under the orchestration of Christopher. The bar was set up, Ian's playlist was on repeat, the food was being set out, and guests were arriving. Olivia's parents who had flown in earlier that day had just arrived. Ian's parents and sisters had come early to help Christopher with the preparations. Zio Paolo and his date Lily were chatting with Olivia's parents, friends were gathering, but Jacq had not yet returned with the poster.

Providing that Ian held to his planned timeframe, he and Olivia should be pulling up to the greenhouse in about 25 minutes and still no Jacq. Christopher busied himself with the final detail of lighting dozens of strategically placed lanterns around the greenhouse. Candlelight and the strings of fairy lights woven among the plants always transformed the old panes of beveled glass of the Victorian structure into a kaleidoscope of reflecting light. The effect was bewitching.

Christopher took in the scene; his design aesthetic was pleasing. When he and Jacq converted her aunt's farm into an events business, he would have never guessed that the site would soon host so many momentous events for close friends and family. As Christopher looked around the room, he realized that at some point along way, many of the people circulating around the room were dear souls he now considered his own friends and family. *Hmm*, he thought to himself, *as I grow older, I get more sentimental—must be some small-town affliction.*

As usual, Donovan and Emmett had made themselves useful and were tending bar. The party was about to get underway, with or without the guests of honor. It was then that Jacq came through the door carrying a poster mounted on foam board of Ian down on one knee placing the engagement ring on Olivia's finger. It was an unexpected "ta-da" moment, as everyone turned and took in the photo with audible gasps or private silent thoughts. Jacq paused and held up the picture so that everyone could see it. The expression on Olivia's face reflected surprise and pure joy. Ian's features conveyed a contentedness that no one had ever before witnessed. The photo had captured a rare moment of unguarded intimacy between two people undeniably in love.

The quiet was broken when Ian's father said, "The lad managed to get on one knee without flashing anyone." Ian's mother swatted at his arm as everyone else broke into laughter.

"What took so long?" Christopher inquired of Jacq as he went over to help her with the cumbersome load.

"I decided to have three photos blown up, not just one, as together they tell a beautiful story."

The two friends went over to the long, narrow, high marble topped table that served a variety of uses depending on the event. Tonight, it was set up with potted ferns, orchids and lanterns. A spot in the middle of the tablescape had a tabletop easel waiting to display the poster sized engagement photo. Jacq and Christopher quickly rearranged things to showcase all three photos to the delight of the guests. When they stood back from their work, everyone in the room broke into applause and excited chatter.

"They're here," someone near the door exclaimed. The guests streamed out of the greenhouse and enveloped the couple with congratulatory hugs, kisses and backslapping handshakes. Olivia had initially been shocked by the gathering of friends and family and it took her a beat to register what was happening. Ian had told her he had a quick stop to make at the farm. When she saw her parents and her zio coming toward her with outstretched arms, the tears she had been holding back flowed freely.

The exuberant group eventually filtered back into the greenhouse and the elated couple were handed glasses of champagne. Toasts were made, jokes were cracked, and congratulations were warm hearted and genuine.

Olivia felt like she was in a blissful trance. Ian was at the center of her ecstasy and the cause of her perfect peace. She looked up at Ian's unreadable face, his attention riveted on something across the room. She followed his eyes to the posters. Olivia could not have been more shocked. She felt like she was having an out of body experience seeing the photos for the first time. "How, who?" her words dropped off as she became lost in the scenes before her. In that instance, everyone and everything in the room fell away from them. They had been transported back to a sacred point in their journey together. *Could it have really only been two hours ago*?! Hand in hand they walked over and studied the photo triptych that captured their deepest feelings.

Olivia felt Ian's hand squeeze more tightly around hers. The first photo was of Ian on one knee placing the ring on her finger. The second photo captured a rapturous Olivia leaning forward, her arms reaching around Ian's neck, her precious whistle on the silver chain dangling between them. Olivia's arms somewhat obscured his expression that mirrored her own. The impact on the viewer of Ian's partially revealed face was that the viewer was peeking directly into his heart and soul. The third photo was a promise of their future together. A kiss that neither one would never, ever forget and a physical vow of unbroken love—as long as they both would live.

Milton Keynes UK
Ingram Content Group UK Ltd.
UKHW040820141124
451205UK00001B/86